my very best friend

Books by Cathy Lamb

JULIA'S CHOCOLATES

THE LAST TIME I WAS ME

HENRY'S SISTERS

SUCH A PRETTY FACE

THE FIRST DAY OF THE REST OF MY LIFE

A DIFFERENT KIND OF NORMAL

IF YOU COULD SEE WHAT I SEE

WHAT I REMEMBER MOST

MY VERY BEST FRIEND

Published by Kensington Publishing Corporation

my very best friend

CATHY LAMB

KENSINGTON BOOKS
www.kensingtonbooks.com

To the extent that the image or images on the cover of this book depict a person or persons, such person or persons are merely models, and are not intended to portray any character or characters featured in the book.

This book is a work of fiction. Names, characters, places, and incidents either are products of the author's imagination or are used fictitiously. Any resemblance to actual persons, living or dead, events, or locales is entirely coincidental.

KENSINGTON BOOKS are published by

Kensington Publishing Corp.
119 West 40th Street
New York, NY 10018

All Kensington titles, imprints, and distributed lines are available at special quantity discounts for bulk purchases for sales promotion, premiums, fund-raising, educational, or institutional use.

Special book excerpts or customized printings can also be created to fit specific needs. For details, write or phone the office of the Kensington Sales Manager: Kensington Publishing Corp., 119 West 40th Street, New York, NY 10018. Attn. Sales Department. Phone: 1-800-221-2647.

eISBN-13: 978-0-7582-9509-5
eISBN-10: 0-7582-9509-X
First Kensington Electronic Edition: August 2015

ISBN-13: 978-0-7582-9508-8
ISBN-10: 0-7582-9508-1
First Kensington Trade Paperback Printing: August 2015

10 9 8 7 6 5 4 3 2 1

Printed in the United States of America

For Rebel Dancing Daughter,
Adventurous Singing Daughter,
and Darling Laughing Son:

We love you.

May you forever be each other's very best friend.

Acknowledgments

A million thank-yous, as always, to John Scognamiglio, my editor, and Evan Marshall, my agent. Also thanks to Paula Reedy, endlessly patient production editor, and Vida Engstrand and Karen Auerbach, marketing geniuses.

1

April 12, 1990

Dear Bridget,

Where are you? I haven't heard from you in so long. I'm worried.

Is everything all right? Are you well?

I planted gladiolus bulbs today after I read an article on free electron lasers. The article was absolutely fascinating.

I also took all four cats for a walk in their pink stroller with the pillows you sent them. Dr. Jekyll and Princess Marie got into a spat and had to be separated into their zippered compartments.

Love,

Charlotte

Chief Constable Ben Harris
27 Wynd Way
St. Ambrose
Fife, Scotland
United Kingdom

Charlotte Mackintosh
3275 Iris Cove Road
Whale Island, WA
USA

April 20, 1990

Dear Charlotte,

I regret to inform you that Mr. Alastair Greer, your tenant, has died. Unfortunately, because he rarely ventured out of the house, he was with our maker for ten days, approximately, before his neighbor, Olive Oliver, checked on him. Olive was missing several chickens. You probably know about their chicken war, with Mrs. Oliver believing that Mr. Greer caught her chickens in the wee dark hours of the night and ate them.

She assures me she entered the home only because she was looking for her chickens, some sign of feathers or feet, and then found the corpse of poor Mr. Greer. The stench was, perhaps I could use the word, pungent?

Mrs. Oliver said it gave her quite a fright. She did find chicken bones in the rubbish, and she is sure they are the bones of Patsy, her favorite black and white chicken, gone missing, but that is neither here nor there.

We had the coroner come out and there was no sign of foul play. Mr. Greer probably weighed twenty-five stones, three hundred fifty pounds in U.S. measurements, so his poor heart was squished. Anyhow, his sons have taken care of

Mr. Greer's body. I'm told that the cremation was a difficult process, but that is not something that needs to be discussed in polite company.

The sons, Duff and Donnell, have cleared out your cottage, so they tell me. As one was recently released from prison because of some business with the Irish Republican Army, and the other is a barrister in London, I cannot assure you that it was done properly.

I can assure you, however, that the purple clematis vine has bloomed early. What a joy that is to see. My own garden is only starting to bloom, but I am delighting in, as usual, the goldenrod daisies and honeysuckle vine that your parents gave us all those years ago. They continue to offer color, both growing profusely, as if your mother is taking care of them herself.

I have taken the liberty of gathering the key from Duff and Donnell. It awaits you at my home.

How is your mother? Your mother and my late wife, Lila, were the best of friends, as I was friends with your father since boyhood. I do remember with enormous fondness so many scrumptious meals with them, the Scotch and turnip broth, shepherd's pie, braised chicken with beer and pepper . . . You and your friends scampering about the cottage. Your father was a good man, a proud Scot, and a tribute to Clan Mackintosh.

Thank you, once again, for sending me a willow tree in Lila's memory three years ago. It is a treasure. Lila would have loved it.

Kindest Regards,
Chief Constable Ben Harris
A friend of your parents, may your father's soul rest in peace with the angels of heaven.

Charlotte Mackintosh
3275 Iris Cove Road
Whale Island, WA
USA

Chief Constable Ben Harris
27 Wynd Way
St. Ambrose
Fife, Scotland
United Kingdom

April 30, 1990

Dear Chief Harris,

Thank you for your letter.

I, too, remember the dinners we shared with you and Lila. It was you and my father who taught me how to aim and shoot, guns and bows and arrows. Superb skills to have as a woman.

I will be leaving for St. Ambrose shortly. I need to get my cats settled before my journey. I will come by your home to pick up the key to our cottage.

I will look forward to seeing both the honeysuckle vine and the goldenrod daisies in your garden. I am glad they are still alive and offering spots of color and scent. I remember the purple clematis. My mother called it The Purple Lush.

Here on my island my wisteria covers my trellis every spring. If I left for a year, I am sure it would take over my home. My hostas have come back, poking through the soil. This year I am declaring war on the slugs that eat holes through the leaves. Do share if you have any slug suggestions.

I hope that Duff and Donnell have retrieved their belongings. If not, I will dispose of them. Please inform them that I expect a clean and emptied home when I arrive, as I shall be putting the house on the market immediately.

I will settle with Olive Oliver and her chicken loss directly.

Yours,

Charlotte Mackintosh.

PS My mother is well but will not be accompanying me. I'm afraid she's busy with standing up for all women, and women's rights, in South Africa at the moment.

2

My name is Charlotte Mackintosh. I am thirty-five. I love science. I have degrees in physics and biology. One would think I would work in a lab or teach at a university. I don't. I write time travel romance novels. My ninth book was released four months ago.

My pen name is Georgia Chandler. My mother was from Georgia, a southern belle, and Chandler was her maiden name.

For me to be a romance writer is a perplexing joke. What romance? I don't have any in my life, haven't for years, since The Unfortunate Marriage. I have named my vibrator Dan The Vibrator. That should tell you about the sexual action I get. Which is, so we're all clear, none.

My late father, Quinn, was Scottish, hence my last name, and his mother had the Scottish Second Sight. She saw the future, all mottled up, but she saw it. Sometimes she didn't understand it herself. I remember her predictions, one in particular when I was seven and we were making an apple butterscotch pie with a dash of cinnamon.

"You will travel through many time periods, Charlotte," my grandma said, rolling out the pie dough with a heavy rolling pin, her gray curls escaping her bun like springs. "All over the world."

"What do you mean?" I rolled out my dough, too. We were bringing the pies to the Scottish games up in the highlands the

next day, where my father was competing in the athletic contests and playing his bagpipes.

"I don't know, luv. Damn this seeing into the future business. Cockamamie drivel. It will drive me to an early grave."

"I want to travel to other planets and inspect them for aliens."

She placed her pie crust into the buttered glass baking dish. "You will live different lives, child. You will love deeply. And yet . . ." She paused, her brow furrowed. "It's not you."

"I don't think so, Grandma. I love science. Specifically our cells. Mutations. Sick cells, healthy cells. Toran and I pricked our fingers yesterday so we could study our blood under my microscope."

She eyed me through her glasses. "You are an odd child."

"Yes," I told her, gravely, "I am."

My grandma was right about time travel. She simply dove into the fictional realm of my life without realizing it. McKenzie Rae Dean, my heroine, travels through time, lives different lives, and loves deeply. But McKenzie Rae is not me. See how my grandma got things jumbled up and yet dead right, too?

Many of her other second sight predictions have come true, too. A few haven't yet. I'm a little worried about the few that haven't. Several in particular, as they're decidedly alarming.

I live on a quiet island, called Whale Island, off the coast of Washington. I have a long white house on five acres. I rarely ever have to leave my view of the ocean and various whales, my books, garden, and cats. I have had enough of the world and of people. Some people call me a recluse. I call them annoying.

My publisher wants me to travel to promote my books. I went on book tours with the first book, hated it, and have refused to go again. They whine. I ignore them. What do they know? I stay home.

I walk my four cats in a specially designed pink cat stroller twice every day. They each have their own compartment with their name on a label in front.

I read gardening books for entertainment, but they are only

second to my love of all things physics and biology. I have a pile of exciting books and articles in my house on both subjects, including astrophysics, string theory, the human genome project, and cellular and molecular biology. Seeing them waiting for me, like friends filled with enthralling knowledge, flutters my heart.

I might drink a tad too much alcohol. Wine is my vice. I drink only the finest wine, but that is a poor excuse for the nights the wine makes me skinny-dip in a calm bay by my house and belt out the Scottish drinking songs my father taught me while cartwheeling.

I am going to Scotland because I must. My mother asked me to go and check on our cottage, fix it up, and sell it. "I can finally close the door to the past," she told me. "Without cracking down the middle, but I need you to go and do this, because if I go, I'll crack."

I told her, "That doesn't make sense, Ms. Feminist."

She waved a hand, "I know. Go anyhow. My burning bra and I can't do it."

I have not been back to Scotland in twenty years, partly because I am petrified of flying and partly because it's too painful, which is why my mother, usually a ball breaker, refuses to go.

I'm nervous to leave my cats, Teddy J, Daffodil, Dr. Jekyll, and Princess Marie. Teddy J, in particular, suffers from anxiety, and Dr. Jekyll has a mood disorder, I'm sure of it. Princess Marie is snippy.

But it must be done.

My best friend, Bridget Ramsay, is still living there. Or, she was living there. We write letters all the time to each other; we have for twenty years.

Until last year, that is. I haven't heard from her in months.

I don't know what's going on.

I have an idea, but I don't like the idea.

It scares me to death.

Truth often does that to us.

Bridget's older brother is Toran Ramsay. I often send my letters to Bridget to his home.

I would see him again. Soon.

I shivered. It was a delectable sort of shiver, not at all based in science.

That evening I called my agent, Maybelle Courten, from my white deck. A whale blew water into the air through its blowhole as a hummingbird zoomed past my tulips and daffodils.

"You're going where, Charlotte?"

"Scotland." I adjusted Dr. Jekyll on my lap and he glared and tried to scratch me.

"For damn and hell's sakes, are you kidding me?" Maybelle almost jumped through the phone to strangle me.

"This is not a joke." Maybelle's house is always noisy. She is a single mother with five kids. They are twelve, fourteen, fifteen, seventeen, and eighteen. Her husband died of a heart attack five years ago. They dated from the time they were sixteen. He was a reporter. When he died she found out he'd left a life insurance policy worth a half a million and a love note in the safe deposit box saying the best thing in his life was her.

She's temperamental, loves whiskey, and calls her kids "My hellions" or "My white hair instigators." They adore her.

"You don't travel, Charlotte. You hardly leave your island. You rarely speak to people. You don't like people. You told me that flying on an airplane gives you panic attacks."

"I have panic attacks unless I'm slightly drunk. I don't like heights."

"You're going to get drunk on the plane to Scotland?"

"That is correct."

"Hang on a second." Maybelle covered the phone with her hand, but I could hear her yelling, "Jamie, you take your sister's underwear off your head right now. Sheryl, that is not a skirt. That is a scarf. You may not leave the house wearing that scarf around your hips, and put your boobs inside your shirt or I will send you to a Catholic school for girls and let the nuns straighten you out. That's right, smart one. A Catholic school for girls means no *boys*. You'd better believe I'd do it. Charlotte. Sorry. What in the blasted world are you going to do in Scotland?"

"I'm going to sell our cottage and find my friend."

"Where is your friend?"

"I don't know. That's why I need to find her."

"When will you find her?"

"When she's not lost anymore." I heard glass clink against glass, and I knew she was pouring herself a whiskey.

"I didn't know you had friends," Maybelle said.

"I have this one friend. And my mother."

"Ah. Right. The Scottish pen pal. And I'm your friend."

"Now I have three friends," I drawled. "Bridget's more than a pen pal."

"Uh huh. Sure. Hang on . . . Eric! Put your sister down. I said put Sandy down right now. No, she is not your hat. You got a D on your last science test, now study. You don't have a pencil? You have a balloon for a brain if you can't find a pencil." I heard more yelling, then back to me. "You know that you have only two months to get a novel to me? You are aware of your deadline?"

"Yes, I'm aware of that. It's going to be late. Have another whiskey."

"How do you know I'm drinking whiskey? Never mind. I am. How far along are you?"

"Did you hear me when I told you to have another whiskey?" I pulled my dark brown sweater around me. It was almost the same color as my hair. I noticed my beige blouse had stains along the hem. Blueberries? Ketchup?

"Yes. How far along?"

"I wrote a sentence." I heard a brief intake of breath, then she swore. She is so inventive.

"That's it? Still? One sentence."

"Yes." Dr. Jekyll hissed at me, tried to scratch. I caught his paw.

"What was it about?"

"Peanut butter and how it makes me feel like I'm choking and how McKenzie Rae Dean does not eat sausages because they're too phallic. Makes her feel nauseated. Two sentences."

She swore again. So creative! "I don't know what's gotten

into you, Charlotte, but you're giving me heartburn. Bad. Bad heartburn."

"I'll get it done." I caught Dr. Jekyll's scratching paw again. "Probably."

"Damn. I'm going to lie down."

"Me too."

"No," she snapped. "You don't lie down. You go work. Now."

"I don't have anything to say. I have writer's block. I told you. Everything I write is stupid."

"Stupid . . . tear my hair out and eat it . . . knock my knuckles together and split them open . . . bang me with nunchucks . . . handcuff me to Antarctica . . ."

"Bye, Maybelle." She makes up silly stuff when she's stressed.

"You're killin' me. Write that book. Hang on. Can you help Eric with his science homework? I don't understand it."

I could. Eric and I talked for over an hour, and we got two weeks' worth of work done. I was pleased with his enthusiasm.

"Randy wants to sing you his latest song. Hang on, Ms. Mackintosh."

I listened to Randy sing and play four songs on his guitar. We worked on the lyrics together. "Thanks, Ms. Mackintosh. You're groovin'."

"I endeavor to always groove."

Dr. Jekyll gently bit my hand. I tapped his head. He blinked a few times, then stood and licked my face. Mood disorders have serious effects on personality, even with cats.

I'm not sure if my female readers like the adventures McKenzie Rae Dean has as she's popping in and out of different time periods in the past or the fact that they get to live vicariously with her popping in and out of bed with new and luscious men in each book.

Variety is healthy for the female mind.

It does not, however, demolish writer's block.

That's a problem.

At least for me.

* * *

I detest flying. You could correctly call it "pathologically afraid." I cannot breathe on planes. I know that I am going to die a fiery death as we plunge into the ocean.

I have studied planes, their engines, and why they stay in the air in depth. My studies took two years. I understand mathematical aerodynamics description, thrust, lift, Newton, and Bernoulli's principle. I even had three tours at Boeing. I have talked to pilots and engineers and examined blueprints for planes. Yet the sensible part of me knows that the plane will crash at any moment because nothing this large, heavy, and rigid was ever meant to be in the sky.

This knowledge is in direct contrast to my physics studies. I acknowledge this dichotomy.

I sat down in my first-class seat. I need room if I fly. I don't want to be sandwiched next to strangers who will be intruding upon my personal space by body part or by air. I prefer to die within my own confines.

Inside my carry-on bag I had these things: Travel-sized bottles of Scotch. My list folder. A handkerchief. Travel-sized bottles of whiskey. My own tea bags—chamomile, peppermint, and for my adventurous side, Bengal Tiger. Three journals to write in if my writer's block dissolves. Pictures of my cats. Travel-sized bottles of tequila. Two books on gravitational physics and evolutionary biology.

I adjusted my glasses. If we're going to crash, I want them to be sturdily placed on my nose so I can see our doomed descent. My glasses have brown rims. I affixed clear tape on the left arm, as it's cracked. I've been meaning to go to the eye doctor to get it fixed, but the tape seems to be functioning well. It does make my glasses tilt to the left, though. Not much of a problem, except if one is worried about appearance, which I am not.

I rechecked the top button on my beige blouse to make sure it was still fastened. I had been able to get most of the blueberry and ketchup stains out of it. If I end up in the ocean, I want to be covered. No need to show my ragged, but sturdy, bra.

My underwear is always beige or white, and cotton. When

there are more than two holes, I throw them out. High risers, you could call them. I like to be properly covered, no tiny, lacy, itchy tidbits for me, even though I put McKenzie Rae, the heroine in all of my time travel romance novels, in tiny lacy tidbits that do not itch her.

If we crash, I can assure you that my underwear will stand up far better to the fire and flying debris than a tidbit would.

I situated my brown corduroy skirt and took off my brown, five-year-old sturdy shoes and put on my blue slippers with pink rabbit ears that Bridget sent me. I took out a tiny bottle of Scotch, as my hands were already shaking.

My seatmate, a man who appeared to be about my age, was white faced. "I hate flying," he muttered. I heard the Texan drawl.

"Me too. Here. Have a drink." I pulled out another bottle.

"Thank you, ma'am, I am much obliged."

We clinked our tiny bottles together. His hands were shaking, too.

We both breathed shallowly. "Close your eyes, inhale," I said. "Find your damn serenity. Think of your sunflowers . . . bells of Ireland . . . catnip . . . sweet Annies . . . wild tea roses . . ."

"Think of your ranch . . ." he said, barely above a whisper. "Think of your cows. Your tractors. The bulls. Castration day."

The vision of castration day was unpleasant. I closed my eyes again.

We inhaled.

We drank.

We shook.

We took off. I started to sweat. So did he.

"My turn," he said when we were done with the first bottle. He handed me a tiny bottle of Scotch out of his briefcase.

"Cheers to aerodynamics, thrust, lift, and Bernoulli's principle."

"Cheers to your green eyes, darlin'. Those are bright twinklers. Brighter than the stars in Texas, may she reign forever."

"Thank you. May Newton's laws reign forever."

Third round on me.

Fourth on him, ordered from the flight attendant, who said cheerily, annoyingly, "Nervous flyers?"

The fourth round did the trick. We decided to sing the National Anthem together, then "Frosty the Snowman" and two songs by Neil Diamond. One was "Cracklin' Rosie," which made him cry, so I cried, too, in solidarity. The annoying flight attendant asked us to be quiet. We sang "The Ants Go Marching Down" in whispery voices, then I taught him a Scottish drinking song about a milkmaid. We woke up in Amsterdam, his head on my shoulder.

I wriggled him awake. "It was a pleasure getting drunk with you."

"The pleasure was all mine, green eyes," he drawled in his Texan drawl. "It seems we have arrived alive."

"We did our part. Praise to Newton."

We stumbled off the plane, shook hands, and I caught the next flight to Edinburgh. I forgot to change out of my blue slippers with pink rabbit ears before I walked through the airport. No matter. The top button on my beige blouse was still buttoned and I was in one piece.

I put my hand to my head. Lord. I hate flying and I hate airplane hangovers.

The green hills of Scotland hugged both sides of the road, smooth and endless. The sun shone down like gold streamers, lambs ambled along, the ocean sparkled.

The sky seems closer here than the sky off the coast of Washington, as if you could climb an extremely tall ladder and scoop the blue up in your hands and take it with you.

The air was different here, too. Lighter, would be the way I would describe it, although that made no scientific sense. It was saltier than the air on my island, and it had the tiniest hint of cool mint tea, I don't know why.

I breathed in, held it. Can you miss air? I had missed Scottish air. I took a swipe at my eyes, which were tearing up. I prefer my emotions controlled, so this brought on some consternation.

Our stone cottage was fifteen minutes, by car, outside of the charming old village of St. Ambrose, which was situated on the eastern side of Scotland on the North Sea. The village had cobblestone streets, at least three ancient stone churches with soaring ceilings and stained glass, and short doors for the short people who had built the buildings hundreds of years ago. I sniffled again. I had loved living near the village as a girl.

I had taken a taxi from the airport, then rented a car. I was starving and stopped by a bar called Her Lady's Treats. There was a full wall of liquor, a stuffed goat on the mantelpiece of the fireplace, and a steel reindeer head attached to the wall above my table. The reindeer had a furry moustache.

I ordered one of my favorites, fish roulades with a side order of kailkenny, then picked up the paper.

ST. AMBROSE DAILY NEWS

FIFTEENTH ANNIVERSARY OF MISSING PRIEST
Part One

By Carston Chit, *Reporter*

Was Father Angus Cruickshank murdered?

It is hard to believe that almost fifteen years have gone by since Father Angus Cruickshank disappeared. Father Cruickshank was the headmaster at St. Cecilia's Catholic School for Girls, ten minutes outside of the village, bordering the Kinsey Woods.

His shocking disappearance, on May 14, 1975, has become an enduring mystery swirling around our village ever since. His wallet, keys, and eyeglasses went with him, which suggests he left on his own. His Bible, however, stayed behind.

Father Cruickshank was at St. Cecilia's at lunch, on a Wednesday, giving a blessing, his dark head bowed, hands clasped, after glaring at the girls, in their plaid skirts and white shirts, lined up at the tables.

After lunch, he retreated to his small home, nestled in the trees on the far edge of campus, after upbraiding two of the nuns who had questioned him about how harshly he disciplined the girls, of which they strongly disapproved.

"I did not ask for your approval or your commentary," he said to former Sister Mary Teresa Doyle, who spoke with me at length for this article. "Please pray that God will hold your tongue."

"You are not to interfere with my discipline," he said to Sister Angeline Aiken, who also talked with me at length. "Submit to my authority."

The nuns went back to their classrooms, furious.

"Father Cruickshank had been with us for five years," Sister Mary Teresa said. "How we missed Father Stephen, a kind and gentle spirit. Father Cruickshank was too punitive. Domineering. And secretive. He always wanted to be alone when speaking with the girls who had committed infractions."

Father Cruickshank did not show up the next morning, and his secretary, a pious, seventy-year-old woman, named Rorie Helene Cantor, was quietly delighted. Mrs. Cantor handled the parents, the students, and the teachers who came in with this or that question or comment. At the end of the day, Father Cruickshank had still not appeared.

"My day was always blessed when Father Cruickshank was not around to spoil it," she said.

The next day Father Cruickshank did not show up, either. Mrs. Cantor did not bother to find out where he was, nor did any of the nuns or teachers. When he didn't turn up for the fifth day, Mrs. Cantor assumed that he was on vacation. Sister

Mary Teresa suggested this scenario, too. They decided to believe it.

This was a wishful assumption to make, as Father Cruickshank took vacations only in the summer, when he visited his brother in various Scottish locations—at least that was what he said.

Mrs. Cantor simply took over running the school, which is what she did anyhow. She was so much more competent at it than he was, in her opinion, and in the opinion of others with whom I spoke.

It took ten days before anyone thought to go to Father Cruickshank's home and check on him. To be completely accurate, Sister Angeline was checking on his cat. She was a cat lover.

Father Cruickshank's cat had silver fur and was especially affectionate. The most peculiar thing was, the cat didn't like Angus Cruickshank. In fact, Father Cruickshank had complained that the silver cat kept biting him and he was going to give her away as she was a "devil cat."

It was then they discovered that Father Cruickshank was gone. Sadly, no one could find the cat.

The police were called, an investigation ensued, and the Vatican was notified.

The rumors started quickly, according to people in town.

Had Father Cruickshank simply left, taking his wallet, keys, and eyeglasses with him? Perhaps he was tired of working at a Catholic girls school? Perhaps it was a midlife crisis? He was forty, after all. Perhaps he had a girlfriend? A mental collapse? Was any money missing from the school? No.

Had Father Cruickshank been murdered for money, his body hidden? That would account for the wallet being taken. But who would do that? And why would a murderer take Father Cruickshank's eyeglasses?

> Finally, there was the question of what Sister Margaret O'Diehl had said to the other nuns. Were her accusations true?
>
> As I have researched Father Cruickshank's disappearance I tried to answer these questions, as he has never shown up again, anywhere.
>
> Was he murdered?
>
> Where is the proof?
>
> Who would kill him?
>
> Unfortunately, as I delved deeper into this mystery, the list of people who might have wanted to kill the priest is quite long.
>
> This is the first of a four-part series on Father Angus Cruickshank.

I put down my fork. I had heard of Father Angus Cruickshank. Bridget had mentioned him in her letters when she was sixteen and went off to St. Cecilia's on scholarship, as her fanatically religious father was so involved in the church and had befriended the priest. She hadn't liked him, at all. Said he was creepy. Scary. I shivered as I folded the newspaper.

I wondered if someone had killed the priest. Maybe. Maybe not.

I thought of Bridget and felt my stomach lurch again.

Something was wrong.

Later, after three cups of coffee and Scottish macaroon snowballs with coconut and chocolate, and when I felt like a human again instead of a lab specimen, I climbed back in my car and drove through St. Ambrose.

I slowed at the ruins of the castle with its drawbridge, then the ruins of the nine-hundred-year-old crumbling cathedral and graveyard, where Bridget and I had often played as children. We had active imaginations, and those two ruins were perfect places for princesses and knights, ghosts and goblins.

I drove by the renowned golf course, stone homes built hundreds of years ago with double wood doors for carriages, the fountain in the middle of an intersection, university housing, and the village stores, including Laddy's Café, Molly Cockles Scottish Dancing Pub, Sandra's Scones and Treats Bakery, Estelle's Chocolate Room, and antique and furniture shops.

I drove out of town when the road ended at the blue gray ocean, then turned a corner and headed down the winding street our family cottage was on, built by my great-grandfather, and passed on to my granddad to my father, then to my mother and me, and now we were going to sell it.

I felt an ache in my gut. As if someone had taken bagpipes and slugged me with them in the face.

Sell it? Sell my family's home? I drove past one farm, then the next, cottages and red barns, cattle and sheep, lambs and horses, rows of orchards, and fields that would soon be flourishing with fruits and vegetables.

I stopped when I came to a fork in the road.

I had gone too far. I hadn't seen our house. I turned around, drove back, and when I hit the main road going toward the village again, I realized I had driven too far, once again.

What in the world? How could I have missed my own home? I was only fifteen when I left, but surely I should know how to do this.

I drove slowly this time, then braked.

It couldn't be.

I gaped at our cottage.

Our home was now a sloping, slipping, bungled, overgrown disaster. I climbed out of the car, then leaned against it, shocked, my knees weak.

The roof of the cottage had partially cratered on one side. The white shutters, downstairs and on the dormer windows upstairs, were filthy and askew. The door was hanging on its hinges, the stone walls weathered and dirty. There was an old green car missing a door where my mother used to have an herb garden and another car, without an engine, parked sideways where there used to be a fountain of a little girl in galoshes holding an umbrella.

The purple clematis was blooming, a purple wave, as Ben

Harris said. It sprawled over the tilting white arch over the pathway into our property, and all along the white picket fence, which now looked more gray than white.

I gritted my teeth when I saw the trumpet vine with the orange flowers near our red barn. That vine had to go as soon as possible. *Immediately*. I would get the ax and cut it to pieces, then dig out the root and trash the whole thing. It was the time of the bees when all that happened, and I didn't need the reminder.

I ran a shaking hand over my hair. It became caught in a tangle, and I yanked it out, hurting my head. I turned my back on that terrible orange trumpet vine and focused my attention on the willow, oak, and birch trees, which seemed to have grown three times in size.

I didn't understand. Mr. Greer wrote a check each month, which was deposited into an account here at a local bank. My mother withdrew the money from there.

Once a year I wrote to Mr. Greer and asked him if he needed anything repaired or replaced. He always wrote back that he didn't, that he had handled the minor repairs that came up. This was positively wrong. He had not handled minor or major repairs.

"Charlotte," I told myself. "You're a fool." Of course the roof would need replacing. It had been twenty years. Of course the walkway would need to be fixed, the bricks all tumbled about and uneven. Of course it would need to be repainted.

Why hadn't I thought of those things?

But I knew why. I tried not to think of this house, and my father, and his death, ever, for several jagged-edge reasons. I was assailed by memories, as if they were charging in on the Scottish wind, over the highlands, across the North Sea, and back to me.

I took a deep, cleansing breath and thought of a complicated math problem to regain my sense of calm.

Something furry ran by my leg and I flinched, my mind still in the dilapidated mess of my childhood home. A silver cat with light green eyes peered up at me and meowed. I automatically meowed back, then settled down on my haunches and petted her. "How are you, Silver Cat? My home is falling down."

She meowed again.

"Meow back at you." I briefly thought about the silver cat that bit the priest in the newspaper article. "Do you have a home?"

I had hoped that I could stay the night here. I don't know why I thought that was realistic. Perhaps my fear of flying blotted out all rational thought.

The two-story stone cottage I remembered had been clean and well tended, my mother's garden flowing, creative, a picture of landscape art.

My dad was a farmer and grew lettuce: Lolla Rossa, Red Salad Bowl, Little Gem, and the Marvel of Four Seasons. The Lolla Rossa was purple and pink, the Red Salad Bowl lettuce burgundy and crimson, Little Gem was green and tight, and the Marvel of Four Seasons was red to green and gold.

He grew strawberries, too: Rosie, Judibell, and Symphony, which he said he grew to be "fancy."

It was like looking at an organic rainbow.

All of that was gone.

I saw my father's face, smiling, red hair, red beard, twirling me around in his arms. I heard him say, "You're my Scottish butterfly, Charlotte. Eyes like emeralds, hair like a mermaid's." I heard his bagpipes, blaring, melodious, as he played "Scotland the Brave," our red, blue, and green Clan Mackintosh tartan over his shoulder.

Then I saw my mother's face, as she is today, her straight, brown bobbed hair, her exquisite clothing and high heels, her lips, painted with red lipstick. I heard her voice in my head.

I groaned.

"Charlotte, must you wear a clip on top of your head to keep your hair back? Why don't you let me take you to a beauty parlor? It's been what, two years, since you've had it cut? Do you want to resemble a human shepherd? Is that tape on your glasses? They tilt. I feel like I have to tilt my head to see you. Oh God. Don't tell me you're wearing all brown again. Brown is the color of blah. Boring. And is that . . . you are *still* wearing the brown monstrosities on your feet, aren't you? A feminist can be stylish."

Finally she told me that I was "wasting your life living alone on an island buying sweaters for your cats and you need to get laid. A feminist can get laid. She can fall in love. You have to say hello to a man without aggression before either of those things can happen. Say hello. Attempt to be polite."

My eyes misted. Sometimes I missed my mother.

If she were with me, she would cry or, more likely, throw broken pieces of brick at one of the cars, stuck in her garden like a curse.

The silver cat meowed again and I meowed back. I lifted her under one arm, put my shoulders back, told myself to buck up, and walked down the crooked brick pathway. I was glad I wore my sturdy brown shoes with the thick heels. I fiddled with my glasses, on the taped part, and gingerly opened the door to our cottage.

I almost dropped the cat. She struggled and screeched.

The stench hit like an invisible wall, thrown at me by a giant, stinky hand. I could not be seeing what I was seeing. I was having an illusion. Or delusion. I had drunk too much on the plane. Surely I was having a Scotch Whiskey–I Hate Flying breakdown.

Our pretty Scottish cottage, the cottage my father had grown up in, that his grandfather had built, all under the proud Clan Mackintosh name, smelled like a dead corpse, which would be Mr. Greer. It also smelled like animal defecation. Dust. Years of decay, as if a graveyard had moved in, followed by a gang of pigs, and farts. A mouse sprinted on by.

Not only did the house smell like rotting dung, it was jammed. Jammed with junk.

I sat in that loaded emotional mess for a minute, then pulled on my underwear, as it had crept up over my right bottom cheek. I tried to open the windows. Two wouldn't open, as they were broken, but I managed to open the rest of them on the ground floor before the stench killed me, then I turned and surveyed the damage.

The couch was clearly a mice home. I heard them scurrying, having a busy day. Two cushioned lounge chairs had dark brown spots in the middle. I didn't want to know what the spots were from. There were two broken wood chairs, three kennels for dogs, but no dogs, fortunately. Inside the kennels were torn blankets and Styrofoam.

An algae-filled aquarium, half filled with water, held three dead fish, floating. There were broken lamps and three ice chests, empty beer cans inside. Boxes of junk, including old clothes that smelled like hell had rotted. There was another couch, gray this time, and spotted like chicken pox. Two beds had old mattresses I did not wish to touch. They looked diseased, same with the blankets and bedspreads on them.

I glanced down at what looked like years of porn magazines. "How does a woman walk with boobs like that, Silver Cat? It's as if she's got watermelons with nipples attached to her chest."

I turned a page, disgustingly fascinated. The magazines appeared to be the only thing that didn't have dust on them. "For the love of biology and physics!" I said. "That is perverted!" I shut the cover. I had never seen a porn magazine. That would be my last one. Another mouse sprinted on by.

"Silver Cat, do not look at this or it will rot your mind."

Everything would have to be hauled out, along with all bugs, and all crawly creatures, including mice and rats.

I watched Silver Cat watching me. "You did a poor job of killing the mice and rats. Step it up next time. You're a disgrace." She meowed. I meowed back.

A wave of exhaustion hit on top of the head-banging airplane hangover I was already dealing with. I'd been up for way too long.

I would drive back into the village, find a place to stay, and get a huge bin out to the house so I could empty out all the junk. I'd also see whether I could hire some people to help me.

I hoped to see Bridget. I knew something was wrong, I knew it. My stomach flipped, twisted, and turned. Maybe something had been wrong for a long time. Her letters were always sporadic. Our calls sporadic, also. One number would be good for a year, then gone, disconnected. My stomach clenched again.

Yes, something was wrong.

The question was, How long had it been wrong? And what had happened?

Suddenly Silver Cat pounced.

"Well done." She tilted her head up as if she wanted me to take the dead mouse from her mouth. "No, thank you. Take it outside." I pointed at the door. She trotted on out. Cats usually obey me.

One less mouse to go.

I started hauling the trash out, one bacterial ridden thing at a time.

About an hour later, my glasses slipping off my sweating face, my butt in the air as I dragged out another box, I heard a truck rumbling down the road.

The truck slowed in front of my house, then turned into the long driveway. I watched, with some trepidation, as it kept coming.

I opened the door to my car, pulled the mace out of my purse, and stuck it into the waistband of my brown corduroy skirt. I was as prepared as I could be. I had also brought my pocketknife, ordered from Switzerland, and handcuffs, but they were in my suitcase.

The man opened the door to his truck and stepped out.

"Hello," he called out.

"Hello." My glasses had fogged up, as I was not only sweaty but nervous because a strange man was in my driveway and we were in the middle of the country. My glasses had tilted too far to the left, so I could see out of only one lens, but I could tell the man was a giant. I would tell him my intentions from the start, I decided. Courage, Charlotte!

"I have mace on my person. I also have a black belt in karate." That was a lie. "Don't take a step closer to crowd, cajole, or catapult me." When I get nervous I sometimes speak in nonsensical alliterations. It's irritating to me. "I will aim for your face with the mace and for your balls with a swift kick."

He had brown curls, I think. He had mile-long shoulders. He stood straight. I think I saw him smiling. Could be a premurderous expression.

"Your grin is odd. Get back in your truck." I took the mace out of my waistband. It had gotten stuck on a hole and I had to tug on it, three times, and mutter "Damn!" aloud before it came loose.

I held it in front of me, arm outstretched. If only my vision wasn't fuzzy and lopsided. Should I take off my glasses and give them a quick swipe to clean off the fog? Would that show weakness? I could feel my knees starting to shake, my heart pounding. Biologically normal, a physical reaction to stress.

"I apologize, lass, for my odd grin," he said, his voice deep, amused. *So Scottish.* Then I stopped myself. So Scottish? I was in Scotland. He would speak with a Scottish accent. "I'll stop grinning straight away."

"I appreciate your acquiescence." I waited. I blinked as stinging sweat ran into my eyes. "You are still grinning in an inexplicable manner. Please get back inside your truck and leave."

"I'll do that," he said. "But first I have a question for you."

"I am under no obligation to answer any of your questions, as you are trespassing on my property." I wished I had my handcuffs. Next time I would have them out of my bag and in a pocket for pesky personal problems such as this.

"You are surely not obligated at all," he said. "I appeal to your sense of neighborliness."

"I am not neighborly. I prefer my own company. What is your question?"

He grinned again, I think, and rocked back on his heels. He was wearing jeans, a long-sleeved blue shirt, and work boots. He was a towering crane. Six five, I'd put him at. A hulking Scotsman.

"My question," he said, "is simple. Are you Charlotte Mackintosh?"

I hesitated, lowering the mace ever so slightly. "Yes, I am. Who are you?"

He didn't answer for long seconds, then took a step forward.

"Do not risk it," I told him, my mace arm straight out once again. "Unless you want mace in your face and your balls squished to pancakes."

"No, thank you. I don't want mace in my face and I certainly don't want my balls squished to pancakes. That would be painful, especially for a Scotsman, we of the better endowed species."

"Yes, indeed." I stopped. Yes indeed to his balls being better endowed? "Indeed not! How do you know my name?"

"Do you not know mine?"

"If I knew yours I wouldn't be threatening to mace you, now, would I—" And then I stopped. I took off my glasses and cleaned them on my shirt, wiped my forehead with my arm so the sweat wouldn't blind me, and put them back on. I peered up at him. He had laughing blue eyes. He was still smiling, but it wasn't an odd smile at all.

He was gorgeous. Huge. Confident.

The years fell away. Twenty of them, to be precise.

"Toran Ramsay," I said, stunned. Then I realized how ridiculous it was for me to be stunned. Toran lived a couple miles down the road, across the stream, and around a curve. I had told him I was coming. He had offered to come to the airport, but I had declined. Sometimes my lack of common sense processing is surprising.

"Indeed, lass, it is."

He was one hunk of a man. McKenzie Rae Dean would be with a man like this in a millisecond. She would know what to do, what to say, how to act in bed. She would be saucy and sassy and sexy.

I, however, am not McKenzie Rae Dean.

"You've grown tall," I managed to utter. I tucked the mace back in the band of my skirt. It fell to the ground. I picked it up. Put it back in. I pushed too hard. The mace fell through my skirt and onto the ground again. I picked it up and put it in the left pocket of my shirt.

"You've grown too, Charlotte. In a pretty way."

"Thank you." I heated right on up. "I see that you still have that annoying habit of creeping up on me."

"Creeping up on you? In my truck?" He chuckled, stepping closer and closer until we were only three feet apart.

"Yes. You used to do that with Bridget and me. We would be walking or talking, and all of a sudden, like some monster from the loch, you'd spring. You and Pherson."

"I'll blame Pherson."

"He's not with you today, so I suppose you can't." Pherson Hameldon had been Toran's best friend since we were very young children. Pherson had been in the military for ten years, now he works for an oil company, according to Bridget. He's out on a rig in the ocean for weeks, or months, at a time. He returns home for weeks, then he's back out. He dives to the depths of the ocean, fixes the pipes in a specialized dive suit, and up he comes. Incredibly dangerous work. "He would spring with you if he were here. You were both talented in your springing."

Springing? What was that? I didn't know why I was being grumpy. Probably because Toran was utterly handsome and I am now a recluse and study obscure science facts with a multitude of cats. I didn't know what to do or say.

"We worked hard on our springing. We wanted to be the best," Toran said, his mouth twitching into a smile. "Twenty years apart it's been. A long time."

"Yes." He was standing so close.

"They've been good to you."

"Who has?" I could hardly think.

"The years. You are lovely."

"You are lovely, too. Delicious." I coughed. "I mean, you look cooked. No." I coughed again. "You look healthy. Good."

"Thank you."

We stood staring at each other. He towered over me. Next to Bridget, he'd been my best friend. He'd been my first kiss, my first love at fifteen. We used to talk about science and farming, and we'd play chess together. My eyes teared up.

"You have the brightest green eyes I've ever seen Charlotte. I have thought, over the years, that I remembered your eyes being brighter than they truly were, but I was right. Give me a hug, Charlotte Mackintosh. Can't believe it's you and I'm glad you're here. Back in Scotland."

He was glad.

Glad I was here.

This time my vision blurred, but that was because of emotion.

"I'm glad, too." My voice cracked on the words as I was engulfed in his arms, his chest warm.

"I like your American accent, Char, and your hair has gotten long. How was your trip?"

I hardly heard what he said because I was, mortifyingly, breathless.

Toran's cheekbones were high, slashes on either side of his face. He still had a slight scar near his left temple from me. I had tackled him when I was ten when we were playing hide-and-seek and he'd hit a log. I had cried and cried when I saw the blood and he had comforted me.

"Char?"

And that mouth! Full lips still, white strong teeth. Last time I'd kissed him I was crying, our tears running into our kiss.

"You okay, luv?"

"What?" My arms were still around his shoulders. He was a devilishly desirable Scotsman.

"Are you all right?"

"Yes, yes. Fine." I pulled myself away, cleared my throat. I automatically gripped the top button on my blouse. Luckily, still fastened! "I became inebriated on the plane and I haven't slept in about two days so I'm not myself yet." Argh. Why did I say that? He would think I was a drunk.

"Jet lagged. Do you usually get drunk when you fly?"

"I rarely fly, because I know any plane that I'm on will crash. When I do, yes, I drink for sound medicinal reasons."

"Sound medicinal reasons?"

I squirmed. "Yes. When I fly my heart pounds erratically and I endure systemic anxiety and panic, which puts a strain on the health of my cardiovascular system."

"You do drink only Scottish Scotch, right?"

"I'm afraid I can't claim that. I drink from the tiny travel-sized bottles. It would be inappropriate, though tempting, to bring a full liter on board."

"Ah, that's a crime. Never drink Scotch that's not from Scotland."

He smiled. Goofily, my knees became weak. Ridiculous. I tried to straighten them. They wouldn't straighten. My glasses fell off. He bent down and picked them up.

"Thank you."

"You're welcome."

He studied the house. "I see that the house has not weathered well over the years."

"No, it's an unmitigated wreck." I was becoming a wreck around him.

"I must apologize to you. I didn't know your house had gone on so badly. I should have checked. I don't drive by here on the way to town. I don't drive this way at all. The last time I went by was probably about two years ago, and it in no way looked as it does today. We did have a wind storm, harsh and completely unprecedented, last year. May be why the roof has dipped. How is it inside?"

"It looks like a tornado entered, whirled everything around, followed by a rainstorm of mice, topped off with a hundred smelly cavemen who drank beer and ate legs of lamb and left everything to percolate for twenty years. It's rumored there was at least one chicken killed inside. It is fully crammed."

He chuckled. "You're still funny."

"Funny?"

"Yes."

"I'm not funny."

"Yes, you are. Can I see inside?"

"Please. But endeavor not to inhale deeply. The stench may knock you over."

We stepped into the house together. He put his hands on his huggable hips and surveyed the damage. "Damn."

"Yes, damn. I can't believe it."

"Okay." We stepped outside as he indicated with his arm for me to go first. "You've had a long journey. Come down to my home, I have a spare room. You'll stay with me. We'll get this"—he nodded toward the house—"cleaned up starting tomorrow. I have to call the Stanleys. They can fix this."

"I could not possibly stay with you." I could, I so could, I-bet-you-have-extra-powerful-balls-Scotsman, but I would be awkward and make a fool of myself, as I have not been around men much in years, certainly never a man like you.

"Why not? I'm still friendly."

That smile of his sucked my breath away. I hummed to cover up my lack of voice. "I can't impose."

"Ah, Char, never could you impose on me. I have been looking forward to your arrival for weeks. I assumed you would stay with me. Come, Charlotte, I'll make you a cup of tea. Home we go."

The way he said "home we go" almost made me blubber about again. As if we were going to *our* home.

"I might not be a pleasant or interesting guest. Since I left Scotland I have become introspective, a loner, reclusive, and I can be moody." And I wear dull panties. But I can take them off.

He laughed. "I have missed your humor."

"I am serious."

"I'm not worried, Charlotte. I am introspective, also. I respect the loner in you and your moods never bothered me. You were always interesting. Pleasant?" He peered into the sky. "Pleasant is dull. You were never dull."

I took a deep breath. "That's kind of you to say. I think I'm quite dull. But thank you, Toran. I'll accept your invitation for one night only."

"Here, fine lady." He held his hand out to help me into my rental car.

"I can do it myself. I am a feminist now. You should know that about me."

"I'm not surprised you are, and you told me endless times when we were kids that you could do things by yourself. Let me help you anyway. It'll make me feel useful. Besides, Scotsmen like to feel manly. You already threatened to spray mace in my face and turn my balls into pancakes. Allow me to be chivalrous."

He gently grabbed my hand. I let him. I wondered if I would shortly begin to pant.

He closed the door when I was fully in. I tried to get the smile off my mouth. No sense grinning like a fool because a man opened the door of a car for me and helped me inside. Feeling protected by a man, having chivalrousness directed my way, hadn't happened to me in years.

I stole a peek at Toran as he backed up his truck so I could follow him in my car. He caught my eye and winked at me. I smiled. Couldn't help myself.

I would need to spray myself down with ice water, then dunk my head in the ocean.

On the way to Toran's I glimpsed the road on top of the cliffs in the distance, the straightaway part, no curves.

It shouldn't have happened. Those were strange, mysterious circumstances. Different scenarios played out in my head. I spun them up and turned them around, analyzing each one.

Would we ever know what truly happened on top of the cliffs? Did Toran or Bridget know? Did they suspect?

Toran, Bridget, Pherson, and I were together from the time we were babies. Our mothers had tea and biscuits together, whenever meek and beaten down Bonnie Ramsay could sneak away from her hellfire and damnation husband, Carney. Pherson's mother, Nessa, would come with Pherson and one little sister, to be followed, years later, by twin girls.

My earliest memory is playing dress up with Bridget. We put on my mother's silky dresses, tutus, sequined shirts, hats, and heels. We danced together, had tea parties. My mother said Bridget and I were three when we snuck off with Pherson and Toran into the woods to play Kings and Queens. The mothers were frantic when they couldn't find us.

Toran, Bridget, Pherson, and I would ride the bus to school each day, always sitting in the back. Bridget and I sat side by side at lunch. I shared my treats. Her father rarely let her have sweets. We baked pies with my grandma, gardened with my mother, listened to the legends my father told, and pretended we were evil scientists. We avoided her house entirely.

Bridget and I whispered our secrets, our thoughts, and our plans, as we grew older. She told me about Carney and what he said, what he did, her fear, her pain. When I was five I remember giving her a hug as she cried under our dining room table.

But it was the four of us, Toran, Bridget, Pherson, and Charlotte, from the start.

Our mothers laughed and said we must have all been related, or in the same clan, in past lives. We didn't know what that meant, but we named ourselves Clan TorBridgePherLotte. What we did know is that we were best friends, which was all we needed to know.

It never occurred to us that it wouldn't last forever.

3

June 12, 1985

Bridget,

I wore my furry purple sweater dress to Olga's gift shop the other day and received some odd looks. When I returned to my car I realized that I was also wearing my pink pajama bottoms with the ghosts on them that you sent me.

I am becoming more strange by the day. I read science journals and send chess moves to two pen pal chess partners. Ah well, Bridget. If all else fails, I can use my chess pieces as weapons. Against who, I don't know. We don't even have handsome bad guys on the island. If there were any bad guys on the island I would probably bore them to death with what chemicals can go together to make explosions or force them to study the geological history of the earth, including all Ice Ages.

My butterfly bush is blooming, beautiful purple flowers. How is yours doing?

I've killed another hydrangea. The pink one. What is your secret to not murdering hydrangeas?

I know you're the queen of hydrangea growing, so do tell me.

Love,
Charlotte

June 25, 1985

Charlotte,

The queen of hydrangeas will tell you that you may have to add a smidgen of lime to your soil for the pinkies and acid for the blue ones. Give it a go. And don't think of yourself as a hydrangea murderer. That's rather harsh. Think of yourself as a hydrangea curse. Less violent.

So you're still the weird loner on your island with the cat stroller, right? Hold your head high. It's something to be proud of.

I have enclosed one of my miniature drawings. I know you like them. As you can see, this one is of the fort we built when we were kids. I added our crowns and capes, Queen Charlotte. As we used to say, Clan TorBridgePherLotte, gather your powers, defeat the enemy!

Never fear about your love life, Charlotte, the right man will come along. If not, go and hunt him down and bring him home by force. Do you have a spear handy? Use that. Do try not to get arrested.

Toran said he would help me plant a new rose garden this summer. Poor man. As if he doesn't have enough to do.

Love,
Bridget

July 7, 1985

Bridget,

There is not a hint of a man in sight to spear even if I wanted to. I have four cats. I put sweaters on them in cool weather. I live in my imagination with a fake woman named McKenzie Rae Dean and talk to her. She talks back. I am pathetic. I am going to die one of these days and people will find me on the ground, all my cats lying on top of me. If I thought a spear would work, I would use it.

Speaking of spearing men. How is Toran?

Love,

Charlotte

July 20, 1985

Charlotte,

Toran is fine. The semi trucks are coming in and out all the time to pick up the potatoes, blueberries, and apples that he's growing. He has more and more clients for his crops, here and abroad. They take his crops across the ocean now. The invitation to come and visit us is always open.

Then you could try out Toran's . . . spear.

Love you,

Bridget

"What happened to your family's home?"

Toran's face hardened across the table from me. He had made cheese and ham sandwiches, warmed on a skillet; a fruit plate; and lemon tea. He was a yummy cook. "I had it demolished."

"Completely taken down?"

"Yes. That was not a happy house to grow up in, and I didn't want to see it again."

"I understand." Carney, Toran's father, was a Catholic fanatic. He was hellfire and brimstone. Obsessed with religion and bible thumping and thunking. That house had been about a half mile away from this one. "I would have helped you demolish it had I been here."

"Thank you, Charlotte."

"You're welcome."

He rolled his shoulders, as if he was trying to shake off the memory. "I told a builder in town what I wanted, and he built this."

"I love it."

"Thank you."

Toran's home, a Scottish cottage, was new, but he had adhered to the traditional Scottish style. Light beige stone. Shaker roof. Two story. White trim, dark blue door. It was charming but solid. Spacious but not too spacious. It was more open on the inside than other Scottish cottages, with few walls. Downstairs was the kitchen, huge family area, and den. Windows everywhere. Two sets of French doors. Upstairs, as he had shown me, four bedrooms and a loft.

Bridget's bedroom was equal to the size of the master bedroom, with its own bath. "I wanted to create a place she wanted to come home to."

A light pink, striped bedspread covered the bed; the walls were white; and a long window seat stretched under the largest window, waiting for her to sit and read.

He had bought a white desk for Bridget where she could draw her miniature, magical drawings. It was placed under the second window, with a view of the farm, and in the distance, the ocean and the cliffs.

Toran's windows framed the views of his farm where he grew blueberries and three different types of potatoes—Shetland Blacks, Dunbar Rovers, and russets. He also grew apples. Discovery; Katy; Red Devils, "For trouble," he joked; Edward VII, "To add royalty to this place." He had Bramleys and Grenadiers and crab apples. "For the bees. Without the bees, we don't work."

He had tractors and farm equipment, three red barns, too

many outbuildings to count, and greenhouse-type tunnels for early growing. He also had two other enormous tunnels for storage of the potatoes.

I was not surprised. His father had done a poor job of farming. Toran had not.

"How do you like farming?"

"I love it. I even loved it when I was at home with my father, the long hours he made me put in. I like to plant things, watch them grow. I like the business end of it. I like to watch that grow, too." He smiled. "It's a challenge. Farming has many challenges. The weather. Blight. Insects. Fungus. Weeds. Water irrigation issues. Long days, long nights sometimes. Fortunately, most of my employees have been working for me for years and I trust them.

"I was not going to work the farm for my father, after university, but then he and my mother died, and it was our land. Clan Ramsay land. My father had sold pieces off, as he didn't want to work and needed the money to give to the church and pay debts, and I was determined to buy it back."

"And you did?"

"Yes. And more."

"I'm pleased to hear it."

I waited to see if he wanted to say anything else about his parents, but it didn't appear that he did, his jaw tightening. I understood his reluctance to speak of it.

"I can't see you inside an office, trapped like a rat, so I'm glad you like to farm." Those blue eyes refocused on mine. They were blueberries and the Scottish blue sky mixed together.

"I think it would kill me, I do. I have to be outside."

The conversation was easy, fast, as we had so much to talk about. I have never talked to a man like I talked to Toran. Farming. Science. He asked me many questions about my life on the island.

We had his homegrown blueberries and ice cream for dessert, with a sprinkle of nuts, sitting together on the couch. It was delicious. He was delicious.

"So, Toran. I'm ready." My stomach flipped, twisted, and turned, as it had earlier. "How is Bridget?"

"Bridget." Toran closed his eyes for a second, sadness covering his face. He rubbed his temples.

"I haven't heard from her since last year." I clenched my hands together. "Is something wrong?"

"I don't know where she is, and yes, something is wrong." He leaned back on the couch and seemed instantly exhausted.

"I told her I was coming. I had hoped that she would be here."

"I wish she was."

"You said in your letter to me that you wanted to have a conversation about her."

"Yes, I do. Perhaps we should have that conversation tomorrow. You look a bit pale. I know you haven't slept in two days."

"Is she ill?" Please, not ill. Bridget was a kind, fun, funny person.

"In a way. But . . . there is much more to it." I thought I saw a sheen of tears over his eyes.

"What is it?" Flip. Twist. Turn.

He clasped his hands together. "Charlotte, there are many problems."

He told me the problems.

When he was done I opened my mouth to speak. No words fell out. I closed it. Opened it. No words fell out again. I finally choked out, "You have no idea, not the slightest, where she is?"

"No."

"Or how she is?"

"She's alive. I believe." He put a hand to his forehead. "I think. Now and then she'll call. Or write. Or someone I've hired to find her gets news that she's okay. But I have nightmares about that question all the time."

"I didn't know." But I knew something was wrong, something was off. I had felt it.

"I know."

"She didn't tell me." Why? Why didn't she tell me? "I thought we were friends. . . ."

"You are friends. She didn't want you to know. She made me swear I wouldn't tell you about it, what had happened, what is happening, the things she'd done and what had been done to her. Her life is messed up, Charlotte. She's in the dark. That's the way I'd explain it. She's lost. She's losing her own battle. I didn't tell you, because I thought it would make things worse for her. There was nothing you could do. You were far away, and she wanted one person to talk to so she could pretend that all was well and she was living the life she wanted. I've tried to help. Constantly. It hasn't worked."

"She lied to me then."

"Yes."

"About what?"

"Almost everything."

And there it was. The truth.

My best friend had lied to me.

I felt ill.

I was in bed by ten that night, crashing from jet lag and emotionally whipped.

I thought of Bridget again and my stomach heaved. I thought I might be sick.

A chill stole over me, like a shadow, stretching up and up until I shook, head to foot.

Toran, Bridget, Pherson, and I played imaginary games together. We explored the hills, the woods, the ocean. We built a fort. We built a tree house. We read books.

We were King Toran, Queen Bridget, King Pherson, and Queen Charlotte.

Clan TorBridgePherLotte. We were the fearsome foursome.

We battled the evil goblin Strike, we overthrew the wicked headless horsemen, we had sword fights with bad guys with horns and scary witches with spells that flew from their fingers.

We broke each other out of traps before we were eaten by voracious giant monsters. We hid in bushes and spied on the enemy. We wore invisibility capes and could fly on our own. We rode horses with wings, crowns atop our heads. We talked to animals in their language.

Toran. Bridget. Pherson. Charlotte.

And in our imaginary lands and adventures, we escaped.

It was only later that I learned how much Bridget and Toran needed to escape from their home.

Oh, how they needed to escape.

I huddled deep into all my blankets and let the tears soak my pillow.

"Bridget will come back to you."

"What do you mean, Grandma? She's right there." I pointed to Bridget. She was helping my mother tie up the trumpet vine with the orange flowers to our trellis. Bridget wasn't afraid of the bees.

"She'll be gone for a while. She'll move across an ocean, she'll run with devils, she'll hurt her arms, she'll keep getting lost. I don't know why she can't find her way home, so confusing, but she'll come back with roses and a statue of four children. She'll bring a long garden. You'll see her again. Do you understand?"

"Yes. No."

She stroked my hair. "Cursed, she is."

"What?"

"It's random, unfair," she muttered.

"What is?"

"Life."

I woke up the next morning to white rays of sunshine pouring through the window and my face puffed up like a pasty white balloon.

Toran had put me in a guest room with a yellow comforter and pillows, a wicker chair in the corner and a wicker desk. It was clean, sparse, and organized. My suitcases were in a corner.

I had a dark brown suitcase and a light brown suitcase. The dark brown one was duct taped shut. I found out the lock was broken a half hour before I had to leave to go to the scary airport, so I duct taped it, round and round. I bought them both at Goodwill. No need to pay hard-earned money for more expensive ones. I would try to fix the one that was duct taped, but I figured that after ten years, I might have to find a thrift shop and buy a new one.

I felt human again except for my exploded face.

Toran was gone, working on his farm. I got up and took a shower. I washed my hair, though I find that chore tedious. I do have thick hair, via my mother, and it can be a nuisance.

I dried off and put on fresh underwear, slightly frayed, only one hole, no matter, and my other beige bra. I clipped my wet hair back from my forehead so it wouldn't get in my way. I put the rest of it in a bun. I pulled on my denim skirt that hung to midcalf and a blue blouse with two red diamonds on the front. I'd found it at Goodwill in Seattle for two dollars three years ago. Still looks stylish. I added a yellow crocheted vest. As I would be at my house today, cleaning, I put on my tennis shoes and my favorite blue socks with white stripes to complete my outfit.

I went downstairs, made eggs and toast, ate half a bowl of vanilla ice cream, and drank four cups of coffee. I cleaned up the kitchen. It was messy, not much, but once I start cleaning I don't quit until I'm done. When I was done, that kitchen sparkled, everything in its place.

I took discreet peeks around Toran's home. So this was where the Scottish Warrior lived. This was where he walked around, this was the den where he worked, this was where he fell asleep.

This was where he ate. If he had girlfriends, this was where he brought them.

I did not like the thought of girlfriends, so I envisioned the women stuck in petri dishes with the lids screwed on tight in refrigerators. Laboratory research is a creative way to mentally exact revenge.

Toran had a huge four-poster bed with a headboard. I thought about tying up Toran's wrists to the bedposts and kissing him down one side and up the other, and then I blushed. McKenzie Rae Dean would not blush at that thought. She would have been proud of herself and excited. She would have grabbed silk scarves for Tie Me Up Night.

I don't think I could be tied to bedposts by anyone but Toran. I would savor the experience.

I saw the Ramsay clan tartan, red and black, hung from a hook on the wall, and his red and black kilt, hung on a hanger, his fur sporran and Prince Charlie jacket. His bagpipes were in a corner, next to his clan's crest, with a unicorn.

I was getting all hot and bothered once again and I had work to do, mice to chase out, moldy couches and mattresses to get rid of, porn magazines to toss.

I grabbed the keys to my rental car and left as visions of bedposts danced through my mind.

I like routines, and I would have to figure out one for my time in Scotland.

Routines mean I can have control over my life, that there will be no surprises.

I lie to myself sometimes. There are always surprises in life.

When I drove to our cottage, I took a slight detour to the place where Toran and Bridget's old home had been. There was nothing left. Any scrap of the building had been ground into Scottish land. In fact, judging by the ground, I think it may have been set on fire.

It was as it should be.

Bridget and I, even as little girls, used to write letters to each other. She told me one time that when she was sad and lonely at home, that's when she would write to me. I kicked a few charred pieces. When we saw each other at school, or when we were playing near the ocean, she would give me the letter.

She wrote me many letters. From right here.

I kicked another charred piece of wood. Hard. Then three more.

I let out a scream, too. It echoed off the rolling hills in the distance and came right back at me.

* * *

I knew what I had to do first when I arrived at our cottage. I could not start anything else until it was done. I heard my grandma's voice saying, "It will be the time of the bees."

I found our old ax with a red handle in the barn and stomped back to the trumpet vine, my hands trembling as one memory after another rushed in, stabbing and cruel. I cut the trumpet vine down, right at the base, my mouth trembling.

Whack.

I remembered everything.

"You stupid vine," I said to it. "You did it. The bees did it."

Whack.

It will be the time of the bees.

The tears streamed down my face.

My mother had taken this very same ax to it, years ago. She had been crying, too. And the damn thing had grown back again.

Whack.

I sobbed, my breath catching.

No, that damn trumpet vine could not stay, no matter how pretty the orange flowers would be this summer.

Whack.

Out.

Whack.

Out.

My grief rushed through, in screeches of pain. It had been twenty years ago, but still, here the grief was back again, mangling my insides.

When the vine was down, and in a dead pile, which I would later set on fire, I tossed the ax, sunk to the ground, and covered my face. I let all my tears out. My glasses fell off and I rocked back and forth.

It will be the time of the bees.

Yes, it was. She had known it was coming.

It was the time of the bees, and that's when it all went to hell.

I lay down on the trumpet vine, in victory. It was gone, and I was here. I won. It was dead. I watched the clouds, my tears sliding out the corners of my eyes. I hadn't won.

Silver Cat came and lay on my chest.

"Nice to see you again, mouse killer," I managed to rasp out.

Silver Cat meowed until I meowed back at her.

I later used a water bottle to clean off my face and hands, then grabbed a plastic trash bag and pulled on thick work gloves I had borrowed from Toran.

A towing company had already been here, thanks to Toran, who had said he would call. The two old cars in front of the property were gone, as were two ruins of cars in the garage, a motorcycle without wheels, and a camper trailer without, curiously, a roof. There was also an enormous bin in front, about fifteen feet long and six feet high.

I took a deep breath and told myself to buck up. I opened the door to our near-destroyed cottage as a mouse skittered across the floor. The mouse was in mouse heaven in a second as Silver Cat streaked in and snatched it up.

"Perfect execution. Take it outside." I pointed. She took the dead mouse out. Cats are obedient to me. I don't know why.

I quickly filled two trash bags and dumped them in the bin. I worked for about two hours, nonstop, and got rid of the porn magazines, the kennels, two tires, a six-foot stack of newspapers, and piles of clothes, among other bizarre things.

A car headed down the driveway and stopped. Two ladies climbed out and walked underneath the tilted arc holding up Purple Lush.

"Hello there!" one woman, with a white braid, called out. "Greetings! I'm Olive Oliver and this is Gitanjali Chavan."

"It's a pleasure to meet both of you." I took off my gloves and we shook hands. Olive was tall and thin, wide boned. She was about sixty-five. Gitanjali was much shorter, East Indian, very pretty, and wore an embroidered blue tunic with small mirrors attached to it. Hard to determine her age. Probably fiftyish.

Gitanjali said, her voice gentle, like molasses on ice cream, "I learning English. Pardon me for mistakes I give and take generously. A pleasure on meeting you."

"It's a pleasure to meet you, too." I turned to Olive. "So you're the one whose chickens my tenant stole?"

"Yes, he did. Mr. Greer, chicken eater." Her face showed her disgust. I noticed she was wearing a knitted green scarf with a white cat on it. The white cat looked dizzy, eyes slightly crossed. I don't think it was intentional. "Did you find evidence of the crime?"

I nodded. "I did. I found chicken bones. One full skeleton in the kitchen sink and two other full skeletons in the bathtub. I don't know why he put them there. I apologize for his actions."

"I knew it. He ate Lieutenant Judith." She snapped her fingers. "And Lizbeth and Smelly Toad."

"You name your chickens?"

"I don't have that many. It's unfortunate that Mr. Greer did not care for the garden, either."

"It's a regrettable mess," I said. "My mother would be disappointed."

"I'm sure." She nodded, wisely. "Do you like to garden?"

"Yes. It's a compulsive habit."

"Compulse iv hab eat?" Gitanjali said. "What is that?"

"It means I have to garden or I get anxious. Nervous." I wrung my hands. "It's a calming mechanism. Some people do yoga. I pull weeds, dump snails in buckets, and design garden rooms."

Olive Oliver flipped her white braid over her back. "That's how I feel. Nothing more emotionally stimulating than gardening."

I thought of a naked romp with Toran. That would be more stimulating. "Nothing more stimulating except for sex." I cleared my throat, surprised by my bluntness. "Pardon me. I can't believe I said that."

"No need for pardon," Olive said, waving a hand. "I agree. My husband knows after I garden is the proper time for post-planting coitus."

Gitanjali's eyebrows shot up and she laughed. "Ah, sex. I know that word. The making loving. That not better than gardening, but still pleasing, I hear. I don't know. It not happy for me. Not much had in long time for me."

"I'm sorry about that, Gitanjali. Me either." I thought of Dan The Vibrator. He didn't count, as he doesn't have testicles or kneecaps.

"Ah," Gitanjali said. "Maybe one day or one week. New man come in the life for you. Say hello."

"Sex could be better than gardening as long as he's talented in the bedroom," Olive said. "I've had both. Sex less stimulating than gardening and sex better than gardening."

"Talent in the bedroom is a requirement," I said. "And lusty. Who wants a prim man in bed?"

"Not me. I like the creative type." Olive put a finger up. "Nothing hurtful."

"I agree with your opinion," I said. "No spanking for me." I thought of Toran. "At least not *hard* spanking."

"I have not making love in my bed for long years, so my garden feed my soul," Gitanjali said, pressing her palms together. "The world down upside. Wars. Starving. I feel I do so little. But my garden is peace. A place for me."

"That's how I feel," I said. "I like to watch things grow."

"Watch things grow, plant, nurture, then drink Scotch," Olive Oliver said. "Scottish Scotch only."

I nodded. "It does have a special smoothness after one has spent time cutting back the roses or tying up a wisteria just so."

"It is thrilling to the heart when pure dirt can be transformed with love and care," Olive said, "with a shovel and your bare hands, to flowers, trees, vines, and vegetables."

"From dirt to color. From nothing to an Eden. From plain to a place where butterflies and birds come to visit." I choked up. "Like friends."

Gitanjali reached for my hand and patted it. "We make the vegetables in dirt. We make the fruits bloomy. We talk, say hi to them, thank you for being over here with me. Then we share with others. Ah, gardening." She tapped her chest. "Here."

"It's a damn gift," Olive said, dabbing her eyes with her dizzy white cat scarf.

"Yes, a gifty." Gitanjali smiled, a dimple in her right cheek. "Damn."

"And I will forgive you for having a chicken stealer in your home," Olive said.

"Thank you. I appreciate your understanding. I had no knowledge of it. I will replace your chickens."

"No need."

"Please. I insist."

"We'll argue about chicken replenishment later," Olive said. "For now, I would like to formally invite you to attend the St. Ambrose Ladies' Gab, Garden, and Gobble Group."

I experienced some befuddlement.

"We get together with a group of women and talk gardening. Plants, flowers, plans, failures, and successes," Olive said, "then we gobble food, tea, wine, and gab. Talk."

"Would you like come?" Gitanjali asked. "Not much yelling at Gabbing and Gobbling Group. Sometimes. We control." She sighed. "We try control."

She was a sweet, compassionate person, I could tell. I wish I still had that side to me. I think it left me when I left Scotland as a teenager, the land absorbing my tears.

"We say what we please about men, marriage, women's roles in our changing society, politics, and social issues after we talk about gardening," Olive said. "We don't always agree about those issues or how to kill slugs. One time one of the ladies threw a bag of daffodil bulbs at one of the women, and another time we had a yelling fight and one woman landed in my geraniums, but that was all the violence."

Violence? In a garden talk group?

Gitanjali cleared her throat. "Not yet all. I be truth. We have one sad and scary incident with apple tree."

"It wasn't sad," Olive argued. "Two of the women were having an argument about who had better apple trees. They brought in apples for everyone to taste in a blind taste test. Well, the Obnoxious One, Lorna, lost and she threw a fit, then threw apples. One forehead was bruised."

"And there Hydrangea War." Gitanjali shook her head, made cluck-cluck sounds. "That another problem."

Olive waved a hand as in, "Let's not bother."

"People feel strongly about hydrangeas and soil composition," I said. "The colors, acid, lime, pruning . . ."

"I will admit our talks on politics and social issues can become a mite heated. Scottish temperaments in the room altogether." Olive exhaled.

Gitanjali's gold bracelets tinkled. "I say the politics not belong in same room as roses and the zinnias."

"Dangerous nights, they are," Olive said.

"I'm in," I said.

"You're in what?" Olive said.

"I mean, I'd like to come."

"Tuesday night is invitation," Gitanjali said, smiling, her dark eyes shining. "It will be delight. No throwing." Her brows came together. "Probably no throwing."

"With a pinch of excitement and minor violence and small temper tantrums," Olive said, playing with the dizzy white cat. "Don't you mind it now."

I wondered at my easy acceptance to the St. Ambrose Ladies' Garden, Gobbles, and Gabbling Group. Was that the correct name?

I avoid people. I don't like them much. I don't like groups of women, either, whose conversations can be too fast and too confusing, sometimes shallow and mundane. Not enough science or math, conversations that don't allow for emotions, which is, I know, partly why I'm attracted to both subjects. But what to say when I can't relate to the subject?

But this was gardening. I had longed for someone to discuss it with.

Maybe I longed for people to talk to about anything?

No.

That could not be true. Could it?

"Thank you, Gitanjali and Olive. I'll be there."

We chitchatted, they drove off, and Silver Cat wrapped herself around my legs. I picked her up and stared into her eyes. "I miss my cats. They are the best company of all, but you're acceptable, too."

I thought of Toran.

"Toran is more than acceptable."

Silver Cat leaped out of my arms and killed another mouse.

"You're an adept killer."

She dropped the dead mouse out of her mouth and meowed. I meowed back.

I put my garden gloves back on and started hauling out junk. Broken lamps, couch cushions (now mice homes), piles of moldy clothing and blankets, a wad of rubber bands, a massive collection of beer bottles, and the entire contents of the refrigerator, which I was sure was growing things that had never been seen before, including something red that resembled an electrified blood clot and something deep gray that appeared to move on its own.

Yuck and yuck. I like biology but not refrigerator biology.

I didn't see it at first. It was covered with food wrappers, a bicycle tire, a truck bumper, and a medium-sized cage. But once I cleared that off, my parents' dining room table appeared, built by my granddad.

"Oh." I ran my hand over it. "Oh." I wanted to hug it. "Oh."

We had eaten here. My father and mother and I. I had rolled bread with my mother and grandma, made jams and jellies, cut out Christmas sugar cookies, and made black buns with currants. I had helped my father make salmon noisettes with watercress and tomatoes. I had helped my mother make honey cake. We sang Scottish songs here. My grandma made her Scottish Second Sight predictions. I couldn't believe the table was still here.

I heard my granddad's booming laugh ringing in my head . . . my father's Scottish stories and legends . . . the bagpipes he used to play . . . my mother singing American rock songs and quoting Gloria Steinem.

I looked underneath it. Yes, there they were.

My granddad and grandma's names, my father and mother's names, my and Bridget's names. One rainy afternoon, Bridget and I had made a tent over the table with sheets and blankets and had played with a kids' laboratory my parents had bought me. We decided to sign the table as Scientist Bridget and Scientist Charlotte inside a red heart.

I ran my finger over our names, and my eyes became misty. Ah, poor Bridget. I sat cross-legged under the table. Poor Bridget. What nightmares came clawing for her later . . .

"What else is here?" I asked Silver Cat before I lost my emotional control. I found our armoire, which was now crooked, in one of the three bedrooms upstairs, clothes strung across it so that it was almost hidden, with a kitchen sink and bicycle handlebars on top. My granddad had built it for my grandma, a honeysuckle vine carved into the doors. The armoire had held my mother's china from her wedding and frames of our family.

I found two of our wood chairs in the master bedroom, upside down, near a car engine, two shovels, a tent, and a tarp. Each had a wobbly leg. My granddad had made them, too. My mother would sit in them while braiding my hair.

All the furniture had to be restored. Every piece needed to be sanded and restained. There were dents and scratches and structural problems, and they were filthy. They would all look much better when a trained hand was done with them. I had never thought of them as special when I was a kid, but now they were priceless.

They had belonged to my parents and grandparents. They were part of our past, our history, and our memories.

I missed my father. I missed my grandma and granddad. I even missed my ball-breaking mother in South Africa already. Contact with her for the next year was going to be sketchy because of the phone service.

I missed our life here in Scotland. I missed Bridget.

I heard a grumbling truck and peeked out the window. It was Toran. I wiped the tears off my face, refastened the clip on top of my head, forced myself to think of Madame Curie and her research to gain my composure, and headed out.

He smiled, then his face grew concerned. "What is it, Charlotte?"

I waved my hand. "Nothing. Dust in my eyes."

"Ah, Char." He gave me a hug. "I know. You have not been home in so long and yet this is what you find. Your childhood home in disrepair, a wreck, filled with the trash of someone else, nothing of what you remember here. The house has changed, but the memories remain of your father, bless his soul, your mum, your grandparents, and how you were as a family here together."

I nodded, sniffled too loud.

"This was your life, your home, and it was all lost to you so quickly. And here you are, twenty years later, a huge task ahead of you, to clean it out, and maybe sell it. Ah, too much. Too hard."

I took a tissue out of the pocket of my skirt. Never travel without a tissue. I couldn't help but snuggle into the warmth of his arms.

"I cannot take away the pain of what you're feeling, the loss, but I can help you. I have taken the rest of the day off to get this cleaned up."

"No, Toran. This is not your problem."

"Aye, it is. I want to help. I got up early to work on the farm. I thought you would be asleep for hours after your long flight. My employees are doing what needs to be done. So I'm here. Let's have a look, shall we?"

He stood in the doorway, those shoulders filling it. "Worse than I remembered from yesterday. Give me a minute, and I'll make a call. We'll get this fixed straight away."

He drove off, went home, came back, and half an hour later at my house there were six men who worked for Toran. They were friendly, cheerful.

"Here's what we have to do," Toran announced.

It was amazing what eight people could do. We had to get another giant bin, but by the end of the day—and it was a long, endless day, the sky dark when we were done—the house was cleared. Even the gross, moldy, yucky mattresses that probably had snakes living inside of them and a pantry full of the worst throat-clogging junk food were cleared out. We also removed an empty hornet's nest, a pair of antlers painted pink, and a freakish clown puppet.

The kitchen had been removed. There was no way to sell the house with it there. The curtains were ripped down, the garage cleared out, the carpets Mr. Greer had had installed ripped up. I did not gape *much* when Toran took off his shirt, as the other men had, and lifted furniture in a white undershirt. He was muscled up, tight and hard.

I chatted with the men who came to help. They were interested to know that I live on an island off the coast of Washington. I was vague about my job when they asked and started talking about the tomatoes I grew, three types, and my garden. I told them I had four cats and enjoyed studying the latest in science research and development. They asked if there were whales, and I said yes, many.

In the end everyone left and it was Toran and I, and Silver Cat, who meowed.

"I will pay you for your employees' time."

"No, luv. It's my favor to you."

"That's against my feminist leanings."

"Your what?" His brow furrowed.

"My feminist leanings. My feminists ideals. My belief system on what it means to be a woman independent of men, rebelling against a society that says women need to be paid for and taken care of."

"I hardly understood what you said, Charlotte, but it's a gift, and we don't need to talk about it anymore. Make me a pie in exchange. Here, let's test your aim." He reached down for a pile of cracked plates. We stood fifteen feet away from the bin.

I glanced at the plates. They had naked women on them. "How can you eat staring at a crotch?" I muttered.

Toran chuckled. "Well, I suppose it depends on whose it is."

I blushed.

"But not these, for sure," he said. "Toss 'em."

"I want you to take the money, Toran. It's my house. I'll pay to have it cleared."

"Make me a pie, as you did before. I love your pies. The best ever."

I admit I blushed with pride, then put my hands on my hips.

"Don't do that, Charlotte. I remember that expression from when you were younger. Stubborn. Accept a gift."

"That's hard for me, especially from a man."

"You're back in Scotland." He grinned. "Let me be the man."

Let him be the man?

He saw my hesitation. "I'm the man, you're the woman, I pay to clean out your house."

"That's not part of the rules."

"Aye, lass. I don't like rules. But I do like you. Very much. Here, let's have a throwing contest. I'll bet I'll win."

He knew that would get me. It always did when we were kids.

I grabbed a naked girl crotch plate. Who would believe that tossing dishes into a bin would make me laugh so much.

We threw plates, then cracked tea cups that said, "Bash Your Balls and Bagpipes." Next we cracked bowls with women's busts barely covered by Scottish tartans. Toran won every time, though I did try to calculate angle, length of toss, and wind velocity, of which there was little.

"I will have to practice this," I told him.

"It's rather fun, isn't it? Takes your mind off things."

We stared at each other and he smiled, his blue eyes comparable to blue heat. The years fell away and we became who we were as kids: King Toran and Queen Charlotte. Two of the four rulers of the Enchanted Woods. Dragon Slayers. Evil Emperor Destroyers. Champions of the Scottish people. Enemies of a tyrannical King of England.

"I'm glad you're here, Charlotte."

"Me too."

He put a hand up. I placed my hand against his. "Let victory unite us," we said, together.

I blinked. It was still there.

"We always knew what chant to say, Char."

"We did." There had been many chants, but we repeatedly picked the same one.

It had been uncanny how connected we were, but I had loved him as if he was part of my own soul.

My soul had missed Toran.

As I drove back to Toran's, I thought about what I was doing. It would cost a fortune to remodel the house. It would be cheaper to bulldoze it and sell the land.

I thought about flattening the house my great-grandfather built.

I absolutely could not do it.

I turned toward the green Play-Doh-like hills in the distance, now covered in nighttime's shadows. Beyond them was the Mackintosh/Ramsay graveyard.

It was where my father was buried. I would go and see my father at his grave, covered in daffodils and bluebells. I would go and pay my respects. Not yet, though.

Not yet.

In my field, romance writing, everyone expects the writer to have a rollicking love life. Panting under the sheets, sexual gymnastics, creative lovers. A change in lovers now and then when you get bored, bad-boy attraction without giving up your power, maybe tattoos, dark hair and smoldering eyes. Blah blah blah.

I know many romance writers—not that I've met many, because I don't go to conferences and conventions and that sort of silliness, but we do write and call—and that image is rarely true. In fact, I don't know anyone who has a man toy. Some of the romance writers I correspond with have been married twenty, thirty, even fifty years to the same man. Most of them write their romance novels in pajamas, ponytail on their head, door shut to the outside world.

One will eat only even numbers of food at a time when she's on a deadline. Forty-two spaghetti noodles, four pieces of bacon, two bowls of oatmeal. Another picks at her left eyebrow until it's gone. A third dresses up like her characters to get into their heads.

Disappointing to hear of their peculiarities, but it is the unvarnished truth.

I won't toss off my skirts, high-riser underwear, and comfortable shoes for any man. I'm not buying into that free sex thing. What is free about it? What if his condom slipped off? What if he had a disease? What if I got pregnant? I don't want him to spend the night, and I don't want to spend the night at his house, either.

What if he wanted to stay for breakfast? What if he wanted to stay for lunch and dinner? What if he wanted to stay, in general, as in, every day?

I don't want a man hanging around every day. I need my privacy. I need to be alone. I don't need his opinion or his thoughts about my life. I don't want to change, nor will I, to accommodate him. Men don't live up to expectations. I know that from my Unfortunate Marriage.

I shouldn't lump all men together, like weeds invading a rose garden, or a comet heading toward Earth.

But, generally, for excitement, women should study the Hubble Space Telescope and the technology there. What else is out there in our galaxy and beyond? Now, that is thrilling.

But Toran would be thrilling, too.

I thought about him naked.

Oh yes. He would be even better than the Hubble Space Telescope.

4

"I found these before I had our old house demolished."

Toran handed me a battered cardboard box after we had fish and chips and white wine on his deck for dinner.

His view was peaceful, panoramic. The ocean spread out in the distance like a blue-black blanket with frothy lace on the ends.

"What's in it?" I fiddled with the top button of my beige blouse. After I had showered, I had paired it with my dark brown skirt and a brown sweater with a blue, smiling whale on the left shoulder.

"Open it, but be prepared, Charlotte."

I studied his face. He had a hard jaw and lines fanning out from his eyes. He was the kind of man who would get even more deadly handsome as he aged. "Okay. I'll be prepared."

Inside the box there was a stack of letters tied with straw. My name was written on the outside of each envelope.

Charlotte

Queen Charlotte

Charlotte Mackintosh

My friend, Char

Charlotty

My hands shook as I took them out. "What?" My voice was stricken. "What are these?" But I knew. I knew what they were.

"These are letters that Bridget wrote to you. She obviously never sent them. She didn't want to tell you the truth. It was therapy for her. It was like writing to her diary, only she wrote them to you, her best friend, as she did when she was a child. I think she wanted the truth of her life written down, and that's why she brought these letters home and placed them in the box.

"I read some, I hope you don't mind. I was trying to find her, find out the truth of what happened. My parents weren't honest with me at the time. They lied about where she was and why. Then they refused to talk about her at all." He paused, clenched his jaw, and groaned. "I'm sorry. Their part in this is still painful—it infuriates me, they infuriate me—and Bridget's letters are an open door to atrocious things that happened to her."

I put a hand to my forehead. "In our letters back and forth she talked only about normal things . . . her garden, a boyfriend now and then, going to university . . . her friends here, her travels . . . sometimes she would talk about being lonely, or alone, but I would, too. It was normal life. . . ."

"Charlotte, the only men she has ever been with have hurt her. She never went to university. She traveled, but it wasn't for pleasure. She was wandering, she was often in trouble. She wasn't lying about her love of gardening. In some of the letters she talks about the garden here. She loved working in our garden. She told me what she wanted and I did it. I built the trellises to her exact specifications. I used a rototiller on the ground so she could plant her roses and bulbs. She bought plants, and together we got out the shovels. The garden was Bridget's haven. Then she would take off again, her nightmares chasing her down."

Toran stood up and stalked across the deck, then leaned against the post of his trellis, arms crossed over his huge chest. "You were her one island. The truth, Charlotte, of her life is in those letters."

"But . . ."

"Read them." He ran a hand through his brown curls. "It'll

take a while. Ask me anything when questions come up. If you hate me by the end of it, I'll understand."

"Why would I hate you? I could never hate you, Toran."

"You might. I did not protect my sister. That was my job as her older brother. That's reason enough. I have looked for Bridget many times when I don't hear from her. I have been to eight different countries, countless cities—three different trips in the last three years. I have paid people to go and find her. Now and then I find her and bring her home, get her help. Then she leaves again. It's up to her to come home this time."

I picked up the stack of letters.

"Start from the beginning, Charlotte," he said, so gentle.

I nodded my head, pushed my hair out of my eyes. "Okay."

In the guest room that night, the yellow comforter around me, I opened up the first letter.

November 30, 1973

Dear Charlotte,

Do you know? Do you know what happened? No. How could you. You weren't there. You were gone.

I am alone.

The bluebells are blooming.

Love,

Bridget

I opened up a second letter, then a third. First came shock, then horror, then the tears. Endless tears.

Toran saw my swollen face the next morning when he returned from working on his farm and hugged me close. I looked like a pale gargoyle. I cried on his shoulder, a blubbery mess. Tears slipped out of his eyes, too.

"I couldn't read all of them." I pushed my hair back, as some had slipped out of my clip. "Only a few."

"Pains my heart, that it does."

"Mine too, Toran." My voice broke, aching for Bridget. I was furious, too. Furious at what had happened to her.

We talked and talked.

Toran wiped my tears away, so gentle. He clenched his jaw, but his eyes kept watering on up, like mine. Bridget, Queen Bridget, dragon slayer, artist, kid scientist. Poor Bridget.

I would read more letters.

But not now. I couldn't.

I made a call, then another call. I wrote a check and mailed it. I hoped.

That afternoon Toran handed me the keys to one of his trucks. It was black. "Please return the rental, Charlotte. You're losing money. Drive my truck."

"No, thank you. I couldn't take advantage of you like that."

"Please. I want you to take advantage." He winked at me.

Baby, I want to take advantage of your body. Thank heavens I did not say that out loud.

"I will rent."

"I'm afraid I can't allow that, as it's a waste of money, luv."

"You need the truck."

"I don't. It's now yours. And you have that stubborn expression on your face again, Charlotte."

"This is, once again, against my—"

"Your feminist leanings, I know. Don't quite understand it. No arguing, or I'll kick you out of Clan TorBridgePherLotte."

"You can't do that. It would require a vote."

He grinned. Dang.

"Thank you, Toran."

"I'll have two of my employees return your car tomorrow. Leave the keys on the front seat."

I would like to strip you naked on your front seat. "I can do it."

"I know you can. Let me do this for you."

Let me do what I wish with you, Scottish stud. "I'll handle it."

"But I want to do this for you."

"Then I insist on cooking dinner for you."

His eyes lit up. "Luv, I think I have the better end of the deal."

I would like to see your rear end. I cleared my throat. I hoped he couldn't tell what I was thinking. I gave him a smile to cover up my rampant, carnal thoughts.

He smiled back.

My father, Quinn Mackintosh, was a huge, blustery, smart Scotsman. Proud of himself, his family, his ancestors, his clan, proud of being a Scot.

I remembered some of his favorite quotes. "A man who does not stand up for what he believes in, is no man at all. . . . If a man doesn't make a decision, that is a decision. . . . A man who cannot provide for and protect his woman and family has fallen down on his responsibilities. . . ."

He told Bridget and me Scottish legends, handed down from generation to generation, but often he'd make up legends and magical stories himself, sometimes on the spot.

"Keep an eye out, girls," he told us one day. "Yesterday I saw a faerie watching me, sprinkling her golden glitter. When I chased after her, she flew up into the trees and right through a hidden green door. The faeries use the trees as secret passageways to their own villages."

"Where do they live?" Bridget asked.

"They live in the clouds, on rainbows, on the tops of stars, in our forests and meadows. Their world is filled with magic, rivers of gold and stars of silver. They have two moons."

"They have two moons?" I asked.

"Aye, lass, and two suns, and now and then they come here to play tricks and maybe make a wish or two come true."

Bridget and I decided to keep our eyes out for faeries in the forests and meadows, but also in the village, as my father said they could hide quickly among the alleys, nooks, and crannies.

"They know the village because they've lived here for hundreds of years. They know where the magic is. They know where they can slip in a crack, or jump through an attic window, or hop through an open door."

I wrote my father's legends down, and Bridget drew the pictures. She liked to draw everything in miniature, down to the most intricate details. She drew tiny faeries with sparkling wings, homes tucked into tree branches, birds with glittering wings carrying princesses, butterflies drinking tea together.

We spent hours making books, in our house, not hers. She had to leave all of her work at our house, as her father would not have approved of magic. Magic was considered ungodly.

My parents delighted in our books, always careful not to say a word about it to Carney Ramsay, or his cowed wife, Bonnie. It was a magical time.

At least for me.

To the ladies of the St. Ambrose Gab, Garden, and Gobble Group—

We will meet at our usual time, 6:00, on Tuesday, at my home. Please bring soup and bread to share.

Charlotte Mackintosh will be coming. I am delighted that she is back at her family home, although I fear she plans on selling it. All these years of dealing with Mr. Greer stealing my chickens. Lieutenant Judith. Lizbeth. Smelly Toad. To think of my edible pets in his massive gut!

How he was able to get that girth of his up and moving fast enough to catch one of my ladies is beyond me. If the man was broke, he could have told me, and I would have helped, but he had to go and steal my precious feathered friends. Maddening!

I will be making my enchilada soup with chips and guacamole. I will be sending Fiona to chicken heaven. You know, the brown and white one, gold feathers on top? Arrogant chicken.

She'll be delicious.

Remember, we need to talk about the fund-raiser. I can put up a couple of my chickens for the event, but we need something to crow about if we are going to contribute money for whatever worthy cause we choose this year, so start tootling that thinking cap!

Sincerely,
Olive

As always, so we don't have to spend all day on the blasted phone, pass this note around. When you've seen it, write your name down, or a message at the bottom, and get it quick as a whip to the next person on the list. You all know the route by now.

To the ladies of the Garden Gobbling group,

Olive,

I'm delighted that Charlotte is coming. I can't wait to see her! She's a few years younger than me. Charlotte's parents were both quite kind. I remember loving Mrs. Mackintosh's American accent. I thought it was so worldly and stylish.

I heard from Dee Dee's boy, Arthur, who works for Toran, and who helped unload all the rubbish from Charlotte's house, that Charlotte lives on an island near Hawaii, has about twenty cats, sells vegetables for a living, especially tomatoes, and she has six types of tomatoes. She's a farmer like her father. She likes physics. She also is against whale killing, but keeps whales in the ocean, which is her front yard. A tad confusing!

Don't kill Fiona. I love that chicken. She's a chicken fashion model and I won't eat her.

On another note, we could kill my soon-to-be ex-husband, The Arse, pluck his feathers, boil him, and feed him to a hog. He has a girlfriend named Chrissy. You might know her by her other name, Bubbles. Can you believe this? He left me for bubbles.

Rowena

Hello garden gang ladies,

Olive, I have to add my own dose of medicine here. Please don't kill Fiona. She is one of my favorites. She does seem to think the world of herself, but more woman power to her, right? Maybe we all should learn to strut like she does. Sorry this is such the scribble! I had a plum busy night. I reattached a toe, put twelve stitches into a man's arse when he cut it open on a wine barrel, and had to operate on a man who had "accidentally" swallowed two beer caps.

He was in his cups. Told me I reminded him of "Doctor Mean Elf."

I'm so glad to hear that Charlotte is a farmer in the States. Her father was an outstanding farmer and businessman, that's what my father says. He still misses Quinn.

Kenna

Ladys,

I come to Gobbling Ladys Club and I bring chicken makhani, which is a chicken that has the butter. It's tasty in the mouth water.

And piece to all of you and joy of life,

Gitanjali

Rowena and Kenna,

Don't be ridiculous. You will love the taste of Fiona.

Olive

Lorna,

I am sending this note only to you.

We have St. Ambrose Ladies' Gab, Garden, and Gobble Group this week, as usual. I want to talk to you about something, and I thought I'd put it in a letter for personal protection. You can come round or phone later if you need to talk after you have calmed your feathers back down.

A few of the women have been complaining because—I don't know how to say it gently, so I won't bother—you're snippy and rude.

When you told Rowena that her garden had not improved for years, that did not have a pleasing result. It was not right for her to shove her slice of Tantallon cake into your chest, and call you an old witch, as you are not old, but you had no right to get so huffy about it, either. Rowena has four kids, and an ex-husband who, as you know, has taken up with that young bartender in town with breasts the size of Edinburgh.

When you had an argument with Kenna and told her she didn't know a thing about roses, which she does, and you realize it, Lorna, as her roses always win awards, it showed your jealous side. You took such offense when she said your garden looks like you, uptight, and as if it had a snake up its butt, but what you said to her was uncalled for now, wasn't it?

As for Gitanjali. You will hardly recognize her presence because she's from India. Don't deny it and stop it this instant.

So, Lorna, as a proud gardener, the president of the club, and a Scotswoman, I'll have to insist that you act like a pleasant human to the women in gardening club or stay home and dust.
Olive

"How does it feel to be back in Scotland, Charlotte?" Toran stretched his legs out in front of his fireplace, which was huge, with a rock hearth and a mantel made of polished wood. He had long legs, hard and muscled. I tried not to stare. My oh my. I had made Partan Bree soup with crab, white rice and sherry, barbecued beef steaks with shallots, bread, and Scottish Whisky Dundee cake with orange and lemon. When he saw what I had cooked when he came in from work, I thought the man was going to swoon. He said, "I wish I had more trucks to loan you."

I had tried not to giggle, because that would have been unbecoming for a person my age, and too simpering to boot. So I blushed.

"It feels like I've returned home only a few key people are missing."

He smiled, soft. "I understand. You must miss your father and grandparents even more when you're here. And Bridget. I'm sorry, I truly am."

He was so quick, so intuitive. We talked, and he asked all sorts of questions about me and my work as a writer. He was truly interested, which is so sexy. A listening man is a sex-able man. You can have wild good sex with a listening man. I think. I mean, I would have if I had been given the opportunity.

I reminded him not to tell anyone about how I write, as I am "part hermit, part recluse, part insanely private," and he said, "Your secret is safe with me unless you refuse to make me this Scottish Whisky Dundee cake again."

I reassured him I would make him the whiskey cake again.

"Dance with me, Charlotte," he asked as the fire burned down.

"Right now?"

"Yes," Toran said, spreading his arms out. "Dance with me."

"There's no music."

"One moment please, lass." He turned on rock music, the dancing sort.

He held out his arms. "Let's dance like your parents used to dance together." He pushed a table and a chair out of the way. "Your father was my role model on how to treat a woman, so let's see how I'm doing."

"The only type of dances I know are the traditional Scottish Highland dances where I'm kicking my heels up with my arms in arcs in the air, back straight. I can also do the foxtrot, some salsa and ballroom dancing, but with this free dancing, wiggling everywhere to a beat everyone hears that I don't hear, I'm awkward and unbalanced."

"Every Scot knows how to dance."

"I think that gene has gone missing."

"No, you have it. It's given at birth. We danced as kids, and I remember you could dance then. The four of us danced in the meadow all the time."

"And in the river."

"And on top of the hill."

"And on the beach."

"Then that proves it. You can dance."

"It's been years. I have no rhythm. You will confuse me with an electrified chicken."

"You see? You are so funny, Char. An electrified chicken." He laughed. "Come on, luv."

He pulled me into his arms. I was stiff at first, rigid like a stick. My long brown skirt didn't help, and my sturdy brown shoes were not slidey enough.

"If you dance I'll let you have some of my Scottish whiskey."

"I can't refuse then, King Toran." I smiled. I sounded almost flirty. Was that flirting? I pulled back and curtsied. I smiled at him. I hadn't seen him in twenty years but now here he was, a man. A heck of a handsome Scotsman.

I placed my hand in his, and his fingers curled around mine.

He twirled me around. He spun me, he turned and dipped me.

I laughed. I twirled, I spun, I tried to dip him. He was too tall. We swayed and boogied and did strange things like pounding our fists into the air, and wiggling our butts around, and swirling our hips while waving our hands. We latched elbows and do-si-doed. We danced back to back and side to side. He pulled me through his legs, then flipped me over his shoulder.

Later, we collapsed on the couch.

"I knew it," he breathed heavily.

"What?" I panted.

"You're my perfect Scottish dance partner."

"And it appears that you are mine, too, King Toran. You're a fine dancing partner. Quick on those feet of yours."

I wanted to kiss him so much, I tingled in my privates.

Did I know how to kiss okay still? It had been a long time.

Would my lips forget?

Would my breath be okay?

What about my tongue? Did he like French kissing? Did I know how to do it right anymore?

I couldn't help smiling at him as he yanked me up and we did the twist. I wanted to pull him down on top of me and link my ankles behind his shoulders.

I was beginning to believe that all of my sex thoughts were disrespectful to Toran's intellect and fine character.

Nah.

I woke up the next morning and stretched in my flannel nightgown. I actually hurt in a few places because I shook my buttocks so hard on the dance floor.

Last night, I'd danced. My whole body moved to the beat. Yes, I, Charlotte Mackintosh, had found my beat. My rhythm. My dancing shoes, which ended up being my bare feet.

I had danced with Toran.

I pulled the sheet over my head, then wriggled myself as hard as I could.

I was a dancing girl again.

Romance Readers and Writers Magazine
By Kitty Rosemary
Books For Chicks Reviewer

MY OH MY, THE LITERARY SECRETS I'LL TELL

This week I'm writing about the mysterious, elusive Georgia Chandler. Her latest book, Danger, Doughnuts, and a Latin Lover, A Romantic Time Travel Adventure, Book Number Nine, *is still topping the charts since it debuted sixteen weeks ago. She has sold approximately ten million books, but who's counting?*

La-di-da, I love 'em all.

Her protagonist, McKenzie Rae Dean, is a saucy, adventurous, lusty character who is afraid of chains, enclosed spaces, and sausages, because of the phallic shape, and thinks pudding is disgusting. She is surprisingly emotionally deep and her problems, fears, and personal pain strikes women readers straight in the gut.

McKenzie Rae Dean rocks my literary world, I am telling you.

We all know everything about McKenzie Rae Dean, but the question that lights my brain on fire and smokes it, as a book reporter is, who is author Georgia Chandler?

I'll tell you what I know. Don't breathe a word of it to anyone else!

As some of you know, Georgia Chandler's real name is Charlotte Mackintosh.

We know that Charlotte Mackintosh received degrees in biology and physics from Stanford and went to work at a research lab after graduation. We know she published her first book when she was twenty-five. We know there are eight books after that and she lives, reputedly, on an island off the coast of Washington.

But there are other rumors that she spends part of every year in Tibet in meditation, in China with monks, and in Africa on months-long safaris. I've heard rumors that she particularly likes watching apes in their natural habitat.

So the recluse part? I'm not so sure about that. The sleuth in me is doubtful.

We also know that she is unmarried, but again, through the grapevine, I've heard there are men. *Men plural, isn't that titillating? She's like McKenzie Rae Dean. Voracious!*

And we've heard that she doesn't tell those men that she's Georgia Chandler, New York Times *bestselling author. In fact, she tells them she's, get this, a fourth-grade teacher! Hilarious! Tickle my tummy, doesn't that give you a giggle?*

But that's all we know. She refuses to give interviews. She refuses to answer questions by letter or by phone. She is a mystery, and I don't like mysteries. I like to open them wiiiide up and reveal it all, drum roll, please!

Her New York agent, Maybelle Courten, says that Ms. Mackintosh/Georgia Chandler wants her readers to focus on the stories in her romantic time travel adventure series and not her.

"Georgia Chandler loves and appreciates her readers, but she likes her privacy." Asked if she traveled in disguise all over the world, Courten said, "Georgia needs to nurture her creative energy. Sometimes she takes herself off on adventures to exotic worldwide locales and uses a fake name and identity. She keeps her love life private. I absolutely cannot comment on the men who are in and out of her life to protect her privacy and theirs."

There have been no photos of Georgia Chandler/Charlotte Mackintosh in ten years. There have been no appearances.

As one fan, Dr. Barbara said (she told me I couldn't print her last name as she's up for tenure), "I'm a chemistry professor at an elite university. I read Georgia Chandler's books to relax. Do I want to go home and read one of those gloomy literary novels where life sucked, life sucks now, and life will suck in the future? Those dreary ones that win awards and pompous people pretend they read? No. Hell, no. I don't. I want to read about McKenzie Rae Dean's adventures traveling through time and the sexy men she ends up naked in bed with."

Samantha Pho, who owns her own import-export business said, "I often pretend that I'm McKenzie Rae Dean. Sometimes when I'm bored at work, I write down where I want to go and to what time period. I even bought a red bag, exactly like hers, so when I'm in business meetings, I can channel her aura. Crazy, I know. And I don't like pudding or sausage anymore, either."

Next year another book will come out.

You will not be hearing from Georgia Chandler.

(Unless I, dear friends, do some poking and prodding and find out the real truth about Georgia Chandler/Charlotte Mackintosh. And I shall pop some champagne and share it all with you!)

Secrets, secrets, they tickle my fancy.

Ta-ta for now!

Kiss, kiss!

Kitty Rosemary

In each one of my books, McKenzie Rae is working as a minimalist artist in Seattle. She draws the exact same type of drawings that Bridget did. A full scene. Lots of color, tiniest details. She sells her work at art shows and sometimes she sits near Pike Place Market and draws and sells her work right off her easel.

Sometimes I keep McKenzie Rae in her new time period for months, other times she stays for a lifetime, then I whisk her back on her deathbed. In the first novel, McKenzie Rae Dean falls in love with her soul mate. They are married for ten blissful years, then she's whisked back to current time and she can't get back to him.

She falls in love with other men, one a book, but she never forgets the soul mate, in the almost two hundred years she racks up time traveling.

McKenzie Rae and I are radically different in a multitude of ways. McKenzie Rae is daring and brave. I like being home and frighten easily. McKenzie Rae is witty and funny. I am not sure I have a sense of humor. McKenzie Rae is outgoing and social. I like to be alone and I don't like people much.

McKenzie Rae dresses in silks and high heels. She flashes her cleavage and butt. I prefer my long skirts, bulky sweaters to cover my body, and shoes that are flat and comfy.

McKenzie Rae is good in bed, passionate and free. She has *experience.*

It's embarrassing to admit how little va-va-vooming I've had in bed. I am probably a sexual dud.

McKenzie Rae would never need a vibrator named Dan, like me.

We do have one thing in common, though: McKenzie Rae has a soul mate she can't have.

I have the same problem.

I understand her angst and longing.

I was married once. He was not my soul mate. It lasted two years. By the end of it, I felt shriveled, exhausted, and defeated. I was surprised and unprepared for what I found out about my husband. On one hand, it was devastating. On the other, it was not my fault. I realize that now. It sure hurt then.

I knew Toran knew about the divorce. Maybe I would talk about it with him.

If I had married Toran, that never would have happened.

Toran told me about two home remodelers named Stanley I and Stanley II. They were cousins. I called Stanley I from Toran's and met both Stanley I and Stanley II at the house the next day. They were about forty-five and have been remodeling and building homes since they were nineteen.

Apparently Stanley I and Stanley II had mothers who were sisters who both wanted to name their children after their father. Neither one would back down. So, Stanley I and Stanley II were born. Stanley II was born one month after Stanley I.

Stanley II asked where I was from, and when I said an island off the coast of Washington, we talked about whales and migration. His knowledge about them was extensive. Stanley I had extensive knowledge about the American stock market. "A gamble, if you ask me, run fast and loose by gamblers and gangsters, sanctified by the American government."

I knew we would be able to relate. They were smart, had ideas already about what to do with my home, and they were experienced, honest, and articulate.

I hired them and promised to get them a check. They would start immediately, but they couldn't work this weekend. Stanley II's daughter was getting married. "Got a temper that one, feisty as a tornado, fiancé is half deaf. I think it will work out because of the deafness, I do."

"Maisie has her mother's temper," Stanley I said.

"And I have been married to that woman with that temper for twenty-five years." Stanley II sighed.

"Must not have bothered you that much, as you have six kids," I said.

"My woman, she does let the steam blow off of her when she has her feelings in a stew and a boil, but, to this day, I cannot say I have ever met a woman I wanted to be with more than my Serena."

"Serena is a blessing, a true Scottish wife," Stanley I said, nodding. "I've been married for twenty years, to my Isla. Five kids."

"You two have a lot of kids," I said.

"Too many," they said together.

We all laughed.

"Any named Stanley?"

Yes, one boy each. Stanley III, Stanley IV.

Dear Charlotte,

I so enjoyed catching up with you when you came to get the key for your cottage. I also enjoyed showing you my garden and your mother's goldenrod daisies and the honeysuckle vine while we had our tea. Please excuse my emotional response when I saw you, the tears that leapt unbidden to my eyes. It was a gift to see you again, to see the daughter of my friends, all grown up now.

I wanted to thank you for buying Olive Oliver

ten chickens. That was certainly kind of you to do, though not necessary. I know that your parents would have done the same thing in this pickle, they being honorable people.

I saw Olive in town and she was infinitely pleased and surprised at your generosity. She said she tried to give five chickens back to you, but you insisted. Olive named them, as she probably shared with you, after flowers: Violet, Snapdragon, Daffodil, Rose, Begonia, Crocus, Dahlia, Marigold, Peach Blossom, and Tulip.

Intelligent and neighborly decision on your part. We now no longer have chicken wars in the village.

Olive said she'll kill Tulip and send her over. Perhaps I will go to Gitanjali's spice shop and buy spices and chat with Gitanjali about how to prepare Tulip. Do you know Gitanjali yet? I am (delicately) trying to get to know her better, as she is an intriguing woman.

So far I have bought twelve pounds of cardamom, four pounds of cinnamon, and two pounds of dill weed. Gitanjali gave me recipes to follow. I have filed them in a new recipe box I bought called Gitanjali's Recipe Box for this particular purpose, but I have no clue how to cook.

Yours,

Chief Constable Ben Harris

A friend of your parents, may the choirs of angels accompany your father as he plays the bagpipes for Our Lord.

Dear Chief Constable Harris,

The pleasure of our visit was all mine. You are right, though. Seeing my mother's goldenrod daisies and the honeysuckle vine did send the two of us down an unexpected emotional lane! Next time I will bring more tissues. I am glad we have reconnected, and I shall tell my mother in South Africa in my next letter to her.... I know she thought the world of you and Lila, as did my father.

I was happy to buy the chickens and have them delivered. I don't want to be involved in any village chicken squabbles, and a chicken crime was committed.

I have met Gitanjali, and you are correct. I liked her. If I am not being too forward, perhaps you would like me to speak to Gitanjali when I see her at Garden Ladies Gobbling Gang and tell her what a long-term and loyal friend you were to my parents, that you are a man of character and integrity.

Yours,

Charlotte

Charlotte,

I would be most indebted to you if you could put in a word for me with Gitanjali. My intentions are honorable. I don't want to offend her in any way or to step in a direction where she would not wish me to step. She is a gentle woman and I don't want to alarm her. I am not a skilled man when it comes to dating. In fact, it confounds me. I am, currently, confounded.

I did, however, buy three pounds of curry powder today from her and two pounds of Indian gooseberry. She gave me more recipes to follow. I have no idea how to cook. I did file the recipes away in the Gitanjali's Recipe Box.

Gratefully,

Chief Constable Ben Harris

A friend of your parents, may your father win all the events in heaven's Scottish games.

Silver Cat showed up at Toran's the next evening. Toran heard a meowing at the front door and opened it. Silver Cat limped in. He picked her up and cradled her against his chest. "Isn't this the cat that was at your house?"

"Yes. That is. I didn't know where she came from. There are a few houses down the road from us, I thought she might belong to them."

"We'll check. I'll put up signs tomorrow."

Silver Cat meowed. I meowed back, then Toran meowed.

I had a feeling we had a new cat.

5

“I want to take a shake of a lamb’s tail minute to welcome Charlotte Mackintosh to our St. Ambrose Ladies’ Gab, Garden, and Gobble Group,” Olive Oliver said, her white braid over her shoulder. Tonight she was wearing a knitted pink scarf with a frog with a long pink tongue. The frog looked inebriated. I don’t think it was intentional.

Seven women, including me, were in Olive’s living room, tea, cream, and sugar ready. Olive lived right outside of town, within walking distance, in a three-hundred-year-old stone home with her husband, their acreage, and animals behind the house. She had a rock wall in front of her house and white daisies surrounding the border. The home reminded me of Snow White’s.

Her husband was a carpenter. They had married ten years ago, and she made and sold scarves, which accounted for the dizzy white cat and the inebriated frog. Her business was called Lady Olive’s Scarves. She was an animal lover who believed, “Animals should be cherished until eaten.” In addition to her chickens, she had pigs, horses, and lambs. She did not eat the horses, she told me. “I won’t eat an animal I can ride.”

“Yes welcome . . . hello, Charlotte . . . nice to meet you, from the States then . . .” the women’s voices blended.

“Your grandma,” Rowena said, “told my own mother that she would become pregnant when two pies were baked and when the moon was full, but colored orange like fire. Sure enough, when Mr. Beacon’s barn burned down and turned the moon orange, my mother was pregnant with me and it was the same day she baked two pies: huckleberry and strawberry."

Rowena has red hair and gold eyes and is bright and confident. She was wearing a funky necklace with a rock wrapped in silver wire. It was earthy. I liked it. Next to her I felt like a dull possum, but I couldn't help but like her. I liked her when I was younger, too. She's about five years older and was always nice to Bridget and me. Her family's farm is down the road, which her elderly parents had sold to Toran.

When Rowena saw me she screamed and hugged me. I am not used to people getting excited to see me or long hugs. I was surprised to find that I became very emotional.

Which made Rowena yell, "For the love of God, Charlotte's crying! For the love of God, I'm crying now, too."

"Your grandma told me that when two birds collided, and a shot went through a foot, I would be free," a blond woman named Kenna said. She's a doctor. "When that horrible first husband of mine saw two birds collide in midair and fall, he thought that was so neat he accidentally shot himself in the foot and died of an infection, the buffoon. I was in medical school then. He used to slug me when we had a fight to 'shut my trap shut.' Said I was getting too uppity for him. When he had the infection he was even worse. He tossed my cat, broke its leg."

I sucked in air, other people made equally angry noises. Cats are furry people and must be treated with respect.

"The cat tossing did it. I moved out." Kenna smiled. "Too bad he died alone."

"Too bad," Olive drawled.

The other women nodded.

"It's been years, but I still miss your grandma," Kenna said.

"Me too." I felt a pang in my heart. "My grandma died two years before my father. She told me she would die after the houses were flipped upside down, thousands of trees were on the ground like toothpicks, and the wind spun hell up from its grave. She died about two weeks after Hurricane Low Q."

They all remembered Hurricane Low Q.

"I would love to see your mother again, prettiest woman in

the village when she was here," Rowena said. "I remember thinking that when I was a child."

"Well," a woman in her late fifties humphed. "She was *one* of the prettiest women here, in an *American* sort of way."

I studied her. Grayish hair. Face set like a bulldog. Her upper body was normal sized, although she had ponderous boobs, but her hips sprawled. It seemed as if she had two bodies, one average sized sitting atop a lap spreading like packed oatmeal. She smiled with irritating condescension at me. "There were others who were as pretty, or prettier, everyone said so."

"So you knew my mother, Ms.— " I paused and waited for her to fill in her name.

"*Mrs.* David Lester."

As a feminist I fought not to roll my eyes back into my head. Why on earth would a woman identify herself by using her husband's name, as if she is no one, only an appendage, like an octopus's leg?

"Mrs. Lorna," she emphasized. "Lorna Lester. And yes." She squiggled her oatmeal butt in the chair. I could tell by her drawn, disapproving expression that she hadn't liked my mother. "I did know Jasmine. Some. We didn't socialize. We had different . . . friends." She pursed her lips. "Her friends had different . . . *values* than myself."

Ah. I got it. Let's imply that my mother had poor values, in front of all these ladies. I studied Lorna Lester. I wasn't surprised that my mother wasn't friends with her. She wouldn't have liked that patronizing, petty personality. My mother liked interesting, outgoing people with an edge. She was friends with prosecutors, professors, doctors, two strippers—one of whom was transgender and made the best banana pie ever—artists, writers, and two ex-cons who now run a floral shop. She was friends with other feminists and political activists, and with one member of the mob in Jersey.

"What would those different values be?" I asked.

Lorna made an impatient *pfft* sound and waved a hand, as if it was "nothing," my mother *nothing*. "We were different . . . women. I valued my home life, and my husband and daughter."

I heard Kenna, the doctor, groan and mutter, "Not again."

Gitanjali murmured, "Unkind. Let us be gentle."

"My mother didn't value her daughter and husband?" I felt my temper rise. I am somewhat shy and socially insecure, but I am no doormat, and don't mess with my mother.

"Well, your mother *worked*."

"You say that in the same tone as if you're saying my mother caught lizards and ripped off their legs with her teeth."

Lorna's eyes widened in surprise.

"Yes, my mother worked. She helped my father run the farm."

"She also wrote articles for the local paper on many . . . let's say, *inflammatory* issues that we didn't need to hear about."

Olive flipped her white braid back, tugged on her knitted inebriated frog scarf, and said, "I liked your mother's articles. I read them in the village I was living in an hour north of here. Some people need to have their minds opened up so they can properly join us in the twentieth century."

"I'm in the twentieth century," Rowena said. "Firmly planted. Go women. Boo men. Especially my ex-husband, The Big Arse. May his scrotum rot."

I nodded at Rowena. "Creative thinking." I turned to Lorna. "My mother wrote about women, women's rights, women's choices and opportunities. I've read her articles." I had met women like Lorna. It was one of the reasons I prefer cats.

"I personally believe that a woman's place is in the home, supporting her husband and children." Lorna tilted her chin up, proud of herself in an oh-so sanctimonious way.

"Well, rah-rah for you," Kenna said. "But not everyone shares that opinion."

"I work," Olive said. "I make my scarves and sell them. Not as many as I'd like, but I'm growing my business. Fortunately, I haven't used them to gag anyone." She dipped her head toward Lorna. "Yet."

"I work," Rowena said. "I recently started making rock jewelry and I'm trying to sell them, too. I call it Scottish Rocks of Love and Lore." She tilted her chin up and held her necklace out. Proud of what she'd done. "I have four children. I stopped working to take care of them, then The Arse walks out the door. Was that the best choice? Yes. I loved being at home. But no, I gave up my career and I can't pay my mortgage. What I can do is make The Arse's life with The Slut as miserable as possible, and I do try my best to do that. It takes time."

Lorna sniffed. "My family needed me at home and thankfully my husband was able to provide for all of us, so I did not have to work."

"Why say it in such a snobby and nauseatingly superior manner?" Kenna said. "That's not the point. Some women want to work."

"No, they don't," Lorna said, shaking a finger. "They do so because their man can't provide."

Wow. Her ignorance was truly stunning. "Some people believe what they want to believe regardless of facts."

Lorna shot a malevolent glance my way.

"Did you not receive my letter, Lorna, about your snippiness?" Olive asked. "This would include inane, piggish comments about women and working."

"I cut people open with knives and sew them back together, sometimes after removing something sick from their bodies." Kenna leaned forward. There was no fondness between those two women. "I worked and I raised my children at the same time. If I stayed home all day to change their nappies, my brain would have dribbled out of my head. Like yours."

Lorna rolled her eyes.

Malvina, Lorna's daughter, hadn't spoken. She was shaped like her mother, although her lap did not have as much oatmeal in it. Her shoulders were scrunched in, her short brown hair flat on her head, and she focused her gaze on the floor. She was an assistant librarian. She and Bridget had both gone to St. Cecilia's.

"I have not job for the many years when I live in India," Gitanjali said, her voice music, but sad music. She was wearing a wispy, yellow embroidered tunic and yellow pants. "It was unbroken. That not right word. It not allowed for me. For girls.

My father, he marry me off when I thirteen to a man my great uncle. He want me, he tell my father, my father say yes for cow. So he give my father three cow. I would have love job because it give me, ah, the word is . . . when you are strong, alone . . . Independence! Money mean independence. Independence mean power not to get hit and marry off to old men."

Gitanjali's words whipped into that room, swung around, and fell hard.

"I'm sorry, Gitanjali," I said, tamping down my anger at Lopsided Lorna.

"Me too," Olive Oliver said. "You've never told me that."

"I know. Please forgive," Gitanjali said. "Trust not come simple to me, but if you will excuse the words, Lorna, I had to give you some thinking, no not right word, I had to give you a tongue, no that not right word, no tongue. Ah yes!" She smiled and stuck a finger in the air. "I had to give my voice to this talk on the women and working."

Lorna glowered.

"When did you leave India?" Kenna asked, pushing back a stray strand of blond hair.

"I escape from hitting husband fifteen year ago. Go to shelter in Bombay, run by American woman. Husband and brothers try to find me, kill me. Say I cannot leave him. I hide. I get new name, then stay ten years. I work in factory making clothes for America, then I a maid and man and wife I a maid for, he Scottish, he in government, he tell me, I get you Scotland. So. He got me papers and I comes three year past. They are smiles in my life to me."

"And now you have your own spice store," Rowena said. "I love the free recipes you hand out."

Gitanjali bowed her head, palms together. "Thank you. Yes, spices, for me. Independence. No choking my neck." She wrapped her hands around her neck. "No hitting on the face." She mocked getting hit in the face. "No push up there." She pointed to her lap. "No man say, you do that, Gitanjali, you dog. Now, I share my love Indian food with every one of the persons here with the recipes and the spices."

"Your recipes are delicious," Olive said. "I killed Mr. Knee to make the chicken curry and my husband said it was mouth-watering. It was worth it to kill Mr. Knee."

"Do you have any spices that will make my ex-husband's scrotum rot?" Rowena asked in all seriousness. "Special red peppers? Hidden Indian spices that will make it wilt?"

"No, I scared, no, I afraid, I fear, I do not. I do have spice that rumored to lower the, uh, the sex push?" Her brow wrinkled. "That not the right word. Hmm. The intercourse lay? No, not that. I have spice that take away the—how you say—the way that a man—" She lifted one finger up, then flopped it back down, up, down. "The spice can do that to the man and the stick."

"You have spice for a penis killer. I'll take five pounds and put it in a dinner I'll make him," Rowena said, triumphantly. "He'll never know what made his pecker not peckable any-more."

Kenna laughed. "To think of the millions spent on modern medicine to give a man an erection."

"Yes," Gitanjali said, her finger flopping. "Erection. Down. I have that down erection spice."

"I haven't tried your recipes," Lorna sniffed. "My husband enjoys roast loin of venison, braised cabbage, lamb, puddings, and Scottish shortbread. Pure Scot, we are. His family has been here for thousands of years, at least, like mine. We are not for-eign to this country and are not interested in foreign food."

I wanted to knock my fist into Lorna's oatmeal gut. I knew what she was doing. She was pointing out to Gitanjali that she, Gitanjali, was the foreign one, that her family, Lorna's family, *belonged.* They were Scottish, not Indian, and they did not like Indian food, they liked Scottish food, as all their ancestors be-fore them liked Scottish food. Nothing foreign. *No foreigners.*

Gitanjali dipped her head. Her English wasn't perfect, but she got it. I got it, too. Racism resides in all places, villages, cities, and everywhere in between. It's subtle and it's blatant. Tonight, it was Lorna.

"Gitanjali's food is delicious," Kenna said.

Lorna waved a hand. "We prefer our *own.*"

"Now I understand why there is violence in this garden club sometimes," I said.

"Don't make others bleed is my motto," Rowena said. "Unless it's The Arse."

"If there's blood, I would sew most of you up," Kenna said.

"Let's begin tonight's discussion about garden design," Olive interrupted, glaring at Lopsided Lorna. She was obviously agitated. She stood up and handed each of us a slice of iced cherry cake, then started pouring tea. "What should we think of when we are designing a garden or redesigning an existing garden?"

"A garden must be proper. Orderly. Organized," Lorna said, her voice brooking no discussion, as if she was the Holy Holder of All Garden Information. "You must not allow any infiltrations by any plants that do not belong. Weeds must be pulled immediately. Native plants flourish best as individuals and for the whole."

Was she still on the India/Scotland/Immigrant thing?

"One's home and garden is a reflection of how you see yourself and how others will see you, therefore it must be perfect," Lorna droned on.

Whew. "Perfect? How can nature ever be perfect?"

She laboriously turned toward me, so put out at this interruption, and lifted a gray eyebrow. "You must tame nature. A Scottish garden must show control. A profusion of color is fine, as long as it's in the correct place, and not wild."

"I like wild," Olive said, her inebriated frog swinging. "My climbing roses are in charge of their own destiny, my dahlias grow wherever they choose, and I think my morning glory would take over my entire garden and cackle about it if I turned my back and got rid of my machete. Wildness everywhere!"

Lorna sniffed. "I am merely saying that a garden must be subservient to its owner."

"Oh, bother," Rowena said. "I don't like the word *subservient*. Gives me the shudders. For some reason it makes me think of whipping The Arse." She tapped her fingers together. "I like that image."

"Subservient. Submissive. Submit," Kenna said. "All words that should be illegal worldwide."

"Except," said Rowena, flipping that thick red hair dramatically as she laughed, "I would be subservient to Tom Selleck in bed."

"Bring me that man and his hindquarters," Kenna gushed. "He could do anything to me and I would agree and smile. I would dress in black leather and ask my husband to leave for the night."

I laughed out loud.

"I'll take Robert Redford," Olive said. "He'd take charge and I'd let him woo woo woo me."

"But that would be the only time I'd be subservient," Rowena said. "Tom Selleck and I."

Malvina kept her head tilted down.

"I not do that servant thing again," Gitanjali said. "No. Not me. That man, that great uncle I force to marry for cows? He yell the word *submit* to me. Submit! Then he hit me with cane." Her dark eyes filled with tears. "I submit to him for years. I had to submit to his mother, who hit me, hit again. I had to submit to his father. That was bad submit."

"If I could explain myself, ladies," Lorna said, disdain dripping from her words like garden slugs. "A garden should submit to your will. You can tend it carefully, water it well, and fertilize, but you must be in control."

"No woman, no garden," Gitanjali said. "I say with pleasant words, no submit. I no ask my garden submit."

"I agree," I said. "Submit is not in my vocabulary. I won't submit to anyone and I don't want anyone or anything to submit to me."

"Me either," Olive said. "Never." She reached over and hugged Gitanjali.

"Please, all the ladies," Gitanjali said as she wiped her eyes. "This is garden gobbling club and I am crying. Go on with your talking conversation as I do an embarrassment on myself with this"—she waved a hand—"sad music recital."

She must have seen our confused expressions.

"I mean, with this sad story I sing."

"You're not embarrassing yourself," Rowena said. "Embarrassing yourself is when you get caught in a car having sex with your boyfriend in the backseat by a constable with a nightstick when you're seventeen and wearing a witch hat and he tells your mother at church the next day."

"Embarrassing is when your children find your sex toys," Kenna said. "Twenty years ago Devon took it to preschool for show and share. It was bring an orange object day."

"Embarrassing is when you can't remember what Es on the periodic table means," I said, chuckling.

They looked blank. Shoot. I cleared my throat, forced a laugh. "It's a joke."

"Ah!"

"I think a garden is about freedom, not submission," Olive said. "Freedom for us to plant, to grow and nourish, and to be in nature's beauty. It's something for my animals to look at before they become my meal."

Rowena said, "I think a garden is where I'll bury my ex-husband and The Slut who had an affair with him and led him home by the dick with her pinkie."

"I think a garden is a place where a woman can put herself back together again," Kenna said. "She can think, argue with herself, philosophize, speech make, tell her herself she can do it, then go back into the world and stand tall."

"A garden gave me back to me," Gitanjali said. "No one hurt or bang banged in garden."

"I think a garden should be restrained!" Lorna said. "A sign of respectable people, living respectable lives."

"I think a garden is a wonderful excuse to learn Latin," I said. "To use the Latin words for each plant in your garden." They all stared blankly at me again. I am such an idiot. "That was a joke." It wasn't. I love Latin words for plants. I forced a smile. "Ha-ha! A tulip's a tulip."

They laughed. "You are so funny, Charlotte," Rowena said. "I remember your fine sense of humor from years ago!"

Lorna rolled her eyes and *humphed!*

Malvina never said a word.

It was a diverse group. But it would be better without Lorna. There was always one wart.

Always.

Lorna and Malvina, the silent, sad one, scuttled out with their oatmeal bottoms, and the rest of us Scottish women—Gitanjali, who sold spices that could make a man's penis flat; Olive, who loved her animals and eating them; Rowena, who wanted revenge on The Slut; Kenna, the doctor; and I—drank too much. We ended up at Molly Cockles Scottish Dancing Pub in the village and then in the town square, dancing and singing old Scottish songs. Many people from the bar and village joined us in harmonic wonder.

I don't know why I ended up leading them like a choir director, swaying back and forth, arms waving, and I don't know how I got a pink flowered hat on my head or whose it was.

I don't do things like that. I am quiet and reserved. I mind my own business. I like to be alone with my cats and physics books.

It must be something in the Scottish air, that dash of salt, a hint of mint tea.

Olive took off her inebriated frog scarf and hop-hopped in front of the choir, swinging it above her head. She said later it was her "froggy dance." She was in her cups.

Rowena introduced a new song, which I led the choir in three rounds, with a high soprano closing. The words were, "The Arse has no dick/Why did I marry/such a limp prick?"

We Garden Ladies stumbled by a long, wide vacant lot, after the constables politely asked us to disperse as forty people singing Scottish drinking songs in three-part harmony in the center of town was too noisy. I saw Chief Constable Ben Harris, tall and sharp in his uniform, speaking with Gitanjali, smiling.

"The old Zimmerman Factory," Kenna said. "Burned to the

ground. Gas leak led to an explosion. Boom and boom boom. City doesn't know what to do with it now, but perhaps if they drank whiskey it would help." She burped. "Whoops. Like me."

"Ugly," I said, leaning on Kenna. "Ugly like my cottage that smelled like corpse and farts. Drunk mice in there, too. I know it."

"This ugly place need spices," Gitanjali slurred. She patted my shoulder. "I think I have too many liquid spice tonight in my glass, new garden lady, Charlotte."

"Gitanjali," I said to her. "Chief Constable Harris is a good man. I forgot to tell you that."

"Good man," Gitanjali echoed, her steps crooked. "I think I sing a song from India right now."

"Gitanjali has the voice of a mermaid," I said, as the notes sailed around the stars. "A swimming mermaid." I felt the need to clarify. "Not a land mermaid."

"I want a merman in my bed," Rowena said, then burped. "Whoops."

"I am so glad I'm not operating on anyone tomorrow." Kenna slung an arm around my neck. "I might cut off the wrong limb. Wait! I could operate on Rowena's husband!"

"Kenna." Rowena put a hand on Kenna's arm. "Would you?"

They both burped.

"Sometimes I miss my dead chickens." Olive's voice was sad. She flapped her wings. "But they are tasty." She burst into tears. Then she hop-hop-hopped. Sappy drunk.

"I could bury The Slut here, too," Rowena shouted. "Right here, right here!" She pointed to the middle of the rubble. "Don't tell anyone. Shush!" She put a finger to her lips.

"You bet!" I gave Rowena my pink flowered hat. "Have a flower hat. It's not as drunk as the mice."

Gitanjali sang Indian songs. Olive hop-hopped, her frog scarf now wrapped around her head. Rowena hummed The Arse/prick song. Kenna said, "I do want to dress in black leather for Tom Selleck. I do." She mimicked whipping him.

My head split with a cranium jangling headache the next morning.

Tequila's curse.

I laughed.

Silver Cat peered through my bedroom door and meowed at me, then snuggled up and went to sleep on my chest. She was a huggy thing.

The next afternoon I found a note in my mailbox at my house.

> *Dearest Charlotte,*
>
> *It was a joy to see you late last night dancing and singing with your ladies garden group. You are a gifted choir director.*
>
> *I was sorry to interrupt you all, and I wanted to make that clear today in my note to you. The singing was melodious, robust, but as a large group from the pubs had joined you, and it was one o'clock in the morning, Officer Telloso and I felt that we had to ask you to engage in whisper-singing.*
>
> *I apologize to you for any offense taken.*
>
> *I am partial though, from my university days, to the drinking songs you sang. Especially "The Stable Boy" and "The Cobbler's Daughter," and also the song "Mermaid Love," about the mermaid who swam away from the sailor, breaking his heart forever.*
>
> *I'm afraid I do have a romantic heart, which those songs sang to. Your father did, too, Charlotte. Tough as nails he was, and I saw him knock flat more than a few men who deserved it, but his love for his wife and you was true.*
>
> *I must say I was impressed at how you were able to get people to sing in rounds as the choir director. It added texture and depth to the music. I was particularly impressed by Gitanjali's voice,*

rich and deep. I bought six more pounds of spices from her recently: turmeric, saffron, basil. She gave me a new recipe and I have filed it in Gitanjali's Recipe Box.

I was pleased that Toran and Kenna's husband were eager and willing to come and get all of you and drive you safely home.

I am having a difficult time with my roses, last season was not as bloom-filled as I would have preferred, and I was wondering if you had any suggestions for a successful season. Roses can be so picky.

Yours,

Chief Constable Ben Harris

A friend of your parents, may the angels of heaven fill your father's heart with joy and exuberance.

Dear Chief Constable Harris,

I apologize for the ruckus we caused in the square last night. I could blame it on the tequila but one must take responsibility for oneself. I had too much to drink after Gab and Gobbling Gardens Group. That might not be the correct name, I shall note that here.

We did enjoy the drinking songs, but did not realize that the men and women from the bars would be so eager to join in. It became a more resounding choir than expected.

I'm afraid I have missed Scottish music, especially "Tuck the Man Down," which we managed in three-part harmony. I am not sure if you were there at the time.

I will be more circumspect with my behavior in future.

As for the roses. Have you used a granular fer-

tilizer? I always do, every three and a half weeks. I also use two tablespoons of Epsom salts per bush. I use my fall leaves, from my compost pile, around the base of the rose and add some lawn remnants. My mother also taught me to put two pennies in the soil on either side of the rose. Says her mother did the same in Georgia.

Thank you for what you said about my father. I know he valued your friendship—and respected your impressive skills in the Scottish game competitions—tremendously. I heard many stories about the trouble you two engaged in when you were boys. Don't think I've forgotten about your shenanigans.

Yours,
Charlotte
PS I did put in a word for you with Gitanjali.

"Would you like to go for a ride in the tractor, Queen Charlotte?" Toran asked me the next day.

Oh boy. Tractor riding with Toran. Bumpity bump bump bump! "I love tractors."

"I know. I remember. Let's give it a go."

From his tractor—growl, rumble, roar—I saw part of Bridget's Haven Farms. We didn't go and see it all as it was enormous. It looked like an organic land quilt, beiges, greens, blues, with a red barn here and there. It was farm heaven, and so much more than what his father had done. More land, better crops, incredible beauty. It was organized, thriving, and efficient.

He had bought land from our neighbors and let the owners stay in their homes. Most of them were elderly and wanted the cash, but not the work anymore. When they died, the homes would go to Toran. It was a fine deal for all.

Toran had called my mother years ago and she'd sold off part of our land to him, too. It paid off the loan she took out, without my knowledge, to put me through college. She thought it was a lucky gift. I wanted to write a letter to thank him, but he was married and I had this shattered feeling in my chest about him, so I didn't. I couldn't.

He told me that his blueberries, potatoes, and apples went out to grocery stores across Great Britain and overseas, and he said he donated to families in town who were struggling. "We put it on their front porch and leave. I know what it's like to be poor, and the last thing I'd have wanted was to thank someone for helping me."

"Toran," I told him later as we walked through a line of his blueberry bushes, my nether-private region still reeling from the unexpected eroticism of a bumpy tractor ride beside the Scottish Warrior, "you must be proud. All of this is yours."

I counted ten tractors, of all sizes, four with wheels taller than me. He had pilers, harvesters, windrowers, spring tine harrows, potato ridgers, grubbers, rollers, rototillers, and reversible ploughs. There were backhoes and forklifts, mammoth-sized trucks, a mechanic's shop, and behemoth pieces of equipment I didn't recognize that took up half a warehouse.

Three long greenhouse tunnels, Toran told me, extended the growing season.

Another set of tunnels, 175 feet long and 51 feet wide, made with concrete floors and galvanized steel, held all the potatoes they harvested. The roof was twenty-five feet high. He called it the cellar. Part of it was underground to keep it cool, but they also had air tunnels, ten feet wide and ten feet high, on the sides, for additional cooling.

"We get mountains of potatoes here, Charlotte. They go to the roof. There's enough storage here for one hundred twenty-five thousand sacks of potatoes, forty-five kilograms each. We harvested seven thousand tons last year."

"That's a lot of potatoes."

"Enough to feed a slice of Scotland, luv."

"I'm looking forward to eating your potatoes." I closed my eyes. *Why did I say that? It sounded carnal.*

"I'll cook them for you tonight."

"Thank you." I focused my attention on the blueberries. It is not always comfortable to have a vivid imagination.

"I'll cut them up into cubes, and cook them in olive oil, parsley, and salt."

I tried to turn off that vivid, graphic imagination by reviewing the periodic table.

"They're delicious, cooked simply."

"I'm sure they will be." Next I tried to list all the elements in my head.

"I eat them three or four times a week."

Iron. Cobalt. Nickel. Copper. "What about the blueberries?"

"We harvested 725,747 kilograms last year." He grinned. "Now for the American in you, that would be one point six million pounds last year."

"I get it." I tried to stop thinking about his potatoes.

"I know you do, smart Charlotte." He winked.

My heart actually fluttered. *Carbon. Nitrogen. Oxygen.*

There were different outbuildings for brushing and cleaning the apples, blueberries, and potatoes with a dizzying array of belts and conveyers, two cooling areas about the size of Nebraska, three different packing and distribution areas, and stacks of crates and boxes with Bridget's Haven Farms stamped on them. There were six semi-trucks, also stamped with Bridget's Haven Farms.

Toran also had two longhouses, clean and neat, with bunk beds for the seasonal staff, a living area in the middle, and a kitchen. Another building, between the longhouses, had a full kitchen and four women cooking the meals for the workers. They smiled, shook my hand, welcomed me to Bridget's Haven Farms.

"All of my workers are paid almost double what I'm required to pay them. They work hard. Most of them have been with me for more than ten years. I have parents and their children working here. They quit only when they get pregnant and want to stay home with their babies or when they die."

I wasn't surprised. Toran would be an outstanding boss.

There was a separate building, painted yellow, with a long room with a wall of windows, comfortable furniture for the employees, and offices on the second story. Toran's office was spacious, in the corner, and had a view of his patchwork quilt. There was paperwork spread all over his desk and on two tables.

I like to organize, so my instinctive reaction was to start in on the mess, categorizing, labeling, making new folders, and filing, but I restrained myself.

"I'm so impressed, Toran. Bridget's Haven is incredible. You built all this."

"Thank you. Aye, it's all mine, and Bridget's. But it's only me here. I love this land. Despite my father, I love it. It's been in my family, all the way back, two hundred years. It's my responsibility. But I am alone out here. Who do I leave this to? Who is it for? Bridget doesn't want it."

I wanted to shout, "I will have our babies. We will keep the land for them. You want four kids? I can squish out four. Five? Sure thing. Six? Pushing it, but okay, baby."

"There's no . . ." I wanted to say the words *stupid, irritating woman,* but I didn't. "There's no woman in your life?"

"No, there's not. I was married once, when I was twenty-three. I think Bridget told you? We dated for six months. Not long enough. It did not work out. We were living in London, but I had to come home after my parents' deaths to run the farm.

"Carissa didn't want to live the rest of her life in the country. I understood. It had not been our plan, and I changed the rules after we were married, as I felt I had to move home. She said it wasn't fair for me to ask her to do so, and I think she was right. You marry someone and you are agreeing to the life that you will give each other. When that changes, some people don't want to make that change. Country life, the village, it was too small for her. She moved back to London, and I commuted back and forth on weekends unless we were in the middle of a harvest.

"I was different after my parents' deaths. I worked all the time. Bridget was in rehab again, then left, and I couldn't find her, so I was constantly worried. I blame myself in many ways for the breakdown of my marriage. I was not attentive enough during that time of my life to Carissa. We started arguing. She met someone else. When she told me, we divorced."

"I'm sorry. I can't imagine a woman being interested in anyone else when she had you."

"Thank you." Those blue eyes softened. "That's awfully kind."

"You're welcome. It's true. Do you miss her, though?" Gag. I hoped not.

"I saw Carissa about a year after the divorce. We met, had dinner, in London, and I remember listening to her talk, and if I had any doubts about whether the marriage should have ended, they were completely cleared up then. We were not well suited. I couldn't wait to leave, which makes me sound terrible, but that's how I felt. It was like having dinner with a stranger, a blind date, and the date was not working out. I had assumed I would be married forever, and that was a struggle for me, for a long time."

"I assumed the same."

"You were married and divorced also, Bridget said."

We talked about my marriage and I was brief.

"You had no other choice," he said, when I was done.

There was no judgment.

No dismissive, minimalizing statements. No shock.

Only, "You had no other choice," then, "You were strong and did the right thing."

"I wasn't strong."

"Yes, m'lady. You were. You just don't see it in yourself."

I wanted to kiss him. Before I said something awkwardly suggestive, as flirting is a confounding foreign language to me, I said, "What I want to know is, how can anyone say no to the Scottish countryside?"

He grinned. "Come, let me show you more of Bridget's Haven."

We walked, and talked, back through the blueberries, and Toran took my hand and we linked fingers. I about swooned like a fragile, brainless maiden. I have not wanted to be around men much in the last years. I think they are basically sexist and want a traditional relationship where the woman is the cook/cleaner and ego booster and penis stroker. What's in it for me? I don't trust them. I can't read them. I'd rather not get hurt again.

But Toran?

He was thoughtful and sensitive.

His fingers tightened around mine, but I knew he was holding my hand as a friend, so I told myself to chill out, simmer down, and quit letting my imagination run amok.

He smiled. He was irresistible.

Lithium. Sodium. Potassium . . .

I started reading romance novels when we moved to Seattle when I was a teenager. I was grieving my father's death. I lost my best friends, Bridget, Toran, and Pherson. I lost Scotland and Clan Mackintosh. I lost our home and our land, the village of St. Ambrose, bagpipes, the Scottish games, the North Sea, the traditional Scottish dances Bridget and I learned for competitions, the songs, and my school. It was devastating.

I lost it all.

We lost it all.

Why did my mother, Jasmine, leave? She loved Scotland, but her grief was all consuming. She could hardly stop crying. She couldn't stand to stay in the hills where she and my father had told each other their dreams, next to the ocean waves she'd jumped over with him, under the white Scottish moon where they'd kissed so many times.

We packed up, found Mr. Greer the renter, and left.

We went to Seattle, where she had gone to college and had friends. She started waitressing at a friend's mother's Italian restaurant, then enrolled at the university and received a scholarship for journalism. My mother used articles she had written for the paper in St. Ambrose in her application.

We lived in family housing on the university campus. We

struggled. The rent from Mr. Greer covered the mortgage and taxes on the home here, and that was about it.

I went to school and did not make friends when I arrived. I had an accent. I had odd clothes, an out-of-style haircut, crooked teeth. All the kids already had their cliques. I sat alone in the cafeteria, and I was frequently the target of bullying. I was gawky and awkward. I was depressed.

It was like landing on a different planet and I did not belong on the planet. I requested to not have a lunch break due to the torture of the cafeteria situation, but my counselor wouldn't let me do that and encouraged me to "socialize, Charlotte. Please."

Now that worked splendidly. Tell a teenager to socialize and everything will be well.

Toran had written me several letters, but I hadn't answered his, or Bridget's. My depression left me almost paralyzed with grief. About a year later I heard that Toran had a girlfriend. I had a long cry.

In 1970, America was on fire. The Vietnam War being one of the flames, the other the civil rights movement. Several of my classmates' brothers, fathers, and cousins were fighting in Vietnam, and the rest feared they would be called up. My mother supported the civil rights movement and was vocal about why.

There were antiwar protests and demonstrations that my mother took me to as well. We marched, we yelled, we made signs. After participating in protests, some of which we drove long hours to get to, we would go back home and she would write articles for the university's paper and, often the city's paper, as a freelancer.

My mother was always a feminist, believed in equal rights and opportunities for women, for *everyone,* but after losing the love of her life she channeled her anger and loneliness into saving women. She couldn't save my father, but she would save her fellow females. She had her doctorate in three years and became a professor at the university, which soon gave her a broader platform on the national stage to encourage women to fight for their rights.

Though she was opinionated, strong-willed, intimidating,

and demanding on the outside, when she shut the door to our home, she was . . . Mum. Funny. Loved to eat popcorn and watch movies. Together we cooked all our Scottish favorites to feel closer to my dad, especially the desserts. Together we mourned the loss of my father, her husband. It was hard to breathe that first year—grief took our breath—but cooking dimmed it.

She would write her articles, plan her lessons for her university students, or craft a speech she would make in New York or L.A., and I would study, read, and write at the kitchen table. She was my best friend and encouraged my writing. I was her beloved, nerdy daughter.

After I studied, my favorite subjects being math, physics, and biology, I would read a romance novel. The romance novel allowed escape. Vietnam. The Kent State shootings, the Beatles breaking up, Elvis starting a concert tour, Jimi Hendrix's death, Janis Joplin's death, my father's death, the loss of my friends and Scotland, it all went away.

I wanted a happy ending and love and to believe there were men out there who were protective, heroic, strong, smart, and madly in love with me, a girl with googly glasses, lanky hair, braces, acne, and awkwardness in a new country that rendered me almost completely verbally paralyzed. In every single book then, as now, I pretended that I was the heroine. I wanted peace in the midst of a country going hippie, going to war, and going crazy with the thousands of deaths of their brothers, sons, and husbands in a jungle overseas.

I read the classics, too. I read *To Kill a Mockingbird,* then *The Prince's Woman.* I read *Lolita,* then *The Mistress of the Castle. The Autobiography of Malcolm X* and *Passion's Purse. The Catcher in the Rye* and *Eden's Love Gift. Uncle Tom's Cabin* and *Twelve Years a Slave,* followed by *Catherine's Throbbing Justice.*

You could say that misery launched my writing career. I think it's true for many writers out there. Misery, loneliness, aloneness, and a natural tendency toward watching people because they don't fit in.

I was the valedictorian and gave a speech at graduation. My

classmates actually gave me a standing ovation. They had gotten used to me. By then they had accepted my brainy, awkward Scottishness. To be even more rebelliously different, now and then I wore a kilt. For the talent show I did a traditional Scottish Highland dance in our clan's tartan kilt and a blue velvet waistcoat with gold trim. Screw them, I thought. They liked it. I had also started to fight back. With my fists. That helped. There was, however, no one giving me a louder standing ovation than my mother, Jasmine Mackintosh.

I would study physics and biology in college, but I kept reading romances.

"You will study how things are. You will study the smallest things in the world, Charlotte."

"Small as a mouse?"

"Smaller." My grandma pushed my hair back, her gray curls framing her face. We were making a Tipsy Laird together. "Something so small we can hardly see it. You'll study what we don't understand and can hardly see."

"What do you mean?"

"I don't know. I have no idea. I see a body, too."

"A body?" I stepped back, horrified.

"Maybe a murdered body," she mused. "I'm telling you what I see. It confuses me. But one thing I know, we don't always have to know all the answers, especially with this darn Second Sight curse."

"I know that I love you, Grandma."

"I love you, too. Where you go, my love goes with you. Where you go, Scotland goes, too. This is your country, your home, your ancestors. Never forget it, Scottish granddaughter."

"I won't, Scottish grandma." I smiled at my own cleverness.

We went back to making the Tipsy Laird, with yellow custard, fruits, whip cream, and a "tipsy of whiskey," as she said. She let me pour in the whiskey.

Then she put in a tip more, "For luck."

* * *

Stanley I and Stanley II had pulled off the old roof of our cottage and put on a new one, after hacking at the vines clinging to the house and trimming back an oak tree that had been short when I lived here twenty years ago.

When the roof was replaced, they started the gutting and remodeling. The electric and plumbing would all have to be replaced.

White, non-custom-made kitchen cabinets had arrived. I had chosen white appliances and a light beige laminate for the counters, except for one expanse near the sink where I was having butcher block put down for pie crust rolling. There would be a white tile backsplash.

I had Stanley I and Stanley II take down a wall between the kitchen and family room to make the kitchen larger and to open up the first floor completely, except for the library. I would then have room for the table my granddad built in the kitchen. I also told Stanley I and Stanley II I wanted to use the armoire my granddad made as a pantry so the kitchen design would need to work around that, too.

Not that I would use it as a pantry, as I would be selling the house. Probably.

The downstairs windows had been replaced, and I could not believe the difference in light. The old trim had been pulled off, and new white trim would be put up soon, as would white wainscoting in the kitchen. The old wainscoting had to go—it was half off, and looked like it had been eaten by beavers.

The fireplace and mantel, built by my great-grandfather, would remain the same, but the stones he had gathered from our land would be cleaned, the wood mantel restained.

I would love sitting in front of the warmth of my great-grandfather's fireplace until I went home to Washington to weed my garden on Isolation Island.

The wood floors were not in as bad a shape as one would expect, because Mr. Greer, without asking, had covered them with brown carpet for the last twenty years.

All the walls would be painted light yellow. I was having

Stanley I and Stanley II build bookshelves for the library so I could read in a leather chair with a light and my tea nearby, until I returned to my cats, their stroller, and my science books.

I walked upstairs, the stairway skinny, to my parents' bedroom and stood in the middle of it. Half the upstairs was their bedroom, with dormer windows on both sides. I remembered how many times I had climbed into my parents' four-poster bed and laughed with them. My father would sometimes play his bagpipes to wake up my mother as a joke.

My parents' bedroom would soon be painted a light, powder blue, easy for me to sleep in. The other two bedrooms and the small loft would be white.

The house I remembered as a child was much larger than the one I saw as an adult. Our stone cottage was medium sized, no more, and cozy. A place for a family. I choked up when I thought of my family, except for my mother, all gone.

I sniffled and lifted my skirt up to wipe my nose. The clip on top of my head came undone and my hair popped out. I re-clipped it.

Nostalgia is a dangerous place to go. It can be very depressing. You can never go back to that place, that time, with the people you want to be with. It's history. I sniffled again.

Unless you're McKenzie Rae Dean, time traveler, who always manages a romance in between the danger and adventure and getting the job of saving people done. Then you wait for the pull and the whoosh and, voila, you're in a whole new time and place.

But I was not McKenzie Rae, and I was spending a fortune.

What was I doing?

It was ridiculous.

It made no sense.

I was gutting and designing the house for me and I was leaving.

It was like throwing dollar bills into the ocean.

I should have bulldozed it, but I couldn't do it. I absolutely could not do it.

When it was done, it would be restored, a family home fit for a Scottish family, who liked huge fireplaces, a small library lined with shelves, an armoire for a pantry, a long wood table in the kitchen with my and Bridget's name in a heart, and dormer windows with views of the ocean.

That thought had me wiping my nose again with my skirt. My clip popped, my hair fell down, a tear rolled into my mouth. It tasted like the sea.

6

"I like the swans," Toran mused, holding up a red napkin that I'd folded for dinner.

"Thank you. I can show you how to make them."

I had set the table while Toran cooked Scottish stew with beef stock, onion, and carrots. And wine. Brings out the taste.

My mother taught me to appreciate pretty table settings. "Candles and flowers, Charlotte. Always. A feminist indulges her feminine side."

I had pulled daffodils from Bridget's garden, put them in blue vases I'd found under the sink, then started folding the swans. I learned origami from Russ, one of my neighbors on Whale Island, who is obsessive compulsive and must always be doing something with his hands. Three whole tables were filled with his origami creations.

Napkin folding was also one of his obsessive compulsive activities. He liked cloth. I now know how to make swans, turkeys, bunnies, roses, and a monster out of cloth napkins.

Toran laughed. "If I made napkins into swans I would not be able to consider myself a manly man Scotsman anymore."

"I won't tell anyone and we'll pull the drapes."

"I don't think I can risk it. What if one of my friends came over? What if Pherson returned early from his time on the oil rig? No. I'd never hear the end of it. He would ask me each time he saw me how my origami was going."

"Then I will have to be the reigning queen of napkin swans here."

"The reign is yours." We clinked our wineglasses together, over two candles I'd lit. "I've read your books."

"You have?" My spoon clattered onto my plate. That was a problem.

I fiddled with my glasses, on the taped part. Did he recognize himself? The love of McKenzie Rae Dean's life, the one she longs to get back to, who looks exactly like him, based on the photos Bridget had sent to me years ago? I was remarkably close in my description. Brown soft curls, blue eyes, hard jaw but a seductive smile. Huge hands, tall, a faint scar on his left temple. Oh no oh no oh no. I felt myself grow hot.

"Yes. All of them."

I could only nod. I was stricken. Speechless. Stunned. And now I was thinking in alliteration.

"I loved them. Gripping. I could hardly put them down to work on the farm."

"Really?" My voice squeaked. And were you impressed with how you made love to McKenzie Rae Dean in the first book? What about the time in the ocean, near the cliffs, her breasts in your mouth? What about the time in the barn, McKenzie Rae up against the wall, her naked butt in your hands? And the time in the ruins of the castle, at night, when you kissed . . . low? I flushed, dabbed my head with a red swan.

"But tell me, Charlotte. Who is McKenzie Rae Dean in your mind? Where did she come from?" He leaned forward, those eyes diving right into mine.

I started off slow, tentatively. I am not used to talking about my writing, as I am an odd duck who does not even admit to people that she's a writer.

"What I've noted," Toran said later, "is that no man has ever truly taken the place of her first love."

That's because no one has ever taken your place, Toran.

"She has lovers, husbands . . ." I shrugged my shoulders, up and down. Then up and down again. One more time. *Stop, Charlotte,* I told myself.

"Yes, a number of them."

"She's discerning."

"She is. They all sound like honorable chaps to me. Strong. Honest. They protect their woman. Madly in love with her."

"Every time."

"I think of the poor men who have fallen in love with her who she leaves in the end."

"They'll live. Sometimes she's there for a lifetime."

"Said so lightly." He placed a hand mockingly on his heart. "Men get hurt, too. We just head to the pub, have a few beers, and try to forget about it."

"Does beer cure heartache?"

"No, it doesn't. Puts it off a bit. How did you create her?"

"She's my alter ego. She's who I would like to be."

"What? Why?" His eyes widened. "I like you better than McKenzie Rae."

"You do?" I fiddled with the top button on my blouse. Buttoned to the neck. I shrugged my shoulders again. Up. Down. Up. *Please stop,* I told myself. *Please.*

"Yes. You're different than any other woman I've ever met. Always thinking. You see everything. You understand. You're funny."

"I have to come here more often to get my ego boosted up."

"There are a few things I don't like about McKenzie Rae."

I bristled. Couldn't help it. "Like what?"

"She doesn't talk about physics or biology, water, the United Nations, farming, weather, international law, that type of thing, as we do."

I relaxed. My shoulders stopped shrugging. I was pleased. I loved McKenzie Rae, but it was relieving and complimentary that he saw the distinction between her and me. "She's busy. She's time traveling, solving problems, saving others."

"But she needs to be more like you, Charlotte."

I sniffled and teared up, and I busied myself with my glasses again. "Thank you, Toran." He was probably the only man on the planet who would think that. The only one.

"You're welcome, Queen Charlotte." He picked up my hand and kissed it.

I wanted to launch myself at him, ripping buttons off my shirt as I flew through the air.

He turned my hand so our palms were together. "Magic powers shield us now," we both said, laughing.

I could not help but think: I will give up Dan The Vibrator for you any second, of any day, Toran.

I talked that night, because Toran listened.

He had more questions. How do you write your books . . . How do you get your ideas . . . How many times do you edit your books . . . What's the best part about being a writer . . . Is there anything you don't like about being a writer?

The sun went down. The candles melted. The bowls were pushed aside. Toran brought Caleb's Kilt coconut chocolate sticks to the table, and we kept talking. I had never, except for my parents, had anyone so interested in me, my brain, what I thought.

"If you were going to time travel, Charlotte, where would you go?"

That started another discussion, as I asked him the same question.

At one point we stopped and stared at each other. I wanted to leap on him and yank open his shirt, buttons flying everywhere. Nervous, I hummed a few notes of a Scottish song about love and heartbreak my father had sung to me at bedtime. I abruptly stopped humming, so embarrassed. But then, joking with me, Toran hummed the next few notes.

Then we hummed the song together.

He held up his hand, palm facing me.

I put my palm against his, then we twisted them and laced fingers. "Clan TorBridgePherLotte powers, activate! Speed ahead and fight bravely," we chanted. We tapped fingertips three times, then pulled them apart, as if they were held together magnetically.

"Victory!" we both shouted, then bounced our closed fists together.

We are a strange twosome.

That night in bed, flannel nightgown on, I said to myself, I have to get back home. I have to wrestle with my writer's block and kill it.

But when I returned to the island I would be alone.

All alone.

By myself.

Solo.

Lonely.

Except for four cats who ride in a specially made stroller.

I did miss Teddy J, Daffodil, Dr. Jekyll, despite the concerning mood disorder, and Princess Marie.

I thought of Toran. The cats could always come here. . . .

I dressed in my denim skirt and a T-shirt that said EINSTEIN RULES and drove into the village a few days later for groceries.

St. Ambrose is small and charming, nestled on the ocean. The sky feels closer, as if it were lowered to bring us a clearer shade of blue. This is atmospherically impossible, but it's how it feels to me. The wind smells like the sea and highland dreams. The moon is brighter, only a few yards away, surely, and if you could jump high enough off the top of the cathedral you could catch it with your hands. It's a village that makes a science nerd like me almost poetic.

The six-hundred-year-old university sprawls all over the village, the ancient buildings practically speaking with all the voices who have studied there before.

I am sure I would have attended this university had I stayed here.

Bridget and I grew up watching the students covering themselves in shaving cream one day in October every year. We watched them in suits and fancy dresses traipse through town on their way to parties. We saw how the girls dressed, always in high style. Bridget would tell me, "One day I'm going to dress like them, Charlotte, you watch me!"

We would have my mother drive us to the ocean every year in May so we could giggle as the students jumped into the frigid North Sea and came out laughing and shaking. We would see them carrying books and bags, looking serious, as they headed to class.

Bridget and I would go to college at St. Ambrose and be roommates and we would buy tea and biscuits together every day.

How we plan our lives and how our lives turn out . . .

I heard the blaring notes of bagpipes and I stopped, unprepared for getting slugged in the chest with such raw emotions. I sat on a bench, the ruins of the cathedral behind me, and listened.

I could smell the sea, a dash of salt, a hint of mint tea. Croissants, coffee, and Indian food, maybe Gitanjali's spices, wafted by. The bells of a church rang out, the waves crashed.

This used to be my village, the village of my ancestors.

It hadn't been mine for twenty years, but I had never forgotten it.

It had followed me to my own island, in the middle of another ocean, where I watched the whales play and my flowers bloom, but St. Ambrose, the history and mystery, the kilts and the legends, my mother and father, my grandma and granddad, had stayed inside my heart.

As had Toran and Bridget.

I was back again.

I breathed in deeply. I was glad to be here.

The next morning I took a shower, then put on my light brown skirt with the ruffle, a blue T-shirt with a whale and SAVE THE WHALES written across it, and my pink fuzzy socks. I couldn't believe I was calling a bedroom in Toran's home "my bedroom."

I had an image of me crooking my finger at Toran and whipping off my whale T-shirt. I would swing my bra around over my head, wiggle my chest, then toss it at him over my back. I would throw up a jaunty heel, then pose seductively in bed while he eagerly followed me in. I would keep my pink fuzzy socks on for warmth.

Yum.

I pulled out the brown box where Bridget had saved my letters—and hers, the ones she wrote and didn't send.

She had filled her letters as a teenager, the ones she sent to me, with tales of fun and adventures with the girls at St. Cecilia's. She wrote about Pherson and Toran. As we got older, we talked about gardening and the farm, the village and the people we both knew, Toran and Pherson, music and science, and the miniature drawings she sent me.

We would plant the same flowers, the same trees. We would read the same books and tell each other what we thought of them. Some were classics, others romances, and everything in between.

We talked about everything. Boys, when we were young; my husband, who became my ex-husband; my work as a researcher then writer; her work as an assistant to an executive; her travels.

I read two of my letters to her.

July 3, 1987

Bridget,

I did love your miniature drawing of the Garden of Eden. Very clever. Thank you for making Eve plump and for dressing her in a rock T-shirt and red heels. I do so hate those skinny models. Feed them a carrot, I say, before they pass out. I appreciated Adam, too. His top hat and jungle pants were particularly fetching.

You should be selling your drawings. I am telling you that for the hundredth time.

How did your date go that you mentioned? Ready to pop him up on your white horse and steal him away to the castle you own like a true feminist? Take charge, be the woman, slay the dragon on your own because who needs a man's help, etc.?

I've planted a full border of begonias, and I've had Charles come and build an arbor for an Oregon grape I bought. I put a table and two chairs under the arbor. Should be a nice reading corner when it's done. I will probably hang a picture of an anatomically correct skeleton out there next to a photo of the galaxy.

What did you decide to do with the east plot of land? You mentioned a patio and fountain with a circular surround. When did you get back from Paris?

Love,
Charlotte

February 1, 1988

Bridget,

Thank you for your recent advice on how I can get a date. No, wearing a sign that says, "Haven't had a date in years. Call if you're interested," during the Whale Island Annual Parade is not an option. Nor is taking out a personal ad. What would I say? Strange woman with a multitude of cats needs a date? If you don't understand quantum physics, or if you believe the earth was created in seven days, don't bother applying?

Your third suggestion that I go to Seattle and ask a man out is equally mind-boggling.

I have beaten two of my chess pen pals in our matches recently. That is the excitement in my life.

But do tell, though, how is your love life? And how did your trip to London go?

Love,
Charlotte

I picked up a bunch of her "real" letters. The Diary Letters, as I now thought of them. With shaking hands I read through a few more.

I was horrified down to the marrow of my bones. I actually hurt for Bridget, my chest tight. I tried to keep control, but I couldn't. It was like walking through the darkness with her, the darkness filled with evil and violence.

Poor Bridget.

She had lied. She had written two sets of letters, ones she sent to me to keep up the façade of her life and the ones she kept.

Though it hurt me, like a pen piercing me in the chest, to know that she lied to me, that things were not as they seemed, that my reality of my relationship with her was utterly wrong, her lies to me were completely irrelevant. My feelings were nothing against the background of Bridget's suffering, the harm that had been done to my friend, the crimes committed.

I put my head between my knees, my hands over my head, and cried harder than I had cried since my dad died.

I cried for Bridget.

Bridget, where are you? Please come home.

"It was my father's fanaticism that set Bridget up for what later happened."

Toran and I sat on the sand, the day sunny, the ocean waves blue-gray silk, the sky dabbled with white, squishy clouds.

"He was obsessed with Catholicism. He thought more of his obsession than he did of his family. Church for us every day, twice on Sunday, as you know. Kneeling and praying for hours on end, sometimes on sand or gravel if he didn't feel we were holy enough. He believed in self-punishment. There was constant memorization of the Bible. He was intimidating and angry. I think he loved us but had no way to show it. I have no mixed emotions about the man, and when he died I grieved only for what could have been, what should have been. I didn't grieve for him."

"He hit you then?"

"Yes. Sometimes."

"You and Bridget didn't talk about that, but I wondered."

"We were humiliated, and my mother told us not to tell. She was humiliated, too. He hit us whenever he thought we were not being 'devout, Christ-filled Catholics,' that's what he told us. He would quote the Bible before he hit us, and afterward. We thought we were bad—he told us we were. What kid wants to tell anyone they're so bad that their parent hits them?"

"When your father would hit you, what did your mother do?"

"Nothing. She was totally and completely cowed and controlled by my father. She was scared. She had no education, no money, and she was Catholic, too. Didn't believe in divorce."

"How do you feel about her, that she didn't protect you and Bridget?" I pushed my brown corduroy skirt between my knees. I was wearing my white sweatshirt with a squirrel on it and a straw hat.

"I could forgive her for not stepping in to help me, as a young man, but I have a hard time forgiving her for not stepping in to protect Bridget."

"I have a hard time forgiving her for not protecting either of you."

"My emotions toward my mother are more," he tipped his hand back and forth. "Undefined. I loved her, because she loved us and we knew it, but she drank too much to block out her life. By drinking too much, she wasn't there for us, and because she wasn't sober, or was hung over, she couldn't find a solution, which would have been taking us to her family in Dublin. She couldn't think straight."

"And by not thinking straight, she didn't protect you from your father, a harsh and creepy virus." I sat straighter, realizing my mistake. "I apologize. I'm being way too blunt and harsh."

"Never apologize to me, Char, for being honest. I loved my mum, but no parent who is drinking heavily is being a true parent to their children. She saw us hit. She saw us kneeling for hours, reciting the Bible in tears, standing in a corner being castigated by a fanatic.

"My father did the same to her, only I often think she had it worse. No telling what that man demanded she do in the bedroom. I would wake up to him yelling scripture at her. She was scared. I felt sorry for her, I still do. But she should have intervened when Bridget went through what she did. She should have saved Bridget, and she did not. That's hard to get past."

Off in the distance, a blue-gray wave crashed, then smoothed out. Another wave followed it and crashed, too. By the time the crashing waves met the shore, they were calm.

"I look back now and I know there was something wrong with him. He had an addictive, twisted personality. He was a slave to Catholicism, would even whip himself at night sometimes. He sometimes wore a barbed chain around his thigh, which caused him to bleed. He wanted me to wear one, but I refused. He wore two crosses on his chest, which he kissed religiously.

"When he met Angus Cruickshank, when he arrived from Belfast, those two would rant and rave about the Bible, yell, pray. It was scary, that's what it was. But he was honored to be friends with a priest, awed. Talked about Father Cruickshank all the time. They performed an exorcism on Bridget once, when I was away at school, when you were in Seattle."

"That would be like participating in your own horror movie."

"She was terrified. She told me later what happened." He gritted his teeth. "Poor Bridget actually believed there were evil spirits inside of her.

"My father's family was Catholic and from Ireland, but they came here to Scotland about two hundred years ago. I think my father always felt that he was not accepted, so he became more extreme. His father had a temper, and I know he hit my father as a boy, much worse than what we got. My father had a slight dent on the right side of his head from a head injury. Perhaps all those things turned him away from a rational, reasonable life."

"I remember you doing most of the work on the farm."

"What I remember is how often you and Pherson, and your father, came and helped me. Your father came only when he knew my father wasn't here. My mother never said a word. Your father—" He stopped. I knew he was trying to rein in his emotions. "He was the one who taught me how to be a man. He taught me about farming. I remembered everything. I'd write it down. But our farm didn't do well for long years, and we were poor.

"Being poor, at any time of life, is very difficult. You feel like you're less than other people. That other people are better than you. Everything's a struggle, a worry. You're thinking of survival so much, you can't get much past that."

"Toran, I'm sorry. I never felt better than you." Not a day did I think that. "I don't think anyone did. You were the most popular kid in school."

"I know you didn't. I don't know about being most popular. I was trying to survive my home life. When I was older, thirteen, fourteen, and could handle more of the farm work, that helped. I was able to hide some of the money from my father, and I bought food, and things my mother and Bridget needed. I hated the way my father treated his own family. He was supposed to be the man of the home. He was supposed to protect us, to provide a life, a living. He was supposed to lead, to be kind to my mother, and to Bridget and me. He was supposed to be involved in our lives, to make things easier, not harder. He did none of that."

"I used to think of him as Le Monster."

"He was a monster. I'm glad he's gone. I'm glad he's been gone a long time, too. He did enough damage. When I am a father, if I am fortunate enough to be a father one day, I will treat my children with respect and love. Above all, love. And I will never lay a hand on them in anger."

I couldn't talk. My lips quivered, and my chin wiggled. He saw it and said, "Ah, Charlotte, I did not mean to make you cry."

"You didn't." He pulled me into his shoulder. "Okay, you did."

The next blue-gray silk wave rushed up to us. I knew we

would get wet. I didn't move. I liked being in Toran's arms. When we were wet, his jeans, my skirt, we still didn't move.

The sun shone above us, the clouds white and squishy.

I was glad that Toran's father was dead. He was a block-headed, raving lunatic.

I felt sorry for his mother . . . but I had a hard time feeling too much pity for her. Her job as a mother was to protect her kids, and she didn't. She should have taken Toran and Bridget to her own parents, who would have welcomed them in. Carney had forbidden her from visiting them, according to Toran, but she had an answer. She said no to it.

I know there are many reasons why she didn't, things that Toran had already said, but does that excuse it? Does that excuse that her children were raised in fear, spent hours on their knees while their fanatical father screamed Bible verses, hit them, and was intimidating and scary?

Does it?

Look what it did to them.

Look what it did to Bridget.

Look what they did, to Bridget and to Toran.

And then they died. Up there, nearby.

What happened?

"She's got a mark on her," my grandma said to me as Bridget and Toran ran back through the fields to their house. "It's dark. It will stain her whole life." She teared up. "Trouble comes to her."

"Mum," my dad said, his face creased in worry. "Don't say that to Charlotte."

"It's true, though. She is old enough to hear it. You must be Bridget's friend always. Never let go. I see cities for her. I see a wanderer in the dark. I see pain in her veins and smoke surrounding her life. I see . . . confusion. Lost. She's lost. Oh!" She covered her mouth.

"What, Grandma, what?"

"I see that they take her away."

"Take who away? Take who?" I watched Bridget in the distance, her red ribbon flowing between strands of her white-blond hair, Toran running alongside her.

"Both of them."

"What? Who?"

"Both of them. Her and . . ." Her eyes filled with tears, and I knew that this time the vision was clear. "Mackintoshes are loyal to their friends. You must always be loyal to Bridget. It is not her fault."

My father went to stand at the window and watched them go. My mother linked an arm around his waist, then laid her head on his shoulder. They sighed, as if on cue, together.

Since I had no close friends in high school, I had a lot of time to study for the SAT, which I nailed. It is not something I am overly proud of. Rather, it's a mark of how much time I had to spend alone and how lonely I was.

I went to college and majored in physics and biology. I was glad to go to college. Physics and time traveling actually go hand in hand. In fact, my love of physics helped propel the original plot of my first book, which launched my career. For fun, at night, I would study time travel.

I knew it wasn't possible.

Logically speaking.

I knew it was a ridiculous notion.

Scientifically, that is.

I knew it was only a fantasy.

For magical dreamers only.

But, I asked myself, over numerous cups of coffee: What if it were possible?

I pet my beloved cats, Pillow Z and Tasmania, long dead now. I listened to symphonies composed by Dvorak and Rachmaninoff, and had more coffee. I was, as usual, alone, so I had a lot of time to think.

What if?

Were time periods simply parallel to each other? Could you cross that parallel? How would you do it? Are we living multiple lives at once and don't know it? Could certain people time travel who had special perceptions or inexplicable universal powers? Are we new people in those lives? What about reincarnation?

What if?

I thought about my lack of romance as I analyzed time travel, scouring books, journals, and articles in prestigious magazines. I thought of my stash of romances under my bed, some contemporary romances, some historical, others so graphic and titillating that I would read in my flannel floor length pajamas and have to fan my face or get Dan, the first vibrator.

I had no romance. I had cats, coffee, and romance novels. After graduating from college, I decided to get a master's in biology. Along with school, I had a job at the university research laboratory which I loved, except for one prick named Dr. Xavier.

What if?

In between school and work I asked myself, Could I write a *time travel* romance?

I started scribbling some thoughts down, late at night. McKenzie Rae catapulted to life as if she were a living person. The plot came. The history. The time travel elements. How she had to save someone in every book.

I was the happiest I'd been in a long time.

Then the book was derailed.

By a man, no surprise there.

And I let it happen. That's what galls me the most. I let a man alter my destiny.

Preposterous and shameful on my part, and on my feminist belief system.

My mother almost choked on her own tongue.

Toran and I drove over to my house several evenings later, the sun beginning its descent, slow and easy, lazy, as if it were waiting for us to tap it down those final inches. The colors blurred, like melting popsicles, with a dark streak of purple.

I liked the new roof. The white kitchen cabinets were halfway up. Because they were premade, it was quicker. It was a mess, but an organized, tarp-covered mess. The Stanleys had a large crew.

"When this is all finished, I'm going to buy curtains and put them up to help sell it," I said to Toran. I adjusted my glasses, then refastened my clip to keep my hair out of my face, as it had popped open again. I touched the button of my blue blouse to make sure it was still fastened. Over my blouse I was wearing my favorite green poncho, with a horse embroidered on the front, and my light brown ruffled skirt.

"I'll use my drill and put the rods up for you, but not so you can sell it." Toran crossed his arms over that wide chest of his. I bet it was hairy. I like chest hair. "So you can have the curtains you want."

"I'll bet you've got some talent with a drill, don't you?" I was thinking of all his farm work.

"Yes. I can drill a hole in anything."

My cheeks flushed as my imagination exploded and took off. I almost tittered.

"I meant," he said, noting my reaction and getting it, both palms up, "I can drill anything with holes."

I slammed my teeth together. Tried, again, not to titter, or laugh out loud.

He slapped a hand to his forehead. "I meant that I can drill anything that needs to be drilled to make something, do something."

I tittered. Couldn't help it. I laughed. My shoulders shook.

He shook his head, sighed. "I don't mean this how it's sounding. Okay, let me start over. When do you need it drilled, Charlotte?"

Right now, baby, I wanted to shout. I laughed.

Whew! Sexual tension whipped into that conversation faster than I could say "quantum physics."

"Hmmm, Toran . . . lemme think . . ."

He ran a hand over his face, laughed, and turned away. I saw his cheeks get a tad red.

I had flirted with Scottish Warrior Toran! Behind his back I did a quick dance. I had never had fun flirting with any man. Flirting would have made me too uncomfortable. How do you flirt without seeming desperate and ridiculous? What if the man doesn't want you to flirt with him? What if you make him feel disgusted? What if you do it wrong? Ugh. No.

Toran turned back around, and I immediately stopped dancing. He seemed a bit puzzled by my movements. I cleared my throat.

"I will hang the curtains for you, Charlotte, and I will also help the Stanleys with this work this weekend."

"Oh no. You're busy with the farm." I clasped my hands together in front of me and my embroidered horse.

"Not too busy to help my favorite lady."

Now he was flirting. Wasn't he?

"You already work six days a week. You need a day off, and I know your idea of taking a day off is different from mine. When I take a day off, I make sure I spend part of it walking, part of it in bed, and part of it eating my favorite nutritional foods, like chocolate. I don't even try to write." Not that I could write now with my brain burned out and sizzling. "You workaholic."

"Write-aholic."

"Farmer."

"Time traveler." He put his hand out and I shook it, then we twisted our palms, clapped them together three times, touched fingertips, and linked fingers. "Clan TorBridgePherLotte, forever we fight, forever we win," we both said.

"We chose the same one," I said.

"We always do."

I smiled, then studied my sturdy, solid, black shoes and tried to breathe. I could feel Toran so close to me, but I couldn't look up.

"You have pretty hair, Charlotte." He reached out and lifted a strand. "Shiny chocolate."

"I eat a lot of vegetables." My head whipped up. Why did I say that? "I also eat fruits and . . . but not peanut butter, because

I'm afraid I'll choke. And not sausages because of . . . uh . . . their shape." I did not say that McKenzie Rae thought the same thing. It would be exceedingly bizarre.

"Their shape?"

"Yes. Phallic." And why did I say that inane thing, too?

"No phallic-shaped food then?"

"No."

"Corn?"

"Yes, but off the cob."

"Zucchini."

I coughed. "No. Don't even grow it."

"Carrots."

"Yes." I cleared my throat. "But only when they're chopped in circles, not when they're in their natural form."

He laughed. "Aw, Charlotte. You are the most unique woman I've ever known. There is no one like you. Come along, I'm taking you out to dinner."

"I'm always up for eating."

"Me too. And you're a skinny thing, so let's go feed you, but not carrots, unless they're cut up in circles."

"Let's go feed me," I echoed. More inane words! "Yes, let's." He held out a hand and I took it, quick as could be. "But we won't order sausages."

Before we left, I glanced up at the Scottish hills, green and smooth, as if they'd been molded by a gentle hand. My father, Quinn Mackintosh, told me once, "Our bones are part of Scottish soil, our souls part of Scottish air, our stories part of Scottish legend." His relatives had died at Culloden and most other battles Scotland had ever fought. "We were warriors back to the time when Scotland was not even Scotland."

Through him I heard of Blayne "The Brave" Mackintosh, who defeated an invading English army with only ten men, and Monroe "The Conqueror" Mackintosh, who kept his village safe for fifty years with Scottish magic. The last story he told Bridget and me, the night before he died, was of a father who left his daughter to fight a battle he knew he would not win but had to fight for the Scottish people; their clan; and, most important, her.

The father, Blackburn "The Protector" Mackintosh, mounted a white horse and rose against an evil sorcerer who was taking away Scotland's moon, which meant the oceans, their tides now in chaos, would drown the country and the people in it. He threw a spear, laced with a mountain of white fire, at the sorcerer. The sorcerer burned up as it shot through him, but the spear, bright white, kept going, and landed in the middle of the moon, which is why, in Scotland, the moon is whiter than on any other place on Earth.

Blackburn Mackintosh died as the evil sorcerer's last curse stopped his heart, as he knew it would.

My father left his stories in my memory. And on the moon.

I found peace in that.

The restaurant Toran took me to was elegant. We had not gone home to change, so I think I may have been underdressed, except I was wearing a skirt, which was appropriate. My clip broke open on the way over, so I had to leave my hair down. I retaped my glasses on the way. I always keep tape in my bag.

Toran asked more questions about my life on the island as we ate sliced bread that came with oils and a side of butter that had been scooped into small circles. "I'm not social. I don't do social chitchat without getting a headache. Remember, I'm cat woman. Not in a cat suit, masked sort of way, but a woman who likes her cats and makes sure they have sweaters when it's cold."

His eyes widened, surprised. "You talk extremely well with people, Charlotte."

"Thank you, but I will have to respectfully disagree. I don't. I'm reserved. Private. I often don't like people. Certainly not groups. Gangs of women make me nervous, too. Can't predict them. They speak of topics I know nothing about, like fashion or men or makeup or kids." I waved a hand. "I'm amazed I actually went to Gabbing Garden group."

He tilted his head at me. "Charlotte, I don't think you see yourself correctly."

"You don't?"

"You may know yourself, Charlotte, but I don't think you understand how others see you."

"How do they see me?"

"Interesting!" He leaned forward. "Easy to talk to. Easy to be with. Funny, sarcastically so sometimes. A true friend, and most of us have few of them. Someone to trust. Someone who will be there for you no matter what. Fun. Excellent at listening, knowing exactly what to say and when to say nothing. Always willing to be a part of Clan TorBridgePherLotte and to have adventures."

"Did you drink before we came?"

"No, sweet Charlotte." He laughed. "I didn't. I knew you when we were kids, and you are the same as you were then, my friend."

His friend.

Would that be all I would ever be to him?

I was leaving, yes, I was, back to my lonely island. But, if on the smallest chance I wanted to stay, could I stay if Toran wanted to be only friends but I constantly wanted to pull off his red and black kilt?

I didn't think I could.

It would hurt too much. It was a sobering thought. I finished my glass of wine, and Toran and I launched into a conversation about cold fusion and nuclear reactions. I was pleased that his love of science had continued.

But sometimes we paused and stared at each other and I could not help smiling. I'm sure I resembled a goofy, lusty, confused nerd. Which is exactly what I am.

"Good night, Charlotte," Toran said to me outside my bedroom door.

"Good night, Toran." You have a devilishly enticing body, Toran, but I can't imagine you would ever be interested in me.

The impossibility of that is enormous. I think you only want friendship. Or a brother-and-sister relationship, who were born of different mothers and fathers.

"I'm glad you're here, Char."

"Me too. But I'll move out of your home soon. Are you sure you don't want me to go to a bed-and-breakfast in town? You said no earlier, but—"

"I absolutely do not. I have lived alone for a long time, and I don't like it."

"You don't?"

"No. I like living with you."

He smiled. I smiled back, tried to read that Scotsman, felt myself getting red and hot in the face and lower. I shrugged my shoulders inward, then out, my odd social anxiety reflex, then told myself to *quit that immediately* and turned toward my door.

I opened it, stepped inside, shut it, and desperately hoped he would knock and I would let him in and fling my clothes off with abandon, my black sturdy shoes flying into the corner; my underwear, not too holey, hitting the desk; my bra ripped from my body. I would wrap it around his neck, then those fine buttocks, to raise the sexual tension while gyrating my hips like a belly dancer.

It didn't happen. No knock on the door, no knock-knock on me.

I was up for a long time staring out at the moon. My father was right. The moon is different in Scotland. Glowing white. You can almost climb up and touch it. Tonight, though, it wanted some action in the bedroom.

Silver Cat appeared from under the bed and sat on my lap. She meowed and I meowed a sad meow back.

My father and Toran's father did not like each other.

My granddad and Toran's granddad didn't like each other so well, either.

The great-grandfathers hated each other, too. The feud goes back for generations.

Why?

What you would expect: Land. Water rights.

And, two generations ago, my grandma. She married my paternal grandfather, Brodie Mackintosh.

Brodie Mackintosh, it was rumored, won the Caber Toss and Open Stone at the Scottish Games one year. Toran's granddad, Rodric Ramsay, lost to Brodie. Both men saw my grandma. Rodric asked her to dinner, but she declined. My granddad asked a minute later, although family lore has it that he didn't ask, he simple whisked her away.

Rodric was furious. Brodie and Grandma's love was soon sealed, and the romance began.

Toran's granddad's anger lasted for a lifetime, too. He always believed that Brodie took Grandma away from him. That was nonsense, as my grandma told me. "I was in love with your granddad when I first saw him. Handsome devil. A smile that undid me."

But my grandma's smile undid Rodric, too, and he never forgot his lost love.

So Brodie and Rodric didn't like each other.

My father and Carney didn't like each other, either, because my father thought that Carney was an "overzealous, fanatical Catholic who was too strict with his children, a poor husband, and obsessed with the church."

Yet from the start my family liked Toran and Bridget.

My father said one time, "I can hardly believe that Toran is Carney's child. Same with Bridget." He shook his head. "They're nothing like Carney. Toran is a hardworking young man. He'll protect you, Charlotte, if need be."

"Though still young, I think he's a feminist," my mother said. "He believes that women should be treated with respect and do what they wish to do, unlike his slobbering father."

My granddad said, "He should have been in Clan Mackintosh. Same with the girl. Bridget's a sensitive one."

My grandma said, "I feel that Toran and Bridget are part of the family. In the future I see one garden."

"One garden, Grandma?"

"Yes." Her brows came together. "One for both families. There are blueberries nearby. An old red barn. A pond with lily pads. Birdhouses. A red table. A blue door. Bottles with candles. A flowered tea set . . . But someone's missing. . . ."

So we had generational relationship problems.

It was like Romeo and Juliet, except that Juliet's parents thought that Romeo was terrific.

In the end, though, Mackintoshes and Ramsays lie in one piece of land. Yes, they are buried in the graveyard over the hills, as it's been for hundreds of years. There are not many people up there who do not come from the Clan Ramsay and Clan Mackintosh lines. Despite the feuds and fights, we all end up together.

I would go and visit my father's grave, but I couldn't do it, not now.

Not yet.

7

I sat cross-legged on my bed in my temporary bedroom in Toran's house the next morning. I opened all three of my new journals. There was Albert Einstein's face and electrified hair. Moody Edgar Allan Poe writing in a shadowy room. Science beakers surrounding Marie Curie.

Usually I wake up in the morning in my island house and write while chugging coffee. I often write by hand or type out on my deck. My morning writing sessions last from two to eight hours.

I'll get inspiration from my garden, my cosmos, Bells of Ireland, snapdragons, zinnias, sweet peas, poppies, and, for a surprising reason, catnip. I like to watch my cats play in their screened outdoor play area. I wait until inspiration hits, a daydream becomes a storyline, I see the story in my head like a movie, and I write.

When I need a break, I sit in my gazebo overlooking the ocean and continue my daydreams, which consist of my being the adventurous and saucy McKenzie Rae Dean and having wildly erotic sex with men who are Toran on the inside, defeating diabolical men and murderous women, helping the innocent, and spinning in and out of time as I see fit.

I don't get out of my pajamas until around two in the afternoon, if I get out of them at all. Deadline time, pajamas all day, every day, for two months. Hair washing: Maybe. Eating: Sporadic. Bizarre and poor diet filled with marshmallows, granola, and for some reason an abundance of tomatoes, which I eat like apples.

I walk my cats in their four-seated stroller or head into the one-street town, if I must, or I read. I read everything from articles on all aspects of biology, physics, and new scientific discoveries and explorations, to fiction, nonfiction, and romance. I garden. If it is wintertime, and raining more, I listen to classical music and hard rock. Sometimes I am inspired to play air guitar, jumping and spinning, then I smash the invisible guitar on the floor, when I'm feeling especially frisky. In the summers I make jams and jellies with fruits I pick on my own property and on U-Pick farms on the island.

After dinner, I read what I wrote that day, tell myself I'm a terrible writer and that no one should have to read my crap as it might rot their thinking cap. I say things like, "Did you write that, Charlotte? Were you drunk? How does that move the plot along? Do you know how to structure a sentence? I'm asking, I want to know. Why don't you write about pancakes instead? It would be more exciting for your readers. You can't be serious. You should quit writing. Buy a nursery and sell plants. Or sell socks."

While I write in the evening I have a glass of wine. Or two. Three, sporadically. Only the finest stuff, though. Wine is made from grapes. Therefore I am drinking fruit.

Before I go to bed, I recheck all the doors and check that my gun is still loaded, as if the bullets could have jumped out of it during the day. We have no crime on the island. It's ridiculous that I worry. Over the years I have had fantasies of Toran creeping in through my window in a cat burglar black leather outfit with the buttocks cut out.

The cats curl up on my bed, exhausted from their day.

I read gardening books to combat insomnia and attempt to expand my knowledge and memorization of the Latin names of plants. When the book hits me in the face, I turn over and try to sleep. I am alone when I go to sleep. I am alone when I wake up. Alone.

Except for the cats.

But now I wasn't alone. Toran slept down the hall.

I liked that. I liked him. My body liked him in a carnal, lusty way. I liked him straight from my brain.

I picked up my journals again. "Help me, Albert. Help me, Marie. Help me, Edgar," I said out loud. I searched around in my head. I had nothing to say, nothing to write.

The writer's block was still blocking me.

Why was that?

Why did I not want to write? Why could I not go anywhere with my tenth novel?

I couldn't figure it out.

So I thought I'd go and help Toran on the farm.

"You want to help me?"

"Yes."

Toran climbed off the tractor with wheels taller than me and stood before me, the potato plants in rows and rows behind him. "What would you like to do?"

"Anything."

"Anything?"

"Yes."

He seemed relieved. "Charlotte, I know you're brilliant, that you like numbers, and I hate doing the books."

"I'll do them." My, he was tall. I pictured him in those black leather pants, cat burglar style, with the buttocks cut out. I wondered if he would wear them, say, if they were given to him as a gift. "My father taught me how to keep the books starting when I was twelve. I was enthralled by the numbers."

"I know. I remember coming over to your house and you were at his desk, papers everywhere, and you were using two calculators at one time. Charlotte." He put his hands up. "If you could do the books, I would be grateful, more than I can say."

"You would?" I felt hopeful! I could be useful. "I love making numbers work, every single one of them, down to the cent."

"They drive me straight out of my head."

"Are your books in your office in the yellow building or at home in your office?"

"Both places. Totally disorganized. Here, there. You'll want to run me over with a tractor when you see the extent of it."

"No. I won't." I tried to push my glasses up my nose, but they fell off. Toran picked them up and handed them to me, chivalrous warrior. "This is going to be fun. Thrilling, even. I'll get the books from both places, then I'll go tackle the numbers. Numbers can hide but they can't lie, and I'll figure it out. It's like a numerical puzzle."

"I'll pay you. You are now Chief Financial Officer and on my payroll."

I waved a hand. "I'll earn my keep."

"No. I will pay you."

"Toran, I—" I stopped. His face was resolute. He put his hands on his hips. He did not smile. He would not argue this point. I heard my mother in my head. "A feminist provides for herself, and she insists that she is paid fairly." Then, "In a love relationship, don't ever emasculate your man."

"Thank you, Toran."

"There's a spare office next to mine. You can work in there."

I turned away, my light brown skirt ruffle spinning.

"Charlotte."

"Yes?" I turned around.

"Thank you." It was heartfelt, sincere.

"Thank you." I stood up on my toes for a second. "Numbers make me giddy." I cleared my throat. That sounded geeky, albeit true. "They get me charged up." Darn. "Numbers make me excited." That was sexual. Keep going, Charlotte, you're bound to get the right word within the hour. "I mean—"

"I know what you mean, Char. I do."

Yes, he did. I could tell by that softened-up hard face that he did. I turned away as another image of black leather cat burglar pants with the buttocks cut out tantalized me.

* * *

As if my agent, Maybelle Courten, could hear my literary struggles, she called me the next day when I was having spaghetti for breakfast, pouring over Toran's books. I could tell he didn't like bookkeeping.

He did not write his numbers precisely or in tight columns. Numbers were missing. There were receipt piles here and there. There were few invoices. There had not been a weekly entry in two weeks except for payroll. I looked for separate client accounts, and they were a mess, too.

I would clean this accounting catastrophe up for him and enter the numbers into the computer. He had recently bought one, but I don't think he knew how to use it competently yet. I wiggled. My feet did a dance under the table. I could be of help! Was that against my feminist leanings to want to help and have him, a man, be grateful? No, it wasn't, I decided. I worked for him and I was living free in his home. Aha!

"How is your novel coming along, Charlotte?"

"Dandy." I swirled the noodles around my fork. I had made garlic bread, too.

"You haven't written a thing, have you?"

"I cannot lie, because then I would be struck by lightning."

"Quit indulging your writer's block. Oh, for God's sake!" she yelled. "Hang on. . . ." I heard her cover the phone with her hand. "Sheryl, your crotch almost shows in that miniskirt. No one wants to see your crotch, least of all me. No, no one else's mother allows them to resemble a hooker, and I wouldn't give a rat's ass if they did." She spoke into the phone again. "Tell me your idea for your next book."

"I am thinking of making a new cement patio with rectangles and squares."

"Hit me in the face with a goose. Tie my hands with a rattlesnake. Make me eat cardboard, this is a disaster. What does that have to do with your book?"

"I prefer to think of gardening types of things right now. Specifically, geometrically correct patios with a nod toward prime numbers and asymmetrical leanings."

"Charlotte, what is wrong?"

"I don't know."

"Yes, you do, what is it? You're not writing. Oh, for God's sake again!" Maybelle put her hand over the phone. "That is not appropriate, either, young lady. You are not going out. You're going to crawl out your window and leave? Fine, then I will go down to that dark and yucky basement that I know you're sneaking off to at the Mulligans' house and I will bring you home. Oh, yes. I would so do it. No, Jamie, you are fourteen, you may not drive me there." She spoke into the phone again, her voice back to normal modulation. "Tell me, Charlotte. What is it?"

"Parenting teenagers sounds like an enjoyable experience."

"It's comparable to a colonoscopy. What's holding you up?"

I put down the fork. "I don't have any ideas. I don't have any enthusiasm. I don't have any excitement for any topic."

"It's McKenzie Rae Dean. She's always exciting. Here, answer me these questions." She asked questions—what country was I interested in, what time period, who did I want McKenzie Rae to meet, what problem could she solve? Save one person, save many? I answered. All of my answers were blah.

"Are you even trying to write?"

"No."

She tried to smother a scream of frustration. "I sent you another one of Kitty Rosemary's blasted articles. Did you get it?"

"I got it."

"Someone from your publishing house obviously talked to her." She shouted, "Randy. Stop singing, it's too loud. He doesn't sound like a sick pterodactyl, Jamie, don't say that. Here, Charlotte, can you talk to Sandy again? She wants to know about mathematical proofs and I don't have a clue."

I talked to Sandy for an hour. It's encouraging knowing the next generation has a passion for the complexities of mathematical equations. When we were done, Randy sang me his songs. He did not sound like a sick pterodactyl. He still thinks I'm groovin'.

Romance Readers and Writers Magazine
By Kitty Rosemary
Books For Chicks Reviewer

GEORGIA CHANDLER AND . . .
YOU WON'T WANT TO MISS THIS!

I've come upon a juicy bit of literary gossip, romance reader friends, but I can't tell you who it's from.

La-di-da, are you ready? Bra on tight? Holding your breath yet? It seems that the famous Georgia Chandler, of the Romantic Time Travel Adventure books, has writer's block. Yes, writer's block. After nine novels.

Her next novel will be late. There is no plot, no summaries, no nothing.

I know, I know, I want to bawl, too. Bring me my lace hankie!

Her readers, who number in the millions, will be sorely disappointed. I can barely stand it. Every time, after I have a bad date, and there are many, the last one with a man named Stuart who I found out later was married with five children and lives in Portland on a street named Oakhills, I pick up one of her books. They empower me, bring out my feisty side.

So what happened to Georgia Chandler?

Well, friends, I have been sleuthing about. There are many scintillating rumors.

Some say that Georgia Chandler has had a nervous breakdown and she is in seclusion in a chalet in Chamonix, France. Others say that she has run off with a Latin lover and doesn't want to write anymore. Someone else, a prominent source, heard that Georgia is in a spiritual retreat in Cambodia, is not speaking to anyone currently, and is perfecting her prayers and yoga.

I wish we knew the truth but, rest assured, as soon as I know, I will pass on this most intriguing information to you, trusted romance reading friends.

My belief is that she's with the Latin lover. I've always thought that Georgia Chandler simply writes about her own life—and adds the time-traveling storyline in. I've heard that she believes in taking charge of her own sexuality, and that means she sleeps with who she wants, when she wants.

Wishing you all wishing wells and romance under starry nights with seductive, polite gentlemen who are able to make a commitment, unlike married father of five (Stuart) on Oakhills Street in Portland, see above.

Ta-ta for now!

Kiss, kiss!

Kitty Rosemary

Molly Cockles Scottish Dancing Pub is in the center of the village in a stone building that looked to be about four hundred years old, give or take a century. Three stories, with a red door and red trim around the arched windows. The windows had that diamond crisscross pattern that reminded me of the castle in Cinderella.

When I arrived, it was dark, the old-fashioned streetlights casting shadows across the cobblestone streets. I could see the candlelight dancing in glass holders on the long wood tables. I squinted at the skinny, minimalized red door. People sure were short back then.

I had told Toran I would meet him here for lobster when he asked. He had a meeting in town with two other farmers. I said, "Yes, thank you. I like butter on my lobster, no hot sauce, no side of coleslaw, no bib."

"Butter it is, then. No bib."

Why do I utter such things?

I don't like bars. Bars are raucous. Too many people. Unpredictable. Dancing, yelling, that new karaoke singing, sometimes punching. I smoothed my hair back and pushed my glasses up my nose. It was a warm night, and my face was sweating. The sweat was probably, biologically, from nerves.

I was wearing my dark brown corduroy skirt. My mother hates it. Last time she saw it, she called it my "pioneer woman who is a bag lady on drugs" skirt. "A feminist stands tall, stands proud, and does not endeavor to dress to hide that she's a woman. Be proud to be a woman, not a bag lady on drugs, and burn that skirt."

I was also wearing my sturdy brown shoes. Her comment? "Are you wearing shoes for pond exploration?" I made sure the button on my white blouse was buttoned up. Not all the way to the top, but the one directly beneath it. I didn't want to be falling out or looking loose.

McKenzie Rae Dean would have unbuttoned two buttons. She would have worn a red bra beneath a black blouse. She would have been in tight jeans and black heels. She would have left her brown wavy hair down instead of in a bun like mine. There would be no clip on top of her head to keep her hair out of her face. She would be unforgettable.

In fact, McKenzie Rae would have strode into the bar, stolen everyone's attention, smiled saucily at her latest love stud, and strutted her strutty self on over to him, no matter what time period she was in. I needed some McKenzie Rae in me.

I shifted, stood on my tiptoes, and peered through the window of the pub, only my eyes and long forehead peeping over the sill. I hoped the dark would hide me. "Strange cat lady" came to mind, but I did miss my cats, so I wasn't that offended by the label.

I saw Toran. He was laughing with a group of men. His smile was . . . inviting. Warm. Friendly. He was taller than the other men, broader. And popular. Everyone liked Toran. He was a force. A leader.

McKenzie Rae would be after his tail in a minute. I cringed.

I stepped back from my peeping and examined my blouse. A buttoned blouse hides everything, including my fraying bra straps.

But my fraying bra straps wouldn't show if I unbuttoned one more button. I heard my mother's voice, yet again, telling me that a feminist is in charge of her sexuality and doesn't let anyone else tell her what to do, how to act, or what to wear. "Don't smother your sexuality, Charlotte."

I unbuttoned the button. There. I sucked in air.

I felt self-conscious. Exposed. I buttoned it back up.

I should let go, be free, embrace my smothered sexuality. I unbuttoned the button again.

Too much skin! I buttoned it up.

I was going to be daring! Bold! I unbuttoned it.

I peered down. I buttoned it back up. Dang!

"Charlotte?"

I whipped around, in the midst of being a proud feminist who stands tall and unbuttons her button.

"Oh. Toran. Good evening." I smoothed my pioneer bag lady on drugs skirt down. "How are you?"

"Fine, there. Are you coming in straight away?"

"Yes, yes. I was . . . I was . . . buttoning. Unbuttoning."

"You were what?" He walked closer to me, smiling.

"Do you think that this shirt looks better buttoned like this, or like this?" I was mortified that I'd even asked the question out loud. He watched while I buttoned and unbuttoned.

"I think you should wear it however you like."

"But I don't know what I like."

He tilted his head, those blueberry/Scottish sky eyes soft. "You don't know what you like?"

"No, Toran, I don't." I took my glasses off. The taped arm wobbled. "I live on an island."

"Yes. Me too."

"Mine is much smaller. I live a pretty isolated life. I watch whales. Play chess against myself. I like my cats. I think of my cats as friends, which is pathetic. Cat friends. I walk them in a stroller."

"You walk them in a stroller?" His mouth tilted up. "I would like to see that."

"Everyone likes to see it. When there are tourists driving by, they practically run off the road to see four furry heads sticking out of a pink stroller."

"So you're the cat stroller lady."

"Yes. I would be that woman. Dull. Eccentric."

"You aren't dull at all, Charlotte," he said quietly. "Not at all. I like the eccentricities."

"You've always been nice, Toran." *And now you're flat-out sexy. And tall. And you have eyes that stare straight at me and listen. I have never met a man like you.*

"I'm not being nice. I'm being truthful. What do you mean when you say that you don't know what you like?"

"I can't even button my shirt without standing and wondering whether I want to unbutton a button. I didn't have that problem until I came to Scotland. I knew how to button before I boldly, brazenly, bravely left America." Why did I have to use alliteration at bizarre times? "Scotland is unbuttoning me."

"It's unbuttoning you?"

I put a hand to my face and fluttered it, trying to cool off. "I am having a button attack."

"You're in a place you haven't been for twenty years and everything's different."

"And the same, in some ways. But I haven't been that person, the person I was when I was here, for twenty years. That person was a kid, but Scottish, and somebody who liked adventures and running around outside, singing Scottish songs, and shooting off guns and bows and arrows with her father and she knew what she wanted to do."

"And you don't now?"

"I'm fighting with my buttons, Toran. That should tell you something."

"I think, Charlotte Mackintosh, that we should find out what you like and what you don't like."

"I think I should, too. Buttons shouldn't confuse, confound, or contradict like this." And there were my alliterations, again.

"I think you should find out what kind of beer you like first. Surely that's the first goal."

"Definitely. I wouldn't even mind a hangover."

"All right, then, in you go, luv."

I woke the next morning with a hangover. I put both hands to my head and groaned.

I opened my eyes slowly. On the floor was my white blouse.

It had red wine on it. I bet it had Scottish whiskey on it, too.

I laughed. That hurt my head.

I had ended up unbuttoning not one button but two, but that was after a shot of whiskey, half a beer, and some tasty red wine. I had not dared go any lower, as then the beat-up bra would have shown through, but if I had been wearing red, who knows what would have happened? Clearly, McKenzie Rae had jumped into me.

Rowena, who came in with Olive, told me her ex-husband, who had the kids that night, had "small balls, like marbles." Olive told me that she couldn't wait to eat Mr. Giraffe, one of her favorite pigs, would I like to come to dinner? I said I would love to come and eat Mr. Giraffe. She moaned and said, "I love Mr. Giraffe, and it pains me to eat him. See, I'm wearing a giraffe scarf. Knitted it myself!"

The giraffe looked baffled. I don't think it was intentional.

I played poker with Toran and several of his friends. I had played poker with my university colleagues in the past and had researched poker so I could win.

That night, with almost everyone watching, I won.

The women in the bar cheered, then heaved me up on their shoulders and paraded me around the room. Toran was second place. He winked at me, grinned . . . and I think he was . . . proud. Yes, proud. I used the winnings to buy drinks for everyone until the money ran out. That was a popular move on my part.

There was a band in the corner, and I danced with Toran. He felt strong and tall. I was stiff and awkward at first, but he pulled me into his arms and smiled and I had another shot of whiskey and things went warm and well after that as he spun me around.

The other couples spun around, too. We all had huge beer mugs and clunked them together in the middle of the dance floor. We sang Scottish drinking songs about a young boy's longing for the dairy maid, another one about offing the English king, and a third about how Sailor Davey missed his momma so let's chug, chug, chug to him.

I'd had way too much by then, so I decided to end the night

with one of the traditional Scottish dances I knew as a girl, and Rowena and Olive joined in. Our knees went out, our hands went up, and our feet flew and crossed at angles, rapidly. We did this holding beer mugs. On the bar. I tried to pretend I was in my kilt, white blousy shirt, and my blue velvet waistcoat from childhood. I wanted to be authentic in my endeavors.

We received a raucous standing ovation.

Toran smiled at me. "You still have it, Charlotte."

He held me close, and wonder upon wonders, I even took off my glasses and tucked them into the deep pocket of my skirt as they kept wobbling to the left. During the night my hair fell out of the bun and the clip flew off. Toran kept smiling. He bought me dinner. We had lobster. I did not wear a bib. It was delicious.

I had unleashed my sexuality by two buttons on an unsuspecting Toran.

I laughed again, and it hurt my hangover.

I kept laughing anyhow.

After I showered I took off my high-necked, floor-length, flowered nightgown and stood naked in front of the long mirror in my bedroom. I avoid looking at myself naked. I think it's because I see no reason to fuss with how I look. I am also somewhat repressed and not exactly a sexy gal. Plus, The Unfortunate Marriage did a number on me, shredding my self-esteem, I know that.

I ran both hands over my breasts. I am "remarkably, blessedly chesty," as my mother refers to it. "Got those guns from your grandma."

"Perfect breasts," Drew had told me. I wear bras that smash them down so they don't jiggle.

My stomach was flattish, but not perfect. I turned around.

My butt was still mostly up. Not huge. There were a few dimples. Some of them appeared to be smiling.

My legs are skinny.

What are we to expect, and want, realistically from our bodies?

To walk, to run, to move? Yes.

To dance and explore and have adventures? Yes.

To be perfect? No. That's inane. That's a pathetic waste of time and almost biologically impossible.

What I want is to be alive and healthy. I don't get hung up on much more than that.

And here I am.

Alive and healthy with a body that wants to engage in panting, rolling intercourse with Toran.

I wondered if he would ever want to make love to me wearing his kilt and tartan.

I jumped up a bit in excitement. My boobs jiggled. That was okay. Totally okay. I jumped again.

I wondered what Toran would think of the jiggling boobs in front and my fat dimples smiling at him from behind.

Ben Harris had been right about the purple flowering clematis that my mother had named The Purple Lush. It was a flowing purple wave, covering our wobbly arch over the pathway, then dancing across the white-gray picket fence. I had planted it with my father while we sang Scottish songs.

I remembered that sunny afternoon. It had been after the Highland Games. My father had won many events, including the Caber Toss, Open Stone, and the Scottish Hammer. He had also played the bagpipes.

When it was planted, he swung my mum up in his arms and carried her upstairs, "for a nap. Your mum is tired, Charlotte. I'm going to tell her a story, then have her lie down for a wee bit." He kissed her, she giggled, and they disappeared. I stood under the trellis staring at the purple flowers, the sky a blue background, smooth and clear, as if I could scoop it right up.

It was probably then that my love of gardening started and bloomed. While they took their "nap," I wandered around. My mother had paths to a picnic table and red Adirondack chairs under an oak tree, the branches spread out like an umbrella, that she said was as "old as time, maybe older." She had another path to a rose garden, one to a vegetable garden, another to a fountain of a little girl in galoshes holding an umbrella.

She had vines growing up steel planters and flowers pouring out of wine barrels, a wheel barrel, a wooden wishing well, even my father's old boots.

She hung silver watering cans on a tall post and a purple three-foot-high metal star on the wall of the house. We had red flower boxes on each window, and she'd painted a mural of red poppies with outdoor paint and hung it on a fence my dad built specifically for her painting. That painting was gone.

"A garden should be natural art," she told me. "A place for peace and serenity. It's yours, for you. You plant and nurture, rip out weeds, and create a place of beauty. Then you get back out into the world as a fighting woman and kick some butt."

Now most of her brick paths were completely overgrown. I couldn't find three of the paths, but I was able to walk down to another oak tree where my father had hung a swing. All that was left was the frayed bits of rope.

I adjusted my straw hat and tried to find the picnic table. My grandma and I always sat there. When I found it, the table was crumbling. It had fallen in on itself, the tree massive above it, the branches gnarled.

I heard my grandma's voice.

"*Let me tell you what I see, sweet Charlotte. There are words in your future, many words. There is an ocean, not this one. It is far away. You'll cross this ocean to get to the next. Come back to this ocean. Come back.*"

"I came back, Grandma." Tears streamed down my face. "I came back. I miss you. I miss the bread we made together, your second sight, your smile. I miss everyone."

I sniffled, took out an old tissue and blew my nose, then stuck it back into my skirt.

I moaned, sniffled again, wiped my face.

There was so much my mother left in her garden. Part of the star was still there. The silver watering cans were rusting. The wine barrels were crumbling. No wheel barrel in sight. I saw one of my father's old boots, the other lost. It hurt to see everything she'd done so ragged and overgrown.

She was in South Africa, my father was dead, my grandparents long gone. They had moved out when my father married, to a new home they bought right next to the ocean, and he and my mother had moved in. My granddad had died the same year as my grandma. He could not have lived without her, my dad told me.

I was here alone, without my family. How could that be? How could they all be gone?

I tried to rein in my emotions. Studying science for years has helped me to be practical, logical, and rational when solving problems, equations, formulas, mathematics. My emotions, since I arrived in Scotland, have been skittering around, overwhelming me. I am used to covering up my emotions, but the truth is that I'm a sap.

A sap, I decided then, sitting under the oak tree that was as "old as time, maybe older," who wanted to restore her mother's garden to its former glory.

Drew Morgan and I were both working on our master's degrees in biology. We'd often stay late, work on our research, and then he and I, and whoever else was there, would eat takeout food together. Monday, Chinese, Tuesday, Indian, Wednesday, pizza, Thursday, Italian, Friday, Japanese. We worked together for eighteen months before he asked me out to dinner one night.

Squirming around, nervous, he said, "Charlotte, I would . . . it would be . . . pleasure . . . an I if our my . . . my honor . . ." He cleared his throat. "Me, I would like to take you to dinner, and dessert, if you want dessert, you don't have to have dessert, um, at Loralee's on Friday night at sixteen o'clock. I mean, six o'clock. Would you please me? With me."

And I said, setting down a folder I was writing in and pushing my glasses on top of my head, "Why?"

"Because I want to have dinner with you."

Drew was tall with thick dark hair and glasses. Our glasses matched almost perfectly. Like me, the glasses made his nose appear more beakish than it was. But behind the glasses his eyes were soft brown. Drew wore the same pea green sweater several days in a row before changing it for a black sweater, which he wore for another three days in a row. He always wore beige pants, which I noticed were different. They were all the same brand, but one was older than the other two, and of the other two, one had cuffs that were slightly frayed.

"Why do you want to have dinner at a restaurant?" I asked him, confused. We had our takeout schedule already, and it was efficient and varied.

He squirmed. "So we can talk."

"What do you mean?" I was totally not getting it, as I had not been asked out in a long time. Like, in years. "We talk here."

He fidgeted. "It's a, well, if you can, want to, um, I, uh, it's a date, Charlotte. I'm asking you out for a date."

"A date?" My voice pitched up. "A date? Why do you want to go out on a date?"

"Because I like you."

That flustered me up. "As a fellow student here, a colleague, so to speak, you like me. You respect my work. You enjoy how we work together on our research and you appreciate my comments and insights into your research. Right?"

"Yes, I like all of that. But I . . . I . . . ," he stuttered, "I like you, too, Charlotte."

I puzzled that one out. I liked Drew. He was brilliant. Soft spoken. Gentle. Everyone liked Drew. Not everyone liked me. One, because I was a woman and there were not a lot of other women in the lab back then. When the men were sexist pigs with me, I called them on it and then I did things to take revenge. For example, I published more papers, completed more thorough research, and when necessary called them out on their misogynistic, sexist thinking and verbally twisted their jocks, in public. Gasp! A woman can, and does, fight back!

It didn't always make me popular. Too bad for the sexist ape-men.

"Okay, Drew. Dinner. I do not eat oysters or clams, because of the slimy texture."

"I know."

"I also do not eat sausages."

"I know."

And when I go to a restaurant, which is infrequent, I order and eat dessert first. I have a sweet tooth."

"I know about the sweet tooth, too. That's why I bring you chocolate cake."

"I can socialize for perhaps two hours, then I'll be tired and need to be alone."

"I understand."

We went to the restaurant. He paid. I tried to pay, but he refused. I told him, "I can pay for myself."

He said, "I know you can, Charlotte, but I want to."

"Then what do you want in return?"

"Nothing, Charlotte." But his eyes teared up.

"Why are your eyes tearing up?"

"Because I had the best time."

"You did?"

"Yes. I like talking to you. You're the only woman I have ever been able to talk to."

"Oh."

"And I think you have pretty hair and eyes, too. I've never seen you with your glasses off."

"And I haven't seen you, either."

"Let's take them off."

"I'll hardly be able to see you if my glasses are off."

"I'll lean closer."

"This is silly."

"Try it. We'll do it together. One, two, three . . ."

We did it. I was surprised. I actually sat back in my chair. "Well. You are extremely handsome, Drew."

"So are you, Charlotte. I mean"—he coughed, then smiled—"you're beautiful. Your eyes are so, so green. Do you remember that lab specimen—"

"From the county health department."

"Yes. Your eyes are like that. That color."

I was pleased. "Thank you."

We smiled. I told him I would pay next time and that I did

not want to be beholden to him for anything, as I was a feminist and independent.

He said I wasn't beholden. But he held my hand on the way out the door and in the car. He was polite, opened my car door, walked me to the door of my apartment.

We went out again and again. It was my first serious relationship.

Between Drew, my research, and school, I had no free time to write my novel. I put it aside, as so much is put aside, I have noticed, in women's lives in favor of a man.

I became the woman I didn't want to be, a woman who would give up interests and passions for her man, a woman who would start to become not exactly herself anymore, a woman who would spend so much time spun up about a man that she spun off her ambitions and dreams, no matter how crazy, and independence.

That was a bubble-headed woman's mistake.

My mother said she lost "a million brain cells watching that antifeminist circus."

Some mistakes in life cannot be undone.

That one, thankfully, could.

Stanley I and Stanley II, and their crew, worked fast. The kitchen cabinets were up, all the window were now in, the trim and wainscoting was nailed up, and the bathrooms were being transformed.

Not only do Stanley I and Stanley II have many talents in terms of home remodeling, they have many interests, too. We talked about herbal versus traditional medicines. Stanley II said that when he is depressed he eats cranberries dipped in butter. Cures it every time. Stanley I said that he had squished daisies and put them on one of his "fungus-ridden" toes and the fungus was killed.

I bought black knobs in the shapes of wineglasses for the kitchen and knobs in the shapes of daisies for the downstairs bathroom towel cupboards and knobs in the shapes of toilets for my bathroom cupboards.

"Right-o. These will be in in two shakes of a lamb's tail," Stanley I said as I handed them to him in a bag.

"I don't eat lamb," Stanley II told me. "They're too cute to eat."

"They do have a special smile that's hard to ignore," I told him.

"I don't eat alfalfa sprouts," Stanley I told me.

"We both eat kidney stew," they said at the same time.

They had sanded and restained, in the same color, our dining room table, with Scientist Bridget and Scientist Charlotte written inside a heart, the two chairs, and the armoire. They looked infinitely better, not crooked, not tilted, not broken. The dents and scratches, made by generations of Mackintoshes, were still there. The character, the history, was still there.

"Old furniture, solid, special," Stanley I said, understanding.

"It's a gift from the people in your past," Stanley II said.

"Yes. They're not here, but what they made is still here." My eyes misted. "Still here." I ran my hands over the honeysuckle vine carved into the armoire. "My granddad did that for my grandma."

"The one blessed with the Scottish Second Sight," Stanley II said.

"She had it, truly," Stanley I said. "She told my mother that when the crows flew backward and the barn collapsed she would get rid of something very bad."

"What did she mean by that?"

"Your grandma told my mother, at the time, that she had no idea what it meant. Not a touch of a blue idea, but sure enough there was a whippy windstorm here, howling like the devil gone mad, and it pushed the crows out of the trees. My mother saw them flying backward and then our father died when the barn collapsed."

"Ouch. That was the bad thing she was going to get rid of?"

"Yep, it was. He was a mean son of a bitch," Stanley I said. He knocked his knuckles on the armoire, pretty hard.

"Used to beat her and Stanley I," Stanley II said. "We were eight when he died and we didn't shed a tear, did we, Stanley?"

"None."

"God crushes the bad among us sometimes, and he came to Stanley I's rescue, and his mother's, and your grandma, she saw it coming wrapped in a mystery."

"We were poor, but happy after that," Stanley I said, "And my mother, she later made a success out of our farm, that she did."

"Crows never flew backward again, to my knowledge," Stanley II said.

They both shook their heads. "No backward crows," they said together, as if on cue.

No wonder the Stanleys were two of Toran's best friends. Kind, strong, honest. That's the type of person he liked. That's the type of person he was.

"Where is the information on Brekinridge's Grocery Stores. . . . I need to talk to the trucking company . . . this bill is incorrect . . . I'll double-check on the blueberries, they received one hundred thirty-six kilograms, not two hundred thirty-six . . . billing issue . . ."

I muttered to myself while I worked in the office next door to Toran's. He was hardly there, always out on the farm.

He had given all books and information to me, some in boxes, some in piles. Ledgers. Receipts. Notes. Notebooks. Invoices.

Thousands of numbers.

I was in number heaven. I pulled on the collar of my shirt. One of my favorites. It had a picture of Julia Child on it. I was wearing one of my two pairs of jeans. Too large, but I had found the perfect rope on my island on the sand to use as a belt.

Toran stuck his head in. "Charlotte."

"Yes." I took a pencil out of my mouth. My glasses slid down my nose and I pushed them back up, as visions of accounts, potatoes, blueberries, apples, shipping containers, and boxes danced through my head. And the cost of a new engine for one of Toran's semis and the cost for an air-conditioner in the cooling unit. I had called Dorian's Cooling directly, and we had worked out a discounted price. Dorian thought I was a "tough negotiator." I could tell by the end of our conversation that he was tired.

"How is it going?"

"I believe I am making adequate progress." I had to smile into his blueberry/Scottish blue sky eyes.

"I'm sorry, Char, that this isn't more . . ."

I waved a hand. "Think nothing of it. I'm getting things together, categorized, organized, in a general sense, then I'll begin on the smaller subunits. Next, I'll analyze and suggest an efficient system of accounting and begin my spreadsheets."

"You have an accounting degree, too?"

"No. However, I have had statistics, calculus, differential equations, and numerical analysis, so numbers are a joy."

"So . . . you are joyful now?"

I pushed my hair back. My hand ran into my clip and undid it. I hardly noticed. "I could not be more joyful if I tried."

"Thank you, Charlotte."

"It's my mathematical and numerical pleasure." I rested my other hand on the rope holding my pants up.

He grinned and headed back out. I swallowed hard. I would find satisfaction in entering all of the numbers from Bridget's Haven Farms into ledgers and spreadsheets, buying and selling, products and shipping, employee salary and benefit costs, overhead costs, and income.

But what was truly tingling and tantalizingly torturous was being near Toran.

The TorBridgePherLotte fearsome foursome could also time travel. We could go back in time, crawling into the fort we built together then bursting out into the Land of the Monkeys, or the Reign of the O'Shaugnasseys, a dangerous family that kept the village people in quaking fear and poverty. We even popped into the future and saved the world from destruction.

To return home, we scrambled into the fort, put all of our fists together, shouted, "Escape, Clan TorBridgePherLotte, back home!" and ta-da! We were back in the hills of Scotland, sheep everywhere.

When it started to get dark, Bridget and Toran would look at the time, their faces would fall, and Toran would take Bridget's hand and we would all trudge down the hills, past the sheep, the potatoes Toran's father grew, the lettuce and strawberries my father grew, and head home.

Pherson would clap Toran on the back to say good-bye. Pherson lived with his parents and three younger sisters, two of them twins who came when, my mother told me, "Pherson's mother was not expecting babies." I was about eight at the time, and since his mother was not expecting babies I assumed she did not know that they would be dropped off at her doorstep like milk bottles.

Pherson's family was loud and friendly, their house in happy chaos. My home was filled with unending love and attention from my parents. As we watched Toran and Bridget leave, I would feel . . . scared. As a small child, that's what I felt: Fear.

Turns out, I had every reason to feel that way.

It would have been better if Clan TorBridgePherLotte had left Bridget and Toran in the past in a magical land far away from their father's fanaticism.

October 16, 1971

Dear Charlotte,

Do you remember Father Cruickshank, who I told you about? I told you I didn't like him. He always wants to see me, always wants to pray with me. He gave me chocolates one time, a game, cards. He's made me drink wine with him. Told me it was Jesus's blood and it would bless me.

Two weeks ago he told me to come with him for a special Bible study at his house in the woods to study, so I did what I was told.

When we were there he told me to lift up my skirt and pull down my panties for a thrashing. I told him no and he grabbed my arms and held me tight and said if I didn't he would tell my father that I had snuck out and had sex with boys in town.

You know my father, Charlotte, and what he would do to me if I was in trouble at school with a priest. Father Cruickshank ripped down my panties and yanked me over his lap and hit me on my bum. It hurt, but then he . . . he . . . he put his finger up me and made me bleed and shoved my head down hard so I couldn't look up. He told me he was purifying me from sin. That I was too sexy and needed to be purged and this was the only way.

He kept saying the Lord's Prayer, but he was panting and groaning. He told me that this time he wouldn't tell my father about my behavior, but he would if I fought with him again.

I pulled up my panties and I ran out of there.

That was the start, Charlotte. The start.

Love,

Bridget

January 4, 1972

Dear Charlotte,

Father Cruickshank shoved me against a wall and stuck his you know what in me. It hurt. Hurt. Hurt.

When I cried and pushed him away, he slapped me and told me to be quiet, to not make a sound or he would smack my dirty mouth again, and he said you like this, lass, you like it, I know you do. Don't lie. There. Doesn't that feel nice? It feels nice.

I don't like it, I told him, and I was crying and said get away it hurts get off and he said you like it bless you daughter of God for you have sinned, you are a sinner, Bridget Ramsay, and I will take your confession. You have made me come to you, you have seduced me. God will punish you. But I didn't, Charlotte, I didn't. I don't want to do that. I bled in my underwear for three days.

I am not a liar.

I am not a liar.

I am not a liar.

I cry all the time. I'm scared. He has a silver cat. Even the cat tries to bite him. He hits the cat.

Bridget

March 21, 1972

Dear Charlotte,

I have nightmares about Father Cruickshank.

Pound, pound, pound. Blood. Rip. Hands on throat. No air. Can't breathe. Hit. No, please, stop. No.

Love,

Bridget

I closed my eyes against my own dizziness.

Bridget, where are you? Please come home.

8

"We're going to begin our discussion tonight with window boxes," Olive Oliver said. She was wearing a blue scarf with a demented-looking raccoon on it. I don't think it was intentional.

"Why do we have them? What are the best plants and flowers for each season? Should we strive for color or texture, or both? Should window boxes reflect our personalities or our favorite colors or, when I make mine, how much I love chickens and pigs? These are important questions to ask."

The Gobbling Gibbling Garden Club ladies were meeting at Gitanjali's house. She lived above her spice store in the village, the building fairly new at only two hundred years old. From the outside the stone slanted, as if a hand had given it a push, but her flower boxes were filled with peppers and her sign GITANJALI'S INDIAN SPICES was in the shape of cinnamon sticks.

We traipsed through her store to get to the stairs to her flat, and I felt like I was in spice heaven. I had to stop and gape at the mounds of cinnamon, coriander, garlic, ginger, mustard seed, nutmeg, turmeric, chilis, and cloves and about thirty other spices I wasn't familiar with. The vibrant colors, the scents, the textures . . . I wanted to run my hands through them, smell them all. The walls of her shop were a deep blue, with pictures of Indian women in saris cooking in each of them. Long paper lanterns hung from the ceiling.

Rowena said to me, fiddling with her rock necklace, "When I

come through here I can barely think. It's like getting hit with little India."

"I could almost live here."

"Me too. Except Gitanjali wouldn't let me talk violence against my ex-husband, who is not paying my child support, which means I'm going to have to move out of our home."

"That scrunched-face jerk. May he be struck by a meteor and smashed to bits."

"I appreciate your vengeance on my behalf. Yesterday he had the kids draw pictures of their "new" family. Him, The Slut, and the four of them. My kids refused to do it, except for my oldest, who drew a picture of her father and wrote *shithead* across it."

"Doesn't sound like they appreciate their father or Bubbles."

"No, they know their father had an affair. The youngest is nine, the oldest is sixteen. Kids know everything. They are fully aware of what's going on. He told them he was not giving me child support anymore because I could get a job. I have a job. I was a full-time mother before he walked out, and I'm trying to launch my rock jewelry business, but the kids live with me and he doesn't want to help feed them."

"He's like a bad virus. What a prick."

"I wish it would fall off. Plunk." She started to cry and I hugged her by the coriander. I was surprised that I hugged her that quick. I am not usually skilled at female friendships, especially not in groups. After high school, I decided I didn't trust them. But here I was, at Gobbling Gibbling Gardening group, hugging Rowena.

"I know you're going to be a rock-solid, proper friend, Charlotte," she whimpered.

"A rock-solid friend who will accidentally trip The Slut if I see her."

"Thank you." She sniffled. "That's loyalty."

Gitanjali had one room upstairs, with a bed in one corner covered in a swirling scarlet-gold bedspread and a kitchen in the other. There were windows front and back.

It was filled with color and Indian decor, including silky scarves hung on the walls, colorful baskets, framed fabric artwork with sequins and mirrors, and paintings of India and elephants. Gitanjali had folded about twenty swans out of thick white paper and hung them from the ceiling.

Burgundy velvet curtains hung to the sides of the windows. A book shelf, painted red with faux jewels glued to it, was packed with books and Indian art. Stuffed green, purple, yellow, and orange elephants climbed up a wall. Everywhere, color, humor, art, creativity. I loved it.

The seven of us sat on the floor on huge red and purple embroidered pillows with gold braid, except for Lorna Lester, who sniffed and said, "I don't like clichés, in speech or in literature. I don't like improper behavior. I don't like spicy food, and I don't sit on the floor." Her daughter, Malvina, was on the floor. I wondered if she'd speak at all tonight.

Malvina saw her mother's glare, sighed, and heaved herself up on the couch. She was wearing black pants and a black T-shirt.

Kenna, the doctor, blond hair back in a bun, came in scrubs. Rowena wore the red dress she was going to wear for a date on Friday night when her "prick-arse ex-husband" had the kids with "his bubble slut."

We agreed she looked fantastic, except for Lorna, who raised a judgmental gray eyebrow and said, "Too tight." She put her palms on the top of her chest. "Breasts in."

I liked the dress. Summery. Light. I could never wear something like that. Could I?

"A window box must be neat and tidy," Lorna said, pointing a finger in the air, her body reminding me of human oatmeal again. "Red geraniums are best. That's what I plant each year. Three of them. There should be nothing in the box that distracts from the original display. Three in a box, no more. Think, ladies: Organization. Control. Neatness."

Malvina studied her short nails. She wanted another plate of food, I could tell.

I couldn't blame her. If I had a mother like that, I'd want to eat all the time to numb the pain and the stress that would undoubtedly produce excessive gas. Plus, Gitanjali had made Tandoori chicken and chicken tikka masala. And naan bread. It was so delicious, my taste buds melted.

Lorna picked at it and said it was "exotic," in a sniffy sort of way.

"I plant mine with petunias, flox, marigolds, and I usually add those swirly branches," Kenna said. "I like different textures."

"Different textures can confuse the display," Lorna said. "It can dilute the purity of the plant in the flower box, usually a flower that the homeowner has planted year after year. My mother planted geraniums, so do I, so does my daughter. No need to change or mix in other varieties."

"I always plant different flowers," Rowena said. "This year I planted nasturtiums and white petunias and put a giant ceramic frog in each one. I liked the humor. I named them The Croaker, Ribbet the Ripper, Froggy Fog, and Jane. Want more wine, ladies?"

We did.

Gitanjali reached out and poured it, then poured herself another glass.

"Red chilis in my flower boxes," Gitanjali said. "I sell spices, so that right spice to do."

"Why spices, Gitanjali?" Kenna asked.

Gitanjali's eyes were liquid black, her skin perfect. She was wearing a red and gold cotton shirt embroidered with elephants, over jeans.

"My mother love spices. They gold to her because then she make her family the food that we like. Nourish us. We so poor in our village. In hills. We were the Untouchables. I was Untouchable, that what I told." She paused and folded her tiny hands in her lap. "An Untouchable. As if no one can touch me as I am dirty."

I put a hand to my throat. How does a society get so out of shape, lose their way to such an extent, that they would call millions of people the Untouchables and treat them like trash?

"We not have the pipies for the loos or the . . . the . . . .

elect-on-tricity. Today, in this house"—she waved an elegant hand—"I still cannot believe I pull lever and clean water come out. I have glass of water. Anytime! I not have to walk to forest, or to well, and carry bucket on my head. Please excuse me, but I cannot believe that I have a loo. You cannot think how unclean village is when there are no loos."

"It would be disgusting!" Lorna said, her face flushed. "All the people would be unsanitary! Disgusting! Living in raw sewage, it's a disgrace!"

Lorna said it as if it were the fault of Gitanjali and her village.

"Yes, it is a disgrace," I said, "when you have a group of people at the top who will live in extreme wealth and lavish comfort and yet you have hundreds of millions of people who are relieving themselves by a river that is the same river people drink from because the government cannot or will not provide for them the basic infrastructure and support, like water, sewage lines, toilets, heat, electricity, and plumbing that they should be entitled to."

"Revolting," Lorna said. "I could never live there. I would refuse. I would leave. I would work my way up."

"You can't refuse, you silly chicken," Olive said, waving her wine. She spilled some on the demented raccoon. "You're born where you're born. It's not a matter of chance."

"If the people living with Gitanjali could have refused to live there, they would have," Rowena scolded. "You don't get to tell God where you want to land on this planet. If I could, I would land on my ex-husband's slut's fake boobs and pop them."

"They could have cleaned around and about. We've had toilets since 1890. Why don't they have them in 1990? They could have made loo lines and bought loos," Lorna said, staring hard at Gitanjali. "There's no excuse to be living in filth."

I sat straight up. Ignorance bothers me, especially when it comes out sanctimoniously. "Lorna, I don't think you're understanding the micro- and macroeconomics here, the governmental ineptitude that caused and maintains this structure, the debilitating societal dynamics, the religious beliefs and the stranglehold those beliefs have on that environment, or the lack of capitalistic, democratic forces and general fairness that we're discussing in this conversation."

"I understand the economics and the . . . the . . ." Lorna was flustered. "Everything else you . . . you *babbled* on about! It's a very primitive way to live. We Scots would never live like that."

"I am having a difficult time understanding why you are not understanding this," I said. Her brain was not functioning in a progressive, analytical manner.

"I understand everything, Charlotte—" Her face was flushed, her cheeks trembling with rage.

"You don't understand poverty," Kenna said. "As a doctor, I see it all the time."

"Or how rich people keep people in poverty," Olive said. "You're giving me a headache, Lorna, and I still have to feed the pigs tonight."

"Perhaps I could give you a lobotomy," Kenna muttered. "Where is my surgical bag?"

"I think it is ignorance that will kill the world," Olive said.

"Or stupid people," Rowena said.

"Or people who don't have lobotomies," Kenna said, "but should."

Gitanjali said, "I understand, Lorna." But I saw those dark eyes. Hurt. She was hurt. Again.

"I don't like the way you're treating Gitanjali, Lorna," I said. "Dismissive. Rude."

"Please," Gitanjali said. "Peace. I am not on the off."

"The off?" Kenna said.

"What that word? Off and the ten?"

"Offended," Olive said. "Why so mean-spirited and domineering, Lorna? You won't keep friends that way. I had a pig once who was aggressive. None of the other pigs liked her. I killed her and she was delicious, but still. Her life was spent making other pigs upset and irritated."

"You're a grouch, Lorna. You need tequila," Rowena said. "I have one whenever I think of The Slut getting near my kids. Those two, happy all the time, as if they haven't destroyed our family's life. Wait until the lust wear off."

"You do need tequila," Olive said. "It'll loosen up that body and rigid mind-set of yours."

"I do not. And I don't drink tequila." Lorna glowered.

I noticed she rarely glanced at Gitanjali, one more way to put Gitanjali in her "place." If you don't acknowledge their presence, you are telling them they're not important. Gitanjali had the audacity to come from a foreign country, with a foreign religion, and she had dark skin. That was too much for Lorna.

"Tequila is for a class that is beneath myself," Lorna said, lips tight.

"Maybe you should go and live in India," Kenna said. "You can experience class there in a shanty."

"I dare you to have tequila," I said. "Are you scared to try a shot of tequila?"

Lorna huffed and puffed, sitting straight up and glaring at me. "I am not afraid of anything, you . . . you . . . skinny pole toothpick nerdy American."

That's what started it all.

Skinny pole toothpick nerdy American. She had what was coming to her.

One tequila shot, then another, some in tea, some not, and Gitanjali's India flat became a noisy, laughing, Scottish-song-singing gang of ladies having a grand ole time. Even Lorna wasn't such a witch. I kept filling her glass.

About eleven, for some inexplicable reason, we decided that we should all go on a bike ride in the village in our panties and bras. It was a hot night. It was a drunk night.

"It's dark out," Rowena said, tottering. "No one will see us. Be quiet, all of you. Shhhh! But if I do see The Slluuuut, I'm going to run her and her fake booby bubbles down."

Lorna swayed. "I'm not going. I am not the type of woman who bikes with bra and panties on at all. Or drinks tequila. It's a class problem. Gas problem. Gassy problem." She farted. "It's a gas problem." She wagged her finger. "I told you." She farted again and waved her hand behind her butt.

"We know," Kenna said. "You're a chicken."

"I am not a chicken lickin'! I eat geraniums." Lorna mimed eating geraniums. "Red ones. Always the same stupid-woopid color."

Lorna's daughter, Malvina, laughed so hard she doubled over in front of her mother. She farted, too. They had eaten a lot of Gitanjali's "exotic" food. "Fart!" she declared. "On my mum!"

"Like mother, like daughter," I said. "Both farters. It is not genetic. Why is the room spinning, Gitanjali? You shouldn't allow your house to spin. It's dizzying and I am dizzy."

"I eat my pets," Olive said, then burst into tears. She's a sappy drunk and wiped her eyes with the demented raccoon scarf. "I still miss Peek-A-Boo pig, but the honey mustard on the side was delicious. I would not eat my horses, though, or a porcupine."

Then, surprisingly, Malvina spoke again. "I'm going to ride a porcupine poking bike in my panties. Porky pig panties."

"I can't bike in my lingerie, I'm a doctor," Kenna said. "What if a patient saw my buttocks? Could never do that. But I have a solution kolution! I will wear a towel around my hair and dark glasses. No one will know like a show. I'll be an enema." She shook her head, befuddled, then pointed a finger in the air. "Not an enema. That makes you poopy. I am an M and M. No!" She shouted. "I eat M&M's. I am an . . ." She paused for effect. "Enigma! A mystery! Like Father Cruickshank who disappeared."

"Mystery!" Lorna shouted. "Gone. Poof! He's gooooone."

"Disappeared!" Malvina announced, then she rocked back and forth laughing. "Never to be found in the hills of Scotland."

Lorna farted, fanned her butt, and laughed again, a cackling sound.

Rowena said, "I am concerned that my V V will get squashed. Gitanjali, do you have a spice that will cure a squashed V V vagina?"

Gitanjali said, with such serenity, "I'm sure there a spice for the V V, the open flower."

"And now," I stood up. "I'm going to make an announcement. First, this house shouldn't spin. Second, I wear high-rise underwear." I put my drink down. "Look here." I pulled the hem of my skirt up to my head and yelled through the fabric. "It's like wearing a cotton chastity belt."

Everyone cheered.

I dropped my skirt as everyone stripped and proudly displayed their panties.

"Olive Oliver wears pig panties." Olive Oliver pulled down her pants. She was right! Pink panties. A white pig on the front. She oinked at us.

"Look at these motherfuckers," Lorna said, hardly able to stand. She unzipped her skirt. "Mine beats yours. I've got a horse's arse."

"You do," I said.

Malvina kept laughing.

I noticed that Rowena had sexy red panties, when she held up her summer dress. "You have lacy tidbit panties," I told her.

"I am going to put my panties on my head!" Rowena announced, and she did, pulling the lacy panties off and over her face like a mask. She peeked out through one leg hole. "I'm Panty Superwoman!"

Kenna grabbed one of Gitanjali's scarves to hide her hair and most of her face after she disrobed. White cotton underthings. "I slice people open, I dice people open, I slice and dice, once, twice, thrice!"

Gitanjali took off her embroidered elephant shirt and pants. Blue panties, surprisingly flirty. "I love silk," she slurred. "So soft." Her bra matched. "Spices. Silk. I like the longer ree."

"The what?" Olive said.

"Longer ree," Gitanjali said. "Pretty."

"Lingerie," I said helpfully. "I am helpful."

Lorna shouted again, "Too big." She spanked herself, both hands. "Too motherfucking damn big."

"An important deduction," I said. "Analysis. Hypothesis. Laboratory results, here come my somersaults." I somersaulted, buttocks in the air. They clapped.

"I hate The Slut," Rowena said through her red superwoman

mask. "I run her over like a dead possum. I look for her! I seek revenge!"

We panty-and-bra-wearing inebriated rebels borrowed Gitanjali's bikes, and we borrowed the neighbors' bikes without asking.

Lorna teetered and tottered on her motherfucking bottom on Gitanjali's bike.

Olive rode behind her, standing on the pedals, singing with Lorna about a woman in love with a Greek God who could "woo woo woo" her and "thump thump thump." I laughed so hard I had to bend over a bush and pee. Peeing outside, I noted to Rowena, was in line with our previous conversation about loos.

Rowena swayed. "No one wants to smell like urine."

"I peed, I peed," I said. "But not on my knee and not on a tree, and not during the time of the bees. I peed, I peed."

We gripped our handlebars and pushed off through the silent village, past the remnants of the cathedral and the castle that had an archbishop with twenty illegitimate children, and two stone churches.

Lorna sang a love song. She had a bellowing, shrieking voice. We circled the square, twice, singing, cackling, my hair loose from its bun and flying behind me.

"I hopie I see the chiefie tonight," Gitanjali said. "I say hi, man. I have too much spice liquid again at Gabbling Gooses tonight. Yes."

"See me, no hands!" I held my hands up, right by the empty lot where the Zimmerman Factory used to be. "I ride a bike, I ride a trike, I ride a kite, I try not to fight!"

Everyone rode with no hands with varying success.

"It's not easy to ride a bike drunk," Olive said, in all seriousness. "This is tricky dicky. I need a goat with me."

"I am a doctor and I'm half-naked here, I'm half-naked there, I'm half-naked everywhere," Kenna sang, high soprano. We joined her, in rounds, at my direction, once again.

Malvina crashed, then stood up and declared, "I didn't hurt my bottom. Bye and bye, geese can fly, no one worry. I'm in no hurry."

"I am going looking for The Slut," Rowena said. "Bash boobies. Smash Cooties. Toodle Tooties."

"No, no." I rode along beside her as she made a quick right. "Let's not."

"When I see The Arse I'm going to pull his balls off, like this." She pulled the air, both fists, then crashed.

Olive started pig snorting. Repeatedly.

Gitanjali tried to ride backward. She was fairly good at it. "Never lookie at the behind in life. Always lookie at the front chest."

We led Lorna home first because she was insisting on going shopping for red geraniums. She actually stopped by someone's house and ripped red geraniums from her flower box and put them behind her ears. She knocked on her own door and shouted, "Open up, Husband. You and your flaxen dick. You and your shriveled balls. You and your flatulence and drunkenness. Open up straight away now!"

She kicked at the door and it opened. She farted again and fanned her butt. "Fart," she said.

Malvina spread her arms out and spun. "I am a panty tequila goddess." She farted, too. "Like my farting mum."

Later that night, tucked up in bed, the moon a white ball in the sky, I laughed, quiet as I could.

I had ridden a bike in my dull and fraying bra and underwear in my old Scottish village. I had ridden with no hands.

I had a vision of myself, from the rear, my butt eating the seat, my hair flying behind me like a messy horse's mane, my glasses firmly attached to my face, tilting slightly to the left, as I teetered down the cobblestone streets with other women who also wore only bras and panties.

It was such a funny vision I started to laugh again.

I was surprised that I was in a garden group. I was surprised I went bike riding drunk in my panties. I was surprised I led friendly people in the village in song. Was I becoming a friend? A girlfriend? Could I do the girlfriend thing?

Charlotte Mackintosh, recluse.

Charlotte Mackintosh, girlfriend?

Charlotte,

I want to apologize for, once again, intruding on your activities last night. I received a call from two elderly people, Mr. and Mrs. Ryeson, who heard screaming near their home. They thought it was ghosts rising from the dead. They are both superstitious. Now I realize that was not screaming, but singing.

I applaud all of you for your athleticism. Riding bikes is healthy for the mind and body. I am relieved that Malvina was not hurt when she ran into the light pole and that Kenna suffered no injuries when she hit Stanley I's truck. She is a gifted surgeon.

Several ladies who approached me this morning at Sandra's Scones and Treats Bakery thought that this was a new tradition in town, a late-night panty and bra bike ride, and have asked if it is open to all women. I told them to contact you. A few seemed rather hurt not to be invited, so you may have to mend some feelings.

The daffodils have all popped up. Looking forward to the gladiolas now.

Yours sincerely,

Chief Constable Ben Harris

A friend of your parents, may your father have God's ears as he shares with him the legends of Scotland.

Dear Chief Constable Harris,
Thank you for your letter.
Gitanjali asked me if she should make you chicken makhani to apologize for the unintended ruckus we caused. I assured her that was a fine idea. She is a superb chef and I'm sure you will enjoy the meal and the company.
Olive told me to tell you that she will kill Harvey for Gitanjali's dish, as he is plump and ready to be eaten. I hope that this will serve as an appropriate expression of our embarrassment for the noise two nights ago.
Yours,
Charlotte Mackintosh

Dear Charlotte,
Words cannot express my gratitude. Gitanjali has already come to me and asked when it would be most convenient for her to make me dinner at her home. I told her any night would be most convenient for me.
I am going to bring flowers. Do you think Gitanjali would like tulips? A mixed bouquet? Something more exciting? I was thinking of a box of chocolates, too. Do you think she would prefer dark or light chocolate? I was also going to bring her a fine china teacup and saucer I saw the other day. It's hand-painted, delicate, like Gitanjali, and she has mentioned that she likes tea.
Do tell me, please. Is this quite too much?
Yours sincerely,
Chief Constable Ben Harris
A friend of yours parents, may your father's bagpipes reach God's ears.

"Care for a walk along the beach? It's raining, but not much. We can catch part of the sunset."

"Yes. I'd love to." I smiled up at Toran and pushed my glasses back up my nose. My finger caught on the tape. I dropped them. Toran picked them up. "Let me change my shoes." I took off my sturdy brown shoes and put on tennis shoes. They seemed clunky with my brown skirt, but that didn't matter. Comfort matters. I pulled on my thick pink wool socks and a blue rain slicker that I'd found at a secondhand shop. There was a parakeet on the pocket. It fell to mid thigh. I added a red and yellow striped rain hat. "Ready."

"Shall we, then?"

We started off down the street, then cut over for the path to the ocean, the rain a light sprinkle. "I love the rain," I said. "I love it in Washington, too. I find it soothing."

"Ah, me too. Love it for my farm. Have to have the rain."

We then launched into a discussion about rain, the weather, and the importance of water for people, food, and animals, but also how a lack of water could cause mass migration and world wars in the future.

It was a stimulating conversation.

We sat down on the sand, the sun setting behind us, turning the sky pink and yellow. The ocean was a dark blue gray with a white, frothy trim. Calm.

"It's nice to have someone to talk to," I said out loud. "I mean. That sounded pathetic. It's not that I don't have anyone to talk to. . . ." I paused. "I do talk to my mother, because she calls constantly and tells me I need to move off the island and quit being a hermit, and I do have a few neighbors I talk to, but not like . . . uh . . . not like . . ."

"Like this?"

"Like this. Yes." He always understood what I was trying to say.

"It's the same for me, Charlotte," he said quietly. "Exactly the same."

"I have writer's block." I ran sand through my fingers. It had stopped raining. "I'm surprised I blurted that out."

He turned toward me. "You do?"

"Yes. I can't write anything at all. The story's stuck."

"I'm sorry about that."

"Me too." The pink in the sky had given way to a dark blue, shot through with turquoise and gold.

"Why do you think you have writer's block, luv?"

Luv? Say it again, Toran, say it again. "I don't know. I don't know what to write. I don't know where I want McKenzie Rae to time travel to. I don't know what country, what time period, what she's supposed to do."

"When is your book due?"

I told him.

"Ah. That's a wee problem."

"Yes, it is."

"What do you want to do besides write the story?"

"I—" I shut my untrustworthy mouth. I almost blurted out, "I want to make love to you in a multitude of positions." I pushed my hair back. My clip came undone on top of my head, and my hair fell forward. I put my clip in my pocket. "The strange thing is, I like what I'm doing now. I like being here in Scotland. I like going to Gabbling Women and Gardening and Eating group, or whatever it's called. I like being on your farm. I like doing the bookkeeping."

"I like it, too." He smiled. "I look forward to coming home and having you there, eating dinner, talking, chess, walks, and reading magazine articles together. And thank you for saving me and handling the books."

"You're welcome." I wasn't done organizing. I was working about eight hours a day, and I loved it. "I have a small, but mostly in control, obsession with numbers."

"I'm glad for that. It's my Scottish luck to have you here."

"Thank you. I like going to the village. I like watching my house take shape. I like watching sunsets."

"You are liking life, then."

"Yes. That's it." I watched the white frothy trim pull in, then back out. "I am liking life."

"Do you want to quit writing?"

That was the hard one. "Maybe. I don't know."

"Let's talk about this. Maybe I can help."

Maybe I can help.

Four of the best words in the English language, all strung together, a warm hand out to hold yours so you can walk through your problem together.

I took the hand, metaphorically speaking, as the sun went down, the moon popped out, white light shining, thanks to Blackburn "The Protector" Mackintosh and his spear.

I told him that all my ideas kept disintegrating, that I had no enthusiasm.

He listened. He asked me questions.

I thought about my own answers, spinning them around in my head.

The rain sprinkled down, not much; the waves with white trim rushed in, then out; the wind puffed through, then turned around.

I smiled at him, pushed my glasses up, hopeful.

He smiled back, loose and easy, sexy.

And it hit then: I loved Toran. Loved him.

I always had. I always would.

I stared out the window in my bedroom at Toran's that night, darkness like a blue-black blanket over the farm. I held Silver Cat on my lap. She meowed. I meowed back.

I was physically humming in Toran's presence. I wanted his naked body on mine. I felt his attention on me, how he listened, how he saw me. But he had never tried to kiss me. Now and then he would hug me, but not often.

We rarely held hands.

I was confused. Thrumming and humming and confused.

There was an embarrassing but realistic chance that the man was not attracted to me, that I was his best friend from childhood and he liked me. That was what a logical person would think, after these weeks together with no rolling and thrusting going on in the bedroom.

I didn't want to think that, though.

I find people who do not live in reality, who do not think rationally, who deny in the face of overwhelming evidence what is in front of their face, to be irritating. That type of intellectual stuntedness and rigid mental clinginess makes friendship or relating to one another a troublesome barrier.

But I was doing it myself. I wanted Toran to bring those full lips down on mine. It hadn't happened. There was no indication it was going to happen.

Therefore, ergo, he was not attracted to me.

But still, with stubborn intransience, I held on to zero factual evidence of attraction and hoped it would change.

I felt myself falling into a black pit. I was alone in the pit. It was a sad pit.

I put on my flowered nightgown. Covered now, from neck to toenails. I noticed a brown stain and a black one.

Super. I was a sad, alone, lonely woman in a black pit in a stained, high-necked nightgown.

What I could not be again, though, is a woman who misreads a man. I had done that before. The ending was an emotional collision.

Silver Cat meowed again. I meowed back. We stared at the blue-black blanket outside together.

Drew and I tried to hide our relationship from our colleagues. They noticed anyhow. I was embarrassed. What was I now? The object of gossip? Was I disrespected because of this romance? I wanted to be seen as a serious student and researcher of biology and gene therapy. Women were not common in labs, and I didn't want to undermine myself or have to deal with any sexist language or condemning behavior.

They smiled. They made comments. Drew smiled back, and laughed. He seemed relaxed about the whole thing. I was not relaxed. When people said things to me about Drew, I cut them off and said, "We're not talking about that subject. What will you be accomplishing today?"

Drew consistently treated me with respect and gentleness. I could tell him anything. He knew how to cheer me up and I knew how to cheer him up. He brought me little gifts, croissants and coffee, chocolates, a collection of rocks and crystals, a book on Marie Curie. He made me a silver necklace with a turquoise stone in it. Another time, he sewed me a scarf. His mother had taught him how to sew.

We did not have sex for a whole year while we were dating. We kissed and held hands. I wanted more, but he thought we should wait and be sure, so we did, and I used Dan Number One, my vibrator, as Drew was an attractive man. Then Dan Number One died and I bought Dan Number Two.

We not only had similar interests in physics, biology, cells, gene therapy, and research, we both liked going to lectures on all things science. We liked *Star Trek*. We liked routine and structure. We liked reading, hiking while discussing nature, ecology, and weather systems. We liked crime shows and, surprisingly, Tina Turner, romance movies, and tiramisu.

He would shop for clothes for me, as I hate shopping, and even brush out my hair at night.

He told me he loved me and asked me to marry him when we were atop the Space Needle in Seattle. I said yes. I loved him. I liked him. I tried not to think about Toran. That had been many years ago. Toran was married, and there was a continent and an ocean between us.

Drew wanted to wait until our wedding night to make love. "It will be special then."

I said, "I think my vagina is going to protest."

He laughed and said, "I will make it up to your vagina." Worry crossed his eyes, a lightning flash, but I didn't think much of it.

"How about we take a few test drives in my bed?"

"A test drive? I don't need to test drive you, Charlotte. I love you."

That I did not see the truth was almost willful ignorance and naiveté on my part.

Our wedding was in the university chapel and the guest list was about fifty people. My mother insisted on paying for it. She had it catered. We had steak and lobster, salads, and breads. She brought in a band and a cake in the shape of a spaceship. Everyone loved it.

I missed my father walking me down the aisle. My mother did the honors.

Drew and I happily danced. We liked to dance. Not only had we taken ballroom dancing but we'd learned the foxtrot and we could even whip our hips around to some salsa dancing. There was a lot of wine and hard liquor, so everyone had an impossibly good time. People in our department talked about it endlessly.

We had our honeymoon in Maui. One would think we'd be sneaking off to make love in the ocean and bays. No.

In seven days we had sex twice, both quick.

I should have seen the warning signs before the wedding.

Blind.

I should have understood the warning signs on our honeymoon.

Confused.

I should have taken action on the warning signs when we returned to Seattle.

Socially inept me, with no clue to life's realities or men in general.

Rippingly, roaringly painful.

It will be a horse and a bolt.

"What, Grandma?

She hugged me close. "It will be a horse. The sunset will be bright orange, on fire." She ran a hand over her face, suddenly drooping with sadness. "It will be the time of the bees."

"What are you talking about?"

I hugged her and she blinked her eyes. They filled with tears. She understood her own prediction this time.

"Charlotte, you must always be strong. There is no other way to get through this life. Promise me, granddaughter, to keep your head and your shoulders back, like a true Scotswoman, like a warrior, like your ancestors did."

"I promise."

* * *

I drove into the village for chocolate. It's telling that I made a special trip for it, but chocolate is a gift that must be received often. I drove past the long blocks where the Zimmerman Factory had been before the fire. It was an ugly place in the midst of a charming place. I wondered why they hadn't cleaned it up. I figured it was because of money.

Estelle's Chocolate Room is on a corner. The sign is pink, as are the shutters and door. Inside, it's pink and white. There are no better chocolates in the world.

Pherson and Toran used to buy Bridget and me chocolates here. None of us had much money, so a couple of pieces brought on some chocolate excitement.

When we were fourteen, Carney Ramsay caught Pherson and Bridget kissing. She had a box of Estelle's Chocolates in her hand that Pherson had given her.

Carney was enraged. He had a creepy, obsessive personality when it came to Bridget. I don't think he ever sexually abused her, but he lectured her endlessly about the importance of virginity and purity and if she ever gave it away before she was married she was a slut and a whore and God would punish her.

He forbid her to see Pherson again. He didn't allow her to leave her house for a month. When she finally did come out, when my mother went over and talked to Carney, and told him that he was being repressive and overly punitive and she had been praying for him (she hadn't), he finally let Bridget come over to our house again.

Carney warned her never to be with Pherson again. *Or else.*

From then on out, he suspected Bridget of meeting up with Pherson and other boys. "You're like my mother. She was a lying whore, too!" he raged at her, and drilled her endlessly, accusing her of sneaking around, having sex.

Carney's mother had cheated on his father, Rodric Ramsay, then left the village with the lover. Everyone knew. It was the gossip of the day. Carney was sixteen, his ego and bullying arrogance apparent even then, according to my father. Rodric had been overly strict, punitive, and a Catholic fanatic, too. No wonder the poor woman cheated and left. It was her last gasp, and in her last gasp she fell in love.

Carney and his father never forgot or forgave his mother, though she repeatedly tried to see her son. Carney's father called the mother a slut and a whore, his own rigid Catholicism a straitjacket. My grandma had definitely married the better man when she chose my granddad, Brodie.

In turn, to prevent any cheating in his marriage, Carney browbeat his own wife, Bonnie, until she was a squeaky, smashed human mouse.

Control was the answer in Carney's judgment. Women must obey and submit or their libidos would take over their feeble, weak minds and they would take off with other men.

He began smashing Bridget down, too, continuing to harp on her virginity, her innocence and purity, that sex was a sin. "Virginity is what a woman has to offer a man. Without it, she's dirty. Spoiled. Used. Do you want that, Bridget?"

It was about then that he met Father Angus Cruickshank.

Angus, too, believed in control.

And he wanted Bridget in his control, too.

For carnal, pedophiliac reasons.

"It must be hard, seeing your mum's garden like this," Toran said as we walked amidst the overgrown mess a few days later.

"Yes, it is. Not a garden anymore, though, is it?"

Three of the arcs my father built for my mother were sagging or breaking. The pergola in the middle of the backyard, over a cement slab my father poured for an outdoor table area, was missing wood slats and tilted. Everything was overgrown, the weeds and shrubs out of control. I was happy to see some of the plants, vines, and trees my parents had planted had survived, but they all needed serious pruning. Much of what she had planted was dead, though.

The birdhouses my mother loved, painted in reds and blues and greens, were now gray, the wood splintering. I found several, broken and cracked on the ground. One was long and green with four holes for birds; another was circular, Japanese style; a third was a tiny cottage; a fourth was shaped like a cat.

My mother had packed up a few of them, the ones my father had given her, and kept them all these years. She had put them on the mantel of our home, and we saw them every day, but there were many she left.

"It's not a garden now, luv," Toran said, "but we could make it one."

"We?" I turned to him and pushed my glasses up my nose. The tape had come loose on the left side and was itching my temple.

"Yes, we. You and I and a few men who work for me. I have a small tractor and rototiller, a roller, and other manly man tools." He winked at me. "We can do this. We can get it ready for you to work your gardening magic."

"Toran, you're busy. You have your farm. The blueberries are ripe. . . ."

"Not busy at all."

"It's a project."

"I like projects."

"I'll do it. Give me the names of the men and I'll hire them."

"I'll send them over. I'll pay them. I'll come, too. This weekend."

"No, I can't take advantage of your time like that—"

"Charlotte." He cupped my face, and I sucked in a breath. "Once again, luv, you are not taking advantage. I want to do this. Your mother's garden gave me a sense of peace, of safety."

"It did?"

"Yes. When I was in your home, your father and mum around, or out in the garden, I knew my father wasn't going to be there preaching, yelling, going off on one hellfire and damnation lecture or another, my mother cowering. He was afraid of your father, and your mother. Next to them, he knew he fell short.

"Your home was safe, happy. I liked helping your mum in the garden. I listened to her, and Bridget did, too. That's why, when

Bridget is home, our garden blooms. It changes under her hands. It's beautiful. She remembers your mother, she remembers us, all together. We can't let it go." He put his hands on his hips, surveying the garden damage. "I see the love of your mother's garden as a link between your family members, even between Bridget and me, don't you?"

"I do." I nodded. How could a man be so tough and hard on the outside and be so intuitive and sensitive on the inside? "A link between my mother, my father, his parents and grandparents who lived here before us who also liked to garden. We have trees planted by my great-grandparents here."

"Let me help you, Charlotte. I want to make you happy, as we were before you moved."

"I am happy here." I paused. I fiddled with my button, high on my blouse. I was happy. Happy in Scotland, happy with Toran.

There was a problem, though. I decided to speak freely. "If I start to love being here, then what do I do? I need to go home and write. I have a house on an island. I have four cats. They'll need new sweaters soon." I kept fiddling with the button. Maybe I would permanently unbutton the button, and not only when I was playing semidrunken poker at a bar. "That sounded breathtakingly bizarre. It's not like my cats are pining to make a fashion statement. They probably don't even like the damn sweaters."

"If you love it here, I think it's the Scot in you recognizing that you're home. You can write here, right? We have pens and paper. I'll buy you new journals. We're on an island. We have an ocean, too. You can bring the cats over. They'll need their sweaters more in Scotland than they do in America. Chilly cold here in the winter."

"Move here, permanently?"

Those blue eyes were so bright. He smiled. "Someone has to take care of your mother's garden, don't they?"

I patted my hair down, made sure the clip on top of my head was on straight.

"Someone has to take care of your mother's garden."

"It is a wreck. The vines are out of control, I'm surprised they haven't taken over the eastern half of Scotland yet." I teared up. "I can see them both here, hear my father's legends and stories, singing Scottish drinking songs with him, playing 'Scotland the Brave' on his bagpipes, my mother trimming her roses, humming Beatles songs and teaching me how to be a feminist. . . ."

"Me too, honey."

He called me *honey*. I felt myself become warm . . . flushed.

I pulled on the top button of my shirt one more time. I think I could undo it.

Toran gave me a hug. In my mother's overgrown garden, with my father's bagpipes playing in my head, we hugged.

Three days later a pile of journals ended up on my desk in my bedroom. The covers told me all I needed to know.

Monet's painting of his garden with the arched bridge in it. A man playing bagpipes. Irises in a vase. Swans, had to be from the swans I made out of the cloth napkins. A sailboat on an ocean. A desk with a quill and feather in the corner. Cats.

What the journals told me? Toran knew me. He got me. He was trying to help.

I almost disgraced myself by giggling.

9

When my mother was backpacking through Europe with her friends Jody and Paula, she met my father, unsurprisingly, at Molly Cockles Scottish Dancing Pub. She told me he was "huge, with a heavy Scottish accent, red hair and beard, and so loveable I lost my head."

She didn't even return to America. Nine months after they were married in our garden, I was born.

My father told me that my mother was "his angel. The winds of Scotland brought her to me." Then he cleared his throat. "On a serious note, your mum took to farming like a unicorn to magic. I think she may know more than me. Plus, she understands the business of selling our crops. She knows how to work with the stores, the middlemen. She is one tough woman, and I am telling you, Charlotte"—he leaned in close and tapped his head—"she's got brains, and thank the ever-loving God you've got hers."

My mother talked to me as an adult starting when I was about five. I remember because the day after my fifth birthday she said to me, "You are old enough to be a feminist. So let's talk about what it means to be one. A feminist is . . ." and she told me what it was.

I remember she had me sign a piece of paper that said, "I am a feminist. When you are a feminist it means that you believe in equal rights and opportunities for women. When those rights and opportunities aren't granted, it is your obligation to fight for them, for you and for your fellow women." I signed it in purple crayon. She signed in pink. My father signed in green.

She would discuss with me social issues on both sides of the Atlantic, particularly women's issues. It was the sixties, and the war was raging in Vietnam. Her brother had been shipped over to fight, and her father was there, I later learned, working for the CIA.

My mother raged against that war, especially when her brother came home in a body bag. I had loved Uncle Tony.

She talked about women's jobs, how women were being discriminated against in education and in the workplace, not getting the promotions and salaries they deserved. She was a raving liberal who could cook, as my father said, "Heaven in a dish. She is heaven, your mother."

I remembered her baking an apple pie for my dad one day, he loved her apple pies, while discussing how women must be independent in their thinking, their careers, and their marriages.

My father had gone to university before returning home to work the land. My mother had a degree in English.

They were both temperamental, intellectual, and passionate. I remember a number of fire-breathing fights. My poor father would cry when they got in a fight. He tried to hide it, but I saw his eyes and he had to leave the house and walk away, or play his bagpipes in a particularly mournful and pathetic way until my mother went outside and gave him a hug.

They would go upstairs and sort things out. Things were cooking in the bedroom. I know this now because I used to hear the bed springs squeaking, slow at first, then faster and harder.

Often.

I told my mother one time—I must have been about six, because I remember I was holding my favorite stuffed alligator, Señor Spook—that her bed sounded like it was going to break.

She said, "Why do you say that, darling?" I made the sounds of the springs creaking, faster and faster. "Are you and Daddy bouncing on the bed? You told me I shouldn't do that because it will break the springs."

They had a new bed in that bedroom the next day.

My mother still loves my father. She has never stopped loving him and has never seriously dated anyone else, like McKenzie Rae has never stopped loving her first love, as I have never stopped loving Toran. Scottish men can get deep into your soul and they don't leave. You live with them, right close to your heart.

My father told Bridget and me a Scottish legend once. He made it up on the spot as he was staring at my mother, who was making his favorite blueberry muffins at the time. He pulled us onto his lap, his red beard tickling my face.

It was about a poor Scottish lad who was in love with the princess in the castle. He played the bagpipes outside her window. The princess had created a garden, filled with a wandering purple clematis over a white picket fence, a statue of a little girl holding an umbrella, a three-foot-tall purple star, a rose garden, and silver watering cans nailed to a post.

She painted birdhouses—one in a Japanese style, another shaped like a cottage, then a cat.

It was colorful and serene, an oasis, and when the princess smiled across the roses at him, his heart wept with love. When the princess's father had a competition for her hand, the Scottish lad worked night and day perfecting all of his skills—marksmanship, bow and arrow, running, spear tossing.

He won, despite a conniving king from a distant land, a greedy merchant, and a "dandy" trying to stop him every way they could. The princess was stubborn and willful, but she agreed to marry him as long as she could still be independent and could attend university. (My father was a feminist and believed in education.) The lad readily agreed, and his life was a "golden song" from then on out.

It was his love story to my mother. She turned and hugged him, bent and gave him a smooching kiss right in front of us. His eyes filled with tears. I giggled and patted his shoulders. "It's okay to cry, Daddy."

Bridget handed him a napkin.

But that's how my mother felt about my father.

That's how he felt about her.

After we left, my mother never gardened again.

Toran came over with three men on Saturday, a pile of tools, wheel barrels, and machines that made loud grinding noises, and we went to work in my mother's garden. Another bin arrived for all the yard debris. I liked the men, all employees of his farm. It was amazing what five people and a bunch of machines that growled could finish in one day.

At the end, Toran and I, covered in dirt and dust, stood back.

"We have a start, luv," he said.

The weeds had been rototilled and dumped. The bushes had been brought under control and looked like bushes instead of ten-foot-tall, green monsters. The vines had been cut back. The earth had been churned, ready for new plantings; the bricks from the pathways were piled up, to be relaid later. The tipping trellises and arcs had been taken down so we could reuse the wood in new trellises and arcs. The arc under The Purple Lush was repaired and cemented. We had saved the purple star, the post with the silver watering cans, and other birdhouses we'd found.

"We'll stick to the spirit of your mother's design when we replant, if you'd like, Charlotte."

"I would love that." It was touching that Toran would think of that. "I would love to put my mother's garden back together, as she had it. It was art."

"Yes, it was. Peaceful. Safe. Flowers everywhere."

I turned to him, my hair in a ponytail, my glasses slipping off my nose because I was sweating. "Thank you, Toran. I can't believe you did all this for me."

"Anytime, luv. Anytime. I will want payment, though."

I grinned. Oh boy! Payment! I envisioned a strip tease if I had two shots of whiskey. Maybe a dance? I could pull off my whale sweater slowly, drop my corduroy skirt an inch at a time, kick off my sturdy brown shoes. . . .

"A Scottish Whisky Gateau cake?"

I tried to hide my disappointment. At least he had the whiskey part right. "I'll make it."

"Thank you." So heartfelt. "You made that for me when we were fifteen, do you remember?"

"I do." We were dating by then. He had kissed me over the mixer.

After Toran left for a shower, I stood in my mother's garden, put my arms out, and spun, one time, not twice, I don't like dizziness. Toran had always been my hero. Today he was my garden hero. He'd helped me because he knew it meant something to me.

That was so romantic—at least to me, not to him probably—that I fought not to giggle.

I would not giggle. I do not giggle. I am Charlotte Mackintosh, feminist, lover of biology and physics and all things science, and I do not giggle. It's ridiculous and immature.

I coughed.

I would not giggle.

So I laughed, then I teared up, then I smiled and felt . . . peace.

Yes, peace, in my mother's garden.

I made a Scottish Whisky Gateau cake with sponge fingers for Toran. The look on his face was all worth it.

"Like it?" I asked him.

"It's the best thing I've eaten since you made it for me twenty years ago."

I am a feminist. I am in the kitchen because that's where I want to be. I love to cook. And I love seeing Toran loving what I make.

Now, that was a treat.

I went back to my cottage the next day, giddy. A clean garden palette. I remembered where my mother had everything, her paths, the picnic table, the rose garden, the herb garden, cutting beds, wild flower borders, the fountain with the girl with the umbrella, the post with the silver watering cans, the birdhouses, the garden rooms. I started planning.

At one point it rained, briefly, then the sun came out, and a rainbow stretched across the sky. I stopped. I had to. I remembered.

My father had told Bridget and me a story about one of our ancestors. Her name was Irene "The Loving" Mackintosh. She had six daughters and sons, all fiery, sword-throwing Scottish warriors. As she grew old, her bones brittle, she wanted to leave something behind so her children would always remember she loved them.

She had six magic paintbrushes and she decided to paint art in the sky. She drew a purple line, then blue, green, yellow, orange, and red. With her bare hands she took the line and made a half circle, then threw it into the air. The rainbow grew and grew, until it covered the land from mountain to mountain.

When Irene "The Loving" Mackintosh was gone, all her children had to do was look up, during a rainy, sunny day, and they would see her love for them. "That's where rainbows come from," my father said. "From love."

When I see rainbows, I think of my father. I still feel his love.

My mother called. I told her about her garden, how I was following her design. I knew it made her cry. The connection was poor. We decided to keep writing letters back and forth. I heard her last comment, though. "I love you, Charlotte. Forever and away, I love you."

April 24, 1972

Dear Charlotte,

He is after me. All the time.

I can't tell anyone. He says I can't. He says he'll kill Toran if I tell anyone.

Who would believe me anyhow?

I hurt.

I wish you still lived here.

What picture should I draw today?

Pain. I could draw pain. Or fear. What does pain and fear look like on paper? How do you draw it in miniature when it's huge and feels like it's suffocating you? How do you draw shame? How do you draw that I am dirty now and used?

He is after me.

Love,

Bridget

May 16, 1972

Dear Charlotte,

Father Cruickshank is coming to dinner tonight. My father has already told me to be good for him.

Be good.

For the rapist.

Love,

Bridget

May 17, 1972

Dear Charlotte,

Father Cruickshank told my father when I was in my room that he was concerned because I sometimes sneak out of the school to see boys in the village.

I don't do that.

My father hit me in the face, twice. My mother did nothing. I had to spend all Saturday in my room, on my knees. My father called me a whore. I can't leave home except to go to school. Slut. Dirty. No man will want you now. Used.

Love,

Bridget

June 4, 1972

Dear Charlotte,
Help me. Help me. Can you help me?
I think I want to die.
Bridget

I closed my eyes. Nausea, dizzying and sickening, hit like a spinning steamroller. I swayed, held on to my chair, put my hand to my mouth, and tried to breathe.

I wanted to kill Angus Cruickshank. *Kill him.*

Briefly, before I curled up in a ball, I wondered who else wanted to kill him.

Toran walked in.

Yes. Toran would. He would have every reason to kill Cruickshank.

I handed him the letters I'd read. He'd seen them already, but the rage on that man's face . . . like thunder meeting lightning in the sky. He slammed out and was gone for two hours. When he came back, he hugged me.

That kind of rage can kill you if you're not careful, take life away from you until you're dead inside.

Had Toran been dead enough inside that he risked jail to kill Angus Cruickshank when he finally found out through Bridget what had happened?

Maybe. I wouldn't have blamed him at all.

Bridget, where are you? Please come home.

Every morning I went to my office in the yellow building. I had met the rest of Toran's staff, all genial, interesting people. They seemed to adore Toran, not hard to do. I was pleased to see he had people, old and young, working for him. His secretary was seventy-two, named Norma. Toran had bought her land, she told me. "Grateful to him I am, as I did not need it after me Harvey died, and Toran says I can stay until I croak off. He didn't say 'croak off,' I did. Free house and a job working for Toran. I go on two cruises a year. Never did that with me Harvey. Harvey didn't like to travel. Norma does!" She leaned in closer. "I had a shipboard romance last time, too. Tickled my fancy. Lucky me."

Within a short period, Norma was giving me calls to take from people who needed to talk money. I took them and at first had to ask Toran questions, but then I started answering the questions myself based on what Toran had said. I also started taking calls about equipment, shipping, clients' concerns, orders, and general business.

I couldn't stand to sit around and think about my writer's block anymore. Working for Toran kept me busy and kept me working with numbers, awesome numbers. Geek me.

I had only initial calculations, but Toran was running a profitable farm.

Extraordinarily profitable. Blueberries, apples, and potatoes were needed products.

I was impressed, and I told him so.

"Ah, Char . . . thank you." He tried to hide it, but I think he was proud.

He should be.

The next morning I took a quick shower. I washed my hair and brushed it out. I don't like washing my hair. It takes so long—what an irritant. I put the clip on top of my head to keep my hair out of my eyes, then wrapped the rest of it in a bun. I put on my glasses; the left side wobbled. I pulled on my light brown skirt with the ruffle and my comfortable brown sturdy shoes. I buttoned up my gray blouse to the neck, then added a knitted gray vest with white teacups. I stared at myself in the mirror.

It was the same self that had stared back at me my whole life.

But this time . . . I tilted my head to the left.

I tilted it to the right. My glasses almost fell off.

I peered down at my shoes. Five years old. Still going strong for daily shoes. Or were they? I turned my left foot to the side. There was a small hole. I turned my right foot to the side. Two small holes. The heels were worn. I would have them reheeled. It would be the third time.

They were comfy. Fit to my wide feet. My flipper feet, as my mother called them. "*You should have become a swimmer. You would have won all the metals with feet like that.*"

I studied my gray blouse. It had been a favorite for three years. Bought this one at Goodwill, too. Had a designer label. I paid four dollars.

I studied my skirt. The hem was out in the back. Not more than a couple of inches. Frayed on the edges. Who would notice?

Comfy, too.

But maybe . . . frumpy?

I peered at my face again, my glasses askew to the left. The tape was rough.

I should do something about my hair. It was way too long.

I remembered what my mother had said to me once: "*Please. Get a haircut. It is not necessary to look as if you are wearing a long brown mop on your head in order to be a feminist. Being a feminist is all about women power, it's a sisterhood, that's what it is, and it can be done with a fashionable haircut. Do you have that? No.*"

I wouldn't have to do anything to my teeth. I am religious about the dentist. Twice a year. And he put something on my teeth last time to make them whiter and get rid of coffee stains. I had to pay extra for that, but I felt it well worth the cost.

I brushed my eyebrows down. Thick. Not touching in the middle. But . . . thick.

Did other women have eyebrows this thick? I would check.

I could hear my mother's voice in my head again: "*Get a supportive bra with lace. That's important. Especially for you, Charlotte, with you being on the chesty side. Get those guns pushed up and together and unbutton another button so you don't appear to be an Americanized, scientific, brainy Mary Poppins.*" Now, there was a feminist for you, magic umbrella to boot.

I stared at the mirror again.

* * *

The Stanleys, and their crew, continued to work on my house. The electrical and plumbing, all new, was done, including canned lighting throughout the house to brighten things up.

Toran bought me a white bedspread with purple irises, because he knows those are my favorite flowers, and a lamp in the shape of a black cat. He said, "I thought, to help you write again, if you had your favorite flowers around you and a cat . . ." I burst into tears at his thoughtfulness and had to blow my nose in a noisy way. It was embarrassing.

The chimney was repaired and cleaned out. The Stanleys had found a dead raccoon in it.

Toran and I sat out on his deck and watched the sun go down over the hills while we drank wine and ate cheese and crackers. We played Scrabble. "I thought playing a word game might inspire your words." I started to sniffle. "Are you going to cry again, Charlotte? It's okay if you do. But let me get the tissues. . . . One moment, luv. . . ."

The kitchen and family room walls were painted a light yellow, my parents' bedroom light blue, and the other bedrooms and the loft white. All the ceilings were painted white, too.

Toran and I made pancakes for dinner. He cut the pancakes into letters. "To make writing edible." My chin wobbled. My lower lip shook. "There, there," he said. "Here's a tissue. I'm keeping them in two places downstairs now, luv. . . ."

A new, white claw-foot tub went in upstairs in my bathroom, as did a pedestal sink. I lay down in the tub. Toran and I could fit together. It would be tight. I liked tight.

Toran treated me to an Italian lunch one day, then a Japanese dinner another day, in the village.

"I've heard that it's important to put food in your manuscripts. So people can taste it with you. . . . Didn't mean to do this again, luv, more tears . . . Here, would a napkin do?"

I had saved my mother's chandelier that had still been hanging over the kitchen table and cleaned it off. It sparkled, though I'd had to buy a number of new crystals. The Stanleys hung it with appropriate ceremony and reverence. "This is where your grandma often made her Scottish Second Sight predictions, according to my mother," Stanley I said. "Always right, she was, though it was a wee jumbled up."

Toran and I played chess until two in the morning. He won twice, I won once. I am a satisfactory chess player. I have two pen pals with whom I communicate about chess and chess moves, but he is more victorious sixty-six percent of the time.

"Chess is a brain activator, isn't it, Charlotte? Thought it might take your mind off the writing worries, luv. . . ."

He is an incredible member of the male species. Total man.

My house was days away from being done.

I would be able to move in soon.

I didn't want to move. That was the truth. I liked Toran's.

Sadness, like liquid loneliness, crept in. I was familiar with liquid loneliness. I liked it less now than before.

I fell in love with Toran when I was a teenager. It hit all of a sudden.

I had grown up with him. He was the older brother of my best friend. He and I, Bridget and Pherson, were Clan TorBridgePherLotte. Secret handshakes, chants. Battling invading alien armies and marauding giants united us.

As we grew older we didn't play our imaginary games anymore, but we were still together, running through the meadows, into the sea, laughing, talking. My father called us The Gang of Four. We hung out at my house and Pherson's, sneakily getting Pherson and Bridget together to avoid Carney's wrath.

Toran and I talked all the time. I told him everything. I told him anything. I told him about the stories I wrote in my journals. I told him how I loved butterflies. I told him that I loved science, and we talked about space, geology, the history of the earth, time travel, black holes, and biology. Endlessly. I told him I was scared of his father. I told him I felt sorry for his mother because she seemed scared.

I listened to him. His fury at his father. How he felt after Carney hit him one day, and he hit his father back so hard, his dad crashed against the wall. His father screamed at Toran to kneel on the floor and pray, then he took off his belt. Toran refused. His father came after him again, swinging the belt, and Toran knocked him out cold. His father didn't hit him again.

I listened to Toran talk about his anger at his mother for not protecting him or Bridget, for her constant, life-numbing drinking.

I often saw Toran protecting Bridget, putting her behind him, as their father raged at her for some minute infraction. Her skirt, he bellowed one time, that dent in his head shiny red, was too short. "I won't have other men thinking Carney Ramsay's daughter is a whore!"

Toran and I were best friends, laughing and goofing off one day, and then, when I was fifteen, we were more. We were at my house. My parents were on a date in the village, at dinner, and he pulled me close and kissed me.

My teenage self almost went up in flames. That one kiss turned into more kisses, and pretty soon he was on top of me and my legs were wrapped around his waist on our couch. When we heard my parents' car pull up, we broke apart, scrambled up, buttoned up, settled down, and said hello.

We smiled at my parents, and luckily my mother had had too much to drink. My father carried her into the house, said a hearty hello to the both of us, and kept singing a Scottish love song about passion and disgrace as she giggled. He followed her into bed. The springs squeaked.

And that was that. The start of Toran and me.

He kissed me good night. That was a crazy kiss, too.

We knew that Pherson and Bridget were already together, despite Carney's possessive wrath, and that night I couldn't have been happier. I remember it as one of the happiest moments of my life.

Bridget and I laughed and giggled. We drew our wedding dresses, Bridget's gown a work of wedding dress art. I had her draw mine, too, as her drawings were better. We thought we'd all be together forever and our kids would be best friends, Clan TorBridgePherLotte Number Two.

Not too long after that, Toran and I were saying good-bye, our tears running into our kiss, and I thought I'd never see him again.

I drove by my cottage the next evening. The men Toran had hired had laid sod, front and back, and the grass added color, structure, and a place to read books.

On one hand, it hurt me to be here, my father and grandparents gone, my mother on another continent, my life on an isolated island in the Pacific.

Yet it lifted me, too. I had happy memories of this house, Scotland, Bridget, Toran, and Pherson.

I could see the undulating green hills, Toran's sprawling farm, tractors and red barns in the distance, and the far meadow, filled with narcissi. The blue-gray sea waited beyond that.

I could feel that Highland wind, a dash of salt, a sip of mint tea.

But I belonged in America.

Didn't I?

Or did I belong in Scotland?

I belong to Clan Mackintosh. I grew up listening to Scottish legends and the stories my father told of our brave, warrior ancestors, both men and women. I grew up listening to Scottish music, bagpipes, fiddles, and harps and dancing the traditional Highland dances, wearing kilts. I grew up going to the Scottish games watching men throw rocks and logs, pipe competitions, and hundreds of bagpipers playing at once in the parade of massed bands. I grew up listening to my father playing "Scotland the Brave."

I am half Scottish. Half Irish and Italian. Yet full-blooded American, too.

Clan Mackintosh.

I heard bagpipes in the distance, a soulful echoing.

The notes of the bagpipes blended with my memories of my father. I felt him hug me, his red beard tickling my face. . . . I heard him telling me an enchanting story about tiny faeries who lived in the ruins of the cathedral. . . . I heard his booming laugh. . . . He picked me up and twirled me around in our garden. . . . He told me to listen to his mother, the seer, for she could tell the future. . . . I heard him say, "I love you, lass. I'll always love you. . . ."

The bagpipes faded, a blast, then a note at a time, drifting off on puffs of wind, to be caught in the branches of the oak trees, the wings of the butterflies, the stems of the bluebells and daffodils. I took a deep breath.

I would stay for a spell in this mysterious land with the whispering wind and the endless ocean, the legends of my ancestors and the spirits of my family.

I would stay until I could seduce Toran into some bed gymnastics. If he didn't want me, wanted only friendship, and started dating a blond bomb, I'd leave. Seeing him with another woman would be worse than having bagpipes thrown in my face a hundred times, worse than never seeing him.

I would try not to run over the blond bomb with the truck Toran had lent me.

That would take some effort and restraint.

Damn. I was a woman I didn't want to be. Waiting to see how a man would react, what *he* wanted. I hated giving up control of my own mind and emotions to someone else, but it's not like I can force him to want me.

On the positive side, it was a charming cottage and my mother's garden did need work.

"Your house is almost done," Toran said. We were walking along the ocean after Toran had taken me to a French restaurant in town for dinner. We'd had ratatouille, hot bread, wine, and chocolate éclairs. We left our shoes in the sand, the sun scooting down to the left, ocean on our right.

"It is." I unbuttoned one button on my blue blouse with pink stripes because I was heating up beside Toran. In the process of unbuttoning, I somehow knocked my glasses off. Toran reached down and handed them to me. He took my breath away. Biologically speaking it's not possible, but it sure felt true.

"I wish it wasn't, Char."

"Why?" My chest tightened. It hurt at the thought of moving out.

He took a second to answer, then stopped and turned toward me. "Because I like having you around."

"I like living with you, too"—so much, you macho stud—"but I don't want to overstay my welcome."

"You could never do that."

"You've let me stay for weeks." Can I stay for decades?

"I've wanted you to stay. I was offended when you asked me not once, lass, but twice about moving to a bed-and-breakfast."

"I'm sorry. I didn't want to . . . crowd you." I kicked the water with my feet. The oceans had been here for billions of years, frozen, melting, frozen, melting. How many tears from lovestruck people had fallen into their waves? "I'm glad I stayed with you."

"Me too. I wish you were staying longer." His voice caught. "Maybe I'll tell the Stanleys to slow down."

I laughed, but I thought, *Please, do.* Tell them to accidentally blow the roof off or cut the kitchen cabinets in half with a chain saw.

"I'll be down the road, Toran."

"Not the same."

No, it wouldn't be the same. I wanted to wake up and see him, see him before I went to sleep. "We'll visit."

"All the time."

"Is that a promise, King Toran?" My feet grew cold in the water. I wondered where the water had been, where the currents had swept it to. Had another couple, one desperately in love with the other, maybe in Russia or China or the Netherlands, walked in this same water?

"It is. I don't break my promises, Queen Charlotte."

"I know you don't."

He never did, never had. When we were younger, if Toran said we were all going to meet, we met. If he said he was going to take care of a bully at school who was bothering Bridget or me, he took care of it. If he said he was going to fix my bike or my wagon, or one time my sandal, as the sole had come off, he fixed it.

"We can still meet for dinner, Char."

"And chess."

"And to talk books."

"And your farm, and I'll be seeing you because I'm doing the bookkeeping."

"Aye." He sighed. "I thank you for that. You're a genius."

"I like numbers. They're addictive." For example, the numbers here. How many women had watched the sun set on one side of the earth and watched the ocean on the other side and wondered if they would live forever without the man they loved and lusted after?

"I'll miss your Scotch lamb chump."

"I'll make it for you."

"I'll miss talking to you, Char." He blinked rapidly.

"Me too." I choked up and turned away.

Where did the puff of wind off the waves come from that was now cooling my hot face? Had it swept by another woman whose heart was aching? Had it rattled the windows of a lonely widow? Had it swept by a war, a broken romance, a kiss?

"I'm sorry that Bridget isn't here, but your living in my home brought light to my life."

"You turned the light on for me, too." What a trite thing to say. "I mean. What is . . . I liked living with . . . you in the light. With you." I let myself drown in that face. His hard-jawed face, the lines crinkling from the corners of his eyes, the blueness. His cheekbones had a touch of red to them.

Was there more here than I thought? I am bad with men, bad with men's signals, bad with being sexy and seductive. If I tried being sexy and seductive, I would probably look like a drunk coyote in heat.

Toran hadn't even tried to kiss me. That, to me, said he was not interested in me as anything more than a friend. Friend zone, that's where I was. Wretched place.

Was I supposed to make the first move, ask him to lie down here and make love to me in the sand?

I couldn't do that. What if he was repelled, like the wrong ends of magnets?

What if he thought it was like having his sister kiss him? That would be incestuous.

What if he was so put off, he avoided me altogether? I'd have to move back to my island in Washington by four o'clock, to avoid mortal, repetitive humiliation.

Please, Toran, I thought, *kiss me. Tell me. Put one hand on my breast and one hand over my buttocks and make it clear what you want.*

I will miss you if I move back to my island, Toran. My tears will drop into the ocean and maybe one day they will reach the coast of Scotland.

I have always missed you.

We picked up our shoes on the way back and didn't say another word, the ocean beckoning us back when we started up the crooked path.

I picked up the newspaper in town after I left Estelle's Chocolate Room.

ST. AMBROSE DAILY NEWS

FIFTEENTH ANNIVERSARY OF MISSING PRIEST
Part Two

By Carston Chit, *Reporter*

Another mystery behind Father Cruickshank's disappearance from St. Cecilia's Catholic School for Girls are the rhymes that the children here in St. Ambrose sing. Who wrote them? When did they start? Are they true? Who believes them? Who doesn't and why?

Was Angus Cruickshank murdered?

Were You Ever True

Father Cruickshank, Father Cruickshank,
Were you ever true?
Father Cruickshank, Father Cruickshank,
Whatever did you do?
Father Cruickshank, Father Cruickshank,
Where'd you run and hide?
Father Cruickshank, Father Cruickshank,
Do they know you lied?

The Man in the Frock

A man came to town one day
Wearing the holy frock.
He blessed us all, and laid us down
Then took out his shrivelly cock.

A man came to town one day
Wearing the holy frock.

God saw his sins, and cursed this man
While the victims cried in shock.

A man came to town one day
Wearing the holy frock.
He hurt the girls, one by one.
Keep the secret or you'll be clocked.

Father Cruickshank, Where Are You?

Oh, Father Cruickshank
What happened to you?
You ran off so quick,
You and your dirty dick.

Oh, Father Cruickshank
Were you killed?
Who did it, we cried.
We'll give them a pie.

Oh, Father Cruickshank
My sister you attacked
Come forth, come back,
We'll nail you to a rack.

Bam, bam, bam!

I felt ill. I dropped my extra-large-size box of chocolates. I felt a rush of fury so thick, I'm surprised I didn't spontaneously combust.

If Angus had been killed, who would have done it?

I grabbed a pen and my list book out of my bag and wrote "List of People Who Could Have Killed Father Angus Cruickshank."

1. Toran.
2. Bridget. She would have been young, and hurting people isn't in her personality, but she had every reason to go after him.
3. Carney or Bonnie Ramsay, one or the other, possibly both.
4. Chief Constable Ben Harris. He would have been enraged at the thought of a man attacking girls. Perhaps he went to investigate and things got carried away?
5. Pherson. He loved Bridget.
6. Another girl Angus attacked, or her brothers, mother, uncles, or especially her father.
7. One of the nuns at St. Cecilia's who knew what was going on.

Clearly, there were many possibilities.

I hoped he suffered.

10

When my mother took Bridget and me to the village of St. Ambrose, she would let us walk down the cobblestone streets without her. We would always meet at Sandra's Scones and Treats Bakery.

Bridget and I would peer into the shops, filled with fabrics and yarn, sweets and cakes, gifts and antiques. We would explore the children's section of the bookstore, where my mother would buy us one treasured book each and check out books at the library.

We could not envision a more exciting future than living in the middle of St. Ambrose. We would live together and have a lot of cats, we decided. She would also have a pet monkey, and I would have a pet lion. She would draw all day and I would do science experiments.

"We could live in a house that was built three hundred years ago," Bridget said. "Like right up there." She pointed to a third-story window, purple pansies in the flower box. "Or right there." She pointed to a window across the street, the lace curtains fluttering.

"And all the people who had lived there before us would be ghosts."

"No," Bridget told me. "You go to heaven when you die, you don't stay here."

"Are you sure? What if they liked their flat?"

She thought about that. "They could visit."

"What if we're in the flat when they visit?" I found that intriguing. "How would we know they were there?"

"They'll make a noise. Maybe they come back to check on someone, make sure they're well. Or to get something they lost."

"We could give it back." A dead person's ghost floating in through the windows fascinated me. Would they be dressed in the clothes they wore when they were alive? Would she wear a bonnet? A corset? Would he carry a sword? Would they be knights in their silver mail? Scottish warriors? "Maybe they're not dead." This was an even more thrilling thought. "Maybe they still live in the flat, only we can't see each other. Everyone is living at the same time."

Bridget's eyes became huge. "We're all ghosts to each other, then."

"Yes!" I grabbed her hand. "We're ghosts altogether, but we don't know it."

"Can we get to the other people?"

"You mean the ghost people who are living with us in their flat?"

"Yes."

"I don't know. We should try to get into their time. We should try!"

We tried. We tried to reach my great-grandparents when Bridget spent the night at my house. We tried up in the hills at the cemetery, where Ramsays and Mackintoshes were buried. "Can you hear us? Can you hear us?" we shouted. We went to the ruins of the cathedral and ran amidst the gravestones. "Are you still here?" we called out.

It didn't work. It did, however, ignite my imagination with thoughts of time travel . . . and, later, my studies in physics took me through a wormhole, a time warp, and a storyline.

"I was at a party the other night."

"Better you than me," I told my agent, Maybelle. I sat down in a chair in Toran's kitchen. I had made Caledonian cream for him with marmalade and a smidgen of brandy. I knew he loved that treat, and I'd made it for him when I was fifteen, after our first kiss.

"You got that right. You told me once that going to all the publishing parties I do would be akin to sticking your head in an oven and turning the heat to four hundred degrees."

"That is correct. I would go to the parties you go to only if I could turn myself into a potted fern and hide in the corner."

"You wouldn't look good with spores."

"I would wear spores with confidence. A fern's spores are how they reproduce themselves. They've been around for hundreds of millions of years. Ferns can also suck out arsenic from the soil. Fascinating plant."

"Why do you have to get all science-y with me all the time?"

"Because science"—I stopped and chewed. Two chocolate creams with pecans at one time were too many in my mouth—"is an all-encompassing interest, impossible to compartmentalize when it's imbedded in our everyday life. I am also secretly trying to turn you into a science nerd like me."

"Banish the thought. I'd rather turn into a toad. No offense."

"None taken."

"So, have you written a few bodice-ripper scenes in your new book?"

"I never write bodice rippers, you know that. I write love-lust scenes with a time-traveling, independent, feminist woman who helps other people and saves their lives in a historical setting that I have researched to death. And no." I popped a vanilla truffle into my mouth. "Not a word. I've been busy."

"No, you haven't been. Torture me with toothpicks. Let spiders eat my toes, you're killing me."

"How would you know? Do you have intercontinental spy glasses?"

"I know these things. You are not writing. Your publishing house lights up my phone at least once a week. Your editor is sounding more and more drunk and hysterical. Last night, at this publishing party, where you could have been a fern with spores, your editor, your marketing people, and even your copy editor came up to me and asked when you would be finished with your book. I told them I didn't know. They know there's a problem. Your editor handed me a vodka tonic, then took it back and drank it straight up."

"Your loss. You like vodka tonics."

"We drank so much, we had to spend the night in the hotel. I slept with your editor last night in a bed."

"You shared a bed?"

"Yes. They had one room left. King-sized bed. I woke up with her curled around me. Her breath was atrocious. It smelled like spoiled eggs."

"And yours smelled like peppermint with a splash of vanilla?"

"God, no. My breath was on fire. Like spoiled fire. Back to your book."

"I'll write it."

"When?"

"Pretty soon. I have to go. The current issue of *Science Monthly* is ready to be read."

"Don't you hang up on me. I slept with your editor, I deserve an answer as to when this book will be done—"

"Soon."

"Charlotte, you creepy writer. Listen, give me one chapter. One—"

"I'll send you a sex scene."

"And a synopsis?"

"No can do. Bye, Maybelle. *Science Monthly* calls."

I love that magazine.

I do not love writing currently. Blocked, blocked, blocked, that I was.

Give me someone sexy, McKenzie Rae said to me.

I looked outside. Toran was coming in. Now, that was sexy.

Drew and I did not have sex often. I was desperate for more. I was hurt at the scarcity of it, but I buried it. I thought twice a day seemed about right; he thought twice a month. Drew most desired having sex with me when I lay on my stomach.

The sex was awkward, restrained, or overly, falsely enthusiastic, as if we were both trying hard and we were on a stage as actors with an audience nearby. We were engaging in this very intimate act, but it didn't feel emotionally intimate. Drew would not hold my gaze when he was inside of me. He most often focused his attention on the bedside clock.

When you are married but your spouse doesn't want to make love to you, you enter into a special kind of hell.

I asked him why we didn't make love more often, why he wasn't interested, and he said he was stressed because of schooling and his research job, publishing and meetings.

I asked again another time, and he said he was tired.

I asked a third time; he didn't feel well.

I told myself I loved Drew. Sweet Drew, who often made dinner, organized our apartment with different colored baskets in the closet, cleaned, and bought me thoughtful gifts like warm socks, subscriptions to science journals, toys for my cats (I still miss Cleopatra and Sticks!), and gardening books with the Latin names.

When I was sick with the flu, Drew made me an I Hope You Feel Better basket with chicken soup, crackers, 7UP, chocolates, and a new romance novel, all wrapped up with a bow. He continued to buy my clothes for me and brushed my hair. We continued our dancing lessons. We listened to Tina Turner and found we loved seeing Broadway shows. He respected my opinions. He was the best husband except for the sex.

I started to fall out of love with Drew. The sex was a huge part of it, I'm sure. It's hard to stay in love with a man who will not make love to you. The hurt kills it, the anger grows, the resentment becomes a bubbling volcano, swirling and burning inside you, chipping away at the love.

The marriage started to deteriorate.

I read more of Bridget's letters.

October 18, 1972

Dear Charlotte,

I am pregnant. The nuns told me I am. I kept throwing up at school and Sister Margaret looked at my stomach and called the doctor. I thought I was throwing up because I am scared scared scared of Father Cruickshank.

Then they told Father Cruickshank and he came in to the health room and told everyone to leave so he could pray over me. I could tell that Sister Margaret and Sister Mary Teresa didn't want to, but he said, "My heart is filled with grief, let me bless this child and take her confession so she will not burn in hell. Show me your obedience to our Lord by giving us privacy for prayer," and they did.

He told me again that if I told anyone, he would kill Toran. He has a gun, he does, he showed me, he put it on my forehead one time. He pretended to pull the trigger. I wet my pants.

Father Cruickshank said no one will believe me, least of all my father, that he forced me to have sex. "You liked it, Bridget. You seduced me. You're the daughter of the devil."

I didn't like it. Hated it hated it hated it. Hate him.

He said I am going away today. He told me he was going to write a letter to my father and bring it to him as soon as I leave. I know what he'll do. He'll hand my parents the letter over the dining room table, probably with tea and biscuits, wait while they read it, then say, "Let's pray and then I'll answer your questions."

He said I can't even go home and get my books and drawing pads and pencils, but I know he's afraid I'll tell. I won't. I love Toran. Don't shoot Toran. Don't shoot.

Sister Margaret and Sister Angeline hugged me.

I love you, Charlotte.

Bridget

October 20, 1972

Dear Charlotte,

I am at the school for pregnant girls. It's called Our Lady of Peace, A Home for Unwed Mothers. We are allowed to plant and weed the gardens. When I'm there, I think of you and your mum and all the time we spent in your garden.

I cry all the time. I cry in the garden, especially.

I draw pictures of this garden, like I used to.

Small. So small. I feel small. Like my drawings.

They said I will have the baby in March. That's why I didn't have my period. It's why I felt sick and threw up in the morning. I signed a paper. I don't know what it said. They said I had to.

The nuns are kind. They say, "All will be well." No, *it won't.*

I am so glad to be away from Father Cruickshank. He's doing to other girls what he did to me. He had a lot of girls go to his house, or to the shed, he did.

I hope he dies. If I could, I would kill him myself. I would kill him. Kill him.

I would not kill the baby, though. I think I should hate the baby, but I don't. I feel the baby moving. I put my hands on my stomach. It is not the baby's fault. I imagine the baby. The tiny hands and toes, the tummy, the eyes. Will the baby have my eyes? My ears? I don't want to see my father in the baby, or Father Cruickshank, but I would love to see Toran.

Love,
Bridget

I dug deep in the box and found the letter Bridget referred to. It was addressed to Carney and Bonnie Ramsay. The letter was written by Father Angus Cruickshank. There was no stamp, no return address, so Bridget was right. He brought the letter to her parents as Bridget was being shuttled off to the unwed mothers' home.

As I read it I felt a gush of rage so strong, so insidious, I thought I would have to scream to get it out of my body.

October 18, 1972

Dear Mr. and Mrs. Ramsay, my good friends in Jesus's love,

I am sorry to inform you that your daughter, Bridget, has obviously had relations with a boy in the village. Who, I don't know. I have heard rumors of several possibilities. I know we have discussed my concerns before this.

It is a tragedy, but Bridget is pregnant. A few months along. It was easy not to see the weight gain, as she is a very slight girl, but the nuns said that she was vomiting in the morning here at school. Because of her unfortunate reputation, we decided to send for the doctor. She has had a positive pregnancy test.

After prayerful consultation with the bishop and archbishop, we decided to send Bridget to Our Lady of Peace, A Home for Unwed Mothers. We will pray for a healthy pregnancy and a healthy baby. After the baby is given up for adoption, we will welcome Bridget back here at St. Cecilia's. Her secret is safe and the other girls will never know.

We are, as you know, a place of compassion, forgiveness, and generosity. I have already spoken to Bridget and told her that God loves everyone, including teenage girls who engage in sinful sexual intercourse with young men. I spent an hour in prayer with her today and I have taken her confession. I asked her to say twenty Hail Marys and twenty Our Fathers, every day, until the birth of the baby.

She is contrite and guilt ridden about her behavior and says the devil made her do it. I, too, believe that the devil led your daughter astray. She promises me that it will not happen again, that the Devil has been purified from her body through prayers and confessions with me.

So as not to cause your family embarrassment, I think we can all agree to say to the students and others in St. Ambrose that Bridget is spending time with a cloister up in Inverness, that she is preparing to become a nun herself, and this placement is an honor. This will prevent any shame from coming upon your heads, as you are God-fearing Christian people.

Do not hold yourselves accountable for Bridget's sin. We have one girl, maybe two, each year who cannot resist their baser impulses and become pregnant by young men in the village.

May God be with you during this difficult time.

I am praying for you both.

In Christ, our love, our deliverer, our savior,

Father Angus Cruickshank

I put on my tennis shoes and ran. I ran and ran and ran. I stopped when I couldn't breathe, when my sobs choked me, when thoughts of my sweet friend being attacked by this vile, Bible-thumping rapist were so overwhelming I thought I'd die if I didn't lie down. I lay down by the fort that Clan TorBridge-PherLotte built years ago

I hated Angus Cruickshank. If he ever appeared before me, I would kill him myself.

Later that night Toran and I talked about Bridget. We talked about her once a week, usually. It hurt too much to do more than that, and there was no new news, anyhow.

Not knowing where someone you love is, especially when she has soul-deep, talon-scraping problems and is not making safe choices, makes you pace at night.

That's what love can do to you sometimes. It nearly kills you with worry. It makes you pace.

So we paced, together.

Bridget, where are you? Please come home.

Gobbling Gardens and Gab Group was held at Rowena's house that night. As she told us when we arrived, "The Arse and The Slut have the kids for the next three days. Let's see how Bubbles, The Slut, likes playing stepmom." She cackled.

Rowena's home, toward the center of St. Ambrose, around the corner from the fountain, was made of stone, possibly rocks from the cathedral, as it periodically crumbled over the centuries. It was, she told me, built in 1780. It had a light blue door and shutters. The interior looked like something that should be in a magazine. Scottish home meets modern color/design and four kids. Upstairs there were three bedrooms. The two girls shared a room, as did the boys.

Downstairs she had set up a place on her dining room table for her rock jewelry business. I loved the necklaces. I had bought four from her, the rocks wrapped in silver wire with bright beading lining both sides. They were earthy.

"I talked to The Arse, and he said he does not have enough money to give me child support again this month, so I'm going to sick that solicitor on him like a rabid dog. Four kids, he walks out, and leaves me with two hundred pounds. He and The Slut bought them all kinds of toys and books and clothes. The Slut has a beautiful home, courtesy of her last husband, and yet The Arse says he doesn't have money for child support?"

"I hope his body is infested with pinworms," Olive said, shaking the end of her knitted elephant scarf in frustration. The elephant appeared drowsy. I don't think it was intentional. "I take care of my pigs. They don't have problems like that, if anyone is wondering."

"Thank you, Olive," Rowena said, passing around tea in pottery mugs. "You are always on my side."

"I hope he has an obscure medical problem that causes his tongue to swell and fill his mouth," Kenna said. "As I am a doctor here, I won't be able to treat him due to the fact that I think he's a eunuch." She clarified, "I would treat other eunuchs, however, immediately. I have nothing against eunuchs who aren't The Arse."

I offered up that I hoped there would be a scientific anomaly and gravitational forces would ebb around him and he would levitate, then fall off the earth. This wasn't possible, but it was the intent behind it that counted, and Rowena appreciated my murderous thoughts.

"I'm the hostess, so I've picked the topic for tonight's discussion," Rowena said. "Today we're going to talk about poisonous and bad plants."

"In India we have plants that hide the poison inside. Secret poison. And kill," Gitanjali said, smiling, gentle, her hands like doves in flight. "Many plants that causes a wrinkle."

"A what?" Lorna asked, mouth twisting in disapproval. She twitched her oatmeal bottom in her seat.

"You understand." Gitanjali scratched her arm. "Plants that cause a wrinkle."

"You mean irritation?" Malvina asked.

We all froze for a second. Malvina spoke and she was not inebriated!

"Yes, you scratch like this"—Gitanjali scratched—"and it's a wrinkle."

"An itch!" Olive said, with triumph.

"Good enough," I said.

"A itchy!" Gitanjali said. "Yes."

Lorna rolled her eyes, impatient. Why couldn't people speak proper English? She could hardly understand that Indian woman!

"I keep all bad plants away from my pigs," Olive said. "Can't lose any of them. I think Dr. Judith had a headache today. She may be in menopause."

"Pigs can go into menopause?" I asked.

"Yes," Olive nodded. "And I think that Faith Sue may be gay."

"A gay pig?" Rowena asked.

"About ten percent of the animal population is gay," Kenna said. "I remember learning that in medical school. Not in medical school exactly, but when we were drinking at night at the pubs."

"I think we should talk about summer flowers," Lorna said. Malvina shrunk beside her. I would try to talk to her tonight. See if she spoke coherent English as she did when we were younger and in school together. Back then she was fun and chatty, super athletic.

"I think we should also talk about how my friend Lulu called me and said that The Arse and The Slut are at Molly Cockles tonight," Rowena said, tapping a foot, shaking her red hair out.

"I thought they had the kids," Olive said.

"They did. But they left them at home because tonight is their anniversary."

"Their anniversary?" I asked.

"Probably their anniversary of their first fuck," Rowena said. "Look at me. I said the f word. I apologize, ladies. It's the anniversary of their first shagging."

"No problem," Kenna said. "When I told one of my patients today he was going to have an operation on his appendix, he said, 'By fuck, I won't let you take it!' and I said, 'By fuck, if you don't, you could die,' and he said, 'Bollocks. Fuck it, then. Go ahead and cut it out.' "

"Can we move right along to a discussion of summer flowers?" Lorna humphed. "Every year I watch my zinnias bloom. I have them in neat beds, in rows, all in order. I even color categorize." Lorna droned on. And on . . .

Rowena paced the room. Caged tiger woman, ready for blood.

Olive said, "Let's not get arrested. The only person who can take care of my edible pets is me."

"If there's blood, I will be medically required to help," Kenna said. "I am warning you of that, Rowena."

Gitanjali said, "I think there be revenge tonight. I center myself first. Calm. Bring peace. Serene. Rowena, hold your hands out to me."

"Summer flowers are a gardener's delight," Lorna bit out. "If everyone can focus—"

I noticed, once again, that Lorna rarely looked at Gitanjali. Don't look at her, she's not there, no one *different* should be in the room. Wrong skin color, wrong origin, wrong religion.

I had grown to strongly dislike Lorna.

"That's it. I'm done." Rowena turned on her heel and grabbed her purse, her red hair a pissed-off mane behind her.

"Where you going, peaceful friend?" Gitanjali said, standing up. "I coming!"

"You know where I'm going. To take revenge on The Arse and his slut."

"Come on, everyone! Let's support a fellow gardener," Olive hollered. She grabbed her bag. It had a pig on it. "Together against weeds, together against cheating husbands."

I grabbed my bag and drank the rest of my wine. Going to the pub would certainly be more fun than staying here with Lorna. "I'm in."

I noticed that Malvina laughed and scurried on out right behind me.

"Hello, Malvina."

"Hello, Charlotte! Can I ride with you?" She snuck a glance back for her sputtering mother. "This will be so exciting!" She darted ahead and climbed into my truck.

I shut and locked the doors of the truck before Lorna could waddle in, her thick body thunking down the steps. She was yelling at Malvina, "Get out of that car this minute, Malvina!"

Malvina giggled. "Hurry, Charlotte, go!"

Molly Cockles Scottish Dancing Pub was filled with people and a rock band. The rockers wore kilts and black T-shirts with cutoff sleeves. Most of them had tattoos and Mohawks.

"They are sexy, aren't they, Charlotte?" Malvina giggled and grabbed my arm. "I read about men like that in my books. I love books."

"Not bad." I preferred my own Scot. The Scottish Warrior who may only love me as a sister. How depressing.

It did not take long for things to become troublesome. On my watch, five seconds.

Rowena charged right up to The Arse, hips swaying, high heels tapping, sitting at a table with The Slut, and said, "Bald man, arse, I need my child support money."

The Arse was shocked. He said, "Rowena, what are you doing here?"

Rowena said, "I'm here to plant a sunflower on your scrotum. What else would I be doing? Give me the money."

"I don't have it."

Rowena glared at The Slut and said, "Slut, you've taken my husband and he won't pay up for his kids."

"Don't call me Slut," the woman protested, flushing red. She had white-blond hair and a lot of makeup. Her cleavage was out and about. She might as well have taken her bosom off and put it in the middle of the table next to the salt for all to admire.

I do not like to place blame when people divorce. There are many valid reasons to shut a marriage down, but what should not happen is a third party deliberately trying to take a husband or wife away. Like Breasty Bubbles here.

Rowena put her hands on the table. "I'll do what I want, Slut Bubbles, as you did what you wanted when you took my husband."

"The marriage was over," The Arse said.

"I didn't know that," Rowena said. "All I know is that you're a combination of a narcissist and an insecure little boy. You're selfish and unthinking. Your brain is flat, your personality drivel and drabble, your character nonexistent."

"If you don't like him, why are you mad we're together?" The Slut protested. "Why so jealous?"

"You can have him, Slut Bubbles," Rowena said. "But don't think you can make my life miserable while yours is so perfect.

Don't think you can cause my kids pain that they will never recover from and walk away. Don't think you can break up a family and then trot off on bonking vacations and tell each other what a miserable and pathetic person I am who you feel sorry for in the midst of your bonking joy. Don't think you can cause devastation, then walk away and be free of all responsibility to start a new bonking life."

"This man is having a midlife crisis. He wants to be young again," I said, trying to be helpful. "In two years he'll be pasty, potbellied, and more hairless on top than he already is. Rowena, once you get over your anger, and you will, you will realize that The Arse leaving is a gift. You don't want to have to take care of this weak man as he grows old, his aches and pains, his complaints because he never became who he wanted to become, his lack of appreciation for you, his poor performance in bed."

"I don't perform poorly in bed!" he protested.

I studied The Slut for the truth. Her head was down.

"Yes, you do!" Rowena roared. "That was one more thing I had to put up with. Limp penis."

She tipped the table and The Arse's and The Slut's food—the lobster, the garlic bread, the salads, the wine that The Arse said he could never afford for her—went sliding right . . . into . . . their . . . laps.

I hate being laughed at. I was laughed at in school in Seattle for having a Scottish accent and for being impossibly socially awkward. Laughing at someone is mean.

Then I thought of how Rowena had told me how she was barely making it, her payment to the bank for her house was overdue, she had twenty-one pounds in her purse, hadn't paid the electricity bill or gas bill in two months, and her husband wouldn't send the money he owed her.

Couldn't help myself. I laughed.

Olive said, "I believe that was deserved, due to past behavior."

Malvina gushed, "I never knew that Garden Ladies Gabble Gobbling Group was going to make me an accomplice to mini-assaults."

Kenna said, "Cheating on your wife, if you study the research, has very poor health results, balding ex-husband. You're at a higher risk of heart attack and high blood pressure."

Gitanjali said, palms upward, "Apologies can heal wounds. You should reach out with your shadow, no not shadow, that not right word, reach out with your sorrow—"

"You . . . You . . ." The Arse started, all huffed and puffed up. I noticed he had a bump of a gut.

"How did you handle that bump gut when you were married, Rowena?" I asked. "It can't have been sexy, that thing rubbing up and down on you."

The Arse's mouth dropped open as he gaped at me, then he put a hand to his gut.

"It wasn't," Rowena roared again. "It was like being rolled by a rolling pin." She then tilted her head back and mimicked the sounds her husband made during sex—gasping, groaning, moaning.

The Slut said, "Why, I never! You bitch!"

Do not call the wife of your boyfriend a bitch.

It would be fair to say that Rowena won the fight when The Slut flew at her with all that cleavage out and about. Rowena, who is strong and was pissed, knocked The Slut across the table next to them, as the first table was already tipped, and landed on her. That table collapsed and Rowena laid flat on The Slut.

The Slut struggled and swore. Rowena managed to grab a lobster off the floor and held it on The Slut's face.

Gitanjali said, "Take but a moment for spirit centering—"

Olive said, "I would have eaten that lobster."

Malvina said, "Go get her, Rowena!"

There was screaming and swearing. I dare say the women were the center of attention. The Arse tried to separate them, but Rowena sat on The Slut's stomach and clocked The Arse in the face. He fell back.

After a delightful minute, allowed for revenge purposes only, I grabbed Rowena, along with Olive, and The Arse grabbed The Slut, who came up kicking, blouse undone, the bosoms out. They were fake.

Gitanjali said, "A peace to all who here. Let us be the loving—"

"Not much blood!" Kenna said triumphantly. "I don't have to treat anyone."

"I have to go to bars more often," Malvina gushed. "I think I've been missing out, indeed."

The Arse shoved and pushed the screeching, spitting Slut out, vowing that Rowena would "regret this, bitch."

Rowena pushed her red hair back, straightened her shirt, then said to the owner, her cousin, "I apologize, Kevin. Lost my head, that I did."

"No problem, luv. I understand."

"Here. I'll get the table and chairs back up."

We helped clean things up and tossed the food in the trash so the waitress didn't have to do it. Rowena grabbed a mop, and when all was well again, the Gobbling Fighting Garden ladies sat down.

We had a few drinks, even Lorna, who had come stomping in a few minutes later, face flushed. Lorna and Malvina danced only after Lorna had had too much to drink, which Malvina encouraged.

When Lorna slurred out, "London. Spaghetti. Curtains and Candy. I spy a girl with a married dandy," I knew the fun would begin for them.

As my cottage was almost done, I would need to buy a few pieces of furniture to hold me over until I could make Toran fall in love and lust with me or until the blond bomb showed up and ruined everything and I had to run her over.

I worked in the morning, then put on my jeans with the rope belt, a blue T-shirt with science beakers on it, and my white blouse over that. No one would notice the slight blueberry stain on the collar.

My first stop was an antique shop.

Antiques have stories. As a storyteller, I relate to them. Who owned them? What were the owners' lives like? Did they meet their soul mate? What did the owners endure that life threw at them, like a sword to the gut? Who did they love? Who did they hate? What was their greatest accomplishment and most glaring failure? What quirks and idiosyncrasies did they have?

I bought a sleigh bed, the curves elegant slopes. I also bought a dresser for my bedroom. The dresser had a mirror, but it also had handles in the shapes of horse stirrups. Humor in an antique! I bought a wardrobe with long, carved doors. It reminded me of the wardrobe in Narnia, the books that Clan TorBridge-PherLotte read together.

I bought three side tables for the family room. Where would I put my tea and books if I didn't have tables?

I bought an antique sideboard for the entry with legs that were carved in a swirly design, and I bought a tall, wide oak bookshelf that I would use in the kitchen for my cookbooks, candles, and extra plates and glasses.

After those purchases, I headed to a more modern furniture store. I bought a long, blue plush couch in an L shape. I bought two chairs in red, the type that seats two people each, both with ottomans.

The store owners said they'd bring the furniture to me. Next stop, the light shop. I needed lights. I like lights. I bought eight lamps from Light Us Up.

Two had crystal bases and white shades, which I'd use for my bedroom; two had bases with a Scotsman and a Scotswoman in traditional Highland dress, which I'd use for my library; two were tall and normal, with white shades; and two were small with red shades and a bagpipe base that I would use in the kitchen.

I envisioned myself reading and writing in one of the red chairs, a blanket over my lap, glasses on, tea in hand, Silver Cat plus my other four cats wandering around, wearing my bunny slippers that Bridget gave me.

I thought of that image.

I groaned.

Frumpy Boring Cat Woman, that's who I was.

That's who I am.

Meow. Hiss.

Boo.

I decided to picture myself in a red negligee sitting on the red chair waiting for Toran to do a strip tease in front of me. His red and black kilt would go flying, his tartan sliding off his massive chest. He would toss me over his shoulder and carry me upstairs while singing a smooth, Scottish romance song about "his woman."

Much better.

Dear Charlotte,

As you know, I was called to Molly Cockles last night because of the ruckus.

After a short chat, Rowena's husband, Gareth, and his girlfriend, Chrissy, who also goes by the name Bubbles, as you know, but who Rowena calls The Slut, have decided they will not be pressing any charges against Rowena.

I did inform Gareth that Rowena told me he is behind on his child support. I told him he needed to pay up immediately, and that I personally would be notifying the office for child subsidies that he was in arrears. Gareth wrote a check when I was there. I asked if that brought him up current, and he said no, so I ripped the check up and we went through the process again. And, indeed, a third time.

I further told Chrissy (Bubbles) that though Rowena did dump the table on her, and there was a squabble, she started it by taking a woman's husband away from her, the father of her children, and I could not possibly charge Rowena, as she was provoked. I told her I had no patience for home wreckers.

I must say that I thought it was sisterly of the rest of you ladies—even Lorna Lester!—to get on the bar as backup singers for Rowena when she sang, "I'm Going to Rip His Manhood from

Him." I had never heard that song, and I was told later she made it up on her own. Impressive, though violent, poetry.

Sincerely,

Chief Constable Ben Harris

A friend of your parents. May your father's soul rest in the palm of God.

PS I am going to invite Gitanjali to dinner once again. She did seem to be pleased with the china cup and saucer with the hand-painted flowers that I bought her, so I decided to take the advice you gave me in the village the other day, about how she loves elephants, and buy her a full tea set with elephants. I drove to Edinburgh and found the perfect one. It only took seven hours of searching, but I do believe it will bring a smile.

Dear Chief Constable Harris,

I would have to agree with you that Rowena does have a special talent in making up poetic, though violent, songs. Which is why I enjoyed singing the songs she wrote for us on a napkin, including, "I Want My Ex-Husband to Lose His Function" and "That Man Has a Wobbly Dick." The lyrics were so simple, all could join in, and many did.

I am pleased by the wide variety of plants and flowers growing here in Scotland. It is an endless state of interest and entertainment to me. I have bought three books on Scottish flowers and I can hardly wait to read and study them each day, along with their Latin names.

Did my advice for your hydrangeas prove helpful?

Charlotte

PS I am sure that Gitanjali will be well pleased with the elephant tea set.

It was time for me to move into my cottage. Stanley I and Stanley II were finished, and they had done a remarkable job.

I had cleaned it all day, vacuumed and dusted, and arranged all the furniture.

I would move in tomorrow, my mattress arriving in the morning.

Toran and I hardly spoke at dinner.

We hardly spoke the next morning.

I was miserable.

He helped me move my suitcase and a couple of boxes to my house. I had trashed the suitcase I'd duct taped. I carried Silver Cat. She slept on my bed and followed me around the house and even up to my office next to Toran's.

Toran stood with his hands on his hips and took it all in, the new kitchen with the white cabinets and white tile backsplash, the refinished floors, the white wainscoting, the antiques, the blue couch, the lights. "I like it."

"I do, too." I will miss you. *I have adored every minute of living with you, Toran.*

"You designed it well. I like the paint colors, yellow and white."

"Me too. Cheerful." *I am aching. Can you see my aches?*

"Lots of light here."

"Let there be light," I muttered. *Please. Let's have dinner together. And breakfast and lunch and brunch and snacks and chocolate.*

"I like the way you kept the beams as they were in the bedrooms upstairs."

"Yes. My mom liked those beams. She liked the tree it used to be, though she felt bad for the tree." *How am I going to live here without thinking of you every minute?*

"Okay." He took a deep breath. "You're all set."

"Yes." *I wasn't set. Living with Toran was the best time of my life.*

He took a step forward and hugged me. I hugged him back.

"Thank you, Toran, totally, truly and terribly." *Shoot. Alliterations!*

He seemed slightly confused about the "terribly" part.

"Aye, luv, anytime. See you soon at the farm."

He turned and left.

I miss you already.

I thought, maybe, perhaps, could I have seen a shimmer of water in his eyes? Was I imagining that? Or was it a pathetic, desperate delusion?

I couldn't see too well, though, as my tears had turned my eyes into little lakes.

Toran had been a part of my life and thoughts since before I could truly think, analyze, synthesize, and evaluate on my own. We were together as babies, toddlers, children, teenagers. We grew up together.

I have always loved him. The love changed, as I loved him when I was a kid to a teenager, and now as a woman, but it has always been there. Loving Toran came as naturally to me as . . . as . . . gardening.

Toran was my garden. My heart's garden.

I should have been happy in my bright home. Instead I curled up on my blue couch and had a sloppy cry. Silver Cat curled up beside me.

She meowed. I meowed back.

With Toran's permission, I had brought the brown box with Bridget's letters with me. That night I settled on the iris comforter he had bought me. I read my letters to Bridget that she'd saved. I chatted about not liking school in Seattle, missing my father, college, my garden, and my research on gene therapy. I had asked her many questions about her life. My letters sounded so shallow and silly next to hers.

I felt like I was breaking inside as I read more, a part of me crumbling, dying.

For her, for my best friend, Bridget.

March 3, 1973

Dear Charlotte,

I had the baby. She was early. I thought she was going to rip me in two. Only at the end did the nuns give me something for the pain. Now I understand why girls scream during birth.

The baby is a little girl. I named her Legend. Remember all the legends your dad told us? That's why I chose that name. I used to pretend, Charlotte, that your father was my father. He was my legend.

They let me hold her for three hours. One of the nuns took three photos. One of only my baby, one of me holding my baby in bed, one of me holding my baby by the window.

Then they came and took my baby! Took her, took her! I told them that I changed my mind and I wanted to keep my baby. They tried to take my baby from me but I fought and kicked and screamed, and they brought in two men and they held me and stole my baby and I kept crying and kicking and screaming and they said calm down calm down calm down and I said bring me back my baby bring me back my Legend and they said no she is gone she is with her real family you can't have that baby you can't take care of it stop it stop it stop screaming Bridget.

Stop screaming Bridget.

Stop!

I screamed until I couldn't scream anymore and they gave me a shot.

Shot. Shot. I was shot.

The baby had Toran's blue eyes.

Love,

Bridget

March 6, 1973

Dear Charlotte,

I want my baby I want my baby I want my baby I kept screaming I want my baby I want my baby I want my Legend they kept saying to hush up hush up hush up.

Hush up, Bridget. Be quiet, Bridget. Stop crying, Bridget. Shut up, Bridget.

I can't be quiet. I want Legend. Where is she? I never said they could take her.

Love,

Bridget

Bridget, sweet Bridget. Where are you? Please come home.

I loved my home.

I loved that I was walking across the wood floors that my grandparents and parents had walked across before me. I loved how I could have Scottish Scrambled Warrior eggs, my father's recipe, with onions, diced tomatoes, and garlic, at the same dining table where four generations of Mackintoshes had sat. I loved the armoire with the honeysuckle vine my granddad made my grandma.

I loved the yellow on the walls, the new windows that were so clear I felt like I was outside. I loved the pitched roof of my sky blue bedroom with a beam that reminded my mother of a tree.

I loved how the cottage looked outside. The stone was cleaned up, the door was bright red again, the shutters white.

It was the home of my soul, the home of my clan and my family.

But there was no Toran here. Even when Toran wasn't home at his house, I knew he would be coming home soon.

He called me that night. We talked for two hours.

I felt better when I hung up. Then I felt lonely again, hopeless, sickeningly desperate, and nervous. I assured myself I could be an independent feminist and brainlessly in love with a man.

I missed him.

Romance Readers and Writers Magazine
By Kitty Rosemary
Books For Chicks Reviewer

GEORGIA CHANDLER AND HER ALASKAN MAN

Keep this under your hats, ladies!

I have more information for you on the mysterious and supposedly "reclusive" Georgia Chandler, our favorite time-traveling romance writer. I can't divulge my source, but it seems that she is in Alaska. Yes, Alaska. Apparently, she had a breakup with a past lover—rumor has it he was from Spain—and on a whim she took off for snowy Alaska. She is now cuddled up with a new man who won the Iditarod last year. A rugged, relentless, danger-loving man, if you know what I mean.

In every one of Georgia's books, McKenzie Rae Dean has a new man, which brings up a question that I heard at the Romance Writers convention recently. How many is too many? What do you think ladies?

Ta-ta for now!

Kiss, kiss!

Kitty Rosemary

11

On Sunday, Toran called and said, his voice quaking a bit, "Charlotte, I must talk to you. May I come down?"

You betcha you can come down. "Yes. Is everything all right? Bridget?"

"I have heard no new news of Bridget. This is of a different subject entirely."

"Do you want to come down now?"

"If I will not be intruding."

"You never intrude." Never.

"See you in a minute."

I hung up without saying good-bye because I needed preparation time. I ran to brush my hair. To be daring I took out the clip and left my hair down. I changed my underwear. Three holes! I threw them out. I took off my blue blouse with embroidered roses because it had scrambled egg on it and put on a pink blouse. The pink blouse had a red strawberry stain. I ripped that off. Gray blouse. Not my favorite, but clean. I put on my vest with two white cats on either side and a skirt.

I brushed my teeth. I whipped on deodorant. I shoved my feet into my sturdy brown shoes.

He knocked.

Shoot. Ready as I ever would be.

"Charlotte, I want to be honest with you."

"Yes." I sucked in my breath. "Please do." Did he sense my

love and lust for him? Did he find me clingy, like a virus? Would he tell me to quit staring at him, like a visual leech?

Toran ran a hand through his brown curls, then clasped his hands on top of my kitchen table. "It's not . . . now . . . if your answer is . . . not what I hope, what I wish . . . it will be terribly unfortunate . . . for me, as least . . . forever . . ."

"Now you've lost me." It was completely uncharacteristic of Toran not to be precisely articulate.

He stood up and paced the kitchen, where I'd set down two cups of Bengal Tiger tea, which neither one of us had drunk. He stopped. "Char, I've missed you. I've always missed you, and not only since you moved out. I've missed you since you left Scotland. I feel like I've been waiting for you to return."

"I feel like I've been waiting to return to Scotland, too. As if my life has been on hold and I didn't realize it was on hold." I stood up, leaned against the counter, and fiddled with one of the buttons on my blouse. "And now I'm here, and everything feels right." Almost.

"For me too, luv." His face registered his relief. "You're back in my life and it's as if you brought the sun in. When I saw you, everything between us was the same. The same friendship. The same trust. I hardly trust anyone. You and Pherson, the Stanleys, a couple of other men I've known since childhood. That's it. I've never felt comfortable around a woman as I do you."

"What do you mean comfortable?" That sounded like a pre-announcement to: You're my sister. Cheerio! My sister's back in the fold. Let's go make mud pies now.

"You can talk about anything—biology, space, politics, books, social issues, all things I like to talk about. I love that you like to walk on the beach and rock on the rocking chairs on my deck. I love that we can talk about farming, my business, and how you've made everything there so much easier, instantly." He snapped his fingers. "Like that. I love listening to you talk about McKenzie Rae Dean and her time traveling. I love that you love Bridget, despite her lies to you."

He took a deep breath, then came and stood right in front of me. "You're beautiful. Your thick hair, the way it curls and waves, and your green eyes, brightest eyes I've seen in my life. I love your hands, I love your smile, I love the way you laugh. You're calm, Charlotte. You're together, you're independent. I love your brain." He blinked rapidly and his voice was rough. "I love *you*, Charlotte."

Hoo. Woo-hoo. La la la! Whew! Did he say "I love you"? Was I hearing things? "You do?"

"Yes, although I feel like a fraud saying that."

"Why?" A fraud? No fraud! None of that nonsense.

"I don't think I've ever fallen out of love with you. We fell in love as teenagers, after being friends as kids, and that feeling, of loving you, wanting to be with you, it's never left. You've always been with me."

I took a wobbly breath. I would be brave, bold, bright. *Stop with the alliterations!* "I love you, too, Toran." I sniffled. Darn. I wish I had a tissue. I usually have them in my skirt pockets.

"You do?" His eyes widened.

"Yes. Always."

"You love me . . ." I knew he was nervous, and I found that so endearing. "As a friend?"

"Yes." You bet I did. I saw him swallow hard.

"Only as a friend?" His face sagged.

"I love you as a friend, my best friend, and I love you as a man and I want to rip off your clothes and I've been wanting to rip off your clothes since I saw you."

He smiled, his chest rose up, then down. He grinned. "I have felt the same, luv."

"But you waited all this time."

"I didn't want to have this conversation with you when you were living in my house. I thought it would make you uncomfortable. It was improper. You wouldn't have anywhere to escape to if you didn't want to be around me. You might feel cornered, awkward. You might feel toward me as you would a brother, and it would make you feel . . . sick, my feelings for you. It wasn't fair of me."

"It would have been fair." Exceedingly fair and yummy. "You're a studly man, Toran."

"Thank you. I have tried. It has been hard since I saw you to . . . to not . . . lose control."

"Ah, control." I waved my hand. "It's overrated. Let's lose it, shall we?"

"Charlotte, my Charlotte." He cupped my face with his hands. "I have missed you every day."

"Me too, Scottish warrior. Now are you going to kiss me or not?"

"Yes, I am, my darling lady, yes, I am."

He pulled me into his arms, my chest tight to his, and he smiled at me. We both laughed, put our foreheads together as a few tears slipped out each, and then all I felt was hot and delicious as his mouth landed on mine. The only man in my life I have been able to let go with has been Toran Ramsay.

He's the one.

And it was one fine orgasm, too.

The second was dandy.

A third for safe keeping.

"Why, Grandma, do you think I don't have the Scottish Second Sight, like you?"

"Child, I don't know."

We mixed the yeast, flour, and sugar for crumpets. "But you have it and your mum had it and her mother before that had it."

She nodded, her hair curling around her face. "That is true. But my sisters don't have it and neither did two of my aunts. I don't know why it skipped you. It will probably come to your daughter."

"Do you like having Second Sight?"

"Sometimes. And sometimes it sends me batty, that it does."

"I don't think I want it. It would be scary."

"Sometimes, Charlotte, it scares the bejeezes out of me."

"I don't want the bejeezs scared out of me."

She laughed, gave me a kiss. "I love you, Charlotte Mackintosh."

"I love you, too, Grandma."

* * *

"Let's jump into the ocean."

I giggled. I'd had a glass of wine and Scottish whiskey. We were lying on Toran's couch together, me on top of him.

Toran had taken me out for dinner at an elegant restaurant the night after we'd engaged in out-of-control naked gymnastics. He had also taken me to a traditional Scottish breakfast a few days later. We had black pudding, baked beans, sautéed mushrooms, Lorne sausage, toast and tea, broiled tomatoes with cheese, tattie scones, fruit pudding, and haggis. There were a couple of food items I refused to eat.

I tried to pay, but Toran said, "No. You are my lady, Charlotte. I will pay for us."

The feminist in me wanted it to be equal, but the woman in me said I would offend my man if I objected, so I made him chocolate chip cookies. Since our first breathless, bouncing copulation we had also gone to Edinburgh to explore for the weekend and did not leave the hotel much, but we agreed, "We had seen enough."

"You want to jump in the ocean, Toran? It's ten o'clock at night."

"Yes, it is, darling Charlotte," Toran drawled. "Are you up for a bit of an adventure?"

Was I? The North Sea is freezing.

It was late.

It was dark.

It was flippin' cold.

"Race you to the truck." I sprinted for the door.

He beat me, then opened the door of his truck with a flourish. "After you, my lady."

The North Sea is filled with liquid ice.

"My buttocks feel frozen just looking at it," I told Toran.

"Mine too. In we go before we change our bleepin' Scottish minds."

He started to strip.

"You're going in naked?"

"Yes, ma'am, I am."

Now this was fun. Whooee.

At least, it was fun to see him. But me? I'm a skinny bird with a hefty chest. "Okay, tough guy." I stripped, quick. "I'm in and out for one second—"

"You have to get wet, head to foot," he yelled at me as we ran for the ocean.

"This is insanity. Icy insanity." I snuck a peek at him. Oh shiver my science beakers, he was gorgeous. Tall, broad, muscled. His genes were scrumptious.

"Hold your breath. In you go."

I saw him glance down at me. Like eye lightning. He called out, over the waves, "Now that is a sexy sight I shall never forget."

He is irresistible.

We splashed through the liquid ice. I shrieked. He shouted. He dove. I dove right after him. Within three seconds we were running up the beach, legs trembling, gasping for breath. He grabbed my hand and pulled me out. He wrapped a towel around me, then wrapped my hair in another one before wrapping himself in one.

"Freezing. Oh, my gosh. I am freeze-freeze-freezing. We're insane." My knees started to shake.

"Yes, we are. We proved it. Grab my hand. I've got our clothes."

We ran to his car; he turned the heater on high.

We did not even bother to dress as he drove to his home, as it would only take a minute.

"I haven't skinny-dipped here since Clan TorBridgePherlotte did it together." My teeth chattered.

"Me neither. Not once."

"You haven't?"

"No. Seemed an activity best done with you."

"You are intelligent and adventurous, Toran. A blend." My lips were frozen. I could hardly speak. "A brave warrior and peach pie."

"I'm a fightin' Scot. I'm only sweet with my sweetheart, and that'd be you."

"Aw, Toran."

"Sweet Charlotte."

And, la la la! There it was again. Sex fire between us. We were frozen to the bone, yet lust was suddenly zinging in the car.

"I want you to know that I love you." He raised my icy hand to his mouth and kissed it.

My chin wriggled, my lip wobbled, and I sniffled, not a gracious sniff, and managed to choke out, "I love you, too, Toran. Always have." I wiped my nose on the towel.

"The same is true for me."

He opened my door to his truck, and we sprinted for his house, like two fast snowmen. Our towels came off quickly as he pulled me in tight.

I have never been kissed by anyone who can kiss like Toran. It's like he's kissing my whole self, my whole body, my whole soul. There is little science in kissing. It's all for the heart.

He lifted me up. I wrapped my legs around his body and he carried me upstairs, because he is made of muscle. We had sex in a hot shower and warmed up lickety-split.

Our lips never left each other's except to travel south. He could not stand my "southerly movements" for long and pulled me back up, telling me he was going to "lose it if you keep doing that, luv." I enjoyed indulging in making his southern parts "lose it," as the hot water streamed down.

"Lose it, baby."

We were North Sea skinny-dippers.

And Dan The Vibrator had nothing at all on Toran Ramsay.

I fell asleep on top of Toran. When I woke up, to him kissing me, we made love again.

In my books I sometimes write that the sex is speedy, shuddering yum the first time and slower the second time to savor, to build the pressure, to stroke, to tease a tad, here and there. . . .

Nope. Didn't happen like that to Toran and me.

Raging heat and thunderous orgasms again.

I collapsed a second time on top of him. We went to sleep.

Third time?

Same thing.

Toran hugged me all night long.

On Thursday and Friday I decided to garden after I worked on Toran's books. I had made headway with his business and I needed to get my hands in soil.

Gardening brings me peace like almost nothing else. I put on my jeans with the rope belt and my black gardening boots and went to the nursery.

I can't help myself in a nursery. If I have a shopping addiction, it's all related to plants. The owner sent her sons back with me to drop off the loot and place it where I needed it planted. The Stanleys came over and helped me, and we worked in my garden for hours.

We planted boxwoods in a circle in the backyard and propped up the statue of the little girl wearing galoshes holding an umbrella in the center of it. It was chipped now, but I loved it. We fixed the brick walk to the front door and lined a path to the back corner of the yard where I would later place two wooden chaise lounges. We planted nine rose bushes, where my mother had planted hers. Three were still living.

There were already many trees, but Toran had brought me three apple trees, and we put those in, too.

The next day I planted marigolds, alyssum, and begonias in my father's leftover shoe, our wheel barrel I'd finally found, and an old, cracked rowboat of my father's. It was still in the garage, and I didn't want to part with it. The Stanleys and I carried it to the back, filled it with potting soil, and soon it honored my father's love of the sea, only now it showed a love of begonias.

After the Stanleys left, the sun sinking, shadows dancing, I picked up my mother's birdhouses and started painting them. Red, blue, green, yellow. When they were dry, I would hang them on a fence, altogether.

Right before the sun went to sleep, I took a walk around. There are many things I love about gardening, but one of the most important is that you can always see improvement. A patch of weeds is gone. Flowers are planted. Bushes are trimmed, garden art hung, a bird feeder cleaned, a patio swept, a vine wrapped around a trellis.

Life is so often not like that. You can't always see the improvement. You can't see that you've done anything, that anything has been accomplished, or made better.

But in a garden, it's right there. You made pretty.

My mother would be pleased. I remembered what she'd told me once. "*A feminist knows what she likes to do and she does it. For you, it's gardening. So do it. Never let society or, especially, a man, tell you what you should like to do or how you should feel. Listen to yourself. You are the only one who knows the true you. Now, get out in your garden and get dirty.*"

The next night Toran and I had dinner, a seafood paella that I made, my mother's recipe, then played chess, at my house. We had all these awkward interludes where we forgot we were playing chess and stared at each other. I realized once that I had moved my pieces three times without him moving, and he realized he'd moved twice without me moving. This was absolutely unheard of for us, as we take our chess games seriously.

When he won, he stepped over the table and wrapped his arms around me, and we made love on the rug in front of the fireplace. He said, "I won, so I choose the position." I was more than willing to capitulate to that.

We played queen and king. Knight and rook. Pawn and bishop.

We fell asleep in front of the fireplace. I woke up the next morning, in bed, his arms around me, blankets and my iris comforter piled over us.

I smiled and started to laugh, he woke up and started to laugh, and then we started the whole king-queen love match again.

I could play chess with Toran, then make love. Checkmate.

I love Toran.

* * *

We didn't talk about it, but we started staying one night at my place and one night at Toran's. Back and forth. We took Silver Cat with us. She likes riding in the car.

I worked in the office upstairs in the yellow building and he'd come by to say hello. He was incredibly busy with the apples and blueberries, harvesting, cleaning, boxing, shipping, trucks in and out, but he would say hello, smile, and we'd stand like that, smiling.

Norma caught us kissing once and said, "Now, this brightens up me day, it does, sure and again. Carry on. Don't let me stop you!"

We kissed again and she stood in the doorway, clapping. "Romance is in the Scottish air, by tea and by crumpets, it is!"

We cooked and ate dinner together. We liked poring over recipe books to plan a menu, or using the recipes I had in my head from my mother. Sometimes we made love when he walked in the door. Sometimes we made love for dessert. Sometimes we could wait an hour.

We went to Molly Cockles Scottish Dancing Pub a few times. We played poker and danced and had dinner with friends, Toran's arm around me. We sat with Olive and her husband, Reginald. Olive had knitted Reginald a Doberman scarf, and he was wearing it. The Doberman had a maniacal grin. I don't think this was intentional. She was wearing a scarf with a mutt on it. The mutt was crazy. Not intentional, either. Probably.

Rowena came when the kids were with The Arse and The Slut, and Kenna came with her husband, bald and friendly Denholm, who is a doctor, too.

We laughed. We were both asked, quietly, separately, if we were together, and we said yes, so they bought rounds of "love potion" beer, as Olive called it, and we went home and made love again.

Toran was a true Scot in bed. He was huge and broad and long-legged and solidly hipped, so he was sexy, au naturel. Sometimes he dressed in his kilt and played the bagpipes. That kilt turned me on.

But his sexiness lay more in the fact that I loved his mind, had always loved his mind. I was with the right person. I was with my best friend from when I was a kid. I was with the first man I fell in love with when I was fifteen.

He kissed me, I kissed him back . . . then I dove right in and rode the passion wave.

Finally, my own passion wave, like I'd written about in my books . . . Ha. It did exist.

Ha-ha!

I put all my clothes—there weren't many—on my sleigh bed upstairs, on the fluffy and warm iris bedspread Toran gave me.

I have always prided myself on simplicity and frugality. It was probably a direct contrast to my mother, who is a clothes horse.

"A woman, a feminist, should look her best," she always told me. "Not for a man, but for herself. For her self-image and self-confidence. Feeling your best gives you courage to get out the door and demand respect, to do what you need to do. Are you presenting your best, Charlotte? No. It takes twenty minutes to transform from looking like a slovenly sloth to a lovely woman. Homeless to Lovely. You can do it."

I studied my clothes again.

I missed my mother. "Don't try to disappear into blah clothes, darling, please," she had told me. "You are much too special to do that. Are you trying to disappear?"

Yes, I was. I had disappeared, in many ways, for years, after my father died. I wanted to disappear in high school when I was teased and felt awkward, lost and lonely. I wanted to disappear after my divorce and what I found out about my husband. I wanted to disappear after that long, loud book tour and all the attention. I wanted to be alone.

Did my clothes reflect disappearance?

Yes.

I thought of Toran. Perhaps I didn't need to disappear as thoroughly anymore. I could appear, instead. Not appear too loudly, but appear.

I picked all my clothes up and dumped them into a black plastic trash bag. Two skirts, six blouses, my cat vest, my horse poncho, my Julia Child shirt, the slicker that went to my knees, my red and yellow rain hat, the brown sweater with the blue whale, and my two pairs of jeans, one with the rope belt I'd found on my island. Black sturdy shoes with holes. I would donate them. No. No one should wear those clothes. I would save them from themselves. I would trash them.

I put on the brown skirt, brown sturdy shoes, and white blouse.

"For the last time," I muttered.

I grabbed my purse and headed to the village.

I think I was the shopkeepers' favorite person that day. At one shop, decorated mostly in pink, I bought three summer dresses, three skirts, three pairs of jeans, and ten colorful tops. The saleslady said the size I wanted to wear was too big.

"Dear," Esther chuckled. "I don't know why you think that's the correct size for you and your bum. It's not. Have you lost weight? No, then. This is your correct size.... No, dear, once again." Esther took from me the shirts that I pulled off a rack and handed me new ones. "This size. This will cling to your bosom, not hang like a grocery sack." She wagged a finger at me. "A woman should not dress like a sack."

"You sound like my mother."

"She is correct, then, in fashion fitting."

In the dressing room, I wrapped my arms around my chest because I felt so uncomfortable to be that... *outlined* in a shirt, but then I dropped my arms and gave myself a personal analysis.

I had boobs.

I was a woman. No need to hide the bosom. Right? I swallowed hard. Right? Could I put my body on display like that?

My mother had been clear about my clothes. "You hide underneath your clothes so you can't see you and so others can't see you. See yourself. You need to want to see yourself. Be brave, honey."

I took a deep breath. Okay, no hiding anymore. It wasn't like my cleavage was bulging out. I bought the clothes. I liked them.

I could barely recognize myself, but I liked what I saw. Esther said, "You have excellent taste," though she'd picked them all out for me. I dropped the pink bags in Toran's truck.

At another shop I bought two pairs of sandals and three pairs of flats—one in red, one in tan, and one in cheetah print because I was feeling free, growly, and stylishly jungley. I bought two pairs of heels—one black, one red. I suddenly liked my flipper feet. They didn't look so flipperish in heels. I bought a pair of red plastic boots for the farm.

At a third shop I bought twenty-four pairs of lacy panties and six bras. The colors? White, black, red, magenta, pink, purple. The lady there fitted me. "This is what you were wearing?" She held my beige bra up with one finger and raised an eyebrow.

"Yes."

"Don't worry, dear, I'll dispose of it here. And it was completely the wrong size. Too small. No wonder it hurt. Your wobbly parts were being smashed to bits."

I lugged the bags out to my car. I felt ridiculous. All these clothes. So indulgent! Materialistic! Unattractive consumerish behavior!

Then I decided today was my day to defrumpify and didn't feel guilty. I rarely bought clothes, and then usually at Goodwill.

I stared at my pretty bags stacked up in the back of the truck.

I laughed. Good-bye, Frumpy Charlotte.

Hello, new dresses and lacy bras that will push my boobies up so Toran can see and touch them.

McKenzie Rae wasn't the only one who could shake her booty in purple zebra stripes!

I decided to get my hair done before I left the village. I saw a salon called Louisa's. It had lace curtains and a red sign.

Louisa was what I called a well-done-up woman. Her black hair curled down her back, her lashes were thick, her lipstick bright red, and her dress clung to curves that should not be allowed as they make the rest of us feel like bacteria. She was stunning. If I saw her near Toran, I'd want to put a brown bag over her head and wrap her in a black plastic sack.

I stared down at my skinny self with my rack of boobs. Then I compared myself. "I feel flat next to you."

"No, no, darling, you not. Stick them out, like this." She pushed my shoulders back and thumped me in the middle of my back, not that gently. "There. Now you are the woman! Be proud of the womanhood, no? The femininity? I say to God, each day, thank God I not stupid man."

Louisa was from Mexico, I learned. She had fallen in love with Erroll Fraser when they were in Guadalajara. She was living there, and he had been visiting on a university exchange program. She was engaged, at the time, to another man. She was twenty. She broke off the engagement, and she and Erroll wrote letters for six months when he returned to Scotland. Then she followed him, after a wedding at her parents' home in Mexico.

"We still in love. Every day." They had four teenagers. Errol was a professor at the university.

Louisa studied me, sitting in her chair. She took the clip off the top of my head, pulled the rubber band off that held my hair in a ball, and said, "*Madre de Dios*. What is this? I no understand the clippy thing. Your hair like long-haired mouse. You *want* to be long-haired mouse?"

"Not really," I told her. "I do have an affinity for mice because of my love of cats."

"Ah yes. I like my cats, too. Adios and Hola, killer of mice. But you no want to look like mouse to love the cats, no? I am right, I know this. Come. Come," she said. "I fix you. Don't worry. You won't be no mouse when Louisa done with you."

Her scissors started clipping.

"Here. I turn you. You no watch. I see you be nervous. No nervous. I fix this"—she swirled her hand in the air around my face—"bad problemo."

Based on the *click click click* of her scissors and her "This not right. . . . I cut this here. . . ." *click, click, click* and "You never cut hair, no?" I would probably be bald when she was done with me.

A bald cat lady.

But we did have a stimulating conversation as I learned about

Louisa's life, including that she makes the best Chinese food, reads constantly about World War II, adores her "rebel teenagers, ah. They so rebel," and loves gardening. "When mad, me, I get out the clippers and snip, snip, like that. Everything I cut. Husband get out of way."

Like I said, a stimulating conversation.

"Louisa," Louisa announced, hands on her hips, black hair thrown back, an hour later. "She work miracle. I work the miracle on you. Not a mouse no more. Now you are va-va-voomimg." She fluffed my hair. She took off my glasses and held them with two fingers, as if holding a wiggly mouse.

"Not these. No more. Tape? You tape glasses? You see." She pointed down the street. "Go to doctor of eyes. He fix you." She dropped my glasses in the same trash can as my hair and my "clippy thing."

"Good-bye tape glasses. Not pretty, Charlotte. No." She waved a finger in my face. "Now you sexy. Go get sexy eyes."

I agreed to go get sexy eyes. As I'd heard one of the lenses break when it hit the bottom of the trash can, I had no choice.

"I do makeup on you, Charlotte. You see. Those green eyes. Bright. Love the eye! But I make brighter." She took some sort of pencil out of a container. "And see? No, no, you no back away. No scared! This mascara. You hold still." I was too afraid to move as she kept waving that black stick near my eyes. "See cheekbones, here. I like yours." She put powdered blush on them. "And you mouth. See? Fat lips. I like the fat lip on you. Lipstick. So easy. Four makeups, Charlotte. Liner. Mascara. Lipstick. Blush for the cheekies. Mucho better. You take these with you, as gift. I turn you now. You ready, Charlotte? Now you are a Charlotte. Not a mouse. Here we go, señorita! I spin you now to mirror!"

Whew.

Couldn't breathe.

Couldn't move.

"See?" Louisa laughed in triumph. "I turn you beautiful. I so good. I so good at this. I the best. Now you the best." She put her cheek to mine. "And I like you, too, Charlotte."

Couldn't speak.

"You no speak, right? I know. I talent."

I shook my head, mesmerized. Was that me?

"New life for you, Charlotte. New and happy love life. Better in the bed now. You feel va-va-vooming, in the bed, va-va-vooming."

Although things were somewhat blurry without my glasses, I hardly recognized myself. My long brown hair, relegated to a bun, was often tangly and fried on the ends and hard to brush through. Periodically I would take it upon myself to cut it. Now it dropped in soft brown waves to right below my shoulder blades. It was thicker and shiny. Louisa cut bangs, straight across, which made my overly long forehead appear . . . normal. The waves cupped my face so my face didn't resemble a skeleton.

My eyes were brighter and seemed much wider, not so googly. I had cheekbones. I leaned forward. Fat lips. She was right. That lipstick did it.

"Yes, see? You have the fat lips. Not from fist. I have that before. No like. But these fat lips are your fat lips. For kissing and for . . ." She nodded down. "For the lower on the man, if you want. He like. That what I think. On the down low for the man only if you love him. You love him? You do with those fat lip of yours. What you think?"

"I think I'm surprised you're talking about that, but I like the lipstick."

She hugged me. "You lovely lady. That truth. Now, you go swing around that man of yours. And what I know now, I have new friend, Charlotte."

I stood up and she hugged me.

"Oh no, Charlotte. No crying! You mess up all the makeup! No cry. See. Oh no. You make Louisa cry, too. Bad girl." She thumped me on the buttocks this time. "No cry, ah, you sensitive lady."

I couldn't believe it.

I was . . . maybe . . . a tad . . . pretty.

I smiled. Braces had done the trick, and I did have white teeth.

"Now you are naughty lady," Louisa said, winking. "Go be naughty."

I did have to spend a few minutes thinking about my makeover and how that intersected with feminism, woman power, the role of women in society, and how I reject what society says a woman has to be and do and look like.

I thought about my own individualism. I had to make sure that it was me, Charlotte, wanting this, liking this, and that I wasn't metamorphosing myself so that I could please Toran.

Was I insecure, down deep, and wanted to be prettier to hold on to him, to make sure no other woman would sweep his tight butt away from me? Was I catering to a man? Was I buying into the shallowness of relationships based on outer expressions of beauty and vanity? Was I allowing myself to be dragged into valuing my external physical relationship with myself over the qualities of my personality and character?

I stared into my mirror that afternoon, hung beneath the wood beam my mother loved. I was wearing a red lacy shirt with a V neckline and a white skirt. My clothes were cooler, more airy.

I had on earrings shaped like gold leaves and a matching gold necklace.

I loved my new contacts. I kept trying to push my glasses up on my nose, but there were no glasses to push, no tape to fight with, no weight.

I loved my hair, too. It wasn't limp or tangled, but silky, smooth. My head felt lighter. My nose didn't stick out like a long toe, emphasized by my heavy-framed glasses. I liked that when I peered at the mirror I didn't see a mix of a brown-haired Cruella de Vil, a spaniel, and genetic material gone awry.

I have never bought into the notion of a woman parading around like an in-heat peacock to lasso a man.

But, no kidding, I looked better. So much better.

I liked seeing my face. I had cheekbones. My eyes weren't hidden by my glasses. I didn't appear so blah and tired, like solidified lab experiments. I felt . . . happier.

I am still a liberal feminist, but I decided that improving my appearance wasn't against my ideals, as the ideal for a woman is to feel strong and proud and happy and to be doing what she damn well wants to be doing.

That would be me. I am doing what I damn well want to do, except for the writer's block.

I smiled. What would Toran think?

I took a peek at my brassiere.

Red.

I bet he'd like it.

I called Toran and invited him to dinner.

"You're calling me and asking me for a date, luv?"

"Yes, I am." I was nervous about what he would think of the new Charlotte. Was that anti-feminist? I should be proud of the new Charlotte and not need a man's approval. I decided I didn't need a man's approval unless he was my Scottish Warrior.

"This makes my day."

"So, will you come?" Will you like what you see? Too much? Too soon? Too much makeup? Fluffy hair?

"It will be my pleasure, luv. What time?"

No one talked about being gay when I was growing up. I didn't even think about it. It didn't occur to me that Drew was gay when we were dating. I respected his decision to wait to have sex.

Drew told me, tearfully one night, the truth. I had begged for sex, for the umpteenth time, thrown a lamp, and burst into a snivelly round of tears because I felt so rejected, my self-esteem swirling around a swamp. It had been over a year of near abstinence.

I told him how I felt, crying, furious, frustrated. "If I had known I was going to live like a nun, I would not have married you, Drew."

His face crumpled and he said, "I am so sorry, Charlotte. I love you, I do. But I'm not . . ." He waved a hand. "I can't . . ." He bent his head, shoulders shaking, "I think I'm . . . I think I'm . . . gay."

It had been in front of my face all that time. I was in denial. I didn't want to see it. I was still in shock, though, as if he'd tossed me a bomb and yelled, "Here, Charlotte, catch this! Don't drop it!"

When I could move my mouth again I said, "You should have figured this out before we were married, you asshole."

"I know, I know!" Drew threw his hands in the air and broke down. "Please forgive me, Charlotte."

I'd rarely seen anyone that upset. He apologized endlessly.

I thought I would lose my mind. I loved Drew. He was the best husband, except for the sex. He paid attention to me. He listened. We talked all the time and did things together. That part, I knew, was going to leave a huge hole in my life.

But the marriage was over, my husband gay. He loved men, not me. Not Charlotte. It was like getting hit in the teeth with a hundred science beakers, each filled with rock-hard reality. I threw a lamp, then I threw all of his research papers out the window. He didn't even try to stop me.

The divorce was simple. Drew insisted I take the nicer car, his, which had seventy thousand fewer miles on it than mine. I moved out; the apartment had been his. He offered to move, but I told him I didn't want to stay there. He helped me move and bought me a new beige couch, a two-person denim chair, and a bed, which arrived the day I moved in. We shared an account. He closed the account and came home with a check for me. He gave me sixty percent of what we had. He insisted.

Drew made me a welcome home basket with honey, cheeses, jams, crackers, wine, and a pink bow. He cried more. Apologized again. I drank the wine pretty quick. I wanted to hate him for what he'd done, for what he'd put me through. The lies he told to himself that ended up affecting me.

I couldn't hate him.

I still liked him. There was still love left over.

We cried together. I was an emotional, mangled mess, my brain a tangled trap of despair and depression.

Eventually, I moved on.

What else was there to do? It was what it was.

A year later I met his boyfriend, Joey. Joey was as sweet as Drew and as handsome.

It sounds ridiculous to say it, but after I recovered from my hurt and fury, we all became friends. They come and see me on the island and stay for several days. Drew and Joey and my mother are the only ones I allow. They're funny and fun, and we play chess and backgammon, watch crime shows and romance movies, listen to Tina Turner, practice the foxtrot, and hike around the island.

Drew and I talk genes and gene therapy. He still buys me clothes. When he's on the island, I wear them. When he's gone, it's back to my comfy clothes.

In fact, Drew and Joey are taking care of my cats in their home in Seattle, where Joey works for some start-up computer company. They'll take warm care of Teddy J, Daffodil, Dr. Jekyll, and Princess Marie. I know this because they are cat lovers, like me. They have already bought each of the cats their Halloween costumes and have agreed with me that Dr. Jekyll has some sort of mood disorder, to which they are sympathetic.

Toran, for sure, is not gay.

Always a plus in a husband if you are a woman.

Toran didn't notice my metamorphosis.

I couldn't believe it.

I waited. He headed into the kitchen with a raspberry pie. "I made a pie for us. Had to take a break from work. Brought vanilla ice cream, too."

"That is a work of pie art, Toran." A pie-making man. Romantic! Seductive! Burn my tidbit panties now so I can show him nude flips on my bed!

"Thank you." He dropped a kiss on my lips, gave me a hug. "Want to eat it in bed?"

I smiled. "Sure do."

Toran started talking while I put our dinner on plates. I had made Mexican food. Enchiladas, chips, guacamole, salsa, fruit salad, and strawberry margaritas in honor of Louisa, miracle worker. I put candles and daisies in vases on the table.

We talked about a science article he read about further space exploration and shuttles. Then we talked about his potatoes, which he expected to reach the twenty-five-foot-tall roof of his tunnels this year. "I think it will be an excellent year for us, Charlotte."

"Have you noticed anything different about me, Toran?" The candles on the table flickered between us.

His brow furrowed, worried. "Uh. Well. Uh. Yes." He was perplexed, I could tell, poor man. "You . . . oh!" His face lit up. He had gotten it! He had not failed! "Did you . . . did you cut your hair?"

"I didn't. Louisa did."

"Louisa?" He was befuddled once again. Surely he couldn't be. Louisa was one of those hip-swinging, leggy, eyeball-attracting, bosom-bouncing women whom no man missed.

"Yes. Louisa. She owns Louisa's Hair and Curl, the hair salon?"

"Does she have blond hair?"

"No. Black. It's longish. Brown eyes. Mexican."

His face was clouded, then cleared. Recognition! "Oh yes. That lady. She's nice."

"Yes, she is."

"She cut your hair?"

"Yes, do you like it?"

"I do." He leaned closer and wrapped a lock around his fingers. "It's all wavy. Soft. Did she make it thicker somehow? I liked it the other way, I like it this way. However you wear it, sweet Charlotte, I like it." He dropped the curl and his head suddenly drew back as if I'd hit him. "Wait." He leaned forward again and examined my face. "There's something else." He snapped his fingers. He was passing the test I'd thrown at him! "Where are your glasses?"

"I have contacts now."

"Oh. No glasses? How do your eyes feel?"

"Relaxed."

"I love your eyes, Charlotte."

"Thank you. Yours too. Anything else?"

"You're wearing something on your lips." He peered at my mouth. I could tell he was searching for the word. "Lipostick."

"Not lipostick." I laughed. "Lipstick. Yep. Anything else?"

"Earrings!" He smiled, proud of himself. He was on a roll!

"And?" I glanced down at my shirt to give the man a break.

"And what?" His eyebrows shot up. "Am I not getting the lady thing here?"

"Toran!" I shook my head, pointed my fork at him, and stood up. "New clothes. New shirt, new skirt."

He blinked. Twice. "Wow." His voice rumbled. "You're right. You do have new clothes and hair. I like the red. It's pretty. Very pretty."

"Of course I'm right. Did you think I wouldn't notice that I bought my own self new clothes and got a haircut and contacts?" We both laughed. "I'm wearing makeup. Mascara. Lipstick." What else? "Blush. See?"

"I see it now!" He was victorious, a man in the know, perplexion gone!

"Toran Ramsay." I spread my arms out wide, making my statement. "I've had a makeover."

"A what?" Dang. Baffled once again.

"A makeover. It's when you get your hair all done up and you get rid of glasses that slide down your nose and you buy new clothes."

"Ah. I get it now."

"Yes. But how do you like it?"

"How do I like it?" He smiled, gentle, smooth, easy. He sat back in his chair. "I like it. I think you're gorgeous. I've always thought you were gorgeous. How do you like it?"

"I like it."

"Me too. You've had an overmake. Wait. What did you call it?"

"A makeover."

"A makeover."

He stood up, came to my side of the table, and kissed me. He ran a hand through my hair and his eyebrows shot up. "Feels smooth."

"You bet it does. It's been hair tortured. She took tweezers to my eyebrows and plucked me silly. Like a chicken."

"Ah, but you are not a chicken. You're my Charlotte. You're still you. You're beautiful. You were beautiful yesterday, you're beautiful today. You'll always be beautiful. I like your new haircut. I like the skirt. You have pretty legs. Very shapely. You're thin, too." He said it as if he hadn't noticed it before. "Any woman who can talk about quantum physics and how important Scottish kilts and tartans are, all in one conversation, is the sexiest thing on the planet, with an overmake or not and lipostick."

"Thank you."

He kissed me, then held me close. "I'm not an eloquent man, Char, and I'm not a romantic one, but I love you. However you are, I love you."

My heart thumped, my body tingled, and my brain synapses popped back and forth with skippy exuberance. I hugged him, laid my head on his chest. I could hear his heart thudding away, quick. "I love you, too."

"I'm so glad, Charlotte." His voice wobbled. "Every day, I am grateful for it."

"Me too." My voice wobbled, too. "You are one handsome stud muffin Scot. And I'm glad you like my overmake."

We laughed and kissed again. My "lipostick" was immediately gone. It was easy to slither out of my new skirt. My other skirts had lots of fabric, but this one didn't. My sandals slipped right off instead of having to be unbuckled. He admired my red bra. "I'm going to lose my head, luv."

We decided to bounce on my new bed. We liked it. Twice we liked it.

Afterward he went to get the raspberry pie and we ate it in bed. He kissed raspberry juice off my cheek.

Pretty soon he was kissing tears off my cheeks, too.

I was happy.

Happy, happy, happy.

It was a moment in life I knew I would not forget, even when I was 101.

I was so in love with Toran, if an alien spacecraft crashed near the cathedral in town and Toran was standing next to me, I don't think I'd spend two seconds staring at the craft. Toran would get all of my attention.

He put vanilla ice cream on my stomach and licked it off. I put vanilla ice cream on his missile and licked it off. The missile shot off.

I thought of the letters, stories, and drawings that Bridget and I exchanged when we were little girls. If I knew where Bridget was now I would write her a letter and tell her I was madly in love with her brother. Still.

March 10 or 11 or 14 in 1973. I don't know the date.

Dear Charlotte,

They said that because I can't stop screaming and yelling at them to get me my daughter get me my daughter get me my daughter and because I keep fighting with them that now I have to go to a special place to get better.

I was hoping my father would come for me. Or my mum. They didn't. I'm alone, alone. I know that Toran doesn't know where I am. They lied to him. Toran would leave university and come get me if he knew what they did to me.

Father Cruickshank came to see me at Our Lady of Peace, and I screamed at him and said he was a rapist and he pretended to get all sad, and said prayers over me, and told the nuns I was mentally disturbed and when they were out of the room he grabbed me by the throat and told me to shut up or else. He told me not to say a word about how he stuck his thing up me. He told me I was going to a place for crazy people and no one would believe what a crazy girl like me ever said. He told me he had talked to Toran recently. He told me that to scare me.

I hit him, twice, and screamed, and the nuns rushed in and he said the Our Father prayer, loudly, and made the sign of the cross. I told him he was a bastard and the nuns said I am lucky that Father Cruickshank is a forgiving man. They had only met him that day so they didn't know. They don't know.

I kept screaming at him and they had two men come in and tie me down and when I was down and the nuns left so he could "pray over this mentally disturbed child, may God bless her," he put his hand on my left breast and squeezed it tight, then he stuck his hand on my privates and told me he couldn't wait to see me back at St. Cecilia's.

No one knows the truth. No one would believe the truth.

Now you know, Charlotte. You know.

Love,

Bridget

April in 1973 I think but I am not sure of the month

Dear Charlotte,

Insane asylum.

That's where I am. I'm not crazy. My father and mum came to see me and say I have to stay here until I quit screaming and crying. I told them I wanted to go home, that I want my daughter, I want my daughter, I want her, they said no, you can't have your daughter, and I begged, then I hit my father and screamed at my mum and they came and gave me a shot.

A shot. Hold me down. Strap me down. Hurts! And another shot. Pills.

I want my daughter. Legend.

Toran can't find me here. Can you find me, Charlotte?

Love,

Bridget

Maybe May is the date

Dear Charlotte,

My roommate talks to herself and yells at voices that I can't hear and there are other people here who do the same thing and rock back and forth and spit and pee on the floor and hit each other and it is always noisy and the nurses in the white coats and the doctors yell too and tell us we can't leave our rooms and I have been here so long so long so long and I want my baby and I don't know where Legend is and I have not seen my mum or dad and I don't care but I want Toran and you and Pherson.

They make everyone swallow pills and I feel nauseated and sick and weak. I told them I wanted out, out, out, out! And two men said the doctor said I can't leave and I tried to get out five times or six or seven and they put me in a room that's padded. Padded. So I wouldn't hurt myself. Padded.

Can you find me, Charlotte?

Straitjacket. Straitjacket.

Come get me, friend. I have to search for my daughter. She's gone. She's with another mother. I want her. I want my daughter even though her father is a rapist.

Rape. Rape. That was a new word for me. Rape.

Baby.

Can you find me?

Love,

Bridget

June or July 1973 (I don't know the date)

Dear Charlotte,

They won't let me send this letter to you, Charlotte.

They search everything.

I will hide it.

I save them. You are my friend, Charlotte, my best friend, but I can't tell you this. I am dirty. I feel so dirty.

I am shameful, that is what my father says, shameful. I have shamed the family. He said I'm a slut like his mother was a slut. She's a whore, I'm a whore.

I. Am. Bad.

You are my only friend. I think you would be my friend even if you knew, but I am not going to risk it. I am a bad person. A burden. Dirty. Better off gone. I can't eat. I can't sleep.

I remember everything. Everything. Hand on throat. Rip. Pain. Blood. Can't breathe. Dark. That's why I scream.

Where is my daughter? I want my baby back. Legend. I love you, Legend.

Love you,

Bridget

I went outside my cottage and screamed.

Bridget, where are you? Please come home.

12

I worked for about seven hours the next day in the office, reconciling Toran's accounts with the bank's statements. I took, and made, many calls. I was getting more and more involved in the farm, and I liked it.

In the late afternoon, I decided to take a hike into the hills. I passed the graveyard but did not yet go to my father's grave. I would soon.

I walked through the meadow, the bluebells and narcissi swaying. I stopped when I came to the viewpoint over Toran's lands. It had been a rainy night, but the skies were clear, the blue low and pure, scoopable.

Someone, somewhere, was playing the bagpipes.

I thought about my writer's block. Writer's block can be explained by having a brick stuck in your head where your brain should be. I seriously wondered if I would ever write another book in my life. The words were stuck, the thoughts were stuck, the storyline was stuck.

The last sentence I wrote, before I left my island, was "Peanut butter sticks to my mouth and makes me feel like I'm choking. McKenzie Rae does not eat sausages because they're too phallic."

Maybe I was done as a writer.

Am I done?

Did I want to write more books? I have written nine books. Is that all that's in me?

But if I didn't write, what would I do?

Go back to research? Work at a university? Teach? Get my doctorate in one of my favorite biology topics?

The bagpipes blasted a long, haunting note, then went back to a quicker rhythm.

Could I become a farmer?

I gazed down at Toran's fields, the different types of potatoes, the long, endless lines of blueberry bushes, the apple orchards, tended and well cared for.

I liked tractors. I grew up driving one on our land. I liked building fences. I liked planting and watching crops grow. I liked helping my father and mother to load produce onto trucks where it would be sold at markets all over Scotland. I liked being outside. I liked gardening. Even large-scale gardening.

I liked being the numbers woman.

A farmer? Again?

I smiled. I could so do it, and I'd love it.

Was I giving up on my dream, though, of being a writer? Was that a dream I had, then accomplished, and now it was time for a new dream? Did I care about being a writer anymore? Was I giving up on my writing career to help a man I was so in love with my brain was now mush?

The notes of the bagpipes swirled around me, a cocoon of music, the songs of Scotsmen and women, all my relatives, who had come before me, whose shoulders I stood on, who stood on the shoulders of Scotsmen and women before them.

One final noted sounded, and I thought of my father, playing for my mother, for me.

I loved it here.

It felt like home.

In my books, McKenzie Rae Dean always saves people. Every time. Sometimes it's one person. Sometimes two. Sometimes it's a multitude of people.

Save, save, save.

I couldn't save him, but McKenzie Rae, she will save. She will win. She will overcome.

She is the me I wanted to be when my dad needed saving.

One would think after all the books I've written that I would have worked this part out.

The saving part.

I haven't.

I looked up at the hills, where he was buried. I would go soon.

Soon.

Not yet.

"Come and sit by me, Charlotte."

Toran was sitting on his leather couch. I sat down next to him. I was wearing one of my new skirts, light blue, and a summery top with blue flowers that was cut low enough for my red bra to peep on through.

When I first arrived at his home that night, we went for a sexual tumble, which ended up with me on his butcher block counter, and then we ate. I did sterilize the counter. Twice. It is important to rid a kitchen of germs, but it absolutely was not going to stop me from having butcher block sex.

He picked up my hand and kissed it. "I want you to know my intentions, how I feel about us and our future. I don't want you to leave Scotland. I want you to live here. We can settle out the rest later. I don't want to push you or make you uncomfortable, or press for something you're not yet ready to give. We have only been together for a short while, but I cannot imagine my life without my best friend, without my best love, ever again.

"If you left, after what we've had, I think . . ." He paused, and those blue eyes shone bright. "I think I'd hide out in my home. Never wear my kilt. Never participate in the Scottish games. Never look at the sunset. Never shave. My fields would go to rot all because of you, beautiful lady, so I'm afraid I can't let you go."

"Never?"

"No, lass, never." He smiled. "If you left I'd have hair to my shoulders, a beard to the floor. I'd be an embarrassment to the

Ramsay ancestors. I wouldn't be able to wear our plaid with pride. I could not look at our family crest without sadness."

He kissed me on the lips, tender and sweet.

"What do you say, Queen Charlotte? Stay with me here in Scotland? Please. Stay."

Stay in Scotland. Give up my island house, the whales, the fox, the deer, the birds. My gardens. I loved my home on Whale Island.

"Yes."

His face, which had been worried, tight, stressed, relaxed into hopefulness.

"Yes, you'll stay? You'll make me the happiest man in a kilt ever?"

"I'll stay. I need my cats. And their stroller. My science book collection. My model of DNA and my telescope. Teacups my mother bought me."

"We'll fly back together and pack up what you want and need." He stood up, bowed low and said, "Queen Charlotte, I thank you."

I stood and curtsied. "King Toran, it is my pleasure. Thank you for asking."

We did a secret handshake, palms together, then back of the hands, then all ten fingers touching. We yelled, "Crusaders against evil forces unite," and he twirled me around and kissed me.

Scotland had called me back since I left. This time, I answered the call. Most important, I answered the call of my Scottish Warrior.

I laughed at myself. That sounded like one of the cheesy, swoony lines out of my books.

We later tried Against The Wall Sex, my ankles locked around him. It worked out well.

My father told me the legend of one of our ancestors, Rose "The Loyal" Mackintosh. She was in charge of the Scottish skies at night. At first, everything was black. The only bright spot was the moon, and it shone across the land because of the courage of Blackburn "The Protector" Mackintosh.

But the sky needed more light. Rose went on an arduous journey, up into the deep, secret forests of Scotland, where few had gone before. Tucked in a back corner, between two rivers, inside a stone cottage, she found the wise woman she had been searching for. "How can we put more light in the sky?" Rose asked.

The wise woman didn't answer for a long time, her blue and black tartan wrapped around her shoulders, her hair in a long black braid. "For light, you must fill the sky with love."

Rose didn't know what to do, and the wise woman would say nothing further, so she turned to go home. Along the way she saw a mother kissing her son on the cheek, a sister hugging her sister, two lovers embracing. She understood then what she must do. She asked each of them for a little of their love. Each of them gave her one of their kisses and she placed them in a glass box.

Rose traveled long and hard across Scotland, gathering kisses. She did not rest. When she was an old, old woman, her back bent, her fingers gnarled, she finally had enough love. One night, on the darkest night of the year, she threw all the kisses up into the blackness. They scattered across the horizon in swirls, arcs, and spirals.

The kisses lit up the sky with their love. Finally, Rose "The Loyal" Mackintosh rested.

"When you look up into the night sky," my father told us, "and you see the stars, think of love."

He was a legendary storyteller.

Dear St. Ambrose Ladies' Gab, Garden, and Gobble Group,

We need to plan for our annual fund-raiser, not only what to sell but to whom to donate the money to. Last year it was the library, the year before that the local school. I am thinking of a pig auction. Please write your ideas at the bottom of this letter. Pass it around to the other ladies.

Olive Oliver

Ladies Olive and Garden Gollys,

I am on my third glass of wine and I was thinking of our annual fund-raiser for garden ladies eating ladies club. I know we have not decided on the winner yet, but I was thinking that we need something to bring in more money this time. Spilled my wine.

We could always sell plants, straight away, that's a fine dandy idea, but perhaps we could buy white ceramic statues, like cherubs, those fat babies with wings? We could paint them yellow, orange, red, purple, banana, apple colors.

Wouldn't that be bright and original? We could add those wobbly eyes you can buy at a craft store spilled more wine and maybe some white feathers for the wings. For people of a more violent nature, we could paint white teeth on the statues with a splattering of blood or for those who like humor, we could turn them into monsters with horns. Spilled my wine. What do you think? Summer garden art with a twisty.

The Arse has promised the kids a trip to London. I'm going to lose the house because I can't make the bank payments and off they go. The Slut is apparently paying for it. I don't know how on her salary. Perhaps she's going to sell her boobies.

I will bring my lamb casserole to garden ladies eating ladies club. What do we call ourselves again? Gab and Garble? Garden Goblets? Hoblets? Boblets? Booblets? Can't remember.

I am on my fourth glass of wine, but thought I'd share the idea of blood red cherubs with wobbly eyes that bite. Spilled again.

I'll give this note to Kenna first because she likes blood.

Rowena

Dear Olive and Garden Gobbling Ladies,

I have an idea for our fund-raiser.

We could see if Denise's brother, Mark, could make us, say, fifty clay faces. He has a kiln. Wouldn't that be lovely to have a clay face in your yard? You could nail the face to a tree trunk, attach a face to a trellis, or hang a face on your fence. A face could even be screwed into the outside wall of your home. Why, when you went out to your yard, you could see all these hanging faces and believe that you had friends, waiting for you. We could call them Clay Face Friends.

After my work with all the blood and bodily organs during the day, I could use some friends in my yard.

Do be honest with me, Olive, I am trying to be helpful and think of something creative. Garden Gabbing Club is the only fun thing I do outside of cutting people open and my kids. Sometimes I don't like either. I'll pass your note along to Gitanjali. I'm going to buy spices from her today.

Cheerio.

Kenna

PS I'll bring my Scottish Highland soup that my husband says keeps the hair off his chest. I think he means it's too spicy. His flatulence would attest to that.

Dear Ladys,

I thinkie about fund-raiser. I have idea. We sell exotic plants from other countries. That new word for me. Add international to our garden in Scotland. We call it, "Bringing strangers home" or "Immigrants Coming to Your Yard" or "Foreign people, foreign plants, copulate together."

My English, it not always good, so let me know how you think it.

I be bringing biryani with saffron and dim sum to Gab On Your Garden Groupie on Tuesday night. (I not remember our name. Apologizes.)
With kindness and love,
Your friend,
Gitanjali.

Dear St. Ambrose Ladies' Gab, Garden, and Gobble Group,

I have an idea for our garden club fund-raiser. We could sell plants, as usual, always a precious link between selling plants and a garden group but we could also sell . . . hold on to your panties . . . garden underwear. This is not a joke! I saw it in a magazine the other day. The panties are rather large, so they don't rise up your crack, sorry for being crass, but I thought it was a fine idea. I'm going to order some myself. I can't stand panty creep!

They come in pink, green, yellow, and white. Some have flowers, like chrysanthemums, bluebells, and ferns, and others have garden hoes and rakes and lawn mowers.

We could call it the Pick-a-Panty St. Ambrose Ladies' Gab, Garden, and Gobble Group Fundraiser.

I'm going to kill Nonie and make a chicken pie for Tuesday night.

Remember! Sign your name at the bottom and pass this note around. The red is not blood, it's Rowena's wine.
Olive

Dear Olive,

I could not believe it when Kenna told me at Estelle's Chocolate Room that she wanted to make clay faces for the fund-raiser. I have seen Mark's clay faces. They're a combination of a drugged witch and a banana, all long like that, just so. I told her that. Kenna is batty. I swear she has a bug in her head. That simply won't work. No one wants to look at a drugged witch/banana face in their yard. I told her that, too.

I'll think of something else. Someone has to do it. It's always me.

Mrs. Lorna Lester

Dear Lorna,

I understand you thoroughly hated my idea of making and selling clay face friends for the garden. I believe you told Rowena, "The entire idea makes me shudder. It's a disgrace. Against what a Scotswoman stands for in the garden."

Have you thought of another idea, then? I am longingly awaiting a new idea for our fund-raiser from you, as you are quick to cut other people's ideas down. I am sure your idea will be fascinating.

May I make another suggestion? Perhaps we could make Garden Butts.

We could take off our pants and sit, briefly, in wet cement to make an indentation. We would make your cement pad extra large, don't you worry. If the cement gets stuck to your fat arse I can scrape it off at the hospital.

From,

Kenna

I received the note from the Garden Ladies about the fund-raiser. I had no idea what to suggest. I would rather write a check than do this.

* * *

It will be the time of the bees.

My father, Quinn Mackintosh, died when our horse, Sergeant Salt, bolted, then bucked, and fell on top of him in the middle of our fields. It was the bees that made Sergeant Salt buck. They had been attracted to our orange trumpet vine. The sky was an unusual bright orange that day from a burning blaze in the Highlands, all as my grandma predicted.

My mother ran to him, wailing, shouting. I have never heard my mother scream like that. I can still hear her raw, unhinged keening, her head on my father's heart, which would never beat again.

Toran, Bridget, Pherson, and I were in the hills, talking at our fort, and we sprinted down. Toran took charge. He was seventeen. He held my father still, did CPR, while I ran to the house to call an ambulance, my whole world crackling, crumbling.

The funeral was attended, I heard later, by almost everyone in town. We buried him in the Mackintosh Ramsay cemetery, sheltered by oaks and willows. Bridget, Toran, and Pherson stood right behind me. My mother cried and cried. I tried to hold it in, but when Toran gave me a hug, I couldn't stop crying.

When everyone else went down to the house after the burial, Bridget, Toran, Pherson, and I went to the fort. We all crawled inside and I sobbed until my whole body hurt, Bridget on one side, Toran on the other, Pherson holding my hand in front.

It will be the time of the bees.

My mother and I left Scotland, after she hacked that trumpet vine down to nothing with an ax, her cries an anguished roar. Ben Harris and his wife helped her throw it out.

I'm still crying, in many ways, for my father.

What if he hadn't been on that horse?

What if he had gotten off one minute sooner?

What if there hadn't been so many bees from our trumpet vine?

What would it feel like to have my dad in my life? What would my life have been like had he not died and we stayed in Scotland? Would I have married Toran, or would we have been best friends? Would I have become a writer or a farmer's wife? Would we have children by now?

I try not to let those questions plague me, because the answer is: It is what it is.

As simple as that phrase is, it's helped me through the years: It is what it is. Acceptance.

I don't like that my father died.

But I accept it.

And that's what brings on the tears, one more time.

For me, for us, it was the time of the bees.

And I would go to his grave soon, I would.

Not yet, though.

"Charlotte, it's Maybelle. Are you done having your nervous literary breakdown?"

"I'm not having a nervous literary breakdown." I put my feet up on a chair in my backyard. At a thrift shop I had found a black wrought iron table and four chairs with curlicue backs. I'd added a pot of marigolds. Excellent place to read my new book, *Astrophysics*.

"Yes, you are."

"No, I'm not." My garden was coming along. I'd hired the Stanleys. Toran came, too, when he had time. I had brick pathways now, created from the old brick, and the wood from the old trellises was being used for a long grape arbor. The trumpet vine had not dared to pop up again.

"You're not writing, I can feel it. It's time to put the breakdown aside and start your story."

"I don't have a story in me." I was in a red summer dress and a rock necklace. Very McKenzie Rae Dean–like.

"You do. Find it. Hang me out to dry, hit me with sticks. Your story is probably hiding behind your intestines. Or your liver."

"I would never hide a story behind my intestines. Too much acid. And I wouldn't have anything unclean near my liver."

"Write for the women out there who need another McKenzie Rae Dean book. They pretend they're McKenzie Rae, especially when it gets to the sex with handsome hunks part. On another bad note, Sheryl was caught with weed at school. Now she's suspended. She said that weed helped her find herself. I told her that weed is helping her to get a job at McDonald's. I drove her there yesterday, dropped her off, and drove home. It's five miles away from our house. I told her that she had so much time on her hands, she could get a job."

"Did she get the job?"

"She did. She called me from a pay phone and begged me to pick her up, but I told her I wasn't coming because she needed to walk the marijuana out of her system, the sneaky pot-smoking brat. I told her, if you have time to smoke pot, you have time to work and walk. Put a Big Mac in that and smoke it."

"Good mothering language." I ran my hand over my hair. The sleek feel was still a surprise. I was putting on makeup in the morning, too.

"And do you know what Randy did?"

"No, I don't. That would be impossible for me to know."

"He's having sex with his girlfriend."

"What did you do to him?"

"What any competent mother would do."

"Which is?"

"I screamed at him and then we went and I gave him money to buy a jumbo box of condoms. Do I look like a grandmother? No, I don't. I am still young and hip. I told him, 'You hormone-driven baboon. I told you not to have sex as a teenager, but here you are, and I know you're not going to stop because you're like a dog in heat, so stick that sock on your pecker every single time you do it with Crystal because if you get her knocked up you are going to work full time next to your pot-smoking sister flipping burgers to support your offspring, because I won't do it.'

"And he said, 'Okay, Mom, thanks.' He was all red in the face, embarrassed that I knew he was doing the naked hump, and I said, 'I love you,' and he said, 'I love you, too, and I won't get her pregnant,' and I said, 'You better not or I will tie your dick in a knot and you won't need a vasectomy. Got that, son?' And then I grabbed a banana when we got home and he and I went into the bathroom and I showed him how to do it, and then I said, 'Don't come out until you can get a condom over your pecker within ten seconds and done right,' and then we all sat down and had my mother's manicotti. Delicious."

"I love manicotti. Can you send me the recipe?"

"Sure. I'll tell you right now if you want. The key to a tasty manicotti is the ricotta cheese. . . ."

I wasn't nagged further about my book and I acquired a new manicotti recipe. It was a fine call.

I've sold millions of books.

Each year a chunk of money goes to the island kids for scholarships. I review all the applications and choose ten kids to get a pile of money for their four years at college or for trade school. They have no idea who it's coming from, and that's the way I like it. I want to help people help themselves anonymously. No attention.

One check each year goes to pay for a full-time art teacher and one full-time music teacher. It's a small school, grades K–12, so the kids get art and/or music every day. I also pay for a former science professor on the island to teach three after-school science classes a week. The kids love watching things explode, and they each make a rocket, among other things.

One check goes to an abused/stray cat sanctuary in Kalispell, Montana. The staff gets them healthy, then tries to find owners for them. Ten cats lived in each yurt with an enclosed area outside so the cats can go outside anytime to play.

The woman who runs the sanctuary, Adelaide, calls me often and we talk cats. I have visited her twice and enjoyed playing with the cats immensely.

The other checks are for "Newspaper People." When I read stories in the newspaper that yank my emotions out, I write checks. I am especially a sucker when kids are ill and their parents have quit their jobs to take care of the kids and their finances have collapsed.

I manage my own finances. I won't pay some slick financial manager 2 percent to do what I can do better, even with all their patronizing, condescending talk trying to convince me they know better, which they don't. I have a friend, Launa, my accountant, send the family a check under her firm's name so the donation is anonymous. She forwards the parents' grateful thank-you notes. More yanking of my emotions ensues.

It is wrong to keep all of the money that I have made. My father would be appalled. My mother likes to help me give it away. As she says, "When we were broke in Seattle, people helped us, so now we help others, especially women. Women power." So we do. She gives money away, too.

I would have to figure out who needed what in St. Ambrose.

A start would be helping with the garden fund-raiser, but I had no idea what we could sell.

Like I said, I'd rather write a check. I'll do it anonymously.

I walked by a lingerie shop—Tea's Naughty Scotswoman's Lace and Lingerie—in the village the next afternoon. A white lace negligee caught my attention in the window. I stopped and gaped. It was low-cut, almost to the belly button! And all that thigh . . . exposed!

I mumbled to myself, "I can't wear that!" Then I mumbled, "Too much leg, too much hip." I tilted my head at a ninety-degree angle to peer at the mannequins. "I'd have an embarrassment hot flash if I wore it." I pointed at it, shook my finger, as if I were accusing it of leading me astray. I stopped shaking my finger when an older woman gave me a funny look and said, "Don't bother scolding the mannequins, dear. They can't see."

I walked on. I went as far as Sandra's Scones and Treats Bakery. I walked backward for a few seconds, then realized how foolish it was to walk backward in the village. People would think I was crazy.

I next studied a red negligee on another white mannequin.

"I could never wear that, either," I said aloud, leaning forward, nose almost to the glass. There were garters, too. "With my luck they would snap right off and hit me in the face." I said that out loud, too. I leaned farther in, and my nose smacked the glass. Ouch! The mannequin was wearing heels with some fluffy, furry thing at the toe. How do you walk in those?

I turned on my flats, the cheetah print ones, as I had been feeling animalistic that day, and got as far as Laddy's Café. I walked backward for exactly six steps, then turned and scuttled back to Tea's Naughty Scotswoman's Lace and Lingerie, head held high. I am not a crazy lady!

The mannequin off to the right was wearing black. Sheer black. My nipples would pop through. I think I have overly wide nipples. I am unsure, because I have hardly ever seen other women's nipples, but they seem large to me.

A woman stepped out of the shop. She was short with a bob of blond hair.

"Hello, luv. I've seen you walk backward several times. Can I help you?"

"I only walked backward twice."

"Yes, dear, would you like to come 'round and take a peek?"

I pointed to the lingerie on the mannequins. White. Red. Black. "I'll take all three. Size medium."

"Do you want to try them on?"

"I will at home."

"Lovely choices. Come along in, then."

I came along in. Twenty minutes later, after instructions on how to use the garters, only snapping my fingers twice and my thigh once, and with instructions on how to tie the back of the red lingerie piece, and how to get into the sheer black one without ripping it, I was back out the door. I stopped at Sandra's for a scone, clotted cream, and black coffee to contemplate what I'd done.

Me. Charlotte Mackintosh. Romance writer with no romance until lately, and now I had bought sheer lingerie for my overly wide nipples.

I peeked inside the bag, nose in. I had never, ever worn lingerie. Not once. Yet, wrapped up in pink tissue, inside a black and silver bag with a silver heart, there the lacy tidbits were. "I cannot believe I did this," I said out loud. "I can't believe it."

I took the lingerie out and put it on the bakery's table. I took out the shoes with the fluffy, furry thing at the toe and the garters. I held each negligee up to my chest.

"Ah, my lady, your man is going to have a lucky night tonight!" The waitress grinned at me. "More coffee, or should I get you chocolate pretzels to take with you? My husband and I always get hungry for chocolate pretzels after shagging. Must be the salty and sweet together."

I nodded. "Yes. Sounds like a delicious postcoital snack. Thank you."

"Frilly and ladylike at the same time," an older woman with white hair piped up. "Ah, to be young and bouncing around in bed again. I miss those scoundrelly days!"

"Very sexy," a woman said, about twenty-five. "But how do you get into the black one?" I showed her. "And the garters? Never worn them myself." I showed her by example.

When I headed out, with my pretzels, an old man said, in a gravelly voice, "Don't kill him, luv! Leave him something for the 'morrow!"

I peeked inside my black and silver bag again and laughed. I remembered what my mother had said about my grandma, seer of the future, albeit often all jumbled up. *"Your grandma knew how to dress for her husband. One time I saw her lingerie in her dresser. It was like looking at a porn star's drawers. She couldn't keep him off of her."*

I didn't want to keep Toran off me at all.

After my marriage to Drew broke up, he transferred out of our lab to another university so I wouldn't feel uncomfortable. He said, "This is my fault."

I held it together by working constantly. I worked long hours, classic workaholic behaviors, and took on more research and writing projects. I was published twice in academic journals that only competitive and jealous colleagues read, and the writer's mommy.

But there was still time at night, and I started thinking about writing my time travel romance novels again.

One day I was driving home and I saw this woman, probably going to a costume ball, dressed in 1890's attire, a flowing, layered crimson dress with a bustle and a ruffled bodice, a wide-brimmed velvet hat, and a lacy parasol.

Soon after that, I saw a man wearing a rock T-shirt and old-fashioned top hat.

I felt exhausted, ugly, divorced, and hopeless.

If I started writing time travel romances, my alter ego, McKenzie Rae Dean, would be an eye-catching rebel. Courageous. Sassy. Sly and dangerous and aggressive when she needed to be. She would wear heels and have my green eyes and my brown hair, only her hair would be sleek and untangled. She would stand up to men, like the toad I worked with in the lab, Dr. Len Xavier, who was a pompous, chauvinistic, credit-stealing ferret. In fact, I would name the first pompous, chauvinistic, credit-stealing ferret in my book Dr. Len Xavier.

No, I would get sued for defamation. Ha! I would call him Xavier Lenson.

Xavier (I refused to call him Dr. Xavier even to his face) believed a person who was promoted had to have a penis.

Those misogynistic feelings about vaginas were the final kick I needed.

I had finished my master's thesis in gene therapy and was passed up at the university research lab I worked at for one promotion, then another. I deserved both. At a meeting with about thirty people in our lab, Xavier promoted a man who was hired after me and hardly had a grasp on basic biology. I'm not sure he had a basic understanding of what cells are. I'm not sure he had a basic understanding that he had toes at the end of his feet and why they were there, evolutionarily speaking.

When Xavier said, "I am proud to promote a young man who has proven himself time and time again"—blah blah blah—"please help me congratulate Darren Scholls!" hardly anyone clapped. I did not miss the looks thrown my way, how a number of people were shaking their heads, how Vil Tourno said, "That is total shit," and Larry Sho said, "Should have been you, Charlotte," and Maureen Levitt said, "I am so sick of women here getting screwed."

I stood up. I stood up in that lab, for myself, for other women, right in the middle of it, and said, "I cannot believe you gave Darren Scholls my promotion."

People clapped.

"Darren Scholls does not know anywhere near what I know about gene therapy. He came here after me. He doesn't have the experience that I have. He hasn't published as I have. He isn't doing original research, like I am. Xavier, you know as well as I do that you are not promoting me because I have a vagina."

Xavier's face appeared ready to pop, red and puffy. Darren said, "I deserve the promotion," which was a mistake, because a whole bunch of people said, "No, you don't," quietly, but altogether it was as if it was shouted through a megaphone.

Darren slunk down in his seat.

"Xavier, you don't have the brain capacity of a ten-year-old science student, and everyone knows it." This was a true statement. "You hide your lack of intellect behind your condescending and patronizing attitude. Vaginas should not be used as an excuse to hold anyone back. I know what I'm doing, and you know I know what I'm doing. I am not going to take this. If you promote him over me, simply because he has a penis, I'm done."

Xavier blustered, flustered. He was embarrassed and backed into a wall with nipping wolves all around. Xavier wasn't popular. He used fear and anger to hide that he was a semi-functioning monkey.

He squiggled, he wiggled, he flushed and blushed and said, "Then you're out, Charlotte."

"Come on, Xavier," Bryan Yeung said, standing up. "That's not right."

"She can't leave." Vil Tourno stood with Bryan.

Others joined in. "She's the head of our team . . . she deserved the promotion, she's deserved it for a long time . . . you can't promote Darren over Charlotte. . . ." Men stood up for me, proving that not all men are against women. Maureen announced, "I am not going to take this sexist, scrotum-loving discrimination anymore. She leaves"—Maureen jabbed a finger at me—"I call my attorney."

Yet Xavier was going to throw his weight and ego around. He was *the boss*. No one could challenge him. Especially not a *woman*. "Thank you for your work, Charlotte. I'm sorry we have had a misunderstanding."

"That's what people and companies say to someone when they know they're guilty, culpable, and trying to defend themselves against a lawsuit. It's said to get people to shut up. It's paternalistic. It makes me sick. So do you, by the way. Will I be promoted or not?"

The silence deafened us all.

Xavier was shaking with anger, but he was scared, too, of the nipping wolves. He hesitated. But wait! No one was allowed to challenge his authority! "You will not be promoted. Darren has—"

Those words were buried in other people's objections.

I turned and left, went back to my desk, leaving the chaos. I walked out with my research. I was told that everyone else left the lab and did not return for a week in protest.

The university was furious with Xavier, especially when my attorney called. No one wanted to work for Xavier. Xavier was let go by the university. Xavier didn't work again at the same level, all because he wouldn't give a woman a chance. It was that lack of a deserved promotion—and a top hat and lacy parasol—that finally had me writing my time travel romance novels full speed. Overt sexism, one could say, was the last impetus that launched my career.

McKenzie Rae Dean evolved for me instantly; she'd been in the back of my mind playing, spying, dancing, time traveling, and falling in love with various men (all Toran) for years.

I worked on the book nonstop, McKenzie Rae talking in my head. I hardly went anywhere. My attorney sent a check from the university.

It took six months. I edited it eight times. I sent it to five agents at once. I didn't hear from one agent because, I heard later, he had left his agency after a nervous breakdown and went to Nepal. Three agents rejected it.

I heard from Maybelle Courten last. I signed on with her. She took my time travel romance, showed a whole bunch of publishers at once, and almost all declined. Only one took it. A small house. Small advance.

I was elated.

I dedicated it to my mother and late father, but at the end of the book, in the acknowledgments, I wrote, "To Xavier, who refused to promote a woman in his department, me, because I have female plumbing. That caveman-like, discriminatory, ignorant attitude helped launch this book. I hear you work at a deli now."

When *Scottish Legends, Bagpipes, and Kilts, A Romantic Time Travel Adventure*, Book Number One, came out, it went nowhere the first few weeks, and my publishing house was disappointed and antsy. I kept writing. I loved writing. Writing was an escape for me. I could escape into McKenzie Rae. Three months later it was on the best-seller lists.

What tossed me onto the list? A national talk show host. Leah Hagen was smart-alecky, blunt, and funny. She said her daughter gave it to her and she liked the "titillating sex scenes. We should all have shuddering orgasms, like McKenzie Rae Dean!"

That was it. The "titillating sex scenes" and "shuddering orgasms" comment. Which was amusing because I felt the book was more about romance and history, with scientific leanings about time travel, parallel time, black holes, worm holes, the speed of light, etc., than titillating sex.

I went from a laboratory at a university to an international bestseller. It about blew the synapses out of my cranium. (From a neurological perspective, to be clear, this can't happen.)

I'm told that the agents and publishing houses that declined the book have been in mourning ever since.

Gee whiz. Too bad for them.

* * *

Toran walked in my door that night, work boots on, and stopped.

My legs were shaking. I had chosen the red negligee with lace and garters, and the heels with the fluffy furry thing. I knew I would hardly be able to walk with those suckers on, so I stood still.

"Hello, Toran."

He didn't speak for a second, but he did slam the door behind him. His eyes traveled all over, up and down and to the side. I stuck a hip out and put my hand on it. I think I stuck it out too far, as my back briefly cramped.

"This is a surprise," he said, eyes wide. "The best surprise. You are . . ." He waved a hand. "You are . . ." He shook his head, his voice rough, low. "Charlotte . . ."

I was still shaking as he strode up like one of the chivalrous men in my books, wrapped those long arms around me, and pulled me to that muscled chest. He bent his head and kissed me, and that kiss was a long one. The long one went into another long one, and a longer one after that, and we ended up on my couch, limbs all entangled and panting.

He knew how to get that piece of red silk off me.

Damn, I thought later, laughing to myself. He was quick.

Afterward, Scottish Warrior grabbed a blanket to put over us, kissed me, and we took a nap.

I am a fan of naps. Catnaps. Even Silver Cat was napping.

I woke up from my catnap on top of Toran and gave him a kiss on his cheek. The cheek on his face, not the cheek on his buttocks.

"You have beautiful eyes that follow me around every day, Char. I can hardly concentrate on my work at all anymore."

"I couldn't concentrate on my work before I came back to Scotland, and now I can't concentrate at all." I thought about that. "I think concentrating is overrated."

He laughed. "Ah, me too." He kissed me slow and easy, then

ran his hands up, and down, and up, and down, all over my body. "I liked the lacy stuff. It was . . ." He made a groaning, happy sound.

"It was?"

"Sexy. Like you, Charlotte. The second I saw you, when you arrived from the States, I thought, 'That is one sexy woman.' "

"You're joking." I thought of my hair, my broken glasses, and my clothes.

His brows came together. "No. Why would I joke about that?"

"I wasn't sexy."

"Oh yes, honey. You have always been sexy. Put that red . . . whatever you call it . . . back on. I want to see you."

"That contraption is rather tricky." He helped me. I tried to walk in the heels. That went poorly. Toran caught me on the way down.

It was Japanese night, so I made hibachi steak, shrimp, and fried rice in the red lingerie and my cheetah flats, to feel animalistic. No need to break an ankle.

We didn't make it to dessert immediately, which was peppermint creams dipped in chocolate. We ate them in bed later. He ate two creams off my breasts. I ate one off his missile. The missile took off again.

"Magic Four Power, begin!" King Toran, Queen Bridget, King Pherson, and I, Queen Charlotte, put our fists in a circle, then spun around. When we were done spinning we were new and improved children, superhero royalty!

Our goal: rescue three children who had been captured by a towering, English-speaking scorpion who ate children for dinner. We ran down to the ocean and threw rocks at him, then sprinted up the beach and into the hills, where we fought him with swinging tree branches and our mighty fists.

King Toran and I climbed a tree. He pulled me up with one hand and made sure I wouldn't fall off while he yelled, "Victory to us all!"

I thought he was so cool. So handsome.

"Victory to us all!" I shouted back. When I wavered on my branch in the tree, Toran stabilized me again and said, "Now, don't fall off, Queen Charlotte."

"Okay, King Toran. I won't."

And I didn't fall off. But that's because his hand was there, making sure that I didn't.

Dear Charlotte,

It was delightful to see you in the village on Thursday. Thank you for offering to bring me one of your butterfly bushes. It will be a complementary foil to my pink valerian and my cuckoo flowers.

Sincerely yours,

Chief Constable Ben Harris

A friend of your parents, may the bagpipes of heaven surround the soul of your father, my friend.

PS Gitanjali and I had a splendid dinner at my house, in the garden, two nights ago. We sat under the clematis vine, next to a new barrel of petunias I planted, pinks and magentas. I bought ravioli, spaghetti, lasagna, and manicotti from Luigi's. She said she might like Italian food, so I wanted to give her a sampling. I do believe she liked it.

She was thrilled with the elephant tea set, and I received a kiss on the cheek.

She has consented to have another dinner with me. She did insist on making it. I don't want to trouble her, but I must say I am delighted.

Thank you, Charlotte, for putting in a good word for me.

Toran and I talked about Bridget. We worried about her. When Toran had first told me he didn't know where she was, I had paid a Swiss detective for three weeks to search in Europe.

He couldn't find her. He was apologetic, offered to give half the money back. I declined. I had gotten his report and I knew he'd tried. He even worked four days longer than I'd paid him.

"She may be living under another name or under a bridge. I was able to trace a few trails, even found that she'd been in and out of two hospitals, one in London, one in Paris, but nothing came of it. . . ."

I knew Bridget was never far from Toran's mind. He himself made a trip for three days, in the midst of so much work on his farm, the apples needing shipping and delivering, and found no trace of her.

"God in heaven, Charlotte, I hope that Bridget is not dead."

I hugged him. I hoped she wasn't, either.

Dear St. Ambrose Ladies' Gab, Garden, and Gobble Group,

We continue to talk and talk and talk until my head splits about what to do for this blasted fund-raiser, and we have not even decided on who, or what, should get the money yet, not that we've had impressive financial results in the past, anyhow.

But I think the answer is simple: we should sell marijuana plants.

We can do it in my barn next to the pigs with grow lights, or we can use my greenhouse. We'll make a fortune.

Olive Oliver

Remember, sign your name to this letter, then pass it around to the rest of the ladies. Rowena, try not to spill so much wine this time.

To the ladies of Garden Gobbling Groupies,

I agree with Olive. We should sell marijuana plants.

How illegal is it really, when one gets down to it?

I would like a joint. The Arse told the children that I had broken up our marriage because I was grumpy. He neglected to mention that he was bedding The Slut for a year before I knew anything. The Slut dropped by yesterday with one of the kid's coats and told me I needed to "give it a go and get over it," and "quit being vindictive," and "let them (The Arse and The Slut) be happy in their newfound love," and I was a "bitter and unhappy witch."

I threw a ceramic toad at her. It broke. Missed its target. So fun to watch her run with those fake boobs, so I threw a second toad at her.

I do think a joint would help me calm down, and I will be our first customer.

I sold ten of my Scottish rock necklaces to Kacie's boutique. They all sold. She has ordered twenty-five more. I am in business.

Rowena

To Garden Gabbling Gob Women,

Is this a joke that I am not in on? We're not seriously thinking of selling marijuana for the fund-raiser.

We can't. We'll be arrested. We'll be fined, have to go to court, maybe jail. Intent to distribute, possession, that sort of thing. No one is going to do well here in jail, especially Lorna. Everyone will hate her. (When you sign this note, do not send it to Lorna.)

No to pot. I'll lose my job, and I like using surgical tools on people's bodies, cutting them open, taking things out, trying not to get sprayed with blood. The human body is an endless thrill for me.

And for heaven's sake, Gitanjali is dating Chief Constable Ben Harris. She can't grow pot.

Perhaps we can sell our husbands? You know, like they do in the movies? Put your husband up in a kilt on stage and see if someone will buy him. No peeking up the kilt unless you buy him.
Kenna

Ladys,
Marijuana is herb. I read on it. Now I know this. I growing herbs. I be part of marijuana grow. I put in soups.
With peace and love,
Gitanjali

Ladies,
Perhaps we should sell poppies instead. Pretty, and not illegal unless one makes them into opiates. This is a complicated process and we might have to work with frightening killers, so I would vote no on manufacturing and distribution and yes on selling the poppies as is.
Charlotte

I truly had no idea what to sell for a fund-raiser. This isn't my field.

13

ST. AMBROSE DAILY NEWS

FIFTEENTH ANNIVERSARY OF MISSING PRIEST
Part Three

By Carston Chit, *Reporter*

The disappearance of Father Angus Cruickshank from St. Cecilia's Catholic School for Girls more than fifteen years ago, on Wednesday, May 14, 1975, has always been a mystery.

The murder theories continue to abound.

When I first started researching this topic I asked myself, "Who would want to murder Father Cruickshank?"

The question later became, "Who wouldn't?"

Yes, there were many people who might have taken aim.

Who, you ask?

And why?

Ah, that.

First you need to know of Father Cruickshank's upbringing.

Angus Cruickshank had a difficult childhood. He was born in County Cork, Ireland, to a single mother who had a series of boyfriends.

In fact, it was rumored that his mother was a prostitute, at least some of the time. There was no known father, and no other siblings, though Cruickshank repeatedly mentioned visiting a brother when he periodically left St. Cecilia's for vacations.

Cruickshank was tall, and hardy, which came in handy when he had to defend himself. By the time he was twelve, he had been arrested for stabbing one of his mother's "friends."

When he was thirteen he was arrested for beating another one of his mother's "friends" until the man was a bloody pulp.

In talking to a number of people in County Cork, who knew him as a boy, the responses all seemed to follow the same theme.

A local grocer, Boyd McDonagh, who employed Angus, said he was a "hard worker, but his head turned round at the girls, and the girls did not return the lad's affection. It infuriated him, damn popped him, that it did."

A teacher, Caileen O'Coughlin, remembers him as a boy with a temper. "He had a quick switch, my Lord he did. He could be polite as could be, don't you know it, then he would fly into a rage. That's why he was expelled."

Darker stories persist. Two women spoke to me about their experience with Father Cruickshank.

They told the same story. When Father Cruickshank was no more than eighteen, he cornered all of them and molested them.

One woman, who wanted only her first name, Keela, used, for fear of Father Cruickshank locating her again, said, "I still have me nightmares. I was thirteen, my wee back against a brick wall and he shoved himself inside of me, then put his hand around me neck and squeezed and said if I told, he would kill me and me brother. You see? How I'm sweating now? I am still afraid of him."

Another woman, Riona, who also refused to allow her last name in print, said that Father Cruickshank used to wait until school got out, then he would chase her to her home. Once he pulled her into an alley, another time to a park. "When my father found out, he beat the living tar out of Angus. He didn't bother me after that. He went after my poor friend, Gwen. Gwen killed herself about three years after that, poor thing. I still feel it was my fault."

There are unconfirmed rumors that he strangled two women, both still unaccounted for and both of whom had rejected his advances. At some point, Father Timothy Borho, of County Cork, took the young Cruickshank under his wing.

Cruickshank was distraught at his mother's death, of pneumonia, according to her sisters. He was twenty-two. He then entered the priesthood at the encouragement of Father Borho.

"He never should have become a priest," Riona said. "Obviously the Vatican didn't do its job."

There are other reasons to believe that the Vatican did not do their job.

We'll cover that in Part Four.

After I read the article, I picked up Bridget's letters again.

September sometime in 1973

Dear Charlotte,

Six months.

That's how long they kept me in the crazy insane asylum for crazy people. I was not crazy going in, but I think I am crazy now. I cry all the time and I can't think and all these pills they make me take. Pills and pills. Screaming fighting throwing punching wall people.

My parents came to get me.

I ignored them even though they both looked old and tired and pale. We left and I did not speak to them. They made me come home and I am not even Bridget anymore.

My father said to me, "I hope you can live a more Godly, virtuous life now, Bridget. I've been praying for you and when we're home we will pray together until you understand what redemption means. You will be at home with us as we cannot trust you to keep your skirt down around boys. You will do penance and spend your time in prayer, reading the Bible to purify your soul and mind. Your virginity is gone, you will be worthless goods to most men, but we'll hope one day a man can look past this mockery of our faith and our church."

My mother said, "I love you."

I didn't answer them. If my mom loved me she wouldn't have taken away my baby my baby my baby and sent me to the crazy insane crazy asylum. I turned around and screamed. My father hit me in the face and told me to shut up or he would take me right back into the crazy asylum crazy insane.

When we got home, I went straight to my room. All that money that my mother's parents gave me for my birthday? I took it. I left that night when they were asleep.

I will miss Toran. I love him. I called him before I left. He didn't know what had happened. He was at university, and in the summer my parents said I was still with the nuns learning how to be a nun. He knew they were lying to him. He said what happened what happened where are you. I couldn't tell him, though. I'm dirty. Slut. Bad. No baby.

I hate my parents. They took my baby my baby my baby. They locked me in an insane asylum crazy because a priest said I was crazy. I will never see them again. They will never be able to do that to me again.

I want my daughter. I will go to Our Lady of Peace, A Home for Unwed Mothers first and ask who has her and go and get her back. I did not say they could take her. Never. My baby is my baby.

Love,
Bridget

Still in September in 1973. A bad time.

Dear Charlotte,

I took a bus to Our Lady of Peace but the nuns said they didn't know who took my daughter. I told them give me the papers give me the papers give me the papers and they said that Father Cruickshank had taken some of the paperwork. I cried and cried and they held me and said, "Poor dear, poor dear."

I went to St. Cecilia's to see Father Cruickshank and make him tell me. Sister Margaret asked me if Father Cruickshank had raped me and was he the father of the baby, and I said yes. She hugged me and said she was sorry sorry sorry. She said she was trying to get him punished, that there were other girls, that she was trying to get the police involved, but the police were not cooperating and neither was the Vatican.

She said he had been in Belfast before his

placement at St. Cecilia's, and she had called a nun up there, a friend, and they had had problems with him, too, at another girls school. He had been in Limerick before that. Problems there, too. The nuns in both places had reported him to the church, but nothing was done. Nothing was done. Nothing.

I asked her where my daughter went and she said she didn't know. She said that a lot of their own paperwork was missing. She thinks that Father Cruickshank burned it. He was not there when I was there. He was visiting his brother.

Sister Margaret said that my parents called and asked if I was there and another nun, not Sister Margaret, said yes, and my father was coming. Sister Margaret gave me some money and she drove me to the bus stop to get away. She said, "I'm so sorry, Bridget. I'm sorry. God bless you, child."

I am leaving. I hate my father. I hate my mother. I hate Father Cruickshank. My parents would never believe me if I said Father Cruickshank did it. Pound. Rip. Blood.

No one will. Then he would kill Toran.

My father thinks I'm a whore. He said that, "whore."

Gone. I am gone.

I saw Father Cruickshank's silver cat. I hope it still bites him.

Love,
Bridget

November 20 or 24, 1973

Dear Charlotte,

I am in Edinburgh. There are babies in strollers with blue eyes and they could be my baby. I cry all the time. I don't know what's wrong with me.

I don't have anywhere to sleep, and I have no money for food. I know I look homeless but that is because I am.

I saw a man who was fat like my father and I hated him. He walked by me when I was leaning against a wall and then he walked back and said are you okay and I said I am and he said you don't look okay and he went away and came back with pasta and I ate it and I said he reminded me of my father who took the baby from me and he said he was sorry and I said it's okay and I ate the pasta.

I don't think he's a good man but he said I could stay at his place and I don't have a job so I said yes.

Love,
Bridget

January, 1974, don't know the day or date

Dear Charlotte,

Bad things happened with the man who gave me pasta.

Bridget

March, don't know the date, 1974

Dear Charlotte,

I am in Athens and Greece is pretty but it is old and old old old I tried to call Toran but I do not have money so I called collect and he sent a plane ticket but I forgot when and when I went to the airport it was gone I could be at the wrong airport but the right airport would be by your house on the island.

And I do not like needles but I like them too because they take away the pain baby do you know where my baby is I do not she is gone.

Pain. When I get home I put these letters in the brown box so you'll know what happened.
Love
Bridget

December 1974

Dear Charlotte,
I saw Pherson. Toran found me in London in the hospital and brought me to his apartment at the university.
I still love Pherson.
He deserves more. Better. Cleaner. Not a dirty person like me. They said what's wrong, Bridget, what happened, what happened, but I can't tell them the truth I am ashamed and they would kill Father Cruickshank if they knew and go to jail or he would kill them. That gun that gun that gun.
I miss my daughter.
I cannot do this anymore. My memories crowd in and they suffocate me, they smother me, they take me away again. Back there. Father Cruickshank. His hands. The shed. The baby. The baby that is gone. I can't find her. Drugs. I can't think. I cry all the time. Where is she? I hate my parents. I am so angry. I am always angry.
Love you.
Love Pherson and Toran.
I want to die.
Bridget

I was shaking when I was done.
Bridget, where are you? Please come home.

The Garden Gobble Chat Group (or something like that) was meeting at Lorna Lester's. Her home was on the east side of the village and plain. Dull. No color. A lot like her.

She opened the door to me and said, "Do take off your shoes, Charlotte. I don't want any dirt, dust, grime, or oils inside." She sniffed.

I almost turned around right there. Not because I have an objection to taking off my shoes. Shoes track in all sorts of unwanted germs including, but not limited to, dog feces, spittle, dead gum, bacteria, diseases, and sewage.

It was the way she said it. Her tone. As if I was dirty, dusty, grimy, and oily.

Olive was right behind me and said, "No problem. Before I came over I was in the barn with the horses and, my my my, Dander and Prince could not stop dropping their presents!"

Lorna's face tightened, like oatmeal instantly drying.

I didn't step over the threshold. I stood and tried to determine if I wanted to proceed. It was one of those times when you wonder if you should say yes or no, and cut the person out of your life altogether and forget she existed. For example, Pluto. We all forget Pluto's out there.

"Come on in. Don't loiter." Lorna stepped back. I saw that Rowena was inside, with wine, her red hair in a ponytail, as was Gitanjali, resplendent in a green tunic, sequined and shot through with silver threads.

I wanted to talk to Rowena, and I wanted to talk to Olive, Gitanjali, and Kenna. Even Malvina, if she would speak.

Olive pushed me in the back as I stared at Lorna's squishy face. Could I do it? I thought of bacteria. I thought of how they squiggled in a petri dish. All sorts of diseases squiggle differently. Under a microscope, they become alive, sometimes dangerous.

"In you go, Charlotte," Olive said. "Gitanjali told me in town today that she was making rogan josh, which is lamb curry. I'm not going to miss it. I brought tipsy cake with trifle sponges." Olive gave me another shove, and in I went. She is a strong woman from taking care of all those chickens.

I had brought beer-battered fish to share. I should have brought laxatives for Lorna's tea. She needed it.

* * *

"Tonight's discussion is about fertilizer," Lorna said, after serving tea. The tea was tasteless. "This newfangled organic type, which I'm sure doesn't work, versus what I've been using all my life, Donald's All Purpose Enricher. Let me tell you about Donald's."

Malvina kept her eyes on the floor. I watched her. She looked up, smiled at me. I smiled back. Poor her. Mother like that.

Unbelievably, Lorna went on and on, her notes in her hand. Who knew there could be so much to say about fertilizer? I tapped my jeans, tight and stylish, at least according to the saleslady. I was wearing a pink shirt with a hint of a ruffle at the neckline. Everyone noticed my makeover, no glasses, haircut, two of Rowena's rock necklaces around my neck, and were complimentary. Except for Lorna, who said, "Well, aren't we all fancy dolled up now? Like your mother. Fancy doll."

I said to Lorna, "She was not a doll. I am not a doll. If I were a doll I wouldn't be thinking what I'm thinking of you, as I would not have neurons and synapses and electro-chemical signaling."

She humphed and said, "I don't know what you're talking about," before she and her belligerent bottom flounced off.

As Lorna droned on, complete with photos and graphs, I saw Olive nodding off, her teacup in her hand, her chin dipping. I took her teacup. Pretty soon she was slumped against me on Lorna's pink flowered couch. The walls matched the couch.

Lorna snapped, "Olive!"

Olive snapped to attention, muttering something about her pigs. She adjusted her knitted horse scarf. The horse, I believe, was stoned. It was probably not intentional. She had confided to me that she needed a broader market for animal scarves. I told her we could sell the stoned horse scarves with the marijuana for our fund-raiser if we changed our minds. She said that was a splendid idea.

"Please listen attentively," Lorna reprimanded. "I have taken time with my presentation. A proper speech, no clichés or extraneous information. I take Garden Club seriously."

Lorna droned on again, like a sledgehammer on low thrum.

Olive slumped on my shoulder one more time. Her breath smelled like beer-battered fish.

I am interested in the compounds of fertilizer, and it's vaguely interesting that it can be used to make bombs. In fact, when I was in college, several of my university friends and I did make a small bomb, which we exploded in the woods in the Sierra Nevada mountain range. It was impressive.

We did, however, decide not to do it again, as we did not want to risk being arrested, but more than that, we killed two squirrels. This was extremely upsetting to both me and my friend, Sabrina Hillenstein.

Sabrina insisted on a funeral service. So the two of us, along with our friends Tara Wong, Rhonda Bronowski, and D'Ambria Jefferson, had a squirrel funeral service.

There we were, proud of ourselves and our bomb, burying two squirrels. Sabrina said a tearful prayer that ended with, "So thanks, God, for furry creatures." Tara said, "Thank you, squirrels, for giving your lives in our pursuit of weaponry excellence." Rhonda said, "I am so proud of us for making a bomb," which did not honor the squirrels, and D'Ambria Jefferson recited a long poem by Thoreau about nature.

Rowena interrupted my fond bomb-making thoughts. "We sure are talking a lot about a pile of shit tonight."

Kenna said, "Too much. Let's talk about women's issues."

"What women's issue do you want to talk about?" Olive sat straight up. The stoned horse shifted with her.

"I think we should talk about our uteruses," Rowena said.

"Me too. I was thinking about my uterus the other day," Olive said. "Right here." She pointed to her uterus so we could find it.

I don't know why, but I looked down at my stomach. I saw Gitanjali do the same.

Malvina wrapped her arms around herself. I thought I saw a tear.

"What do you want to say about the women's U, medically speaking?" Kenna asked Rowena.

"I want to ask if a uterus is a positive thing or a negative thing for a woman," Rowena said. "What are the pros and cons of a uterus, according to you all, my fellow gardening women and uterus owners?"

"The pros are you can have a baby," Olive Oliver said.

"I have not finished," Lorna Lester snipped, wiggling her imperious bottom, "my talk about fertilizers. I was going to begin Section C, fertilizers and birds."

"Birds don't need fertilizers," Rowena said. "They'll grow without it."

"You fertilize birds? That mistake," Gitanjali said, worried, hands fluttering.

I almost laughed. I squeezed my knees together tight so my bladder, which is now and then a mite weak, wouldn't leak.

"I know birds don't need to be fertilized," Lorna huffed. "*Gitanjali.*"

And there it was again. Putting Gitanjali in her place. Foreigner. Different culture, religion, color. Threatening.

"But how do we fertilize and make sure that the birds are never harmed," Lorna said with an edge, "except for blackbirds. They can all fall out of the sky and die as far as I'm concerned. Cursed birds. And seagulls." She pursed her thin lips. "And I am not enthusiastic about eagles, either. With those talons. My thorough fertilizer research shows—"

"The negatives are cramps," Rowena said. "I have them right now. It's like I'm being stabbed in the gut with a sword. Why did God give women periods when they don't want to get pregnant? Why can't we turn them on and off based on when we want to get pregnant?"

"Thoughtful question," Olive said, nodding her head, her white braid over her left shoulder. "There was a mistake made." She pointed upward. "In heaven. We all make mistakes."

"Why were we made to bleed once a month?" Malvina said. "Why not the men?"

We were, again, shocked to hear a noninebriated Malvina speak, but I gathered myself, quick as I could, so as not to embarrass her.

"That's easy," I said. "Men wouldn't be able to take the pain. Men are the weaker sex. In addition, a menstrual cycle is an evolutionary defect. In modern times, this should have changed.

"In the past, people didn't live long. Girls regularly got pregnant in their teens. We don't need girls to get pregnant in their teens now. From a world population perspective, if women could get pregnant only from the time they were twenty-five to, say, forty, the population would take an enormous nosedive."

I did the mathematical calculations, the numbers staggering. "The math is boggling my mind. Millions of people, billions soon, would not even be here. No future water wars."

"My uterus is sad and bored," Malvina said. "Nothing to do. Nothing changes. Same thing, every day. No hope. No light. No action. It's afraid it will die without living life the way it wants to live. It's scared that something bad could happen, but more scared that being alone will kill it. It gets tired of reading books every night. Alone."

My mouth dropped open, as did everyone else's. I tried to push my glasses up my nose, then remembered I didn't wear them anymore. I glanced over at Lorna. Shiver my science beakers, I think her eyes filled with tears.

"My uterus is old and cranky and giving me hot flashes," Kenna said. "It's middle aged and I am not that interested in sex anymore. How can I have interest in sex? I operate on people, I go home, my husband and I have dinner and clean up and pass out in bed. Last time we had sex I had a hot flash. Sweat flowing. He had to get off and fan me with a sheet. By the time he was done we weren't in the mood anymore. But it's okay. The older he gets, the more he farts. We laugh about it. I sweat profusely and he farts easily."

"I'm an old woman who has been married only the last ten years," Olive said, "and I find sex freeing. A gift." She raised her fists in the air. "One, two, three, boom boom me! Four, five, six, let's see that dick. I give it to my man!"

"I am trying to *give* the rest of my talk about fertilizer," Lorna huffed and puffed. "The second part of my presentation involves the pH balance of soil, which, as you can see by my garden, I have mastered." She eyed me with dark disapproval. "Some people don't understand how critical it is to understand pH."

"I understand pH," I said.

"Do you?" She raised her eyebrows.

"Yes." I tilted my head and tried to calculate her IQ. Sometimes it's possible with people to get a range. Hers was on the lower end.

"Men are not as intelligent as women," Kenna said. "I see it in the doctors I work with. Give me a woman with a uterus any day. More detail oriented. Listen better to their patients, less ego, harder working."

"Men think with their—" Gitanjali pointed down at her crotch. "Their wiggly stick. But not Chief Constable Benny Harris. He kind man."

I think she blushed.

"He honest man."

Now I knew she was blushing.

"The wiggly stick hampers their judgment," Rowena said. "Hence, The Slut."

"My husband thinks with his wiggly too much. It's like a snake that pokes me. Poking around," Kenna said. "Sometimes in my head I call him The Poker. That's a secret."

"My uterus would like a poke, I think," Malvina said. "I think."

Third time Malvina speaks.

Lorna said, "Malvina!"

Malvina said, "Yes?"

"I'm waiting for wine," Olive said. The stoned horse looked like he could use some, too.

"Wine?" Lorna arched an eyebrow. "I am not serving wine. Wine is the devil's punch."

That was hypocritical, given our last garden ladies drunken meeting.

"What? No wine?" Rowena said. She actually gasped.

"Don't worry, ladies," Kenna cackled. She opened her flowered backpack. "Scottish Scotch, for medicinal reasons only. Best in the world. You do have glasses, right-o, Lorna?"

We should not have done what we did after Scottish Scotch. It was crazy and impetuous. But Rowena was furious with her ex-husband for not paying child support again. I don't blame her. You have children, pay for them. Her car broke down. She couldn't fix it. The house payment was late again. The kids had things that had to be paid for. The telephone bill was overdue.

So we went to get one of Olive's beloved pigs. Olive drove, as she'd only had one shot. She tightened her stoned horse scarf and off we went. The pig's name is Hallelujah. Rowena wrote out a total bill for child support and we poked a hole in the top of the note and threaded a rope through it, then put the rope around Hallelujah's neck.

Lorna, drunk as a skunk and more fun now, straddled the pig to keep it in place and said, "I have caught a pig with a uterus. Here, piggy piggy, here, piggy piggy."

Malvina helped with the tying of the note and said, "I am doing things I've never done before with Gobbling Group."

Kenna said, "He looks tasty to me. Bacon! I am so hungry. Had to take out three badly infected appendixes today. Shredded my appetite at lunch."

When we were back in the car, Gitanjali said, slightly inebriated, "I think I sing a song from India," and she did. It went on for a long, melodious time, and we swayed to the notes.

Hallelujah is a quiet but small pig. If he was a person, he would definitely be a physicist.

We went to The Slut's house, where Rowena's husband lived.

What we did was immature.

Inappropriate.

Possibly a tiny bit of animal abuse, as Hallelujah was confused and not snug at home.

Kenna, for medicinal reasons only, rubbed Scottish Scotch on the pig. "Now he's drunk," she said.

Olive gave Hallelujah a shove in the butt, and Kenna shut the door, ever so quietly. Gitanjali sang, "Find your peace and love, piggy friend, sing a song and la la la, lo lo lo," and I put my hand over her mouth. "Lo lo lo."

Malvina said, "I hope we get arrested for this. I never do anything wrong and I'd like to be seen as a naughty woman."

"Naughty, naughty," I said. "Naughty!"

"I want to be seen as competently vengeful," Rowena said.

Lorna said, "Men are motherfucking pigs." She farted.

I laughed so hard when I heard the pig knock into something and squeal that I bent over double, Rowena leaning over me, laughing and cursing The Arse.

We ran away, lickety-split. I had to stop periodically because I thought I was going to wet my pants. I squirted a tiny squirt but kept running. My bladder is not strong. We sprinted past the lot where the Zimmerman Factory had burned down.

Next time I went to Gobbling and Gabbing Gardening Gangsters I would wear a diaper. I thought of myself in a diaper and laughed again.

The next day I called Ben Harris about the missing child support check. He got right on it, even though it's not his job to do so. Rowena was paid that afternoon, and The Arse returned the Hallelujah pig, as ordered by the chief.

Toran and I worked on his farm during the week. He worked twelve to fourteen hours a day harvesting the apples, his muscles strong and tight, squeezable. On the weekends, for a few hours, we worked together in my garden. We both found it pleasing and relaxing.

We put in a wooden wishing well I'd found at a thrift shop. We planted perennials. I like to see plants and flowers come back, year after year. We also planted violets, bluebells, celandine, and poppies.

I had no idea that being covered in dirt could be so romantic, but with Toran it was.

I kissed him. Pretty soon we had to put our shovels down.

It's best I live way out in the country.

* * *

Toran and I have torrid sex.

It's the same heavy gymnastics panting sort of sex I write about in my books.

Sometimes he walks into my home and we can't wait to get to the bedroom, so we use the floor. We indulge in the shower. We stroke and sigh outside at night under the stars, on top of a blanket. We try all the positions that I know about because I have a wild imagination and because I have bought a number of books on sex positions.

I bought the books on sex positions only because of my research for my writing, which goes without saying, as there was no one on my island to do sex positions with.

Our love making is passionate and lusty and I let myself go. If Dan The Vibrator was here I would toss him out and say, "I will not miss you, Dan. I have my own vibrator now. His name is Toran."

Our foreplay can last a long and lush time or only fiery seconds.

But we laugh during sex, too, sometimes. We smile, we are gentle, we are sweet, and then that passion rocks through and Toran grabs my naked self and lifts me right onto his . . . ah . . . *Scottish sword.*

The Scottish sword knows exactly what to do as it thrusts and parries and drives in again. . . .

After my first book hit the best-seller list, I felt like I'd been run over.

It was overwhelmingly busy. My publishing house insisted I go on a book tour. I had to talk to people—some on TV, others in a radio station. I had to go to book fairs and conferences. I had to make speeches. I came off stiff, forced, like a dysfunctional robot. Even Maybelle said, "Loosen up, you're scaring people." I allowed that robotic, incessant workload to go on for three months.

I hated it. I am reserved and private. I am not socially adept. I know I'm awkward. Polite talk bores me. I don't like shallow conversations, as they seem pointless. I don't like being the center of attention. I don't like people gushing over me. I am not comfortable with praise.

As a whole, I wish people well. As a group, I do not like being around them. I like to be alone.

The only group I've been comfortable around, ever, was Clan TorBridgePherLotte, fighters of the Crusading Giants, defenders against the marauding monsters of St. Ambrose.

After three months of the book crap, I was exhausted and shaky. I'd had a scare on a plane. It wobbled in the air, then sank, then landed quick, flight aborted. My flight paranoia bubbled over. I refused to do any more publicity, told my publishing house that they were making a ton of money off of me and that PR and marketing was their job.

I escaped to Whale Island. I bought my house, whale view, and five acres for cash; bought a ten-year-old pickup truck that rumbled and growled; saved the rest; and disappeared.

I watched the whales spouting off and the deer trying to get through my fence so they could eat my garden vegetables. I studied an old raccoon I named Chesterfield as he came out in the daylight, that crazy fool. I grew calendulas and marigolds, purple phacelias and delicate sweet peas, coral fountain amaranth and bachelor's buttons.

I was entertained by squirrels and chipmunks, seals and red foxes, none of whom wanted me to give speeches or take hugs from strangers who loved my book.

I had an extensive playground built for my cats outside, two story and enclosed by wire so they wouldn't get eaten by wild animals. There were catwalks, perches, and open areas. I watched them play while I wrote.

I told no one on the island I was Georgia Chandler.

They knew me as Charlotte Mackintosh. No one asked me many questions. The island is like that. We mind our own business.

Sometimes I loved it, sometimes I thought the loneliness was going to kill me down dead. I had McKenzie Rae Dean and my cats and garden, talks now and then with the obsessive-compulsive origami man, and Olga, my friend at the café/art gallery. And I cooked. I cooked all the meals and treats we ate in Scotland, many that my father made. It made me feel closer to him.

My best friend, though, was a woman I hadn't seen in twenty years whom I wrote letters to and reached by phone now and then. That was pathetic and sad when I thought about it too much, but the truth was, I loved getting letters from Bridget and writing back to her.

And my life went on. Alone.

The woman stumbled in front of Toran's house but caught herself before she fell flat on the driveway. She yanked herself up, stopped, walked two steps, and braced her hands on her knees.

I dropped my cutting scissors into the daisies I was dead heading and ran toward her.

"Are you all right? Can I help you?"

She didn't answer, but ambled toward me, swaying like a reed in a pond, pushed this way and that. She was thin, too thin. She was wearing a black knit hat, odd in this warm weather; jeans; scuffed boots; and a plaid work shirt.

She had white-blond hair.

I caught Bridget when she pitched forward and fell straight into my arms. She said one word: Charlotte. She smiled before she passed out.

Toran and I held hands as we watched Bridget sleep in the hospital. It was hard to call it sleep. Bridget seemed half dead. The doctors had been in and out, as had the nurses. They had taken blood, performed their examinations, done their tests. Bridget had hardly moved. When she did periodically wake up, she would smile at Toran and me weakly, then pass out again.

Bridget had scars up and down her arms from drugs. There were no recent marks, though. She had a horrendous scar on her left shoulder that looked as if a crow had dug a claw in and pulled. She had another scar on her collarbone, like an S. She was pale and gaunt. Her fever was 104 degrees, her skin flaky with open sores.

She was horribly ill.

We waited for the test results, for the doctors, for the answers. Looking at her, I knew none of the answers were going to be good. This was not the flu. I braced myself, my hand gripped in Toran's. I often wiped the tears off my cheeks, then wiped the tears off Toran's.

My poor man. He was shattered.

Three doctors and three nurses entered Bridget's hospital room ten days later in full hospital garb. Scrubs, hoods, masks, gloves, booties over their shoes. They were all worried, fidgety. Three stayed as far away from Bridget and the bed as they could.

"What is it?" Toran asked, standing up.

"What's wrong?" I stood up, too. We had spent the night, again, leaning against the wall, leaning against each other.

One of the doctors indicated a table for us to sit at while another doctor opened the window.

"Mr. Ramsay. Ms. Mackintosh, I'm afraid I have bad news," the doctor said through his mask. He was about sixty. Overweight, out of shape. Gray hair. Eyebrow cocked.

I held Toran's hand.

"We were unclear of her diagnosis. We ran many tests, all negative, as you know, so we began reaching further afield."

"Yes," Toran said. "And?"

"Your sister," the doctor said, with doom, "has acquired immune deficiency syndrome. It is also known as AIDS." He crossed the fingers of his gloved hands together and leaned back in his chair.

Toran and I squeezed each other's hand at the same second, stricken.

"You may not have heard of it—" The doctor had a pompous tone.

"I've heard of it," Toran and I snapped at the same time.

"By her symptoms I believe she's had AIDS for some time. Years. It's advanced, by my diagnosis. She is riddled with it, riddled."

I slumped in my chair, hardly able to breathe. When I first learned about AIDS, having been married to Drew, a gay man, whose fidelity I became unsure of, I immediately went to get tested.

I was negative. In the ten-day wait for the test results, I studied the disease to its minutest cellular detail, my slight hypochondria swelling in my throat until it dang near choked me.

I knew it killed. I knew there wasn't a cure. Now, in 1990, nothing had changed from nine years ago when it first burst onto the scene.

I turned to stare at my friend, Bridget, a friend I didn't know but thought I did, a friend who did not tell the truth to shield me from her shame, a friend who had been crushed by an evil man, along with her health.

My eyes traveled up the tracks of her arms, one needle scar for every emotional torture.

I stifled a cry with my hand.

"AIDS," the doctor said, with unhidden disapproval now, "is quite contagious. A plague-like disease. She will have to be quarantined. Usually it is only gay men practicing immoral behaviors and their promiscuity who have it, and drug users." He steepled his gloved hands together, peering at us over the tips. "Your sister, being a drug addict . . . needles and so forth, sharing, becoming drugged together . . . that's how she acquired it, probably, but it could have been from a man. Promiscuity is common with these types of people. . . ." He wrinkled his nose, a tiny scrunch, *disgusted*.

An older nurse with gray hair said through her mask, "I hope she hasn't contaminated us." She was accusatory, angry, as if we had engineered this tragedy.

A young nurse spoke up. "As long as you don't have sex with her or share drug needles you'll be fine. You should know that already, Myrna."

"We don't need that type of commentary right now, so don't make it," Toran snapped. He was pale white, his shoulders slumped, his face aging almost as I watched.

The old nurse narrowed her eyes.

"We will keep her here in the hospital," the doctor said. "Away from the other patients, far away, behind closed doors, so they don't catch it. Could be plague-like, as I said. No one will touch her. We'll shut off the ventilation to the rest of the hospital from this room. You must shower after seeing her and wear full hospital gear when you visit so you don't catch it and spread it to others."

"Catch it?" I said, my brain starting to move. "Do you know nothing about this disease? You're a doctor, aren't you?"

He straightened. "Yes, I am. Renowned, if you must know. But this is a new, communicable disease to us. We know little. It started with the homosexuals. The fags. San Francisco. New York. Could be airborne. It could be spread by casual contact, a touch of the hand. Spittle, even." He shivered, his eyes darting to Bridget, skinny Bridget who hardly made a bump in the blankets. "She could be a threat to the health and safety of our staff and to the village. We need to prevent her from spreading this contagion."

"You need to educate yourself." What an ignorantly arrogant piss ant.

"I beg your pardon!"

"I do not beg yours," I said. "If you are going to practice medicine, practice it by knowing the facts, not indulging in unfounded hysteria and fear. She is not contagious to you or anyone here unless you decide to shoot drugs up her arm and then use the same needle to shoot them into yours. Are you planning on this activity?"

"I will not be spoken to in that tone!"

"And I will not stand by while a frightened old man, who is supposed to be knowledgeable about different diseases, just about wets his pants when discussing one of his patients."

"Excuse me!" he said, wagging a finger.

"You will need to do more than excuse yourself. You need to

study this disease so you don't engage in spreading rumors about AIDS or demonizing people with it. Surely you can pull yourself together enough to do that."

My heart was pounding. Not from the irritated, sanctimonious doctor—I was used to old/middle aged, rigidly thinking men like him—but because of poor Bridget. Sweet Bridget and her brother, my beloved Toran, who was now sitting beside his sister, holding both her hands as she lay weak, her eyes closed, a half-dead sleep claiming her. He brought their hands to his forehead. I knew he was crying.

I was going to lose it, too, in about one minute, and I'd be a sobbing mess. Sobbing messes cannot take control of situations. The ability to make sound decisions is curtailed by emotion, and first I would deal with this patronizing doctor.

"It is my job to protect my patients and my staff!" He held up his pointer finger, pompous, predictable.

"Then do your job." I pointed my pointer finger right at him. "And do it correctly."

I looked around the room. Several of the medical personnel seemed downright frightened, wanting to bolt. A couple were calm. This was their field, after all. They took care of sick people. They were professionals. One of them winked at me, another smiled. This ego-inflated doctor was another Len Xavier.

The hospital room was sterile, cold. I didn't like it. Depressing. Lonely. Alone. I could not guarantee that the employees would treat Bridget with kindness or with disgust and disapproval.

I was going to say it, but Toran said it first, his voice deep, strong. "She won't stay here. We're taking her home."

I stood up. "I'll bring the truck around."

I saw the doctor's expression of relief. "Courage, doctor," I drawled. "Be brave, little man. You'll be fine."

"I am not a little man! How dare you!"

He was, in fact, tall. "You're a little man in your heart. You lack courage, and that's all that counts, isn't it?"

He flushed behind his mask. "I will not tolerate this impertinence."

"And I will not tolerate you and your sluggish mind. Not for one more minute. You are a plague." I saw Bridget move in bed. Her eyes were open. "We're leaving, Bridget."

She nodded. "Take me away, Clan TorBridgePherLotte. We'll battle the dragons tomorrow." She mimed sword fighting, weakly.

She laughed, also weakly.

I laughed, too. Couldn't help it. It was laugh or fall apart.

On our first day home, with Bridget barely conscious, Silver Cat leaped onto Bridget's bed. She licked her cheek as if they'd been best friends forever and meowed.

Bridget's eyes widened, then she held the cat's face with a weak hand. "Father Cruickshank had a cat exactly like this. The cat used to bite him. This cat is a twin to the other one, I swear." She shivered in remembrance. "He hit the cat once, and later shot it three times."

Silver Cat settled in near Bridget's arm and stared up at her.

Silver Cat, from that moment on, would not be separated from Bridget.

14

"How are you?" A week later I reached out and held Bridget's hand. It was tiny, like the broken wing of a dying bird.

"Feeling better?" Toran asked.

Bridget was in her bedroom, the room that Toran had lovingly designed for her on the second story. Light-pink-striped bedspread, white walls, the window seat so she could read, the wide white desk where she could draw her miniature pictures.

Toran had picked two bouquets of wildflowers for her, one for her dresser and one for her nightstand next to a white lamp. He had also given her several drawing pads and handfuls of colored pencils that he'd stored for her, waiting for her return.

"Perhaps I have been better," she said, laying her head back on the pillows. She was gaunt, her cheekbones sticking out, lips pale. She had bathed, with my help, and I had washed and brushed her white-blond hair, so it looked neat, certainly better than the ragged mess it had been. Tears streamed from the corners of her blue eyes, so like Toran's, only a deeper blue, crushed blueberries.

"I'm sorry, Bridget." We had told her about her diagnosis three days after we arrived home. She was fully awake then, more rested, clean, fed, and she'd asked us what she had been diagnosed with. She had not seemed surprised and said, "I thought I might have it." I thought she would collapse, burst into tears, but she didn't. She said, "I love both of you so much."

Poor Toran. Huge Scotsman, repeat champion in the Scottish games, proud man, crying.

I wrapped an arm around him.

"I am so sorry, Toran," Bridget said.

"No, no," he said, voice cracking. "I'm sorry. I didn't protect you."

"You did, you did. Char, I am so sorry."

"You have nothing to be sorry for," I told her, wiping tears off my cheeks

"I know you're both furious with me. I lied. I caused you to worry. I didn't call you."

"Please, Bridget—" Toran said.

"I have caused you pain my whole life, I've been a terrible burden—"

"No, you haven't. Pain has been caused to you. Years of pain." Toran's neck was bent, the tears streaming down. My whole body ached from the pain in that house. "Which caused more years of pain."

"I should have tried harder, Toran. Should have stopped. Shouldn't have left all the rehab places you paid for. They reminded me . . ." Her voice pitched, raw and edgy. "Of the insane asylum. I couldn't breathe. I was so scared there. Out of control. I kept remembering all those people tied down, beaten up, hurt, yelling at themselves, hurting themselves, the staff mean . . . but I should have stayed at the rehab places. They tried there, they cared and they tried to help me."

"I understand, I do—"

And Toran did, he understood. He was a sympathetic, compassionate man who was introspective and intelligent. He had a mind that could see all angles, with depth and accuracy.

"Those drugs, they . . . I tried to stop, I did, and I would for a while, and I'd keep thinking of Father Cruickshank. I felt his hands on my neck, I could hear him ripping my clothes off. I couldn't get rid of it. I kept thinking of Legend. Out there. Without me. Gone. I never said they could take her, I never did."

"I know, sweetheart, I know."

"Taking drugs was the only thing that took that away." She tipped her face up to him, then looked at me, sick and hopeless. "Char, please forgive me. Toran, please. I can't die without you both forgiving me."

"I forgive you," we both said together.

"Bridget, we love you," I said. "I know what happened to you. I know about your daughter. I can't imagine what you've gone through."

"Aye, me too," Toran said. "A child gone. Endless heart-ache."

"I've been clean for a year. I wanted to make sure I could do it, be sober, before I came and saw you again."

"I am happy to hear it." Toran's voice broke. "So happy."

"But then I thought I shouldn't come because I was sick and getting sicker, and I'd be a burden again, but I wanted to see you. I knew . . . I knew I was dying . . . I'm so sorry."

We talked. We cried over the hopeless, devastating truth of it all. We ended up laughing, Bridget, even now, so funny.

She said, "Do you think I look more like a pasty scarecrow or a ghost? What do you think of my new look? I call it AIDS chic. I've travelled the world, and I know one thing—the drugs are bad everywhere."

We hugged.

We forgave.

What was the point of anger now, anyhow? Toran could be angry with his sister for not staying in rehab, for continuing down her destructive path. I could be angry that she lied. There wasn't enough time to be angry.

And what was there to forgive? A sixteen-year-old girl, one nightmare after another, piled on her innocent head. What she had done was heroic. Angus Cruickshank said he would kill Toran if she told. So she didn't. Her intent was to save the life of her brother.

This is what happens when nightmares claim the lives of young girls. They become women who are haunted. Then they reach for things to take away the pain.

And the cycle begins.

"There is one thing I can't forgive you for, though, Charlotte," Bridget said.

"What is it?"

"That American accent. You must start talking like a Scotswoman again."

Bridget told me later, "You are gorgeous, Charlotte. Absolutely stunning."

"Thank you. I had a makeover." We laughed about what Louisa said to me.

"You're not a mouse, Charlotte."

"Gee. Thanks, Bridget."

I picked up Bridget's letters again that night as she slept the sleep of the half dead. I thought of her writing these letters, The Diary Letters, saving them, bringing them home, so one day I would know what happened, so there would be a record of her life. I felt as if I were being ripped inside out.

February 12, 1975

Charlotte,

How do you live without a child that you love? How does life go on? I know she's alive, and somewhere out there, but she is not with me. I am her mother. I have told myself that I shouldn't want her, that she was the child of a rapist, but I can't help it. I fell in love with my daughter when I held her in my arms that day in the hospital. She had Toran's smile, my nose, our blue eyes.

My baby, not a baby any longer. Are they being kind to her? What does she look like? Does she have brothers and sisters? Is she healthy? Is she happy? Does she dream about me? I dream about her.

She's gone. She's lost. She's somewhere. Where? It hurts me. I can't hold her, can't hug her. She's mine. They took her. I never wanted them to take her.

He made me watch him throw his silver cat.

Love,

Bridget

March 16, 1975. Or the 17th or 18th

Charlotte,

She's gone. Legend's gone. I try to live without her, but I can't. I try to work without her, but I can't. I try to walk by little girls with blond hair and I try not to check to see if they're Legend. How would I know? I try to hold my arms, empty, they're empty. I can't hold empty. I can't hold air. She was mine. Lovely daughter.

I try to breathe without her but I can't.

Love,

Bridget

April in 1975. Don't know the day or date. Maybe the 5th or 12th.

Charlotte,

What does Legend look like? What is she doing? Is she safe? Do they hug her and read her stories? Can she draw or paint? Is she scared or sad?

Does she feel me? Does she know that she's not with her mother? Does she feel lost? Will they tell her, will she look for me when she's older?

Will I see her again? I don't think I will.

They took her. I never said they could.

Love,

Bridget

Could Bridget have murdered Father Angus Cruickshank?

She would have been only twenty years old. She was gentle, sweet, and sensitive.

But women who are gentle, sweet, and sensitive can be driven to murder. Happens all the time when they're continually abused or feel that their life—or worse, someone else's life—is at risk. In Bridget's case, not only was she raped, Angus Cruickshank was directly responsible for taking her daughter away from her.

Could she have done it during one of her trips home, maybe high on drugs and raving?

Would I ask her?

Would I want to know? If I found out, what would I do with that information?

I certainly wouldn't tell the police. I laughed out loud at that. Me, telling the chief about Bridget killing her attacker. Hell, no.

Was it fair to ask her that question and put her on the spot? What would be my motivation for asking?

I knew that answer, quickly. I would want to know if Angus was dead and gone and couldn't hurt other young Bridgets. I would also want to know if Bridget got her revenge.

Bloodthirsty, I can be, yes, I can.

"I want to save Bridget." I held Toran's hand as we walked on the farm, the blueberry bushes in rows, undulating with the land, the leaves of the apple trees whispering when puffs of wind traveled by. "I want to take her to a doctor, to a hospital, and I want to save her."

"We've talked to everyone, Charlotte. She's too far along. There's no one who can do anything."

It was true, we had. I had called contacts at home from my college and master's degree days, including Drew, who had a college friend who had recently transferred to a university in San Francisco to study AIDS. The doctors had nothing on this disease yet. They talked about clinical trials going on, new research, studies, developments, but there wasn't much hope for them anywhere and Bridget was too advanced.

"It's new," Drew's friend, Dr. Jess Lewis, told me. "Five years ago most of us weren't even aware HIV and AIDS existed. We're scrambling to catch up, to understand this, Charlotte. It's wiping out gay men, addicts, and their partners. Blood transfusions, mother to child. It's spreading to the heterosexual population, especially in Africa. We want to stop it. We want to cure it. Education is the way, but we don't have any medication that can help Bridget. There's nothing. I'm sorry."

I made more calls, so did Toran. We researched and studied.

We were at the hopeless acceptance part. Bridget had gotten there long before us. "I'm going to die. I know it. I accept it. In a way, I'm ready. In a way, I'm not. The most important thing is that I beat Charlotte in poker. That was an embarrassing loss the other night."

The three of us had played. Bridget had run out of chips first.

"I can't save Bridget." I felt my voice pitch. "I want to save her."

"Hush, love. Hush." He wrapped an arm around me, pulled me close.

"I can't save her." I could feel myself start to hyperventilate. "I want to save your sister."

"Char, take a breath." Toran cupped my face with one hand and held me with the other.

"I can't . . . I think I'm having a . . . a . . . a . . . panic attack." I tried to breathe.

"One breath with me, Char, one breath." He leaned in close, eyes worried.

I locked my gaze with his, my heart thumping, my nerves shot, my breath shallow, quick.

"One more breath, luv, one more."

He hugged me close, he stroked my hair, he murmured and reassured. I breathed again. My hands shook. "I want to save her."

"One more. . . ."

I took one more breath, then another, until I could breathe, between the whispering apple trees and the undulating blueberries, Bridget upstairs dying.

* * *

The desire to make love can come from many emotions. Passion, for sure. Lust. Laughter, fun, connection, friendship.

Making love can bring comfort, escape, a respite from life, a gift.

It can mask grief, if only for a short period.

Toran and I cried together, in his bedroom, over Bridget. I cried so hard, I soaked his chest and tried to dry him with the sheet.

"Don't bother, sweets, don't bother."

So I didn't, but then I lifted up and kissed the tears from his cheeks and temple. I kissed the tears that were on his mouth, that had trailed down his neck.

He kissed mine and we held on tight, riding that passion into oblivion.

We cried again afterward.

Bridget had made improvements since we brought her home from the hospital. She had slept, she had eaten, though not much, and been taken care of. It wouldn't last, but I'd take this respite.

For the last year she had been living with a friend, an ex-addict, on her family's remote farm in England. "It was the only way we knew we wouldn't get hooked on drugs again. Tristy and I went to rehab, then took off for her parents'. I didn't want to contact Toran until I knew I could stay sober. I figured he was better off not having me in his life than having to deal with seeing me sober, then getting on drugs again. It hurt him so badly when I did that." She groaned and started to cry. "And it hurt him badly when I disappeared, too. Honestly, Charlotte, sometimes I hate myself so much, I can hardly get up.

"I kept the photo of you and your cat stroller. I looked at it every time I needed a laugh, needed to know you were out there, when I was depressed, and felt dirty, lonely." She took a deep breath. "I am so sorry, Charlotte, that I wasn't the friend you thought I was. I was so ashamed. I wanted to be someone else, someone not dirty."

I held her hand. Guilt had swamped me since she'd been in

the hospital. "You have never been dirty, ever. You've always been beautiful." Though she was sick, exhausted, despairing, she was still stunning underneath the fragility, and the scars that spoke of a thousand lasting hurts.

"I want to apologize to you, Bridget. I failed you. I'm sorry that I didn't fly over. I should have. I hate flying. It's this debilitating fear I have, and I didn't want to return to Scotland because of my dad, but now and then I sensed something, I didn't know what, and I should have come. I am so, so sorry. I feel awful. I was not a friend to you."

What would have happened had I flown over sooner? Maybe when we were twenty, twenty-five? I would have seen what was going on. I would have insisted that she fly back to the U.S. with me. I would have paid for her rehabilitation. Counseling. She could have come to live with me.

But I hadn't. A decision not to act is a decision. And now I had to live with that.

"You never failed me. You were my escape. I knew I had a true friend in you. I loved getting your letters, hearing about the island, the cats, your garden, your work, your life."

We talked, raw and open. In the end we decided that the only thing that could help us was chocolate ice cream with chocolate chips.

"I wish I wasn't dying, Charlotte." She swirled the ice cream on her spoon.

"I wish you weren't, either."

"Thank you for not lying to me, telling me that I'll get better."

"You're welcome." What would be the point of that? False hope? She knew she was dying, and if Toran and I were pretending that she wasn't, then who did she talk to about her impending death and how she felt about it? No one. She'd be more alone than ever. We had to take care of her and make sure whatever time she had left was as happy as we could make it.

We held hands.

"I'm sorry about your daughter. I know you love her."

She made a tiny whimpering sound in her throat. "I do. I love her. I worry about her. I hope she's well, healthy, happy. She was a beautiful baby."

I held Bridget and rocked her as her weakened, diseased body shook with grief.

"It's too late now. I'll never see her," she gasped.

"Bridget," I whispered, holding her tight. "I am so sorry."

"I have missed her every day." Her face fell. "Every minute."

I hugged her. Sweet Bridget. She wasn't crying because she had AIDS and was dying, she was crying for the lost daughter whom she loved with everything she had.

"I can't get over losing Legend," she whimpered. "I can't."

I held my Edgar Allan Poe journal on my lap late one night after checking on Bridget. My writer's block seemed even more unscalable, a brick in my head, grief holding it in place.

I had no energy to write my tenth novel. I felt like I'd been hit by a meteor

I was with my best girlfriend.

She was ill and dying.

The block in my head was not going to move.

"They will condemn her. Hate her. Pitchforks and fire."

"Who, Grandma?"

"Bridget. That dear and lovely girl."

I watched Bridget helping my mother dig in the dirt. They were planting marigolds and begonias. "Why would they do that?"

"Because people are scared. I see fear for her. They're scared of her. It's a mob, yelling."

"No one's scared of Bridget."

"They will be." She hugged me, then whispered in my ear, "Stand by her."

"I will," I whispered back. "She's my best friend."

A few days later, when Bridget was sleeping, I drove to the nursery in town, then home to my garden.

I found peace in planting petunias. It was late to plant them, but they were what I needed. Petunias are simple flowers, but they are vibrant bursts of color. I planted pink, purple, and white in clay pots, two wine barrels, and three silver buckets that leaked. I placed them on my deck. I had bought four more clay pots for Toran's house and filled those, too.

I mowed the lawn, front and back. I picked weeds. I deadheaded the roses and the daisies.

Then I lay on top of my new picnic table, bought at a thrift store, under the same oak tree, spread like an umbrella that was as "old as time, maybe older," where my mother had placed her table. I watched birds flit back and forth.

I watched two butterflies.

I listened to the wind.

I breathed. I smelled the faintest hint of the sea, a dash of salt, a hint of mint tea. I grieved, deep, harsh, calm, all at the same time.

A garden softens out life, that's what I know. It does not take away the pain, but it blunts the harshest angles of it.

"It's the best thing ever," Bridget told me. We were sitting on Toran's deck watching the waves crash on the shore in the distance, breathing in crisp air, the leaves beginning to change, orange, yellow, brown, green, a new season coming up.

"What is?"

She smiled, the corners of her blueberry eyes crinkling up. "You and Toran. La la la, romance is in the house."

I laughed, crossed my legs. A vision of a new position last night with Toran hit quick. I am flexible. "Yes. It is."

"I'm glad, Charlotte. I always thought you two would grow up and marry each other."

"We might have. Who knows? If my dad hadn't died, we wouldn't have moved to Seattle."

"If your dad hadn't died, I think a lot would have been different."

"Me too. I've thought the same thing."

"I think I would have told your parents what happened."

"My father would have been an avenging, fire-blazing angel

for you. My mother would have had the police on it in seconds."

"Yes. It wouldn't have helped everything, but it would have helped a ton. But anyway"—she cut that conversation off—"I am grateful that you'll be my sister-in-law."

"We're not there yet."

"You'll be there soon, and you'll have a whole bunch of tiny Torans and tiny Charlottes running around."

I thought of that: brown-haired mini Torans and mini Charlottes. Then I thought, Bridget won't be here to see them, which set everything in black for me.

I reached for her hand. "If we have a baby, we'll name her after you." I knew Toran would want that.

Bridget's chin trembled, then the tears fell.

"Bridget." I put my arms around her.

"Hopefully she won't be a hellion."

"If she is, we'll love her even more."

She sniffled. "I don't think you should name your son Bridget."

"Nah, you're right."

"Talk about school yard bully cannon fodder . . ."

We laughed together.

It tore at my heart that Bridget would never know her namesake.

"And I do think," she said, sniffling, "we should include your cats in the wedding ceremony. We'll dress that stroller of yours up in pink, ribbons and bows . . ."

"They can be the cat ring bearers."

"Only if they don't meow during the vows. They would have to promise to keep quiet. It's a solemn occasion. . . ."

Bridget is so funny.

I had read about AIDS victims rejected by family members and friends, towns flipping out, neighbors turning their backs, schools refusing entry, and general torch-wielding hysteria.

People were afraid. They were uneducated. Their fear often

manifested itself in group think, which has never been known for rational thought. They didn't like what AIDS said about the person, either. It was against their own morality code of what they thought was acceptable. Gay? That was an easy judgment call: Sinful! It's a choice to be gay, they choose it, they die for it! It's a lifestyle! God's wrath! Amoral! Disgusting, repulsive. *Contagious!*

Drug user? They got what they deserved!

And in St. Ambrose? How would they respond? We were not going to make any announcement about Bridget's diagnosis. Why should we? It wasn't spread casually. You couldn't get it by walking by her in the park or breathing the same air. Bridget was no threat to anyone.

But things like this got out.

It would only be a matter of time.

I knew that.

And then we would see what people were made of.

I dreaded it.

Toran was working long hours on the farm, the potatoes were being harvested, but he was also delegating more of the responsibility to the people he trusted so he could spend time with Bridget. I continued to do the books, take calls, and write checks. I worked when Bridget was asleep, bringing my work to Toran's house. I set up a table in his home office, across from his desk. Sometimes we would work together, in silence, then look up, smile, and work more.

There was something intimate about it. I had Toran, I had my numbers, and together we were taking care of Bridget.

We participated in naked gymnastics on his desk.

Maybelle Courten called and left a message.

"I can't believe this. I call. I've left two messages. You don't call me back. Why don't you write me a letter, Charlotte? You love letters. You love letters more than anyone I know. So use your stationery with Einstein's face or the green stationery with 'Save the Whales' written across the top and write to me. You have writer's block, I get it. Write anyhow. And call me. Hang on. The kids are monsters."

She tried to muffle what she was yelling at her kids. I still heard it.

"Randy, put that beer down right this minute or I'll crack it over your head. That's mine. Jamie took the keys to my car. Go and get him before he takes off. No. He's fourteen, he does not need to practice driving. Get him!

"Sorry, Charlotte. Write or call me immediately. Hit me in the face with a pan, pull my toes with pliers, I can't believe this literary disaster we're in. I have a whole bunch of things to talk to you about. First, get that book done so my hot flashes don't get worse. Second, a book tour. I know you want to vomit at the thought and you're going to say no because you hate people, small talk makes you nauseated, and flying on a plane sends you into a tailspin. Sorry. Wrong word. I want you to think about it. And don't ask if you can present with a bottle of tequila in your hands. The answer is no."

I called Maybelle back. She wasn't home. I talked to Randy.

We sang together and worked on his lyrics for about an hour. "Well done, young man," I told him later. "Your voice is melodious and it has a hard-rock overtone."

"Thanks, Ms. Mackintosh," he gushed. "Thanks."

"Take out that one line about guzzling beer with naked women so I don't get in trouble with your mother."

"Okay, ma'am, I will. Hey. Can you talk to Sandy about math? No one here understands what she's talking about. You can? Radical, man."

I did math with Sandy. Once again, it was encouraging to talk to a young person as enthralled with numbers as I am.

"How are you doing, Toran?"

He held my hand as we walked toward the hills, through the blueberry bushes, the fruit gone now. "I'm not doing well. How are you, luv?"

"Same." From the second I saw Bridget, heard her diagnosis, understood the limited time she had left, I felt as if I were falling through the black holes of the universe, fast, irreversible, suffocating.

We walked and didn't talk for a long time. We went up the hill to the lookout point and studied the ocean waves in the distance. There were storm clouds coming in. Grays and darker grays, streaks of white, a hint of blue, the waves frothing.

"I cannot believe, Charlotte, that you came back into my life, into Bridget's life, right now, but I cannot tell you how grateful I am that you're here." He put an arm around my shoulders.

"I am, too. If Mr. Greer hadn't died, if Olive Oliver hadn't gone looking for her chickens when she did and discovered him, I would not have come. I wouldn't have been here."

We watched the storm clouds hover, the rain pouring through a funnel in the distance.

"We're going to get wet if we don't leave soon," Toran said.

"Yes, we are."

He put up a hand. I put my palm flat on his. "Clan TorBridge-PherLotte together always," we said together, then I stood on my toes and kissed him.

We stayed there, on the hill. The storm clouds came closer and closer, thick and dark. The rain when it came was soft.

We let it shower down on us.

It was easier that way.

It blended with the tears.

I went too far out into the ocean once when King Toran, Queen Bridget, King Pherson, and I were playing mermaids and mermen when I was twelve. My parents had strict rules about how far I could go out into the water without them—to my knees only.

I swam out too far because I was a magical mermaid. I was tossed through a wave, the freezing cold North Sea pouring over my head. My mermaid tail did nothing to help me as I struggled to get above the waves, my body somersaulting, the water chilling, slowing my movements.

I felt a hand on mine, yanking me to the surface. I gulped in air before another wave crashed over my head.

I was pulled up again, I breathed, and the water slammed over my head. That hand never left mine, the grip strong and sure.

My feet touched the rocks, then sand, my magical mermaid tail gone. Toran yanked me out of the water with both hands, then picked me up in his arms. Bridget and Pherson helped me, too, and the four of us collapsed on the sand.

I threw up water again and again as Bridget hit me on the back.

"I don't think I want to play mermaid and merman again," King Toran said, his chest heaving with exertion.

"Me either," Queen Bridget said, bursting into tears. "I was so scared for you Charlotte." She turned and hugged Toran. "Thank you for saving her."

"Excellent work, King Toran," King Pherson said. "I crown you King Hero of the day."

I threw up again.

I knew who my hero was.

Later, before we went home, when Toran and I were way behind Pherson and Bridget, making a pathway through a field strewn with blue narcissi, I thanked Toran.

He smiled at me, his brown curls still damp. "You're my best friend, Charlotte. I'd come and help you anytime."

"I thought Pherson was your best friend."

"No," he said, yanking on my hair. "He's my second-best friend. You're my very best friend because you like science and biology and chess and making butterscotch treats and you always listen. And I like your green eyes."

I ran home through our fields, the sun going down, shooting lush pinks and thick golds through the sky. I had almost drowned, but I was happy.

I was Toran Ramsay's very best friend!

"I'm drawing you a plan for your and Toran's garden, Charlotte," Bridget said. She was propped up on a couch I had bought in town and put on my back porch. The couch was red. It was elegant and old-fashioned, with a curving back.

I had added red pillows with gold thread and planted pink geraniums in clay pots. Bridget had wanted to see my parents' home, after I told her about the remodeling, so I drove her there for lunch. She loved the house and she loved sitting on the old-fashioned red couch. "I feel like I'm in an outside parlor," she'd drawled. "Where's the butler?"

"You're drawing a plan for my and Toran's garden?"

She grinned, her blue eyes twinkling, though she was having a bad health day and was wrapped in a blanket. "Yes."

"I don't have a garden with Toran."

"You will." Silver Cat jumped on her lap. "It will happen soon. I want to create a garden for you two so that when I'm gone you'll both still see me and know that I love you."

"That's so thoughtful, I think I'll cry and sniffle." I sniffled, blinked my eyes quick. I didn't want to think about the time when she was gone.

"Sniffle away, Char. I want there to be color all year long. I want a place where you two can have meals, read, relax. A water fountain for hot days."

She started drawing, those weak hands strengthened somehow when she held the colored pencils. She drew birch trees, three in one corner, a willow in another. Sweet cherries, ash, aspens. I watched as she added pathways. One led to a pond in the corner with lily pads.

One pathway led to a deck with a trellis, painted blue, with two wire chairs and a red wood table between them. A flowered tea set sat on the table. "This is your garden planning corner, Charlotte." She drew petunias in hanging baskets on either side.

She would never garden there with me.

Another path led to a red picnic table on a patio, a bouquet of pink roses in a glass vase in the middle. "This is where you and Toran can have dinner together with the kids."

Our kids. Here, without their aunt Bridget.

She drew a shed but colored it with purple, yellow, and red swirls, with blue and shimmery green hummingbirds between them. "You need a shed, but a shed need not be ugly."

She drew grass in the center, "for the kids to run on," and off to the right a rose garden. "Your mother had roses. I know you love them."

"I'll plant them, Bridget." I wiped tears from my cheeks. *She would never see them bloom.*

"Hang your mother's birdhouses." She drew the red schoolhouse birdhouse, the Japanese one, the cottage, and the cat birdhouse.

Bridget knew how important those birdhouses were to me. She knew me. *The person who knew me best would not be here long.*

She drew a raised cutting bed with daffodils, irises, and tulips. She drew pink roses dripping from an arch and wisteria hanging through a patio overhang. She drew a blue door that opened to a private garden, and drew steps down to another expanse of green lawn. She drew glass bottles with candles inside hanging from tree branches.

"And this, in the back, is your writing house." She drew a small house and colored it yellow. "Inside it will be one room, lots of windows, a fireplace." Outside the writing house was a white bench. On the white bench she stacked our favorite books as kids and sketched in the titles. *The Chronicles of Narnia. Charlotte's Web. Beezus and Ramona. A Little Princess. The Secret Garden.*

We had read those books together, at my house, her father forbidding them in her house. We would not read many more books together. Our reading time was ending.

"This is your vegetable garden." The vegetables, orange carrots, fluffy green lettuce, sweet peas, purple turnips, stalks of golden corn, appeared in minutes.

Silver Cat meowed, soft.

Bridget drew everything to its finest detail. From the craggy bark on trees, to every vein in the leaves, to the gray rocks in the pathways, to the mosaic design on the birdbath, to our old red wagon filled with marigolds, to a swing hanging from a willow branch.

She drew and drew, her face pale, her body emaciated, her fingers sure. I watched art come to life, a garden come to life, sitting close to her on the old-fashioned red couch, the breeze floating over the hills where Mackintoshes and Ramsays had been buried for centuries, where she would be buried, too. Soon.

We did not comment on the tears we both shed as the afternoon passed. We did, however, make absolutely sure that they did not smear the mango orange, eggplant purple, and soft cotton candy pink that swirled across the paper under Bridget's talented fingers.

"It'll be the love garden, Charlotte. Now, that sounds appropriately silly, doesn't it? From me to you and Toran forever."

I couldn't even talk.

The Love Garden.

The loss of Bridget into drugs, of what she could have done, could have become, had she not been forced, with such violence, on such a wretched, lonely path, took my breath away so hard, so fast, it felt as if my lungs had deflated.

Silver Cat licked a tear, then jumped back up on Bridget's lap. Sometimes I think that cat's part person.

"Thank you, Bridget," I wobbled out.

She patted my hand. "Thank you, Charlotte. I love you."

"Love you, too."

Loving a person who is dying is a horrendous experience.

When an older gentleman named Mr. Adair died in our village, my father told Bridget and me a story about a white unicorn. "When you're dying, the unicorn up in heaven gets a note from an angel telling her there's a person who's going to need a ride up soon. The unicorn finds out what the person likes. Favorite foods and books, colors and activities, pets and games. She gets a room ready for him, or her, near people who she knows they'll enjoy being with, maybe other friends and family who have died before.

"When the unicorn is done, she jumps off of heaven's perch, flies through the blue sky, around the clouds, over any rainbows, and down to the person. She's invisible to everyone. She patiently waits. When the person dies, she gathers them up on her back, using her hooves and horn. All of a sudden, they sit up straight and smile, they laugh, because they're on top of a unicorn and alive again. They hold on tight to her golden reins and the unicorn takes them to their new home, where they're happy."

"You mean heaven?" Bridget asked.

"Aye, lass, yes, I do."

"A unicorn takes you there?" I asked, enthralled.

"Yes, she does," my father said.

We loved that story.

A unicorn would come for Bridget. Too soon.

Pherson Hameldon came over to Toran's the same day he arrived home. Pherson is almost as tall as Toran, with black hair and brown eyes. He reminded me of a black lab when we were younger. He stood straight and smiled hugely.

"Charlotte," he said, arms outstretched for a hug, "warms my heart to see you. You are a beautiful lady."

I hugged him. "Pherson. It's been way too long. Glad they let you escape from the rig in the middle of the ocean."

"They let me out now and again. And yes, it has been way too long, Queen Charlotte." He mock bowed and I curtsied back, as we had when we were kids.

"Your majesty," I said, trying to nod regally.

"Your highness," he said back, grinning.

We did one of our secret handshakes. "Clan TorBridgePher-Lotte united again!"

"How's work in the ocean, battling storms, sharks, and oil leaks? I understand that you dive all the way down to the bottom of the ocean floor like an overgrown fish, fix pipes, and come back up. A nice, calm, quiet, safe profession."

Pherson laughed. "Yes, that's what I do. Couldn't sit behind a desk in an office. I would rather knock myself out than be trapped like that. Toran and I have to be outside."

He shook Toran's hand, then his eyes widened and held . . . as Bridget came down the stairs.

He couldn't talk. She couldn't talk. Pherson walked right past us and wrapped Bridget in his arms. Toran had told Pherson she had AIDS.

They both cried, and Toran and I took a walk on his property so they could be alone.

Pherson and Bridget had been in love when we were teenagers. They were supposed to be together. I know they would have been had Angus Cruickshank not ripped them apart. They would have been married, had a bunch of kids, built a home.

That would never happen now.

It's hard not to feel like killing Angus Cruickshank.

Two days later, Bridget and I walked, slowly, through part of Toran's farmland. She stopped and stared at the cliffs in the distance.

"That's where it happened," she said.

"I know."

"It was my fault."

"No, it wasn't. Not at all."

"It was, Charlotte."

"You have no responsibility for it."

"I do."

I could not have predicted, with any statistical success, the venom from some people in town.

How they found out about Bridget's diagnosis, I don't know. Maybe a nurse told her husband in the quiet of their bedroom and he told his brother as they built a brick wall . . . that sanctimonious doctor told his sister who was an awful gossip . . . maybe it was someone in the lab who told his mother and she told her best friend over tea and hot cross buns.

They knew. Everyone knew.

The reaction was instantaneous. Toran took the brunt of it.

It started three weeks after Bridget came home from the hospital. Two men from a neighboring farm drove up to the office. I walked out with Toran. I knew the men—Baen Lusk and his son, Gowan. I remembered both of them from when I lived here. My mother had called Baen a "knuckle scraper," as in, a monkey, and of Gowan she said, "Think of a slug with legs. No determinable brain. That's Gowan."

"Toran. Charlotte," Baen said. He was in his sixties. He had slitty eyes in a fleshy face. His son, brawny like his dad, thick in the body and thick in the head, nodded slightly at us.

"Hello Baen, Gowan," Toran said. He was wary, I felt it.

We exchanged pleasantries for about one second, then Baen said, "I want to talk to you about your sister, Toran."

Toran stiffened beside me. "What about her?"

"We hear things."

"Good to know," Toran drawled. "I had my doubts."

I stifled a laugh, coughed. "It's been something we've wondered about."

Our comments went straight over Baen's head. He seemed momentarily perplexed, then let the confusion slide. He had to let a lot slide in his life. "We hear she's got a contagious sickness and it can be spread to all us innocent peoples through the air and we want to make sure you're keeping her inside and locked up tight."

Toran's face stilled. I had seen this anger before when we were younger. Toran never had a temper with Bridget, Pherson, or me, but he could blow if he saw a kid getting picked on or anything else he didn't think was right.

All of his anger toward his father came out—flaming bright and crushing. A couple of times a group of boys at school cornered me, once against a wall and once in the cafeteria. Toran knew because I ran home, crying.

By the next day all of them came to school with bashed-up faces. Same when it happened to Bridget. Two of the boys grabbed her, and she screamed and kicked and they laughed. Pherson jumped in on that fight, and those kids were mincemeat when Pherson and Toran were done, blood and teeth everywhere.

None of the boys bothered us again.

"Locked up tight," Gowan said, smashing one fist against the other. "Tight!"

"I remember when we were kids, you were in love with Bridget, Gowan," I said. "You always chased her and wrote her love notes."

Gowan flushed.

"I'm so glad she didn't end up with you. It would be like living with nuclear waste."

Toran's jaw clenched, then his voice became low and slow, as if he was thinking. "What do you mean?"

"We don't want to get the sickness that God gave her for being a sinner," Baen said.

"A sinner?" Toran asked.

Hmmm. Now, that was surprising. I had expected Toran to swing his fist at that exact second. I was incorrect in that assumption. "We're all sinners, but there are only two people here without brains." I held up two fingers, then pointed them at Baen and Gowan.

They glowered at me.

"Fact is," Gowan said, his small mouth opening to form a black O, "we're afraid you two are going to get sick and then give it to us. That's why we're not reaching out a hand to shake. We're letting air between us."

"She was always wild," Baen said. "We know where she went when she was but sixteen. Had a baby, she did. Didn't even know the father, that's what Father Cruickshank said. He prayed for her. Then she went crazy and had to be locked up, and now she's gone ahead and given herself the AIDS gay drugs disease and she's going to give it to us. She shouldn't go to the village—"

"Bridget will go to the village whenever she wants," I told them. "She is not contagious. You believe she is because you are uneducated and unintelligent, slow to process truth, easily led by your natural inclination toward a caveman style of thinking."

"I am not an . . . uneducated and not that . . ." Gowan had already forgotten the word. "Not that other word."

"Don't insult me, young woman." Baen shook his finger, his fleshy face reddening like an infection. "If she goes to town, then I'm not responsible for my actions, because I will protect other Scots from this fornication and disease and sin."

"I think your mind is diseased." I knew what was coming from Toran. I could feel it. "Some people's minds are filled with filth. It's the same thing as a disease, although without the bacteria."

"My sister is a wonderful person," Toran said, fury practically humming off of him. "She is not contagious. She is sick, and you will not do anything to upset her at any time."

"I will upset her if need be. She is to stay out of St. Ambrose," Gowan said, pointing at us. "We don't need the likes of her in the village!"

"Have you had a head injury that could explain your mild retardation, your inability to assess a situation, and your poor understanding of basic medical information?" I asked. "Where is your brain, and does your brain work properly?"

Gowan was again baffled. "Yes." He tapped his head. "It's right here and it works, dummy."

"I will drag her out if I have to, Toran!" Baen said, chest out. "Don't make me do what I don't want to do!"

Whew. Toran's temper had soared straight up and imploded. It was impressive. He hit fast. Boom, boom. Baen and Gowan were on the ground before they knew what happened.

"That was spectacular, Toran," I said. "Two at once. So fast, I could hardly see you."

"Thank you, luv. Looks like he's going to give it a go again."

Baen stumbled up, swearing, and took an awkward swing at Toran, his belly jiggling. Toran hit him again. Down he went. Gowan struggled up, calling Toran a "donkey's ass," and back down he went. Straight back. Blood streaming from both their noses.

"I'm turned on, baby," I said.

"A state I particularly like you to be in."

When both men teetered up together, I jumped on Gowan's back, squeezing his thick neck with my arms and distracted him while Toran took care of Baen once again, who made a sound like a punched pig. When Toran was free, I jumped off Gowan.

Toran hit him, and we had two piggy men flat on the ground, moaning.

"Well done, Toran. I see the warrior in you. If only you were in your kilt." I had seen him in a kilt. I had peeked under it to find out if he was going commando. He was not.

"Thank you, luv. Next time I'll wear it." He nodded at me, then leaned over both groaning, moaning, bleeding men and said, "Keep off my property. Never again come near my home. Never again talk to me. If you come near Bridget, or Charlotte, I will kill you."

Gowan spit out a tooth. "You lost me a tooth!" His tongue roamed around his trash pit mouth again. "Two! It's two out now."

"You can count, Gowan!" I declared.

"I can count. I just did."

Baen groaned, coughed, groaned. "You broke my nose, Toran. I'll get the chief after you for this."

"Get off my land now or I will bury you on it today." Toran crossed his arms. "You are a disgrace to all Scotsmen. Your clan has always been a drain on the other clans."

"I am not a disgrace," Baen whispered, through his swollen mouth.

"Yes, you are," I said. "All men who are high on ignorant arrogance and monstrous behaviors are a disgrace to Scotland. That would be you."

Toran said, "Leave now."

They pulled their sorry selves up and headed for their truck, stumbling.

It would not be the end of them, or others, I knew it.

When they were gone, I wrapped my arms around Toran.

"If they come near Bridget, I will kill them."

I nodded.

In the back of my head, I wondered if he had already killed a man. . . .

15

"Charlotte?"

"Yes?"

"Let's have some fun before I die. Like we used to do."

"I'm up for fun."

"You and I, and Toran and Pherson, too."

"The Kings and Queens."

"Yes. Clan TorBridgePherLotte."

I put my forehead on hers, and our tears ran together. Then we did one of our famous handshakes and chants. Shake, twist, clap twice, pull back. "May all our adventures end in peace."

"You want to what?" Toran asked.

"I want us to go to the fort, like we used to," Bridget said. "The four of us."

"It's ten o'clock at night," I said. "Aren't you tired?"

"I took a long nap."

She looked pale, and way too thin, but excited. "What do you say, Pherson?"

Pherson looked drawn, his thick black hair a mess. I knew that watching Bridget die was excruciating. He stared at her with those dark brown eyes, at her smile, her delicate hands as they swept through the air. "I say, let's go."

We went.

We built the fort when we were children. We dragged up

saws, hammers, nails, and old slats of wood that my father had in the yard. It had taken a couple of weeks, but we'd done it.

My father had climbed up the hill and given us advice, but he had wisely let us do most of it ourselves. We found a flat spot and nailed a wood floor down on a frame. We built walls and a flat roof with a support beam. My dad showed us how to make a door. We put blue plastic over the top of it when it rained.

We brought wood boxes and put games and cards in them and played for hours. We ate brownies, Tartan toffee bars, and Kilted Meringues my mother made us. We were Clan TorBridge-PherLotte, kings and queens, battlers of two-headed dragons and evil sorcerers.

That night we brought wine, grapes, crackers, and cheese. We brought poker chips, two lanterns, candles, chairs, and a camp table we popped up.

We drove most of the way there, in Toran's truck, so Bridget wouldn't have to walk far. Pherson and Toran helped her, and when she faltered, Pherson swept her up in his arms and carried her the rest of the way, her blond hair swinging.

We lit the candles and turned on the lanterns. We played poker. We drank too much wine. We laughed and sang songs, many of them drinking songs from our childhood.

We held our fists together and shouted, "Clan TorBridge-PherLotte unite!" And "Activate our magical powers!"

We drank more wine and played more poker.

The candles dimmed.

"Thank you," Bridget told us.

Toran teared up and studied the door.

Pherson said, "Anything for you, luv."

I couldn't say anything, so I held her hand.

Bridget won at poker. She announced, "Beat your arses, now, didn't I?"

"Charlotte, let's go into the village. We'll have tea and cakes at Laddy's Café. Remember we used to love it there."

Bridget and I were shoulder to shoulder in her bed. We'd

both been reading. I was reading a biography of the incomparable Rachel Carson. She was reading a book on how to get better at poker.

"I used to daydream about the tea and miniature pink cakes at Laddy's and how your mother would take us there."

"Delicious. Do you have enough energy to go?"

"I think I'd do anything for her Scottish pear and cherry tart. I'll muster up my muscles and we'll go." She patted her legs. "Come on, muscles! Give it a go."

I drove into the village. I knew it was exhausting for Bridget, but if she wanted Scottish pear and cherry tarts, we'd get them. I held my breath and swallowed hard, wondering what Bridget's reception would be. Surely people would be polite. Baen and Gowan's visit had me worried. We had not told Bridget what had happened.

It was rather crowded that day in the village, as there was some sort of event at the university, but I managed to pull into a space about a block from Laddy's Café and opened the door for Bridget. She was thin and fragile. I grabbed her elbow, as I didn't want her to lose her footing on the cobblestone streets.

"Thanks, Charlotte, you old lass."

We laughed. "Come along, then, other old lass."

The bells of the church rang and the scent of croissants wafted toward us. In the distance I could see the ruins of the cathedral and the gravestones. I tried to stop thinking about the gravestones.

Bridget inched along beside me, my hand around her waist for balance, and said hello to several people. She seemed excited to see them, smiling, happy.

A man with blond curly hair saw Bridget and quickly crossed the street after she said to him, "Hello there, John." He said, "Good day, Bridget. Right. Yes. Pleasure to see you . . . uh . . . bye now." He darted off.

A mother with three children, named Claudine, whom Bridget and I had gone to school with, said, "Why, hello, Bridget. Must run. The children are late for their lessons." She practically dragged the children away.

I tightened my arm around Bridget's waist, my anger on low simmer.

"I thought this might happen," she said. "I had the fanciful hope that they wouldn't find out. I wish they knew that AIDS cannot jump from person to person like a frog. As I will endeavor not to have sex with anyone in the middle of the square or force anyone to shoot drugs up their arms with me in front of the chemist's, I think they'll be safe."

"They're not being rational." I felt my face flush as a man with a teenage boy firmly took his son by the shoulder and steered him away, after Bridget said, "Hello, Graeme."

"Run away," Bridget whispered. "When I speak, one of my words might catch up with you and it'll turn into full-blown AIDS by teatime."

She tried to be offhand, but I heard that crackling hurt.

I was relieved to reach the tea shop.

"Hello, do you have a table for two?" I asked the teenage girl at the front desk.

"Yes, right this way, ladies." She smiled, turned, and led us to a table by the windows. The shop was half full, mostly with women. I heard the whispers, which sounded like tiny threats, and felt the stares, which felt like larger threats.

"Hello, Mrs. Thurston," Bridget said, so gently, her voice soft as we passed a table.

Mrs. Thurston, a shriveled bird, did not bother to reply, her face shocked, angry.

"Mr. Coddler," Bridget said, to a potbellied man wearing a hat. The hat had a white feather in the band. His face twisted, and he deliberately turned to the side.

"Hello, Holly, a pleasure to see you," she said to a woman in her thirties who was sitting with two other women. I recognized all three of them. We had gone to school with them until I left for Seattle. They stuttered out a hello, and "Nice to see you again, Bridget . . . hello, Charlotte . . . how are you?" then quickly, as if Bridget's disease would smother them, they shifted away.

I saw the brokenness on Bridget's face, and I regretted bringing her to town. I helped her into a chair. "Thank you," she said to the girl. The girl smiled and said, "Laddy will be out in a minute."

"You remember that Laddy is Lorna's sister, right, Bridget?"

"Yes. Laddy's kids couldn't stand her. Moved away as soon as they could and never moved back to visit her. The woman can bake, but she's a spitting spider."

"They moved to get away from their mother and their aunt. Gargoyle women."

We put the napkins on our laps, and Bridget and I started chatting about how much the village had changed; how we had run through the streets together, our ribbons flying; how we had brought a few coins to Sandra's Scones and Treats Bakery for a treat; how we'd pretended that there were ghosts living at the same time we were. We talked quickly so the tears building in Bridget's eyes wouldn't spill over and fall out.

I felt ill. I thought my anger might eat me alive. It hurt to sit there watching her hurt.

There was a flurry of activity by the door to the kitchen. Mrs. Thurston stood up, wriggling with indignation, then whispered to Laddy, stabbing her finger at us.

Laddy hustled over, her face scrunched up, red. She was a stout woman, firm in her stomach rolls, her hair graying and pulled on top of her head like a ball of gray rope. She had been a stern woman when we were younger, and her three children were all rebels. Who would want to live with that? It would cause rebellion in a saint.

"Bridget, Charlotte." She was panting.

"Hello, Laddy," Bridget said.

Laddy put her fists on her hips. "I'm sorry, Bridget, you must leave immediately. Immediately!"

Bridget—tiny, thin Bridget—swayed in her chair.

"Are you kidding me?" I asked.

"No, this is no joke. Not a one! Bridget must leave this establishment right this very second. Come along, now. Out you two go."

"Why?" I asked.

"Because of the AIDS. I can't have her infecting other people."

"She can't infect other people," I said.

"Yes, she can!" Laddy's chins trembled. "And I won't have my customers infected."

"You can't be that intellectually challenged." I studied her. "Surely."

Her face flushed, her eyes bulged. "I'm not intellectually challenged, you impertinent girl. Daughter of your mother, an outspoken, irrational woman if I ever met one—"

"Don't talk poorly about my mother," I said to her, standing, my voice low. "Don't you dare."

"I'll dare as I see fit, and I see fit for Bridget to leave. Don't touch a thing. We'll have to throw out the dishes and the silver. I'll send a bill to Toran."

"You'll do no such thing," I said. "Because if you had a brain cell, you would know that AIDS can't be caught through forks and teacups."

Bridget put a hand on my arm. "Charlotte, it's all right. Let's go. Thank you, Laddy, for making delicious desserts. I have remembered them fondly over the years."

Laddy seemed taken aback by Bridget's gentleness.

"Why . . . why . . ."

"I loved the scones, the chiffon cookies, and your apple tart was the best I've ever had. Those were my favorites. You're a talented chef, and my brother and I, and Charlotte and Pherson, when we were children, we always came here for your pastries and looked forward to it."

"Well . . . I . . ."

"We'll leave. I'm sorry to have upset you," Bridget said. She tried to stand, she wobbled, and I grabbed her. "Please don't worry, though. You can't possibly get AIDS from me. Send me the bill for the items and I'll pay you."

"I'll do that," Laddy said, but some of the anger seemed to deflate out of her. "Yes, I will. Directly."

I glared at her, told her she was a "fat, prehistoric, bleating cow," and we turned to leave. I propped Bridget up, my arm around her skinny waist. Mr. Coddler, Mrs. Thurston, and Holly glared. Mrs. Thurston said, "Stay out in the country, Bridget. We can't have this spreading to our bodies. The children. Think of the children. And the elderly."

Bridget said, "I'm sorry I frightened you, Mrs. Thurston. There's nothing to be frightened of, though."

I said, "Mrs. Thurston, I studied cells in petri dishes for years. May I say that you remind me of chlamydia?"

Mrs. Thurston made a choking sound in her throat.

"You know what chlamydia is, don't you?"

Holly said to Bridget, "I'm sorry, Bridget, but you're contagious. Henson and I are trying to have children and I can't take a chance on the baby."

Bridget said, a slight smile on her face, "Your baby will be fine, Holly. Healthy as can be."

I said, "Holly, I remember you from when we were kids. You were a tattling, nosy, irritating girl, and I see that you've grown up to be the same. I'm surprised a man is willing to have sex with you."

She gasped, and I gasped back, imitating her.

Mr. Coddler, with the feather in his hat, said, "I'll let Toran know that you need to be kept at home for the duration."

Bridget said, "That's not necessary. I won't come in again."

I said, "Do call Toran, Mr. Coddler. He's helped you with your fields many times, hasn't he? I'm sure he'll be ever so happy to help you again after I tell him how rudely you've treated his sister."

He paled, blinked, and his face sagged.

"You're a closed-minded old man and have lost your compassion."

He said, flustered, "I am appalled! I never—"

"You've never what? Offered compassion or care to anyone? That's abundantly clear." I said this loudly.

There were other people in the café. None of them said anything. None of them spoke up for us. Laddy was still red, but there was something else in her eyes. Maybe tears. Bridget was leaning heavily on me, her skin a ghastly white. Holly kneaded her fingers together, her two friends stunned. Mrs. Thurston appeared ready to pop, like a can of worms under pressure.

"You cannot get AIDS from being in a restaurant with someone who has it," I announced to those illiterate idiots. "You cannot get AIDS from hugging someone or being their friend. You cannot get AIDS when you're having a conversation about the weather. But you can choose to stay uneducated and ignorant and cruel your whole life, which is obviously how you people have chosen to be. That you would choose to be this mean to one of your own is shameful."

I saw jaws drop. I think I saw guilt on a few faces.

"Shame on you."

They were shocked. They hardly moved. Perhaps it was the thought of getting AIDS through the air. Or perhaps it was my last three words.

No matter. What did I care what they thought?

So I said it again, "Shame on you."

Bridget smiled weakly and said, "Good-bye everyone. Have a nice day."

I helped Bridget back to the car. No one stopped to help us. She cried silently all the way home.

I raged against AIDS at dusk that night as I stomped across the hills behind my house and down to the ocean, unusually frothy and noisy that evening. I raged against it as the pounding waves dissolved my footprints behind me. I raged against it as the sun went down, the colors muted, the fog dense, gray and darker gray. I threw rocks into that thudding, churning ocean until my arm hurt.

I raged.

My mother called. She had broken her foot on the stairs at her university in South Africa. I didn't know what to do. I wanted to go to her, to help, but I couldn't leave.

"Charlotte, my students are all helping me. You stay there and don't move. I've read all your letters, twice. You tell Bridget

I love her, I've always loved her, that poor woman. Women must stick together. You stick with Bridget."

I stayed. I felt horrible about my mother, but she was right. I needed to stick with Bridget.

Dear Charlotte,

Once again, I will say to you that I am extremely saddened to hear about Bridget's AIDS diagnosis. I know that the two of you are the best of friends.

I am also sorry about the response of some of the people of the village. We cannot invite people to leave town because of a lack of intellectual prowess, unfortunately. I wanted to let you know, and Toran, too, that I will do all I can to protect dearest Bridget, so undeserving of this, the poor thing, that lovely girl.

Life can be terribly cruel, can it not?

Your rights are thus: You may go anywhere in town with Bridget that you wish, including cafés and bars and other restaurants, despite the lunatics who are protesting otherwise.

Don't go to Lizzie's Café. Honestly, more people get sick eating there than they do from the flu. She's only been in business a year, and she'll be out of business in a month, but this is not a risk Bridget should take with her health.

If you have any trouble, get to a phone, and I will be there for you with my men. (And Officer Mary Adele, a new hire, tough lady she is.) I will never accept discrimination of any kind in St. Ambrose, in particular against the needy or ill.

For a personal story: My mother was Jewish, killed in the camps in the war. We later learned she lived three years in Dachau, a direct recipient of the Nazi's torture.

I cannot write of this further. I apologize for

the smearing of the ink. Those are tears that never quite stop when I think of my brave mother. My father got me out of Germany as a young boy. Being half Jewish, I was at risk. I was blond, though, and that helped. We escaped, and my father, being a Christian, did not have a problem. Lost everything, he did, but we got out alive.

Twice he went back into Germany to get my mother. One time he was beaten by the Nazis but managed to get out again. Missing two fingers on his left hand and had a limp the rest of his life, courtesy of those monsters.

I wanted to tell you so you would understand why I believe that discrimination and bigotry of any kind is wrong, in all circumstances.

I am behind you, Bridget, and Toran. I will defend you all. I will stand in your father's place.

Yours,

Chief Constable Ben Harris

A friend of your parents, your father the best of bagpipers. He was my best friend. I will be the father that you, Toran, and Bridget need now, in his honor.

Dear St. Ambrose Ladies' Gab, Garden, and Gobble Group,

We must take immediate action. The way that Laddy treated Bridget on Thursday in her café was deplorable. She kicked Bridget out. My pigs are far better behaved!

I will not be going to Laddy's again, and I told her that yesterday. She told me that she didn't care, and I said, I'm glad you don't care because you are a scared nit, and she said you are a pig-loving hustler, and I told her that she owed Bridget an apology for being herself, a petty and spiteful overcooked woman, and she said that

Bridget needed to be quarantined. I told her that she needed to be quarantined for improper obnoxiousness.

My pigs are smarter than Laddy is. (I told her that, too.)

St. Ambrose Ladies' Gab, Garden, and Gobble Group, at Charlotte's house next time.

I'll be killing Frieda so we'll have ham and potatoes. I will miss her.

Sign this note and pass it on. Do not pass it on to Lorna.

Olive

Ladies of Gabbing and Gobbling,

I will not be going to Laddy's again, either. I already heard about what happened. One of my patients was there at the time, and I asked her why she didn't speak up for Bridget and she started to cry.

People in town are being paranoid and hysterical. I've had many calls already to my office. One woman wanted to know if she could get AIDS from Bridget if Bridget's "air cells" didn't leave St. Ambrose. Someone else wanted to know if the whole village would be infected and would we have to live under a giant plastic bubble. A man called and asked if Bridget could give him AIDS if he touched the same door handle as her.

I'll get on the agenda to speak at the next town meeting.

I'll be bringing homemade cock-a-leekie soup with prunes that I'll buy at Trudy's Market. A pump up for the digestion system.

On another note, I need ideas for fall flowers. I need to look at bright colors after hours of using knives on people and all that blood. Blood every-

where sometimes. People have a lot of blood. What are your suggestions?

Kenna

Hey wild ladies and Hallelujah!

Olive,

Please don't kill Frieda.

She is my favorite pig of yours.

Ex-husband was not pleased that we let Hallelujah loose in his house.

I told him to pay up child support, on time, every time, or we'd do it again, and this time we'd use one of your horses.

I received a check today. Hallelujah!

Rowena

PS I like Laddy about as much as I like Lorna. Why is she in Gardeners Who Gobble Gab Club with us? What is our name again? I can't remember. Don't send this note to Lorna.

Ladys,

I come to Garden Ladys Gobbling Giblet Club at Charlotte's. I bring Papri Chaat with potatoes and the yum yogurt for Bridget. It heals. She need heals.

Chief Constable Benny Harris drives me up the road to Charlotte's, but thank you for saying you come get me for the vacation to Charlotte's.

Love and joy to you.

Gitanjali

Hello, everyone.

I know what my Aunt Laddy did to Bridget. I am so sorry. I will apologize properly to Bridget.

May I still come to Gardening and Gobbling Gang?

Malvina

> *Malvina,*
> *Yes, silly lady. Bring a salad. I'm killing Frieda, despite internal protests that I not. She will be delicious.*
> *Olive.*

"Who do you think killed Angus, Bridget?"

Bridget put her feet up on a chair in the kitchen. We were making highland toffee cookies. A sliver of anger rushed through her face, then it softened, as if the energy for anger was too much.

"I don't know. He may have run off." Silver Cat jumped on her lap.

"I don't think he ran off. My guess is someone killed him." I thought of Father Cruickshank. Who would have killed him? There were other victims. Fathers, brothers, sisters, husbands, mothers—all would have wanted revenge. "He deserved it."

"Yes, he did. Everyone who hurts children like that deserves it."

"Who do you think could have done it?" I looked right at her, and she held my gaze.

"I didn't."

"I wouldn't blame you if you did, nor would I tell."

"I know." She looked outside. Toran and three other men were on tractors in the distance.

"I have wondered the same thing," I said. "He could have done it."

"Yes. He could have."

"Excellent move."

"I feel the same."

"Anyone else you suspect?"

"My parents."

"Because of the timing."

"Yes. That was suspicious."

"Damning, actually, given the circumstances."

"Yes." We sat in silence.

"I love Silver Cat," Bridget said. "She never leaves me. I can't believe that she looks identical to the one Father Cruickshank shot."

"Think she's a grandcat?"

"Could be. I hope her grandma clawed Father Cruickshank's eyes out."

The nastiness continued.

Someone threw bricks through Toran's front window in the middle of the night, sending shattered glass everywhere. He got up so fast, I went flying off his chest. He was out the bedroom door practically before I'd landed.

Toran found out later, from Pherson, that the bricks were thrown by a man who lived about ten miles away. The man talked about it at the pub as he drank. "Threw bricks through the window to show 'em we don't need an AIDS drug addict in our village. She needs to head on out or we'll take her out, even if she is Bridget Ramsay. She's got to go."

Toran, Pherson, Stanley I, and Stanley II and I went to the man's house late that night. We built a wall of bricks—mortar between them—in front of his door so he couldn't get out of his house.

Someone slashed the tires of one of Toran's tractors. It was rumored to be a young, obnoxious man named Inek. Toran saw him in town, walked straight up, and said, "Do you not like my tractor?"

The boy stumbled, mumbled. Toran asked him to apologize, and the boy said, his voice shaking, "Keep your sick sister away from the rest of us."

"Okay, lad," Toran said. Then in old Scottish form, Toran and Pherson packed him into Toran's truck and drove him ten miles out of town. "You won't get infected out here, Inek." They left him.

Toran was shunned by a few people he had known all of his life, which was the most hurtful. They avoided him in town, the pub, everywhere. They thought they would catch AIDS if they associated with him, as he may have been infected by Bridget.

His best friends, however, did not, starting with Pherson. Pherson was no more afraid than we were. They were smart, measured, learned men.

Toran Ramsay inspired true friendship. He was loyal to his friends, and most of them were loyal to him. I knew that the people who walked away from him now would never be allowed inside his life again.

"I am finding who my true friends are and who aren't, Charlotte." His voice was heavy, shoulders back, strong and hard, but he was hurting.

I nodded. "Yes, you are."

"The true friends, they are my brothers. In another clan, but Scotsman brothers." He sighed. "I was right about many of my friends—who would stick with me, who wouldn't. Yet there are people I would have guessed were not true friends who have been. And there are men who I thought were true friends who have backed away."

I hugged him tight. He hugged me back. I felt him shudder and I was instantly furious. Who were these harsh, judgmental people who would hurt sweet Bridget and Toran, people they had known their whole lives? How dare they make Toran shudder and Bridget cry.

"People can be very disappointing," I said, blinking rapidly.

"That they can, luv, that they can. But you, you have never disappointed. You have always been the truest of all the trues."

I kissed the bottom of his chin. He tilted his head down and gave me a proper Scottish kiss.

"Give me another kiss, Charlotte. I do believe I need one more . . . and another one . . . a third for tomorrow . . . a fourth because I cannot resist you. Shall we take a nap?"

I thought about kissing that night.

Some kisses on the cheeks are between friends, an air-kiss, very shallow, a casual greeting. Women air-kiss other women whom they hate all the time.

Then there are kisses on the cheek, in affection and friendship and love. Mother to daughter. Father to son. Sister to sister. Man to woman.

There are passionate kisses, and kisses that one person wishes would be more passionate. There are kisses that are light and fleeting, a tease, a whisper, a wish, a promise for more. There are kisses that have been given to the same person for decades, and others that have one chance and one chance only.

There are kisses that fill loneliness, that comfort and soothe, that are fun and funny.

Then there are passionate and lusty kisses, like the ones I share with Toran, that reach all the way to my heart. I love him with all that I am.

On Wednesday night someone set fire to one of Toran's barns. He, and the other men who worked for him, tried frantically to put it out as best they could, but in the end, as the fire engines and firefighters raced toward us, nothing helped. I stood outside, a hose in my hand, as the roof caved in

Toran came running, grabbed me with one arm, and pulled me away as the sparks flew, the wood split, the flames took hold, and debris careened through the black night.

"Are you all right, my luv?" Toran asked, panting, sweating, on top of me.

"Yes, yes. Are you?" Our hair was singed.

The walls of the barn collapsed behind us, and Toran picked me up again and shoved me in front of him as we ran, the wood transformed into mini torpedoes, the fire scorching hot. The barn burned to the ground, gas cans exploding, which sent another round of objects spinning through the night. When the flames died down some and the explosions stopped, Toran, the employees, and the firefighters did their best to contain the fire with multiple hoses. The barn was a black, charred, crackling mess. I was so glad he did not have animals.

Bridget watched from her window, too weakened to move.

Later, when I comforted her, the black smoke billowing into the sky, the acrid smell invading the house like living hate, she cried.

"I cause him pain all the time. I do, Charlotte." She wiped her wet face with the tissue I gave her.

"No, he loves you."

I crawled into bed with her and rocked her, the scars on her arms reflected by the moon's beams. "I have caused him pain and trouble. I am pain and trouble."

"Bridget, please—"

"Don't tell me I'm not."

"I won't. You're a pain in the ass and you are trouble on wheels."

"I know, I know!" she said, wiping her face again.

"And if you keep whining and being pathetic, I will continue to be sarcastic when needed, as that self-pitying crap is irritating."

"Oh. Argh. I sounded self-pitying then? Can't do that. I won't do that. No one likes a whiner." She took a shuddery breath. "Okay. Whew. Let's start over."

"Fair enough."

"Those assholes burned down our barn!"

"They did."

"I should get up and set fire to them and their skinny arses!"

"You should."

"I curse them from here to hell and hope that snakes crawl up their buttocks and lodge there indefinitely."

"A righteous punishment."

"I hope they get lice."

"Also righteous."

"I hope they never have a lover again in their lives. Enforced abstinence."

"They deserve nothing more."

We did the Clan TorBridgePherLotte handshake and said, "May our enemies rot in the fires of hell."

"I'll make Bonnie Prince Charlie chicken tomorrow to make it up to him," Bridget said.

"I'll eat it."

"And we'll have some Scotch."

"I'll drink it."

"And we'll play poker."

"I'll try to win."

"You won't." Bridget shook her head sadly. "But you'll try. Try as you might."

"I'll try."

She couldn't stay awake any longer, too weak. When I had her covered, I headed back outside. The engines and firefighters were still there, as was Pherson, Stanley I, Stanley II, Ben Harris, and three of his officers.

I saw Toran in the shadows, directing, leading.

He had lost his barn. This was a direct attack on him, and on Bridget, sweet Bridget.

My fury flamed as high, and as burning hot, as that fire.

The next evening Chief Constable Ben Harris and two other officers came to Toran's home. They had found out who had burned the barn down. Two brothers named Ennis and Ewan Matharnach. They were cousins of Baen and Gowan.

That figured.

"Arrested, in jail currently, will be prosecuted," the chief said. "They'll be in jail for a long time."

"And I will take them to court for the damages," Toran said.

"They don't have any money, Toran," the chief said. "They do have, however, land."

Toran crossed his arms over his chest. "Looks like I have acquired more land."

"Looks like it," the chief agreed.

Clan TorBridgePherLotte had Bonnie Prince Charlie chicken and Cloutie Dumpling parfait with whip cream and Scottish Scotch the next night.

We played poker.

Bridget was wrong. I won. I have, after all, studied the game, too.

We went to bed early, the charred scent from the burned barn still drifting in and out of the Scottish winds.

Toran came upstairs with the newspaper two days later, dawn barely gone. He climbed into bed with me and said, "Editorial written by Chief Constable Ben Harris. Look."

I scooted closer to him, the silk of my purple nightie wrapped around my legs.

ST. AMBROSE DAILY NEWS

A LETTER FROM CHIEF CONSTABLE BEN HARRIS

To the people of the village of St. Ambrose,

I want to be clear with all of you about the law, specifically how it relates to Bridget Ramsay.

Ms. Ramsay is a citizen of this grand country. She was born here in St. Ambrose, as was her brother, Toran, who employs many people in the village.

Because Bridget has AIDS, she has been shunned from many businesses and has been harassed and ridiculed.

Bricks have been thrown through the windows of her and Toran's house. Toran's tractor tires have been slashed. His barn was set on fire two nights ago. That was arson, pure and simple. The perpetrators are in jail and will stay there for years.

There will no discrimination in this town. There will be no more harassment or intimidation. You will not attack, in any way, one of our own.

Some of you have made a member of our community unwelcome. You have made her feel unsafe. You have disrespected the Ramsay family. You have disrespected this village and the values and ethics of Scotland.

That a few of you have excluded her from your bars and restaurants indicates an ignorance I can hardly comprehend. We all know which bars and restaurants have blatantly excluded Bridget. You, friends, are free to choose not to patronize those places anymore. I hope that you will do so.

For those of you who have been kind to her, well done. You have been true Scots, a proud example of who we all aspire to be. Thank you for your compassion, loyalty, and friendship.

I will, once again, hand out flyers I have made detailing what HIV and AIDS is and how it's transmitted. This time, read them.

There is no way—I repeat, there is no possible way—that you can catch AIDS from Bridget. Do not buy into unfounded fears, allegations, and general, unattractive panic. You are safe. We are safe.

But let me be very clear, friends. If anyone causes more trouble for Toran or Bridget Ramsay, if there are any more crimes committed, I will take action again. I will arrest you. I will have you prosecuted under the laws of this land. You will go to jail.

Thank you for your time, and have a pleasant day.

Chief Constable Ben Harris

"True friend," Toran said to me.

"Yes. To my parents and now to us, as he promised."

We entwined our fingers.

When word got out that Bridget had AIDS, one of our grocery stores cancelled their order for potatoes. It was a large order. I drove out to see the president of that company so I could explain that Bridget's breath on a potato was not going to get the potato sick with AIDS. I didn't explain it exactly like that, but I was clear about how AIDS was transmitted. I found out he was interested in cooking. We had much to discuss, including how to delicately spice clapshot and smoked mackerel.

In the end, he put his order back in and we shook hands, and I promised to send him three of my mother's recipes.

This event happened two more times. I explained to the grocers that Bridget would not be having sex with the apples and then sending the apples on for customers to eat. I also explained that she would not be injecting herself with a needle and then plunging the needle into a potato to get the potato stoned.

I didn't explain it exactly like that to the men, but I was, once again, clear on how AIDS was transmitted. One of the grocers and I played chess for three hours. The other grocer and I found common ground over a love of cats. I told him about the cat sanctuary and their yurts in Kalispell. He was fascinated.

Both grocery stores reinstated their orders.

When Toran found out, he hugged me, then swore at people's ignorance.

"We have to make sure that Bridget doesn't have any fruit or potato orgies," I said, "or we're going to have a problem."

"You are so damn funny, Charlotte." He dropped a kiss on my lips and I kissed him right back.

I brought Bridget over to my house so we could make leek and potato soup together, one of her favorites, and homemade white rolls. I brought the ingredients to the table so she didn't have to stand. Later, we crawled underneath the dining room table to look at the Scientist Bridget and Scientist Charlotte signatures in the red heart. I handed her a pen. "Draw something."

She drew Queen Charlotte and Queen Bridget with our crowns, capes, and swords. It was like watching art magic.

I already missed her. That is a harsh place to be: missing someone who is dying when they are still living. You feel like you're on the edge of a cliff, and when you fall off the cliff you're falling into jagged, ripping pain. You know it's coming. You can't stop it. You can only be as brave as you possibly can be.

That's what I was trying to do. I was trying to be as brave as I possibly could be.

Lorna and Laddy put up a petition in Laddy's Café, then both scurried around town asking people to sign two other copies. I heard about it through an indignant Rowena. The petition was to keep Bridget out of the village for the "safety and health of the good people of St. Ambrose."

I thought Toran was going to combust and explode.

I headed to Lorna's house and banged on the door. She opened it up, her tight face squished.

"Charlotte," she said. "I'm busy today. Important matters. Can't chitchat."

"Why, Lorna?" I was so mad, I almost kicked her. I stuck my foot in the door before she shut it. "Why a petition?"

"Because Bridget has the AIDS sickness and we could all get it." She leaned toward me, shaking a finger. "Like the flu. Through the air. Person to person at the grocery store, the tea shop. She should be quarantined. We quarantine people here in Scotland with malaria and diphtheria and the black plague, why not the AIDS? You know what they say about the AIDS and what it stands for? All I Did Was Drugs and Sex."

"I was right," I said, vindicated by my earlier analysis. "Your IQ is on the low side."

"It is not! I had high marks in school. But you listen here, Charlotte, Bridget could infect us. One cough, a sneeze, and all of St. Ambrose could come down with this AIDS and HIVE, too. We could get HIVE! We have too many vulnerable, innocent children here, and we have old people, poor dears, and I don't want them coming down with the AIDS or the HIVE. This is my duty and responsibility, under God—"

"It is your duty to treat people with kindness and respect and to attempt to navigate life with a modicum of intelligence and knowledge that makes rational analysis a priority in your thoughts and behavior." She seemed confused, so I clarified. "It's your duty not to be a dumb cow."

"Well! I don't understand what you blathered on about, but how dare you let Bridget contaminate my sister's café! Using the glasses and possibly starting an epidemic here in St. Ambrose. I don't think you understand Scotland, Charlotte. You are *exceedingly* American, after all. Pushy. Your mother was always too fancy-dancy for her own good, too. Too much pride. Those articles she wrote in the paper, getting the women all frothed up. Women's lib! Women's rights! Feminist thoughts! Ridiculous. Always dressed up. Skinny! Everyone loved her garden, but I thought it was like her, fancy-dancy! And all that art. *In a garden*. Not planned out well, if you ask me. Not organized."

"My mother's garden was beautiful. She was never fancy-dancy. She is a woman who believes in other women and treating people as humans who have worth. Her articles were meant for women like you, Lorna, to wake up whatever part of you is still peeking out from underneath your crushing lack of mental capacity, personal absurdity, prehistoric mind-set, and your sanctimonious arrogance that make you so ignorant you don't even know you're ignorant."

"Why, you! I won't listen to this nonsense a moment longer. I have important matters to attend to. Keep Bridget out of town. I will give you the petition directly. If she doesn't follow it, I'll have her arrested."

"You remind me of space trash, flying around, doing nothing except polluting."

"There is no such thing as space trash, and I am not it, anyhow."

"Keep away from Bridget. Do not come near her. Stop the petition."

"I'll do as I please."

"Then, Lorna," I said, "I will do as I please, too, and you won't like it. In the end, you will lose."

"Ha. Go and drink some tea, Charlotte! You're exactly like your mother. Fancy-dancy!"

She slammed the door. My foot was out in the nick of time.

I wanted to strangle Lorna and Laddy.

> *Dear St. Ambrose Ladies' Gab, Garden, and Gobble Group,*
>
> *I would like to suggest that we sign our own petition and kick Lorna out of St. Ambrose Ladies' Gab, Garden, and Gobble Group. Who is with me?*
>
> *Please sign this note and pass it on to the next person. (But not Lorna.)*
>
> *Olive*

I noticed that everyone had signed Olive's petition, even Malvina. Lorna had been kicked out.

Quarantined.

* * *

I was trying to follow Bridget in terms of what she wanted to talk about. Now and then she cried. She cried from grief and from feeling ill, but she was remarkably courageous and upbeat, too. She was happy, often. She laughed. She was strong. If she wanted to talk, I listened.

We lay on top of the picnic table in my garden one afternoon after I had worked on the books for Toran. We watched the branches of the oak, spread out like an umbrella, as old as time, maybe older, way above us. Silver Cat came and lay on her chest. Bridget petted her.

I waited, we rested, and I wondered what she was thinking about. Her imminent death? What the last days of her life would be like? Would it be painful? Would she be able to stand how debilitating it would be?

"I wish I had had a chance to play with Pherson's balls."

"What?" I turned to her.

"I wish I had had the chance to play with Pherson's balls." She groaned. "And everything else on that man."

"His balls?"

"Yes. Pherson has big balls. I mean, the man is hung like a bull."

"How do you know?"

"I spied on him and Toran when they went skinny-dipping in the ocean one time when I was a teenager. And I saw." She looked wistful. "If only I had been with Pherson from the start. My life would have been totally different."

"Yes, you would have had Pherson's balls to knock around."

"Knock around balls," she mused. "I could have knocked Pherson's balls. What do you think of Toran's equipment?"

"I'm not going to confirm or deny that Toran has incredibly full balls, and I think he needs a ball jock. Nor will I comment on the effectiveness of his missile."

We laughed.

"Okay, Charlotte. Glad you enjoy them."

"I do. No wonder they think about sex all the time with all their gear on the exterior and right between their legs. I look at

Toran's balls and I think, how do you ever stop thinking about something that's hanging off you like that? We're tucked up and private, polite and neat, but they're sticking out, swinging along, jangling about."

"Proud and bouncy."

"Yes, proud and bouncy and so easily stimulated. There is little I can think of in science that is as easily stimulated as men's gear and reproductive weaponry."

"But I think their prominent and proud pistols are a Scottish thing. Genetic. Must have something to do with the air flowing down from the Highlands."

"Big ball air."

"Yes. Indeed. Big ball air."

We found ourselves so amusing.

We would need our sense of humor and amusement of ourselves to battle what was coming next, yes, we would.

Silver Cat licked Bridget's face.

It is a sad, tormenting event in life when you are watching someone you love die. You know they're leaving. You know that train is coming. You don't know exactly when the train will arrive, but you know it's on its way. You can hear the whistle echoing in the distance, out over the sea. You can see the steam above the straight line of the horizon. A bare puff, but it's there. Each day the train chugs closer, the puff of steam rises higher, the whistle becomes more strident.

You want to stop the train. You want to delay it at another station. You want the train to go off the tracks, make a U-turn, and return to where it came from. You want the train to disappear. You want a miracle.

There is no miracle.

You deny this is happening. You are angry. You beg. You grovel. You try to bargain with the train's engineer. It doesn't work.

The train is coming, and you finally realize the only thing you can do is love the person as much as you can before they climb aboard and the doors shut behind them.

So you do.

When the train arrives, your beloved hops on. They turn around once, waving, smiling, young and healthy now, and begin their next journey.

You want to get on the train, too, but the engineer won't let you. He is gentle but insistent. It is their time, not yours. He will take care of them now.

The whistle blows, the wheels lurch forward, the engine groans, the puff of steam rises into the sky, into heaven. You wave to your loved one, and they wave back, blow kisses.

You watch, broken and crying, on your knees, hands outstretched, until the train is too small to see anymore. The whistle is silent now, the puff of steam evaporates, the earth stops rumbling. You watch until you can't see anything any longer, even the tracks, the station, all of it gone, and you are alone, still on your knees.

Alone.

Alone.

The train is gone.

Bridget asked for two people to come and see her at the same time. One was the reporter Carston Chit, and the other was Chief Constable Ben Harris. Toran and I sat in on the conversations.

Ben and Carston brought along tape recorders. She told them what happened with Angus Cruickshank in his quarters, in a shed, in the basement of St. Cecilia's. Toran had to lean over several times, his head in his hands, then pace the room, his fury a living, pulsing landslide of hate.

She told them about her baby being taken from her at Our Lady of Peace, A Home for Unwed Mothers, despite her objections. She told them about being forced into the insane asylum by her father, and Angus, who had convinced her father she was crazy because she wouldn't stop screaming about her baby being taken away and her "blatant devil lies." She told how the insane asylum had made her feel insane, the drugs they'd forced her to take, the shots they'd stuck in her.

She told them how Father Cruickshank had told her he would kill Toran if she told.

It was an incredibly difficult story for Ben to hear. She had to stop twice for Ben to compose himself. Ben keeps the law upheld in St. Ambrose, but he has a soft heart. "I'll do this, straight away," he said, his voice thickened by tears. "Have to get myself together, pull my bootstraps up. Chin up, now. Here we go again, poor dear. I apologize for the delay."

As Bridget said, "I want it to be official, what Angus Cruickshank did to me, so if another girl comes forward, she'll have my story behind her, too, and people will be more likely to believe her with the two of us. Then he will be prosecuted and jailed. But I hope he's dead and I hope he suffered before he died."

Carston Chit, a young, eager man with horn-rimmed glasses, nodded. "After what I've learned, what I continue to learn, that would be a just punishment."

Later, Bridget told me she needed to talk to Kenna, too. Kenna came over and Bridget told her what she wanted. Kenna nodded.

"You will be famous, Charlotte."

"That's silly, Grandma."

"You will be."

"What will I do?" We were making bread together—flour, salt, yeast, kneading, waiting for it to rise. Kneading again.

"You will be a storyteller. It's who you're destined to be."

"And a scientist." I patted my hands together, the flour billowing.

She smiled. "That, too."

"And a gardener. I like flowers, like you and my mum."

"I'm seeing it, child." Her face creased. She was confused by her vision. "But you'll be behind whales. On an island. There will be a lot of cats in sweaters." She groaned. "Scottish Second Sight. 'Twill be the end of my blinking mind."

"Will I like being famous?"

"It will be an annoyance to you." She stared out the window. "You will hide."

"Forever I'll hide?"

Her face cleared, and she placed the bread into a cooking pan. "No, sweet love, you won't hide forever. You'll come back to this ocean."

16

I put my feet up on my old-fashioned red parlor couch on my deck, the stars a white sweep across the sky, as if billions of white marbles had been thrown about in arcs, swirls, and spirals. Many of those white marbles are now dead, their light still shining. All of the white marbles are larger than our own white marble, the sun. There are about 350 billion white marbles in the Milky Way galaxy, give or take ten billion.

I thought about space and the infiniteness of the universe for a while to calm my mind.

I had decided to spend the night at my house to attempt to begin my tenth novel. Two reasons. I didn't want to invade on Toran and Bridget's space every day. They are brother and sister, and they need their time. Both said they wanted me there. Toran said he couldn't sleep anymore if I wasn't in his arms, "snuggled up," but I still felt I should go.

Second, my career is hanging over my head like the blade of a guillotine, and I needed time to think about how I felt about the guillotine.

My writer's block is a wood block in my head. I was trying to see around the wood, heavy and immovable, as it sat on my imagination, squashing McKenzie Rae Dean.

I had tried to write in my Edgar Allan Poe journal but couldn't get anything down. I had even called out, "Help me, Edgar."

I tried to write on a napkin with a purple pen, which for some reason sometimes works for me. No go. I tried writing on the back of a cereal box, which has also produced success in the past, including the ending of Book Four. I tried to write on my wrist, with a pink marker, which launched Book Number Three. Zippo.

I knew McKenzie Rae Dean inside and out. She was who I wanted to be in so many ways. But I couldn't be her. She was herself. I wasn't her. I was me.

And "me" could not write a thing.

I wondered, yet again, if my writing career was over.

Did I want to write anymore?

After nine novels, was I done? Was I burned out?

How did I feel about that? How did I feel about being done?

I didn't know. I didn't know much of anything except that my best friend was dying.

Hard to get around that, yes, it is.

I looked toward Toran's house, a speck of light in the distance, and thought of him.

My writing is, when boiled down to truth, simply a job.

The pain from my heart, where Toran and Bridget lived, that was life. My life. Our lives.

I went to bed reading a garden book, memorizing more Latin names for plants. It did not get rid of my insomnia. I finally got up, went outside with a coat and blankets, and stared up at the arcs, swirls, and spirals, and thought about the infiniteness of the galaxy.

"I have bad news." Toran and I met halfway between our homes the next morning, fall leaves fluttering between us, a cool wind meandering through. The potato harvest had been massively successful, so he was no longer working twelve-to-sixteen-hour days. I knew he was relieved. More time for Bridget.

"What is it?"

"The town meeting that's coming up is partially dedicated to whether Bridget should be forcibly quarantined, and if she won't stay quarantined, arrested. The chief would never do that, but that it's even been suggested . . ."

"I think I'm going to be sick."

"Me too." He ran his hands through his curls, paced back and forth on the road, swore up and down like I hadn't heard him swear before, then said, "Got your walking shoes on, luv?" We headed out and walked for miles, fast.

I didn't say a word. He didn't, either, but I felt that smoldering anger, that insidious fury, and underneath it all, raw pain.

Do not interfere on a Scotsman's anger. Let them quiet down, let them think it out, let them be.

Let them roar, rage, and rumble until they're ready to talk. Alliterations again. Always when I'm stressed.

Bridget and I took a short stroll through the lines of blueberry bushes.

She stopped at one point and stared upward, toward the cliff.

I put an arm around her frail shoulders.

"I feel guilty about it," she said.

"You bear no guilt, no fault."

"I do."

"It is their guilt to bear, Bridget." All theirs. "You were blameless. They failed you."

"If you had read all of my letters, you would know why."

I hadn't read all of them. I would. "I won't change my mind, no matter what your letters say."

"You might."

"No, I won't."

"There was one last conversation. . . ."

"And hopefully they finally admitted what they'd done to you, which was so, so wrong, and apologized for it."

Her shoulders sagged. I gave her a long hug in the blueberry bushes.

That woman's burdens were as heavy as bags of rocks on her skinny shoulders.

"I'll open this Gobble and Gabbing Garden meeting by thanking everyone for coming," I said. We raised our strawberry daiquiris over my parents' dining room table and clinked them together. "Cheers, gobbling and gabbing ladies!"

"Cheers to gobbles!" Olive said. "I got a new rooster."

"Cheers to gardening," Kenna said. "Although I've decided not to plant red flowers again, because I have had enough blood in my life."

"Cheers to being with all of you again," Bridget said.

"Cheers to The Slut losing her job at the bar," Rowena said. She was wearing two of her rock necklaces. I loved both of them, silver wire, purple and black beads, and decided to buy them at the end of our evening. "She was caught snogging with a waiter who is married to the owner's sister."

Oh, we loved that one! Poor Arse.

"Cheers to spices and dices and rices," Gitanjali said.

"Cheers to me, I moved out," Malvina said. "Here's to living on my own. Finally. Fat and unhappy and I made my break. Like a break out of prison." She took another drink of her daiquiri. "Must start over, get away from my mother. Sorry for the problems she caused, and I'll have another daiquiri."

We all cheered and clinked our glasses together. Everyone had given Bridget a hug when they walked in, but Malvina had given her the longest hug, then they'd had a private conversation in the library. I heard Malvina apologize profusely to Bridget for her mother and aunt.

"Cheers to this Mexican food," Bridget said.

It was Mexican night, so we'd all made a Mexican dish. I made paella with garlic, shrimp, and paprika. We also had chalupas, burritos, and enchiladas. Kenna made "homemade" sopapillas with vanilla ice cream, cinnamon, and honey, with help from Sandra's Scones and Treats Bakery.

Then we had more daiquiris.

"Tonight's topic," I said, "is creating secret rooms in a garden. I'll have to say it, remember the book *The Secret Garden*?"

They did. We talked about secret rooms, and Bridget started drawing with her colored pencils, in miniature, on long white sheets of art paper Toran had bought her.

She looked tiny to me, but she was laughing, smiling, calm, Silver Cat sitting right beside her. We knew her immune system was broken, and getting sick could trigger carinii pneumonia, but as she said, "What's the point of worrying about that now?"

"If I had a secret garden, I'd do yoga," Kenna said. "I'd want pink climbing tea roses hanging from a trellis all around me. Then, when I was up to my elbows in blood and squishy body fluids during surgery, I would know I could come home, be zen-like, and hide."

I put down my sopapilla as the image of blood and squishy body fluids entered my unsuspecting mind.

"My secret garden would have a torture chamber for Ex-Arse-Husband," Rowena said. "Chains, whips, prison bars."

"I would have a secret garden room with a gazebo. The gazebo would have a locked door, then my mother could never get in," Malvina said. "I would store my weaponry in it."

"Your weaponry?" Kenna asked.

"Yes. My bow and arrows. I used to be an expert archer."

"I would have a secret garden for my pigs," Olive said. "They could go back there and run around. I'd have a mud pond, too. I love my pigs. They taste so good."

"My secret garden have swimming pool," Gitanjali said. "For the naked swimming. That make you free. Free and cool. At night. Sometimes, I still can't believe. Fresh water everywhere. I have pool and that . . ." She waved a hand. "Paradise. Maybe I put in slide, too. Tall slide. I like to slidey."

We talked about how to establish secret gardens, or secret rooms, what vines to use for trellises to give the room privacy, what kinds of patios could be poured, how trees could offer privacy and shelter, rock walls could seclude, fences could protect. Would we have an outside fireplace for those cool Scottish nights? A pond? A fountain?

Time flew by, the laughter became louder, garden topics petering out as we talked about strange love-making techniques that men had employed with us in the past.

"I had a stockbroker boyfriend in college who recited the names of stocks when he was trying not to come too soon," Kenna said.

Rowena said that Ex-Arse "thumped up and down on me, coming six inches off my chest, then collapsing back down, again and again. It was like being pummeled by a human jackhammer."

"I not like that sex at all but I might like it with other man," Gitanjali said. "The Spice Man, that what I call him." She blushed. "In my head. Benny. Ben Harris."

"Gitanjali," Kenna said, smiling. "A romance for you!"

"I think he be better in the bedroom than that other husband I force marry as child for cows."

"I think so, too, Gitanjali," I said.

"I might like." She smiled. "I think yes. But he like giant. I think gentle, too. No blood this time. No hand on my neck. No hitting, I no think he do that. No, Spice Man, he buys pounds of spices from me all the days. So much spices." She seemed confused.

"Chief Constable Harris is an honorable man," I said. "I've known him my whole life."

"I ask about his wife, Lila, poor lady." Gitanjali's lips trembled, her dark eyes filled. "Too young. I feel bad for her, nice Lila. I think he good to her, so he be good to me."

"I was close to Lila," Olive said. "He was a perfect husband."

"I happy hear that, Olive, thank you to you. So I think I might enjoy him in the bouncy bed."

"Menopause has brought my sex drive way down," Kenna said. "It's a natural progression. We should not be breeding anymore at this age, so we don't want it as often. Why do we try to force this as a society? Why put pressure on women my age to want to have more sex? I don't want more sex. I get plenty of sex. Once a month, good enough, twice a month, okay. More than that? Not so much. I'm tired. When I'm not in the mood and my husband is, I recite to myself the names of the bones in the body until he's done. I fake an orgasm to get him off me. He can't stay in very long, either, because it's too dry down there and it hurts."

I crossed my legs. Dry sex didn't sound pleasant.

"My sex drive is high!" Olive said. "High. And I insist that my husband meet my needs."

"Does he?" Rowena asked.

"Yes, he does, or he doesn't get dinner. Sex for food," Olive said. "That's how it is at my house."

We discussed bribery and sex. Was it fair?

"I want to have sex," Malvina said. "But with who, there's the question. I have to find someone who wants to have sex with me who I want to get naked with. But I'm fat. I don't want some man to see me naked. And I'm not good in bed."

"How do you know you're not good in bed?" Kenna asked.

Malvina shrugged. "Not enough experience. I don't know how to move. I feel awkward."

"Nonsense," Olive said. "You let the passion sweep you away. And don't give up until you've had your orgasm. Sex is not fun without an orgasm."

We agreed that that was a true statement. "It's like having an ice-cream sundae without the ice cream," I said.

"I haven't had a date in years," Malvina said. "I need a makeover."

"Go to Louisa," I told her.

She nodded. "I do like your hair, Charlotte. It's so pretty. Thick and shiny."

"Thank you."

"I want to have sex, too," Rowena said. "Hot, rolling, arching, wild sex that gives me a screaming orgasm."

We agreed screaming orgasms were the best.

"What are you drawing?" I asked Bridget. She drew all the time. She'd told me why. "My hands shake, probably from nerves, maybe the disease, but drawing calms them down."

"I'm drawing everyone in here their own personal secret garden."

"You're what?" Rowena asked.

"Oh, my gosh. Me too?" Malvina asked, hope in her voice.

"Yes, indeedy, Malvina. I'm drawing everyone the secret garden they described."

"You drew me a secret garden for my pigs?"

"Yes, I did." Bridget handed the drawing to Olive. Silver Cat yawned beside her.

"Would you take a gander at that?" Olive exclaimed, her face lighting up. "This is genius. Pure pig genius!" She laughed, and we scooted over to see it.

The drawing was colorful, happy . . . and filled with pigs. Pigs resting on lounge chairs, pigs at a table with pink drinks with umbrellas, pigs swimming in a mud pool, bellies up, pigs planting flowers.

"This is spectacular. You have captured perfectly my love of pigs."

"Oh. My. Spank me with a spoon," Rowena gasped, as Bridget handed her a drawing. "You drew a torture chamber for me!"

"Yes, I did." Bridget laughed. "But see the flowers I added? You said tonight that your favorite flowers were orchids, zinnias, and lilies, so I added them around the handcuffs attached to the brick wall and the chains."

"Bridget." Rowena sighed. "Thank you. It makes the revenge I want to take on The Arse sweet and flowery. I love it."

For Kenna she drew her with her legs crossed, palms out, in yoga clothes, pink tea roses pouring through the trellis overhead. "I'm framing this sucker," Kenna said. "For my office. After moving people's organs about, or taking them out altogether, I need to see this yoga-peace picture. Thank you, Bridget."

For Gitanjali, a pool as she described, only she had a hot tub in the corner and exotic, tropical flowers surrounding the pool and a twisty, tall slide. "Bridget," Gitanjali said, her face crumpling. "This one of best thingies ever done for me. You gift me. Thank you."

For me she drew a desk in the middle of a meadow, with my Einstein journal and a quill in an ink pot. Beyond that was the blue-gray sea, and whales, and a sunset turning the sky into liquid color. It wasn't a secret garden, but it was pure me. It was where I loved to work, how I loved to work. In nature. I couldn't even speak. I stood up and hugged her.

And for Malvina? A white gazebo. A blue table in the center of it with purple and yellow chairs, a huge bouquet of daffodils and narcissi in the center. Three candle lanterns hung from the ceiling. There was a long box with a glass front with Malvina's bow and arrows inside.

"Bridget." Malvina could hardly speak as the tears ran down. "My mother has been so cruel to you. . . ." She choked. "And I did nothing. I was quiet. And in being quiet I let it happen. . . ."

"Malvina, I've known you my whole life. You. Are. Not. Your. Mother." We were quiet, still. Malvina needed to get this.

"No. No, I'm not my mother."

"You're Malvina."

"Yes." Malvina wiped her face, both hands. "Right. I am. I am Malvina. I'm trying to figure out who Malvina is."

"Malvina is a kick-butt woman."

"Thank you, Bridget. I know I'm a woman. I'm trying to do the kick-butt part."

When we were younger, Bridget would always know these insightful details about people. Why they acted as they did. What they really meant when they were talking. What they chose not to say. What pained them. What they wanted. She was terribly sensitive, and thoughtful, and she wanted to know people. She listened. She cared.

Her gifts and love of people were reflected in the secret gardens she had drawn for us.

"Damn, but I love Gabble and Gobbing Garden group," Rowena said.

"I know," Kenna said. "This is my favorite night."

"I love it so much, it's not even hard to leave my animals," Olive said.

"Friends," Gitanjali said. "I love the serenity friends."

"Eating, gardening, and talking," I said. "What could be better, except for a thorough analysis of nuclear fusion and where the country will head in the future regarding the use of clean nuclear power for energy."

They looked at me blankly. Dang.

"It's a joke!" I said, and laughed, overly loud.

"Ah, Charlotte, you are so funny. . . ."

"I am loving this daiquiri," Bridget said. "Shall we have another?"

We should, we decided.

Later I watched Silver Cat stick her nose in Bridget's glass and lick up her leftover daiquiri.

We were pretty well smashed by the end of the night. We went outside to my garden, joined hands on the grass, and ran around in a circle until we all fell down. It was a tad hard for some of the ladies to get up, so we lay there, together. Bridget put her head on my stomach, then everyone put their heads on someone else's stomach and we laughed and laughed.

Daiquiris will do that to you.

The stars were white and pretty, arcs and spirals, the sky so close, you could scoop it up with your hands.

Bridget did not wake up until noon the next day. She felt ill, nauseated, and had a fever of 101.

She said it was "headbangingly fun" and "totally worth it."

I heard the train's whistle.

Most people in the village were at the meeting to discuss quarantining Bridget. Hysteria travels fast. So does panic, ignorance, general stupidity, a lack of education, a need to spread gossip, and a general desire to get freaked out about something.

Toran called a friend who called two friends. Two doctors from London were now coming to speak at the meeting. Both were AIDS specialists. Kenna would also speak, as everyone in the village knew her.

Toran and I went to the meeting. We sat with Pherson and about ten of Toran's and Pherson's best friends, including Stanley I and Stanley II. Also sitting near us was Olive Oliver and her husband, Reginald. They were both wearing knitted snake scarves. The snakes had friendly eyes. That was probably intentional.

The rest of the Gardening, Gabbing, and Drinking group was nearby, as were many of the people who worked for Toran. Gitanjali sat next to Ben Harris. She looked tiny and fragile next to him.

Olive said to me, "I may have to cut Lorna's tongue out tonight. Look, I brought my gardening scissors." She then pulled out clippers, the long ones, from a huge flowered bag.

"Intimidating," I said.

"I think I'll wave them in the air when she stands up, the old stiff bottom."

Lorna arrived, shoulders back, her bottom imperious, as bottoms can sometimes be. She strode down the aisle, indignant, followed by Laddy, self-righteous. Baen and Gowan were there, too, lockjawed, cavemanlike, ready to fling their fat fists around, but probably not at Toran, the nose smasher, again. Their noses were definitely still bumped, and moved to the side.

The town mood was anxious and angry, the division between those who defended Bridget and those that wanted her quarantined in the Arctic firing off at each other. Those that wanted her quarantined—like Mr. Coddler and Mrs. Thurston—were near hysterical, sure they could catch AIDS if a butterfly landed in the proximity of Bridget, then flew and landed on the roof of their home.

I thought of what had been said and done these past weeks, from one person to another. Two bar fights, with both Stanley I and Stanley II taking our side; one fight at the local school, Rowena took our side that time; tempers flaring in the grocery store (Kenna); and even a smackdown in the ruins of the cathedral between one of Toran's friends, Athol, who defended Bridget, and a man named Lennox, who would never be Toran's friend again. There were relationships in this town that would not heal.

Mayor Niall MacBay went through boring business first. Honestly, it could put you to sleep.

"And now we will invite Dr. Takamoto and Dr. Hirsch to stand and talk with us about AIDS, along with our own Dr. Kenna Thorburn, as we are sorely in need of an education." Mayor MacBay glared at the people in the rows, taking time with Lorna, who was still huffing; Laddy, who was sanctimoniously angry; Baen, hoping for a fight; and Gowan, too dim to realize he was a fool with brain cells that would not show up in a petri dish even if they were dug out of his skull.

Toran and Pherson had gone to school with Mayor MacBay. He was blond, giant sized, and had six daughters and a wife who had had a traumatic brain injury and was loving but couldn't remember a thing.

Both doctors, serious, intent, spoke. This is what HIV is. This is what AIDS is. This is what happens to the body when you have it. AIDS is contracted through sex, needles, blood transfusions—although they were working on that—and can be transmitted from mother to baby. No one in the room was even remotely threatened by AIDS from Bridget Ramsay. There is no evidence that it is contagious in daily life.

You are safe.

You are safe.

You are safe.

Kenna addressed the crowd, and she said the same thing, only she added the personal. "Most of us have known Bridget Ramsay for years. We know Toran. She's our friend and neighbor. We need to treat her with kindness and care. . . ."

The doctors took time for questions.

Could they get AIDS by touching Bridget, Mrs. Thurston wanted to know, though that question had been answered ad nauseam. Can the virus hop from skin to skin?

"No," Kenna said, authoritative and impressive up there.

"Not unless you're hopping like a frog at the time," Stanley II drawled. "Then, watch out!"

What if they touched someone who had touched Bridget? Mr. Coddler asked. Could they get it then?

"No."

"Only if you had Chinese food for lunch," Stanley I drawled. "The noodles make your cerebellum more vulnerable to the virus, Coddler."

Was AIDS floating around in the air because of Bridget? Gowan asked. Is it catchable through the air?

"No."

"You won't get it from the air," Rowena called out, "but you might get it if you did three cartwheels in a row."

"Bridget Ramsay should be quarantined," Lorna said, standing up, shaking her fist, "Quarantined! She should never, ever be allowed in St. Ambrose again! She has chosen her own death. She has indulged in sinful behavior, a common harlot, and now she's being punished, rightly so. The AIDS is a curse upon this earth, sent to people who are not walking on God's road."

There was a loud rumble of derisive anger, but a number of people clapped in support.

"You should be quarantined," Olive shouted. She stood, held up her garden clippers, and cut the air three times. I gently pushed her back down.

Bridget should not be quarantined, the doctors said, speaking over the noise. Remember what we said about how a person can be infected with AIDS. You will not get it from her.

Someone had heard that a sliced onion could catch bacteria and germs. Should they cut up onions and put them in their homes? Should they wear garlic around their necks? Would it work the same? Why, my aunt Dee did it and she died at 101, or was it 91? It was 101. Garlic works!

Olive stood, pushing her snake scarf to the side as she cut the air again with her clippers, and shouted, "Garlic won't work, but a rabbit's foot stuck in your ear would."

This is a new disease, a few villagers said. You doctors can't possibly know what you're talking about. What are you hiding from us? Is this a government conspiracy?

They were not hiding anything. There was no government conspiracy.

Couldn't they get the disease if Bridget ate in a restaurant and the plate wasn't thrown out? What about a drinking fountain? Could they get it then?

"No," Malvina called out, "but if she thinks of an elephant the same time you do, you *will* get infected."

My jaw dropped. A hush filled the room, then laughter. Was that silent *Malvina*?

I snuck a peek. She looked proud of herself. Good for her.

You are safe.

You are safe.

You are safe.

Gowan barked in his throat, then said, "You don't know nothing."

Baen said, "Lies, I think it all is. Lies."

"I'm glad you're thinking," Stanley I said.

"We weren't sure if there was much going on in there," Stanley II said.

"A lot of hot air," they said together.

Gowan glared at them. Olive stood again and clicked her clippers. I gently pushed her down.

As the doctors calmly, patiently, answered the questions, I felt the mood shift. Information takes away fear. Learning creates knowledge. There were still people in there who didn't believe that Bridget was not going to contaminate the entire village by breathing or smiling or brushing her hair on Tuesday at eight, but I felt the relief, the minds of rational people kicking in.

Lorna's, Laddy's, Baen's, and Gowan's minds stayed the same: Locked down. Rigid. They thought what they thought and they weren't thinking any different. I can't stand people like this.

"I still don't think that Bridget Ramsay should be allowed in the village," Lorna said, standing, quivering, her butt making its presence known again. "Here's my petition!" She waved the petition. "My petition is signed by all the people in this village who believe in protecting one another. This is a moral issue. We cannot condone her illicit, immoral behavior."

Pherson swore. Toran tensed. I thought Toran was going to lose it. I put my hand on his thigh.

"All this hocus pocus medical advice," Laddy said, standing by her sister. "This is catchable!"

"Your fears are irrational and not based in medical science," Kenna said.

"Science doesn't know everything. They're guessing! It's a guess! This could be contagious. It could be an epidemic."

Baen, beetle faced, spittle flying from his gnarly mouth, yelled, "This is the disease of the gays and the drug addicts. All who say quarantine Bridget, all for keeping St. Ambrose safe from a demonic disease, raise your hands."

Gowan stood with his father, still the angry boy who never got his chance with the girl of his dreams. He would take his frustration out tonight. "I want Bridget to stay out of the village! This is from the devil!"

That about did it for everyone. People stood and yelled and said inflammatory, rude things that would probably not be forgiven for generations. Things to do with others being stupid beyond belief, wooden-headed, and willing to sacrifice the lives of innocent women and children, and can pets catch AIDS, too? What if Bridget gave it to the cats? Could a cat give it to a person? Do rats have AIDS?

Pherson stood and told everyone to sit down and shut up, which quieted people down. He was, like Toran, a Scotsman, tough, ready to fight, and he was pissed off. He spoke, with furious tears in his eyes, about how Bridget didn't deserve their scorn, how their fears were unjustified, their cruelty shocking.

Gitanjali, graceful and elegant, in a pink dress, her black hair in a ponytail, stood next and said, with soft gentleness, "My friend Bridget, beautiful woman in her heart. No one here judge. I not afraid of this AIDS. What I afraid of is I do not see love and kindness in room here. That is all. Thank you, friends." She sat down.

Some people have a way of wrapping things up with more kindness than me.

I stood and said that Bridget and I had been best friends forever and I was not the slightest bit concerned about catching

AIDS. "If you are worried about catching AIDS from Bridget, you should also be worried that a comet with a leprechaun riding on top of it is going to land on your head, as that is about equal to your chance of getting AIDS from her." I did discuss cellular biology in terms of AIDS, briefly, to strengthen my argument.

When I was done, Toran stood and walked to the front of the room. He turned and waited until everyone sat down and was quiet. Mayor MacBay stood one step behind him, as did Chief Constable Ben Harris. Toran was calm. Controlled. Towering and strong jawed. I loved him more than ever. I wanted to see him naked.

"I want to thank everyone here who came today to this meeting, to listen, and to learn. I'd like to thank the doctors here, too. I won't go over the medical information, the irrefutable proof that you will not get AIDS from Bridget. I will, however, talk about Bridget." He stopped, collected himself.

"My sister, Bridget, is the kindest woman I have ever known. She was kind when we were growing up with a father who was not often kind to her. She was kind to all of you. She was kind to our mother. She was kind to her best friends, Charlotte and Pherson." He stopped and looked around the room. "She's even kind about all of you now. She knows about the petition. She knows many of you don't want her in town. She is unbearably hurt by your rejection, yet she told me, yesterday, 'I'm not angry at them at all.'

"She is ill. She is suffering. There are people in this town who are making her life worse, but she isn't angry at you. She has a giving, forgiving, angelic spirit." He paused, took a deep breath, and I could see that simmering anger. "I, however, do not. How dare you demand that my sister stays away from the village of her birth. How dare you slash the tires of our tractors. How dare you throw bricks through our windows and burn down one of my barns. How dare you threaten us." He glared at Baen and Gowan. "How dare you say the horrible things you have about my sister. Your lack of compassion and understanding has stunned me. It's hurt Bridget, worst of all. You shouldn't even be calling yourself a Scot. Bridget didn't deserve to get AIDS. No one does."

No one moved. No one shifted.

"Bridget is dying. She has little time left. She has endured more in one lifetime than any one person should ever have to endure. If I told you what Bridget has been through, and I won't, because it is her story to tell, not mine, most of you, those of you with a heart, would be shocked.

"Bridget told me to tell all of you . . ." He wiped his eyes, which made me cry, and I am not a quiet crier, so I grabbed my tissues. "She told me to tell all of you not to worry. She doesn't want to upset any of you, doesn't want to bring any worry to your lives, so she says she will not come into the village again. Yes, for you, she is doing that. She is banning herself from a village she loves, from a castle she loved to play in as a kid, from a cathedral she ran around, from shops she loved to visit, from the pubs and bookstores and cafés"—he glared at Laddy and Lorna—"because of your undeserved hatred and inexplicable fear of her.

"Bridget is the same woman whom you all knew when she was a girl. The same girl with a bright smile who is a talented artist. I'm sorry that at the end of her life, so many people here, who have known her for years, are willing to easily, without any remorse, condemn her, harshly judge her, and make the last part of her life worse than it already is."

He stopped talking, scanned the room. Some people bent their heads in shame, in sorrow. Others looked away. His friends, his true friends, looked him straight in the eye.

"If any of you do anything to harm Bridget, or to bring her more grief, I swear to you, you will regret it. With everything that I have, I will make you regret it." His voice softened. "To our friends, and I have found out these past weeks who they are, I thank you. Your friendship has meant everything to us. Your kindness will never be forgotten. You may go ahead and take a vote, if you want, to ban Bridget from the village, to quarantine her. Go ahead, if it makes you feel better. The result makes no difference to me.

"I, however, will spend the rest of the time that Bridget has laughing and talking, and grateful for every minute of every day that I have with her."

I could hear people crying.

Toran sat back down.

The meeting abruptly ended when Olive Oliver stood, her husband proud beside her, in their matching friendly snake scarves and declared, "We have all the information we need, from reputable doctors. Bridget is welcome in the village. She is not contagious. Stand with me if you believe the same." She held those giant cutting shears up in her hand victoriously and waved them.

Rowena stood up and said, "I'm with Bridget," and so did Gitanjali and Malvina. Malvina glared at her mother.

I watched as people stood from their seats. Almost everyone. The doctors on stage, including Kenna, stood, too.

Lorna and Laddy had bright red, squished-up faces. They did not lift their jiggly, imperialistic bottoms from their seats. Baen and Gowan glowered, like bacteria.

When everyone sat back down, Olive said, clicking her gardening shears together with both hands, "Now I want to take a vote on Lorna, Laddy, Baen, and Gowan. Stand up if you think these people should be banned from the village. *Quarantined!*"

I couldn't help myself. I stood up. Most of the other people did, too.

Too bad for them.

Olive cut through the air with her clippers three times. "The vote passes! You four are now quarantined!"

I kissed Toran on the cheek in the car, then on the mouth. "I love you, Toran Ramsay."

"I love you, too, Charlotte. Always have, always will."

He sighed, his shoulders tight. We held hands all the way home.

We checked on Bridget, who was asleep, then we made love in front of the fireplace. We ate lemon squares, a recipe from my mother's Georgian mother, together.

On Saturday, Bridget said, "Clan TorBridgePherLotte must reenact our King Toran, Queen Bridget, King Pherson, and Queen Charlotte roles." She tapped Toran's dining room table with her knuckles.

"You're kidding," Toran said.

"No, I'm not. Let's do it," Bridget said.

I looked at Bridget. For an inexplicable reason she was having a fine day, I could tell. She had eaten and she'd slept well last night.

"Fair Queen Bridget, I don't have my crown," I said.

"I know where it is."

"I don't have my sword," King Toran said.

"I'll get it," Queen Bridget said.

"I'll want to rescue you with my cape on," King Pherson said.

"I'll let you. I'll tie the cape."

"I'm in," I said.

"Can I rescue you, Charlotte?" King Toran asked me.

"I'll rescue you. I am a feminist and do not need a man to rescue me."

"What if I say please?" King Toran said.

I sighed dramatically. "If you must."

King Toran smiled, slow, easy, sexy. Biologically we clearly had cells in love.

"Thank you, Queen Charlotte." He stood up and bowed. "I am at your service."

Baby, I would like to service you.

We trooped upstairs, Bridget swaying some, so I put an arm around her waist. She knelt, slow and careful, and opened her hope chest. "All here," she announced. "Come along, kings and Queen Charlotte, get your royal clothing."

It was like opening a box of royal memories.

We each put on our metal, sparkly gold crowns with plastic jewels that my mother had bought us. We pulled on four sheets—two pink, two blue, with a few holes—that we used as capes. We wrapped gold belts around our waists, made from shiny fabric my mother had let us cut apart. The gold was fraying but still bright.

Bridget and I pulled on red ruffled skirts that fell to our knees.

"I remember how I loved wearing this skirt," I said.

"Me too." Bridget's voice was wistful.

"Way too tight," I squeaked out, as I pulled it up over my jeans.

Pherson and Toran pulled on plastic, gold-sprayed armor. It was too small for those monster-sized men, and it had us all bent over, laughing.

"It might stop a spider," Toran said.

We all picked up our four plastic swords, then stood in a circle. We automatically put our fists in.

"Clan TorBridgePherLotte," we shouted. "Activate our powers! Make us mighty, make us strong!"

We left in Toran's truck, but not before Pherson accidentally broke his sword. "I have been emasculated," he intoned. "A man without a sword is not a man."

"You're still my man," Bridget told him.

"Alas, fair lady, thank you for that."

"You can have my sword," she generously offered.

"Aha! I am a man again," Pherson announced, taking it. "Come along and I'll rescue you, Bridget!"

"You're my Prince Charming," I told Toran.

"And you're my Princess Charming," Toran drawled.

"Don't forget I'm a Princess Charming who is independent and a feminist."

"I shall not. As long as you remember to let me be the rescuing knight."

"As long as I get to fight the dragons now and then, I'll agree."

"Done." He kissed me.

* * *

That day, the sun shining down like liquid gold, the wind crisp, fall leaves swirling, we fought the enemy, The Dragon Foes, who were part human, part dragon.

We spied on the highland knights.

Bridget and I allowed ourselves to put aside our feminist leanings and let Toran and Pherson rescue us after we had been captured by the Evil Phantom, Fang.

I pretended to faint as Toran carried me away. I will admit that I enjoyed it.

Bridget was protected by Pherson, who shouted, "Away, my princess, away!" He picked her up and spun her around.

The four of us activated our powers, flipped back our capes, declared ourselves victors, and laughed so hard we could hardly stand.

We righted our crowns, tied our shiny gold belts, and chanted, our fists in a circle, "Nothing shall defeat Clan TorBridgePher-Lotte, not man, not monster!"

Then we went home and had turkey sandwiches and beer.

"I like your sword," I whispered to Toran, eyeing his crotch.

"Ah, my lady," he whispered back. "My sword will offer your maidenhood my eternal protection."

"I don't think I want protection." I kissed his cheek and he laughed.

Bridget stayed mostly in bed the next few days but said, "Clan TorBridgePherLotte Day was one of the best days of my life. I'm glad I gave it a go." She ached and we gave her pain killers. She couldn't eat.

I saw the puff of steam in the sky from the train. It had grown.

And there it was, the whistle.

I went to the grocery store to pick up some ingredients for meals I thought Bridget might like. At the end of the aisle I saw Lorna and Laddy. They did not see me. When I heard them mention Bridget's name, I immediately scrunched down behind a stack of canned corn and leaned in to hear what they had to say. Nothing like spying on the enemy. Lorna was speaking, her voice pitchy.

"Laddy, some people signed my petition so that Bridget would not be allowed to ever come to the village again, including Mr. Coddler, Mrs. Thurston, and Mrs. Golling, who lives in the old folks' home down on Brighton Street.

"Did you know Mrs. Golling is over ninety now? She said she would look at my petition because she liked apple pie, and when I told her about the AIDS and that it stood for All I Did Was Drugs and Sex, she signed it because she said she is tired of not having sex.

"One old man, Mr. Galing, said he would sign nothing that had anything to do with bigotry. He said he had been Bridget's and Toran's teacher one year at school and would do nothing to hurt those fine people. Fine people! My arse!

"I was offended! A few of those old biddies, well, many, perhaps most, *all,* then refused to sign the petition. Mr. Galing followed me around and told them his side of the story, after I gave my speech—he often interrupted me—and what he thought of my petition.

"Remember Jamilyn Hoover? She told me I was an old bat and I didn't know the first thing about AIDS, and she told me that what the town had to fear was me—*me*—far more than we had to fear Bridget. She accused me of being a busybody and a gossip.

"I told her we could get AIDS from Bridget, and she interrupted me, too, and said that we couldn't get AIDS from Bridget unless we had sex with her or did cocaine together. She said, 'I am not a lesbian, and I do not do drugs, so therefore I am safe. Are you a lesbian, Lorna? I've wondered over the years. Do you like women? Your haircut indicates you do.'

"I almost fainted! Mrs. Hoover held her head up high as if I were nothing but a slug and said, 'LaRhodia, ask Mrs. Lester to leave,' and LaRhodia, you know that dark black woman from Africa, she asked me to leave. A black woman! Asking me to leave! I was aghast.... What do you think of all this...."

I clamped a hand over my mouth to keep my laugher muffled.

Then Laddy spoke, equally aggrieved. "I went to the library for signatures. I saw Alyce Mosher there. She told me I was like a cuckoo clock, repetitive and annoying. She actually said that, and her father's a vicar!

"I shouldn't have been surprised, though, with Alyce having those wild years in school, then she went off and became a biologist and stopped going to church! I went right to her father and said I was disappointed in his daughter's inexcusable behavior, and Harold told me he was disappointed in my inexcusable behavior and he would be happy to sit down and explain Jesus's love to me and how Jesus cared for the sick, including the lepers, and he would care for anyone with AIDS, too.

"Some people don't seem to understand the gravity of this situation. Jestin, the butcher, took my petition when I asked him to sign it and used a butcher knife to cut it in half, then he put it through the meat grinder. He told me Toran was one of his best friends and he would never do anything to hurt Toran or Bridget. He told me to get out and not shop there again. Now where will I get my roasts?"

I laughed behind the corn, then scuttled on out of there.

> *Dear Charlotte,*
>
> *I understand you had an altercation with Mr. Coddler yesterday in the village square.*
>
> *He said that you put your leg behind his, gave him the old one-two push, and he fell on his arse. He said, "My buttocks are now injured." He did admit to saying to you that Bridget was "a fearsome wart on the town of St. Ambrose," and I could imagine why that would have struck your temper. He also admitted that he said that I should arrest Bridget and keep her in her home, like you would "another leper."*
>
> *Obviously, this was a poor conversation, and I told Mr. Coddler his behavior was reprehensible*

and that if he approaches you or Bridget again I will arrest him for harassment and he will stay in jail until I am in a better mood.

I wanted to rest any concerns of yours about Mr. Coddler's unpleasant behavior.

Sincerely,

Chief Constable Ben Harris

A friend of your parents.

Your father knew all the songs and stories of Scotland. He taught me after I arrived, as a boy, lucky to have escaped from the Nazis in Germany. I was a broken soul, grieving the loss of my mother, petrified. He was the one who welcomed me here and taught me how to be a proper Scotsman. I shall never forget him. I shall continue to do my best to protect his daughter and her friends.

17

ST. AMBROSE DAILY NEWS

MY INTERVIEW WITH BRIDGET RAMSAY

By Carston Chit, *Reporter*

I recently met with Bridget Ramsay. I have been attempting to meet with Miss Ramsay since she returned home and was found to be infected with the AIDS virus.

I thought I was being called to her and her brother's, Toran Ramsay's, home to discuss AIDS and the town's reaction to her diagnosis, about which I have written previously.

We did talk about her AIDS diagnosis, but first, and at length, we talked about Father Angus Cruickshank.

This is her story.

For those of you who may not believe Ramsay's story, I will add that her story does not differ from others that I have heard, on multiple occasions, all involving criminal behavior by the missing Father Angus Cruickshank, which will be printed at a later date. . . .

* * *

I read the article aloud to Toran, Pherson, and Bridget as we drank tea on Sunday morning.

"I know that part of the reason Father Cruickshank targeted me was because he knew my father, a Catholic fanatic, wouldn't believe me, even if I told him what happened," Bridget was quoted as saying. "He knew I would do anything to protect my brother. I was vulnerable and scared. He took advantage of that."

She talked about the attacks, the threat against Toran, losing her baby, being committed to an insane asylum by Cruickshank, the abandonment by her parents, and the downward spiral that followed.

"I didn't kill Angus Cruickshank," she said. "But I hope that someone did. What he did to me, and what I know he was doing to other girls at St. Cecilia's, was criminal."

As for the baby that was taken from her?

"I have missed her all my life. Every day I have thought of her, and now it's too late. I will never see her again."

Finally, why did she tell her story? "So that there's a record. I want other girls, women now, who were abused by Angus Cruickshank to come forward to get help. If he's ever found, I also need to leave my voice here to help prosecute him."

When told that there were complaints from parents about Father Cruickshank, before his stint at St. Cecilia's, Bridget said, "The priests who knew, the bishops, cardinals, the archbishop, the Vatican, anyone in the church who knew that Angus Cruickshank was raping girls and who looked away, who didn't call the police, who then sent him to other parishes so he could attack again, all of them should be arrested for aiding and abetting in the rape and molestation of children.

"They hid the criminals amidst them at the expense of children's safety, so they could protect the reputation of the Church. And they call themselves men of God? Servants of Christ? Christ would not have done that. God would not condone it."

Carston Chit also included in the article two damning letters written from Bishop O'Callahan to Father Cruickshank.

October 15, 1973

To my dear friend, Angus,

I was much distressed to receive your letter about Sister Margaret O'Diehl, poor woman. It seems she has lost her mind. I could not believe it when you said she tried to cook a live chicken in the oven and danced naked in the woods several months ago.

As you know, when she came to see me recently, she was quite upset, in a rage about you. She told Cardinal Donovan and me that you had attacked and impregnated Bridget Ramsay and two other girls. I was shocked by her accusations, as I am well aware of your impeccable reputation as a Godly, prayerful man. I told her, as gently as I could, that sometimes when women go through the changes at midlife, they become slightly delusional.

She told me that I was the one who was delusional and blind to the crimes being committed at St. Cecilia's by you.

I forgave her immediately for her intemperance, and explained to her what was going on in her body that would cause these delusions to surface. When women get older they have mental upsets based in their innate weakness as females. Women are naturally less resilient than men, as you know, through your devoted service—their thoughts ruled by emotion instead of reason. I also told her that at her age, some dementia was to be expected.

She did not respond well.

As a side note, my own mother became so enraged at my father one day when he was in his cups that she threw a plate at his head and wounded him. He rightfully slapped her down. She left after I left home and moved back in with her elderly mother, where she remains today. She says she's happier without my father, but without a male influence in the house, I doubt this.

You were visiting your brother at the time, but the cardinal and I went to St. Cecilia's and took Sister Margaret to St. Maria's Care Home for Nuns. We had to tell her she was going to talk to the archbishop about her claims, or she would not have gotten in the car.

She had served the Lord well by teaching young Catholic girls for years. I know she was a popular teacher, but now it was time for her to relax and work in the kitchen serving nuns older than herself their daily meals. They put her in charge of the potatoes, sweet and white.

Sister Margaret threw a potato at me, then another one, and a third and fourth. Twice with both hands. It was embarrassing for her, for all of us that day. We were mortified, but it did back up what you said about her declining and deteriorating mental health. She did continue her accusations against you and said she would be going to the police.

I prayed over her and she threw yet another potato, so Cardinal Donovan and I decided to leave. I told her that God would forgive her her lies if she confessed and repented. She said that I needed to confess to being a "blooming idiot."

Poor woman. They do seem to lose their faculties when they're older.

Yours in the love of Christ,
Bishop O'Callahan

October 25, 1973

To my dear friend, Angus,

I have been contacted by the police, my friend, as I know you have, too, because of Sister Margaret's absurd accusations, poor woman. In fact, it was a pleasurable experience for me. One of the constables, Bill, is the brother of Father Mick Magnuson, with whom I attended seminary. I was able to hear all about Father Magnuson, a devout follower of our Lord, and his flock.

I told them to be gentle with Sister Margaret, as she was suffering from women's hysteria and delusions. It was my pleasure to quote the Bible with these fine men about the spirits entering the body and taking over, which is exactly what has happened here. They did admit that she was very upset, ranting, when they talked to her. Her age was a factor, too, being sixty-five.

Sister Margaret's outrageous complaints against you were dismissed. We are sorry that she attempted to besmirch your stellar reputation. Serving in the Lord has many challenges, does it not? With his grace, we persevere.

On another note, it seems that Sister Margaret has left the order. She will no longer be serving the other nuns at St. Maria's Care Home for Nuns. Perhaps that is for the best. We cannot have her throwing potatoes again.

Yours in the love of Christ, (and looking forward to our next fishing trip!)

Bishop O'Callahan

My final note: Bishop Cameron O'Callahan, Cardinal Owen Donovan, Archbishop Dougal Quigley, Constable Bill Magnuson, and Constable Paul Riordan were all contacted for this article.

> They all refused to speak to me. It should also be noted that Chief Constable Ben Harris was in training in Scotland Yard at the time, for another assignment, and was not then the Chief Constable of St. Ambrose. The late Larry Halloren was in that position.

When I was done, we sat in silence for another minute, then Toran turned to Bridget and said, "You are the bravest woman I have ever met."

Pherson said, "Bridget, you are my hero, honey."

I said to her, "I love you, Bridget. Always have, always will."

Bridget said, "We should celebrate."

"What?" Pherson said.

"Celebrate revenge. The Catholic Church has finally heard my voice."

"Aha!" I said. "Revenge is sweet. I'll make Loch Ness monster chocolate squares with icing."

"And I will, yet again, pledge to kill Angus Cruickshank if he ever surfaces," Toran said.

"Friend, I will be beside you when you do," Pherson said.

We played poker. Toran won.

Poor Bridget. She doesn't have a poker face. She smiles, she cackles, she frowns. She went back to studying her poker book.

The next day Toran and I went on a long walk, holding hands.

We didn't say much. We were at that place in a relationship where silence was soft, like a hug.

Carston Chit's interview of Bridget had a huge impact. As Ben Harris told me later, through his contacts on police forces throughout Great Britain and Ireland, the calls came streaming in from women, many who were girls at the time, who were victims of Angus Cruickshank.

What also came to Chief Harris's attention, as it had to Carston Chit, was that there were letters written, complaints made, by victims, by their mothers, their fathers, to the parishes, to the archbishops, to the Vatican, all outraged about Angus, for years.

Nothing was done.

Father Angus Cruickshank was given a slap on the wrist and moved to another parish, to rape and abuse again. Until he disappeared from St. Cecilia's.

The Catholic Church clearly went into denial mode.

They buried the information. They minimalized, dismissed, intimidated, denied.

And the attacks continued.

In America and Ireland, the reports were coming in, too, mostly assaults against boys. The Church had refused to prosecute. They shuffled the criminals to a new parish. Ta-da! Here's your new priest! He likes children, in a bad way, but we won't tell you that.

Rapists can come in any form at all.

They may wear jeans.

They may wear tuxedos.

They may wear crosses.

There were no more bricks. No more slashed tires. No fires.

Neighbors and friends came by to visit with us and with Bridget.

Bridget was tired by the visits, but she loved them. She talked to our friends from school. Friends who had attended St. Cecilia's with her came by. They knew of two more girls, in their class, who went through that same abuse.

Bridget told me later, wrapped in blankets on the back porch, the ocean in the distance, calm, that this was one of the happiest times of her life. "The happiest time was playing with you, Toran, and Pherson when we were kids, but this is a good time in my life, too."

It broke my heart. This time of her life, ill, exhausted, feverish, coughing, weak and too thin, dying, was one of the best times?

"I'm here with you, Toran, and Pherson. I'm in Scotland. I'm clean, I'm sober. And people come all the time to visit, have a cup of tea, to laugh. I'm home, Charlotte. Scotland is my home.

St. Ambrose is my home." She reached for my hand. "You, Toran, Pherson, you're my home."

I am a crybaby now. It is fortunate that I know that tear ducts cannot run out of tears. They are replenished.

Actually, it didn't help to know that at all.

You are my home.

I saw Carston Chit in town. We sat down for a cup of coffee.

"How did you get the letters from Bishop O'Callahan to Father Cruickshank?"

He cleared his throat, played with his horn-rimmed glasses. He's a serious young man. "Perhaps I waited until the weekend, when few people are around and about at St. Cecilia's. It may have been late at night when I made my visit, and then perhaps I might have stepped through an unlocked door and went through a few file cabinets at Angus's former residence, which is no longer being used, has not been used for years, and is in the woods."

"Ah. Perhaps you did."

"Not strictly legal or following the rules of the ethics of reporting."

"Was there anything, Carston, about Bridget, about where her baby went?"

"No, there wasn't. None that I have ever found on her, or any other girl, during that time frame, and I have been there many times." He cleared his throat, played with his glasses. "That information would have been, in a normal situation, at Our Lady of Peace. They don't have it either, though.

"I believe, they believe, Cruickshank took it and burned it. There were a number of girls from St. Cecilia's impregnated by him. He had things down to a science, how to intimidate the girls, who to choose, how to hide the evidence, as psychopathic serial rapists often do."

"Thank you, Carston, for writing about Bridget. It's freed her, I think. The truth is out there."

He teared up. "She's a lovely woman. Unfair, all of it."

"Yes. Indeed it is."

* * *

"I've been thinking," Bridget said from the porch, rocking gently. Silver Cat sat on her lap and she stroked him as fall leaves drifted by.

"About what, Bridget?" Toran held my hand, our fingers linked.

"I want to leave a garden."

"A garden?"

"Yes. A garden and a park for the children of St. Ambrose. So they can play and learn to love flowers and nature, like we did. Like the four of us."

Pherson coughed. He does that when he gets upset and is trying not to cry.

"I want this to be my gift to the village," Bridget said.

I was not surprised by her way of thinking, even though I would like to pack up many of the people of St. Ambrose on donkeys, have them ridden into caves and left in dark, bat-filled caverns. Bridget was a more compassionate person than me.

"But so many people here, Bridget," Pherson said. "They were awful to you."

"And that is the best reason of all for a garden. For them. For their children. Because I want to leave love and friendship. To everyone, even those who were awful, and paranoid, and wanted to lock me up. Maybe, when they're there they'll remember and be kinder to the next person. Can I use my money for a garden, Toran?" Bridget and Toran jointly inherited the land and home from their parents. Toran had put her share of the profits of the farm, from that land, into an account for her. It was substantial.

"I already phoned and talked to the mayor about that piece of land where the Zimmerman Factory burned down. The mayor said if we commit to putting some grass in, flower beds, he'll get the city to donate the land."

"You talked to the mayor already?" Toran asked.

"Yes. I called him." She smiled. "And Chief Constable Ben Harris, who's on the town council. And Stanley I and Stanley II, who are on the council, too, and Owena Woods and Rhona Skeates, also on the council."

"They said yes?" Toran asked, grinning.

"Yes. So we'll give it a go?"

Pherson gave a thumbs-up. He coughed again, added a sniffle.

"I love gardens," I said. "It's a small but healthy obsession. I'll help." I thought of the old Zimmerman Factory. That was a multiblock building and parking lot. The park would be enormous.

"It looks like we're going to plant a garden, Bridget," Toran said.

He is the most outstanding older brother in all the land.

Silver Cat meowed.

Toran and I had a tumble in his bed that evening. We took a break from all our worries and talked about a science article he had seen about neurons. It was fascinating. Then we set up a chess set on his bed and played a game. I wore my white negligee. He won.

"You are the most loyal person I have ever known, Char." He kissed me.

"I think the same thing about you, King Toran."

"I don't know what I would have done without you."

"And I, you." I was straddling him, and I bent down and cupped his face. "You're a man in every sense of the word, Toran. You told me once that you are not a romantic man, that you didn't have the words to be romantic, and that isn't true. Romance isn't words, although it can be, but for me, it's what you do. When I see you smiling at me, that's romantic. When you helped me with my mother's garden, that's romantic. When you helped me clean out my house, that's romantic. When I see you reading to Bridget, propping her up on her pillows, that's romantic. When I see you working hard on your farm because you value the land and your work, you value growing healthy food for people, that's romantic. When I see you sticking up for people you love, that's romantic. You, dear Toran"—I leaned down and kissed him—"are the most romantic man on the planet."

I gave him another smackeroo. And a third.

"What also makes you romantic is how awesome you are in bed, Scottish warrior. Creative."

"Ah, Charlotte, it is you who is creative in bed. All those love scenes you've written." He pulled me down to him, and our kisses smiled at each other. "I have read all of your books and I would like to reenact each love scene. Many times."

"It's a plan."

He picked me up and put me how he wanted me. He obviously had read my books.

"Bridget," I told her the next morning as we lay in her bed together, drinking coffee, "draw the dream. Draw what we would have wanted as children if we were playing in a park."

Silver Cat, sitting right by Bridget, stared at her, then licked her arm.

"I have the dream in my head." Bridget had a sanded piece of wood on her lap that Pherson had cut for her so she could make large drawings. On the wood was a long, rectangular piece of paper and her colored pencils.

Her chin trembled. "When Legend comes here, if she does, I want her to see the park, to love it, to know that I wanted her here and that I thought of her when I designed it. I want her to know, despite all that I did that was wrong, I did this one thing right. This is my gift to her, to the children and people of the village. I left something right."

"Oh, Bridget." My chest was tight, my mouth wobbling. She had never stopped thinking of her daughter. Never stopped wanting to be with her, to be her mother. Never stopped loving Legend. I slung an arm around her, our heads together. "Start drawing before I turn into a bawling mess. No one likes a bawling mess."

"Right. Keep it together, Charlotte. I certainly don't want you dripping all over me."

"I'll try not to."

"Give me a tissue, then you can use it."

"What? I have to use it second? How come you get it first?"

"Because."

I handed her the tissue, she wiped her eyes and nose and gave it to me, with ceremony. "I present to you, the royal tissue."

"That's gross, Bridget."

We laughed.

She drew.

She drew the dream for her daughter and for the children and village of St. Ambrose, a town with cobblestone streets and short doors, the ruins of a cathedral and castle, a rich history, and people who had been unbearably cruel and astonishingly gentle.

When she was done, Silver Cat walked up her legs, her stomach, her chest, and licked her nose.

That cat was Bridget's cat, no question. It seemed like Silver Cat had simply been waiting for her to arrive.

Bridget's design for the garden was, as usual, exquisite and detailed, a work of art.

She showed it to Toran, Pherson, and me after we had Chinese food, homemade by Stanley I and Stanley II, who came with their wives to have dinner with us, then left. The Stanleys and I discussed the future of nuclear energy, the joy of mathematical proofs, and the likelihood of extraterrestrial life coming to Scotland. (Slim. We decided that they would probably prefer Mexico, for the sun.)

Bridget had drawn garden rooms here and there, separated with dogwood bushes, a picket fence, pathways, trees, and shrubs. She drew islands of plants and trellises, two small fountains, and three birdbaths. She had chosen a red, blue, and yellow castle play structure, complete with a drawbridge, towers, tunnels, and a lookout point, specifically because of King Toran, Queen Bridget, King Pherson, and Queen Charlotte.

There were three sets of swings next to that, a merry-go-round, a fountain that spewed water straight up for kids to play in on hot days, an oversized gazebo, a rose garden with benches, grass everywhere to run on, a wide concrete path around the edge of the park for walkers and bike riders, and a statue. . . . I peered closer.

It was a statue of us. The four of us. Toran, Bridget, Pherson, and me. Clan TorBridgePherLotte. We were children, facing each other in a circle, our hands clasped together, crowns on our heads, capes flowing behind.

My chin wobbled, hot tears spilled out.

Pherson coughed, as usual when he's overwhelmed, then buried his face in his hands. Bridget leaned over and stroked his head. "Baby, I'm sorry."

Pherson, the baby, hugged her.

Toran's eyes filled.

I put my fist out before we all embarrassed ourselves. "Clan TorBridgePherLotte!"

We fist bumped and said, "Clan TorBridgePherLotte powers, activate! Speed ahead and fight bravely."

The plot of land where the Zimmerman Factory had been would be transformed. Eternally transformed, for all of the children of St. Ambrose to play in.

And for Bridget's daughter.

Legend would know her mother loved her.

"I want to pay for half the cost of Bridget's Park," I said, hugging Toran later that night in bed. I had worn my black negligee with garters. He had taken it off, quick as a lick, and we continued our goal to try out love scenes from my books. I am proud of my flexibility. "I'll share it with you and Bridget."

"No, Charlotte."

"Let me pay for half."

"Never. I will not take money from my woman."

I pulled his head down to mine and kissed him. I sure liked contacts better than glasses. The glasses used to get in the way of my kisses with Toran.

"Yes, Toran. Don't be a beast."

"No."

"Yes."

"No."

"Then I'm going to pay for the gazebo, the fountain, the rose garden, and the play structure."

"Aren't you the funny one? That's much of the cost."

I smiled and kissed him again. I kissed his mouth, his neck, his chest, then moved lower. He thought nothing more of the park.

We discussed it later, again and again, over the next week. It never became mean, never heated, always ended in a hug and a kiss. It's important to know how someone is going to argue.

In the end, Scottish Warrior agreed I could pay for the roses for the garden, trees, and the statue. He and Bridget would pay for the sprawling two-story play structure with bridges and tunnels, the swings, the fountain, the flower beds, etc.

I wrote the checks. He said, firmly, "That's enough."

I knew he meant it.

A feminist knows when to allow her man to be a man.

And I liked the manly man in Toran.

I saw Bridget and Pherson sitting together in front of Toran's fireplace, rain splattering down the windows, their heads close together, blond and black. Pherson, a literature lover, had been reading to her.

I turned to leave, then stopped. The lights were off and the flames danced.

If I squinted my eyes and ignored how emaciated Bridget was, if I forgot that she was sick, if I pretended that she had married Pherson, I would see only a glow.

A glow of love.

Of light.

Of a life lived together, filled with children, Scottish games and legends, songs and bagpipes, kilts and tartans. Clan TorBridgePherLotte and their children and grandchildren, growing old together.

That was taken from them. What should have been was stolen. Ripped away. Violence and blood.

I stood in the glow that did not exist for a second. I closed my eyes and pretended.

It is unfortunate that we all have to open our eyes sometimes and see the truth instead of what we want to see.

I turned away before what I wanted to see, and did not, could not, smashed me down again.

Grief is impossible to bury for long, and I was fighting it, hard, every day. We all were.

"I want to contribute to the cost of developing Bridget's Park," Pherson said when Bridget was upstairs sleeping.

"No," Toran said.

"Yes," Pherson said. "I insist."

"I insist you don't."

"Why are you doing this to me, Toran?" Pherson said, frustrated, shoulders back, offended. "I want to be a part of this. You know how I feel about Bridget." A tear fell from his eye.

Because Pherson was crying, Toran cried. They sniffled at exactly the same time, then at the exact same second ran an impatient hand across their faces.

Two tall, strapping, strong Scotsmen, who minced people at the Scottish games each year, facing each other down, crying.

"Don't push me out of this, Toran," Pherson said. "We're best friends. All of us. Let me in."

Toran glared down at his work boots. It was against his pride to take money from anyone, ever. He was a proud, independent man, but he would understand the significance.

"Okay, Pherson. Thank you."

"Thank you, friend."

They both cleared their throats at the same time and looked away. Crying was not part of that relationship. Then they both, again at the same time, rolled their shoulders and ran a hand through their hair.

I almost laughed.

"Let's have a couple of beers," Toran said.

"I'll get 'em," Pherson said.

Dear St. Ambrose Ladies' Gab, Gardens and Gobble Group,

We have had many glorious suggestions for making money for our annual fund-raiser, including clay friend faces; colorful cherub babies with feathers, teeth, and googly eyes; gardening panties; and selling marijuana.

I was out with my pigs last night and decided to make an executive decision. We are going to have an Indian Feed. Yes, an Indian Feed. All money will go toward Bridget's Park, where the old Zimmerman Factory used to be. The council recently approved it.

The Indian event will be in two weeks. Friday night at 6:00. The entire town is invited. Gitanjali has two simple recipes that she says we can easily re-create. I talked to Dominigo, and he says we can buy the ingredients from him for cost. Gitanjali will donate all the spices. I talked to Mildred at the school, and she said we can use their kitchen for the cooking and the cafeteria for the event. We'll charge per meal, fair price, plus more. It is for a park!

So what we need to do now is make advertisements and put them everywhere. This is what I think they should say:

Indian Feed!
6:00 Friday night at
St. Peter's Independent School
A fund-raiser for Bridget's park
Bring your appetites for Indian.

What do you think, gardeners?

Send the note around quick as the crow flies, write what you'd like, and sign the bottom, as usual.

Olive

Ladys,

Special sweet greetings.

I think we make fun time together cooking to eat Indians for Bridget Park. I have idea. We make advertisement say, "Eat me." And we make signs say, "Eating Indians." Or "Cooking Indians For Food for Bridget Ramsay." I think that tasty idea. Then the peoples knows they can eat tasty food on Bridget.

Serenity and peace to my friendlies.

Gitanjali

Hello to Gobbling Gardens ladies,

I don't think we should emphasize eating Indians. It sounds rather cannibalistic. I did go and operate on a man at the prison recently who told me before the operation that he was a cannibal. Except for that, he was friendly. I watched to make sure my fingers didn't get too close to his mouth, though.

Kenna

Hello ladies,

You are right. We should not call it an Indian Feed. We will not be eating Indians. That did sound carnivorous and cannibalistic. Whoopsy-do! Sorry!

Kenna suggested that we call it the Celebration and Fund-Raiser for Bridget's Park.

That sums it right up.

Olive

PS I will kill the following chickens as my donation: Portsmouth, Monty Jr., Salamander, Mint Ice Cream, and Tornado. I had Tornado on my lap the other day, the dear bird, and he is going to be scrumptious, now, you mark my words.

Garden gals,

If we do need to do anything cannibalistic, I will kill The Arse and we can eat him. He'll need to be boiled first, and plucked. Don't expect any meat off his penis. It was small.

Rowena

Gabbling Gals,

I'll help cook. Guess what? I have a date!

Malvina

Friends,

Thank you. It sounds delicious. We will bring dessert for everyone.

Love you all.

Bridget and Charlotte

Bridget, Pherson, Toran, and I talked. We had the money, between us, for the park. The fund-raiser initially had us stymied. We didn't want to take money we didn't need, and yet it excluded people if it wasn't taken.

"If people want to donate, we should let them," Pherson said. "If we say no, that would be hurtful to them. It's like we're saying they're not needed, their money, their efforts and time, aren't needed, that they need to step aside and let us take over."

"And some people are trying to help because they feel bad about the way they treated Bridget," I said. Toran and I had heard that several times, and every time the person talking to us was emotional, shamed, and apologetic. There were those who still glared and avoided us, too. We didn't expect them to donate. They would use the park, though. As Bridget said, maybe they would rethink what they'd said and done when they were there among the rose bushes. "We need to let them make amends for it."

"I agree," Toran said.

"Everyone needs to feel included," Bridget said.

"Excellent, then," I said. I bit my tongue so I didn't laugh. "Who feels like eating an Indian?"

"Tornado is going to be delicious," Bridget drawled. "I can hardly wait."

"I want to make the sign that says 'Eat Me,' " Toran said.

"I thought we should sell the marijuana," Pherson said.

"We could have smoked it while we were wearing gardening panties that don't creep," I said.

"Or we could have decorated baby cherubs in red paint and added googly eyes," Bridget added, widening her eyes with her fingers. "While stoned and wearing the gardening panties at the same time."

"I am not going to eat Rowena's husband, no matter how she plucks and cooks him," Pherson said.

"I will not eat a penis at the Indian Feed," Bridget said. "No matter how small."

"I could have made a clay mask of my face and hung it on the fence," Toran drawled. "Maybe a hundred masks. It would be Toran everywhere."

We think we're funny.

I had an idea for the dessert. I talked to Sandra Bao at her bakery. She loved the idea. I wrote a check, and we were set. It was a flamingly fantastic idea, forgive me for my lack of modesty.

Maybelle called and left a message.

"Charlotte, it's Maybelle. I'm sure you know, no, I'm sure you don't know, because you don't look at these things, but your latest book, you do remember that it's titled *Danger, Doughnuts, and a Latin Lover,* don't you? You left the reader with a cliff-hanger about McKenzie Rae wanting to get back to her soul mate. Anyhow, still on the *New York Times* bestseller list. Still. We're on, what, week a zillion? And you are . . . where in your next book?

"Gee whiz. That's right. You have writer's block. Gag me.

You are going to give me a heart attack. You're going to make my stomach tie itself in a slip knot, my colon in a braid. I lied to your publishing house—once again—yes, I'm a liar, and I told your editor that everything is going well, that you're working hard. Almost done!

"You've turned me into a liar. Hello, hello? I need to talk to you, you stubborn author.

"Hang on, Charlotte . . . Eric! Why did your principal call me today? You did what? Okay, Charlotte, talk to you later. Eric exploded half of his science lab today . . . the little shit. You are grounded, Eric! Forever! No, I am not impressed with your explosive abilities. Don't try that on me, young man. . . . Randy, I looked in your backpack and found a beer. You are grounded, too. Don't talk to me about your privacy. See this? That's your beer, down the toilet. How do you like toilet privacy? Please call me back, Charlotte. Please."

I kept balancing the books and working for Toran's farm.

He kept trying to help me break the insidious block in my head so I could write my next book. We tried looking at a map to locate my next setting. We tried reading different books on history to see if that would spark an idea. We tried reading books in different genres, hoping that opposites, literarily speaking, would attract.

No go.

"We'll keep trying, Charlotte," he told me.

"I might be out of steam."

"I don't think so. You tell the best stories, right like your father. It'll come to you again."

"Maybe. Maybe not."

"How would you feel if the stories didn't come back?"

I thought about that for a long time. "I don't know. What I do know is that having you to talk to makes this whole writer's block disaster easier to take."

"We'll get that block out of your head."

"Thanks. I don't want to be a blockhead anymore."

We laughed because we are so geeky, then we played chess naked. I moved the chess pieces with my boobs. The game did not last long.

I saw Bridget, in the distance, the next afternoon, standing near one of the tractors, staring up at the cliffs again. I wished that she hadn't gone—she had so little energy left—but I understood why she was there.

She was trying to comprehend, to work it through, to plow a line through a tangle of conflicting emotions that threatened to strangle her. Silver Cat stood right beside her.

I saw her bend her blond head.

It had not been her fault. It was solely theirs.

She would never believe that it wasn't.

18

Before we left for the Celebration and Fund-Raiser for Bridget's Park, the Garden Gobbling Ladies came over. Bridget could not attend; she was having a poor day, plus she didn't want to make anyone nervous and ruin the night. We didn't try to encourage her. She looked hollow eyed, weak, and limp. Pherson would stay with her.

They each had a gift for Bridget. Rowena brought her rock earrings, a bracelet, and necklace, all with purple beading. Gitanjali brought her a basket of soaps and oils, "for the healing." Olive had knitted her a scarf with a pink bird on it. The bird had a huge smile, with teeth. That was intentional. Kenna brought her a stack of new romance novels. "I read them all the time." I briefly wondered if she'd read mine. Malvina brought her pink slippers and a robe.

"Thank you," Bridget said. "Now get on out of here. Don't burn the food. Don't pluck and boil Rowena's ex. No marijuana. Don't eat Indians."

We laughed, we left.

The Celebration and Fund-Raiser for Bridget's Park, with mouthwatering Indian dinners from Gitanjali, an armful of chickens provided by Olive, no Indians themselves eaten, was a success.

Gitanjali and Olive had a crew of women, including me and the rest of the Gobbling and Gabbling Garden ladies, and men, including Toran, Ben Harris, the Stanleys, and the mayor, prepare tandoori chicken and chicken tikka masala. We added Indian rice, naan, and sliced pineapple.

We decorated the cafeteria of the school as "Indianish" as we could. We put down purple, orange, yellow, and green tablecloths and hung colorful paper star lanterns over each table. In the center of the gym we hung pink, purple, green, and yellow fabric out from the center of the ceiling to the corners. Gitanjali let us hang all of her saris around the room.

The schoolchildren, taught by Gitanjali, made white doves, and we hung those from the ceiling, too, in flocks. In the middle of each table we made a diorama-type box about a foot wide and tall, and on each side we glued photos of India, the Taj Mahal, decorated elephants, women in saris, and Indian marketplaces filled with spices. From gold, shiny paper, Kenna and Rowena cut out elephants holding each other's trunks and attached them to two walls.

We turned the lights down, lit candles, and strung white lights.

Gitanjali said, palms together, "It perfect is. Oh, yes, India, here in Scotland, for the Indian Feed."

It was a Scottish fund-raiser with East Indian flavors. People loved it and the turnout was high. After the tandoori and chicken and tikka masala was served, the evening began with Indian music and Gitanjali herself, resplendent in a sparkling orange sari. She mesmerized all of us with a traditional Indian dance. She received a standing ovation, loudest from Chief Constable Ben Harris.

Toran, Ben Harris, the mayor, and other men played their bagpipes, which brought the tears to the fore for me. It reminded me of my father. Toran stood in his clan's red and black kilt, fur sporran, Prince Charlie jacket and plaid, his blue eyes full of concentration, brown curls ready for my fingers to run through them. People stood and clapped when they were done, too.

Several groups of girls, in traditional Highland dress—tartan kilts, matching hose, and red velvet waistcoats with gold braid—performed Scottish dances.

Toran and I thanked everyone together in front of a microphone. We individually thanked the Garden Gobbling Ladies for all their work, in particular Gitanjali, who received another standing ovation. I could tell she was pleased, palms together, slight bow.

We also thanked the mayor, the Stanleys, Pherson, and Chief Constable Ben Harris. We explained Bridget's vision. We had made numerous copies of her design and passed them out. People loved it. Using an overhead projector, we put that colorful work of garden art on a screen and talked about each part of the garden.

When we were done, Mrs. Jamilyn Hoover stood up, leaned heavily on her cane, pointed at us and said, "You tell your Bridget that we're proud of her. We love her, and we thank her for the park."

"It's a delight," Mr. Galing announced, also standing. "Forever, St. Ambrose will have this park because of Bridget. Bridget, one of our own."

They clapped, they cheered. Toran and I tried not to embarrass ourselves by blubbering about. It took all our control. We again thanked everyone for coming, said we appreciated their donations.

Olive stood then, as planned, and showed them where they could donate more money. She had made an elephant out of cardboard, Rowena had painted it, and money and checks could be placed into the elephant's mouth.

"You've named the park, right, Toran?" Ben Harris stood and asked.

"No, we haven't named it yet."

"Well, then, it's easy. How about this? Bridget's Park. A Place for Everyone."

It was perfect.

Toran nodded. "It's perfect, my friend."

So we had it. Bridget's Park. A Place for Everyone.

"And now, for dessert." I was nervous about this part. I trusted Sandra at the bakery, but it was still a fiery undertaking.

I nodded at Mayor MacBay. The lights went off. Gitanjali, Rowena, Kenna, Olive, Malvina, Chief Constable Ben Harris, Stanley I, and Stanley II each came out with a Baked Alaska, made of ice cream, sponge cake, and whipped meringue. They set them on the tables in front, still in the dark. As one, they each struck a match and set the brandy on each cake on fire.

Everyone went crazy. They loved it. Burning cakes, flames leaping!

Baked Alaska is not Indian. It's not a Scottish dessert. But I knew it would be a huge hit, and it was.

In the dark, and quiet, people relaxing into the mood of cake burning, the camaraderie and friendship of the night, I said to Toran, "I'm going to set you on fire tonight, Toran."

He said, "Ah, luv, there's going to be a bonfire in our bedroom, then?"

"Yes, there is. I'll be wearing the black negligee with the garters."

"It won't stay on you very long."

"It's not supposed to."

We did not know the microphone was still on.

We couldn't figure out why everyone started laughing.

Stanley I shouted, "Think you can properly keep up with your woman, lad?"

Stanley II shouted, "We'll understand if you're limpin' tomorrow."

Together they said, "Good luck, Toran."

We ended the evening with a popular rock band banging the tunes out. The leader of the rock band was Ben's nephew. His rocker name was Pulsing Brother. His real name was Tye Harris.

When the Pulsing Brother and the Scissor Gang band walked in, the young people went absolutely crazy, screaming, yelling, waving their hands. Pulsing Brother and the Scissor Gang played for an hour and a half, and I must admit, they were awesome. We pushed the tables back after the Indian Feed, no Indians eaten, and danced. Toran and I swung each other around, dipped, wriggled, shimmied, hands swaying above our heads, my short red skirt flying, my hair swinging.

The Indian Feed evening, as Gitanjali called it, was a massive success. People donated extra money into the mouth of an elephant.

The best thing? The donations told Bridget that the people of St. Ambrose were behind her and Bridget's Park, A Place for Everyone.

Dear St. Ambrose Ladies' Gab, Garden, and Gobble Group,

Thank you, one and all. Last night was better than we could ever have dreamed, was it not?

And we didn't have to sell one marijuana joint, either. Gitanjali, the food was scrumptious. Was I not right about Portsmouth, Monty Jr., Salamander, Mint Ice Cream, and Tornado? So flavorful and plump.

(Sign this note and give it to the next lady.)

Olive

Ladys,

Thank you for helping me cooking with my spices. I think everyone have pleasing night eating Indians and their food on Bridget.

Serenity to you.

Gitanjali

Gabbing ladies,

I couldn't believe The Arse brought The Slut. She seemed sad. She was sitting alone. I almost, not quite, felt sorry for her, the fake-boobed pariah. Wasn't my fault that The Arse ended up wearing his wine on his head.

Rowena

Everyone,

What did you think of my date?

I like him. I have lost ten pounds. Louisa is cutting my hair on Tuesday.

Malvina

Gardening Gang,

What a night! Malvina, I liked your date. I pulled my back doing the twist on stage with Pulsing Brother and the Scissor Gang. I'm glad we didn't sell marijuana. I wouldn't do well in jail. I'm positive they wouldn't let me cut people up in there. The flaming cakes were a hit. Loved them, Charlotte!

Kenna

Friends,

Thank you. More than we can say, thank you.

Love,

Charlotte and Bridget

I could not believe how many people turned out to help us clear the lot where Zimmerman's Factory used to be. The rubble and trash, including two dead cars and a sink, were hauled away by volunteers, including Toran, Pherson, me, the Garden Ladies, and everyone else we knew. As the fall leaves floated by, Bridget's Park, A Place for Everyone, began.

Bridget declined further. She got a red rash. Her cough was hard to control, no matter what medicine we gave her. Her fever was up and down, spiking. Silver Cat never left her side.

The land was flattened straight across, ready for planting, ready for Bridget's garden design.

Bridget had trouble eating, her throat hurt, her glands swelled, her neck stiffened.

The grass sod was laid, the cement paths were poured, the rose garden planted.

Bridget had problems with coordination, with walking and balance.

The white, oversized gazebo was halfway built, the play structure was being installed, the bark dust was laid and waiting for the swings, the fountain construction began.

Bridget was nauseated. She kept vomiting. Toran or I held her hair back when she was bent over the toilet.

Maple and oak trees were planted down the middle of the park and along the pathways. Pink cherry trees lined the edges to offer shade and blooms of color in coming years.

Bridget's headaches and fevers increased in intensity and duration. She had trouble breathing.

Steel arcs were constructed at both entrances to welcome people to the park. The flower beds were filled with chrysanthemums and pansies.

Bridget had a seizure. When she stopped convulsing, when she could breathe again, she said, "I think I'm almost ready to go." Her vision started to blur.

A wind swept through, bringing the last of the fall leaves to the ground. The trees were bare. The volunteers and the professionals, tons of them, kept working on Bridget's Park, A Place for Everyone.

"I want to see it," Bridget whispered, petting Silver Cat, asleep on her lap.

"You do know it's ten o'clock at night," I said.

"Yes, silly lady, but I took a six-hour nap. Let's give it a go. Help me up, my friend, and let's sneak out of this house like cat burglars."

"Okay, cat burglar, here we go." I wrapped an arm around her. She didn't bother to get out of her robe and nightgown. She slipped her feet into rain boots. I grabbed a jacket and stuck her arms through. I was in sweats, my hair on top of my head, in a ponytail. My contacts were out, and my new glasses, without tape on the frames, were on.

She leaned heavily on me as I slid her into the truck. She was on a painkiller, but she still hurt, her bones brittle.

I hurried back into the house and grabbed blankets, covered her, then ran around to the other side of the truck.

We drove through the empty streets of the country, over the stream, around the shadowy hills, past the rumbling ocean, and into the village. She insisted we leave the windows down so she could smell the salt in the air.

"Stop here."

We stopped in front of the ruins of the cathedral, built nine hundred years ago, gravestones wobbling crookedly over the land.

"It's morbid to stop at the graveyard," I drawled.

"True. Rather gruesome, given the inevitable. Tell me a bone chilling ghost story."

"I don't have one at the moment, except for the one about the headless woman with the hook for an arm we used to tell each other."

"She was scary, but not as scary as the ghost story we told about Hatchet Hunter and Chain Link Man."

I raised my eyebrows. "Correct. Hatchet Hunter and Chain Link Man. They scared me so much, I had nightmares."

We stared out at the darkness, the cathedral looming, the tilted gravestones reminders of those who were here . . . then gone.

"Don't come to my grave, Charlotte."

"Why?"

"Because I'm not going to be there."

Damn. She makes me cry. "You make me cry, then my nose runs."

She held my hand. "You are a true friend, Charlotte, and I love you even when your nose is running like a sieve."

"Thank you. What a special image you've given me of my nose."

We drove three blocks, in silence, then stopped at the castle, the ocean splashing up on the cliff behind it, the drawbridge opening a gaping hole. It was a place where prisoners were dropped into holes in the ground, tunnels were dug to attack and defend, battles were fought and lost, and Bridget and I played.

"Remember that game we invented near the tunnel? The one about being chased by French knights?" I asked.

"Yes. We defended ourselves each and every time. They were afraid of our sword-fighting prowess."

"Powerful girls, we were."

"Other girls pretended they were princesses in distress."

"Dull. Anti-feminist. Too dreary for us."

"Your mother would have lost her pretty head."

I drove past Sandra's Scones and Treats Bakery, Molly Cockles Scottish Dancing Pub, the golf course, Estelle's Chocolate Room, university buildings, two ancient churches with stained glass windows, the fountain in the center of the village, and the bookstore where my mother used to buy us one book each.

I drove on the wrong side of the street and rolled down the windows so Bridget would be closest to her park.

"Look, Bridget." I pointed to the ten-foot-tall steel arc at an entrance to the park.

She inhaled, quick. "My goodness." She put her hands to her face.

The arc was engraved. It said, "Bridget's Park. A Place for Everyone."

"Oh, my goodness," she said again, as I drove to the other end to see the same arc, the same engraving.

"The arcs were Toran's idea."

She sniffled. "I love that brother of mine."

"Me too."

"When Legend comes, she'll see this. She'll know the truth about my life." She struggled not to cry. "I want you to be honest with her, Charlotte, but she'll know that in the end, I gave everyone a gift. My name was on a gift. Her mum's name was on a gift."

I wondered if my heart would burst from the pain of losing Bridget. "Legend will love it. She'll know you're her mother. She'll know from Toran and me that you never wanted to give her up. She'll know you loved her your whole life. I'll tell her. We'll tell her."

"I lost myself that day when they ripped her out of my arms. I lost it. My baby. I screamed so loud, Charlotte. I fought. I hit, I kicked, and I remember they took her out of the room, and she was crying, too. My baby was crying for me, I know it, and I could hear her screaming down the hall and it got fainter and fainter and pretty soon I couldn't hear Legend at all. Silence. Silence except for me yelling for her, trying to get her, and everyone holding me down, telling me to calm down. Calm down. My daughter, my baby, was stolen from me, and they want me to calm down." She had started to shake, and I held her hand. "Calm down." She took a deep, jagged breath. "Calm down." She wiped her brow.

I couldn't even imagine. Someone comes and rips your newborn baby out of your arms and you never see that baby again. Never. How do you live with that?

"Tell Legend I planned it with her in my mind the whole time."

"I will. I promise I will."

"Let's go sit in the park before my memories kill me. They come back like that, they always have. That one awful time won't leave my head. It's an ongoing nightmare."

I helped her out. We walked twenty feet, me carrying most of her weight, and sat on a bench by the rose garden in our pajamas. It was cold, and I ran back to the truck for the blankets and wrapped them around her. She was bones and skin now, bones and skin.

The park was almost finished. It would be one of the best parks in all of Scotland for children and families, at least that's what we believed.

Bridget was shriveled and exhausted beneath her robe, her cheeks sunken, but she was smiling, and I felt her joy.

"It's a beautiful park, Charlotte." Her voice broke. "It has everything for children. They can be happy here. They can play and run and laugh. They can escape if they're from homes that aren't happy, like Toran and me. I would have loved a park exactly like this when I was a kid."

I was an emotional wreck, trembling. "I will miss you. Bridget, I can't tell you how much. I will miss everything about you. I can't imagine my life without you. All these years. Since we were babies."

"I'll be here in the rose beds with you, my friend," she whispered.

I burst into tears, and she hugged me.

"I'll be walking with you down this path right here."

My shoulders shook uncontrollably.

"I'll be sitting by you, here, on this bench, listening to Toran and Pherson playing their bagpipes in the gazebo."

I gasped for breath, my forehead to hers.

"I'll be with you when you lie down on the grass and write your books."

I kept crying . . . and crying . . .

"I'll be with you when you watch the fountain with Toran."

I tilted my head back to the black sky and moaned, my tears drowning me.

"I'll watch your and Toran's children play."

Our children. Here. Without their aunt Bridget. She held me under the night sky, the stars a sprinkle of kisses, the moon a circle of white fire. Bridget comforting Charlotte when it should have been me comforting her.

My tears were a river sliding down my cheeks and onto Bridget's, where they mixed together, two broken, sad rivers.

"And when you're an old Scottish lady, Char, I'll look out for you, and smile, as you watch your grandchildren playing in the castle."

"I'll miss you." It was all I could manage, all I could do. Losing her was killing me. "I will miss you, Bridget."

"I will miss you, too. Thank you for being my friend. Thank you for building this park. Thank you for helping me leave something behind, something beautiful. For Legend, for everyone. I love you, Charlotte."

"I love you, too."

I could hear the whistle of the train. It was on the tracks and headed straight for us.

I held Toran close to me that night after we made love.

"I feel like I'm dying of grief, Charlotte."

"I feel the same. I can hardly breathe through it."

We kissed, and held the kiss until we fell asleep, devastated.

Utterly devastated.

Pherson and Bridget sat on a bench in Toran's backyard, hand in hand, their heads bent toward each other, black and white-blond, Bridget wrapped in blankets. Silver Cat sat right beside her.

I looked away when I saw Pherson swipe a hand across his eyes. I knew he was crying. Tough and rough Pherson, Toran's best friend, another tough and rough man.

They were gentle on their women.

And Pherson was losing the woman who had been in his heart from the time we were kids.

Day by day, that's all we had with Bridget.

Soon she would be gone.

Pherson would never be the same. He had told me he had not married because he had not found any woman he loved as much as he loved Bridget.

Bridget had been his soul mate, and they should have been together. It was there in their script. But the script never made it to completion. Someone shredded the script. Someone burned it. Someone decided his evil should wipe it away.

I felt another rush of rage for Angus Cruickshank.

Whoever killed him, if he was killed, had done everyone a favor.

Bridget kissed Pherson's cheek, soft, so soft. She whispered something to him.

He would remember it forever.

I cried that night for Pherson.

For his total, forever loss.

* * *

Bridget wanted me to drive her to the top of the cliffs, so I bundled her up in blankets and took her up. I knew exactly where she wanted me to go.

Before we left, she dug in the brown box for letters that I hadn't read yet and brought them with us.

I read them when we arrived, the ocean whipped up in the distance, wind blowing the trees like rubber bands.

April in 1975. I don't know the date. Maybe the 25th?

Dear Charlotte,

My father and mum came to see me in London in my flat when I was done waitressing at a bar. Waitress. I waitress and I draw my pictures.

It is not a nice flat. I am having troubles with bad drugs. Arms hurt. And bad alcohol. Too much of everything, but the memories don't go away. He's forcing me, hurting me, wearing black and white, a choker on his neck, a choker on my neck, a choker . . .

Where is she now? How is she? How is my baby? Do you know?

It has been months since I talked to my mum and father. Toran is at Cambridge. Smart Toran. So smart. He doesn't know it all.

My father said to me Sister Margaret told us what happened to you but he did not believe what she said. She had dementia Father Cruickshank told him later and tried to cook a live chicken in the oven and she danced naked outside and she lies but he said Bridget was Sister Margaret telling the truth?

Bridget was Father Cruickshank the father of the baby did he hurt you and I said yes and he started to cry and cry but I did not comfort him because he put me in that home said I was a slut and a whore like his mum and he took my baby away from me then he sent me to live with people who scream at voices and knock their heads into walls and rock back and forth for that long and I also had straps on me and shots there too.

And he said why didn't you tell me and I said you would never have believed me you didn't even believe Sister Margaret you would have believed Father Cruickshank because you love the church more than you love your family and Father Cruickshank said he would kill Toran if I told and my father he put his head in his hands and cried and cried again.

Legend she would be two years old. Two. My girl. I will never see my girl again because of this crying father this stupid man who shrieks Bible verses.

My mum cried, too. Bridget she kept saying I am sorry sorry sorry and I said it's too late for you to be sorry why didn't you help me Mum why didn't you come get me why didn't you save the baby why didn't you get me out of the asylum and she said she couldn't Dad wouldn't let her and I said why do you only do what Dad says why didn't you help me your daughter?

And she cried and rocked herself hands on her head. But I said to her now you cry Mum but where were you for me for your daughter? What happened to your granddaughter? I was not a whore or a slut and you believe the priest and your husband who is mean to you.

And I say go home crying father. You took my baby from me and you believe Father Cruickshank that I had sex with other boys and it was him who forced me to for a long time. Blood on me. Choked me. You get out now and take your cross with you and your Bible and don't you quote scripture here where was God in my life? Where was he?

So my father he says he's sorry he has never said he's sorry and I say it's too late because it is and then gets up and tries to hug me but I pick up a pan and I hit him on his shoulder and then his shoulders sag like they have the weight of potatoes on him. I hit him again and again. Then I'm sad I hit my father.

I might love my mother a little because she tried when she wasn't drunk but why was she drunk? Drunk mum means she couldn't be a mum. I told her that she said sorry sorry sorry, I love you. She tried to hug me and I said get out and never come back never talk to me again never come here and outside the flat I heard them fighting and my mum said I knew it she was not a whore look what you did to her Carney and I want a divorce and my dad said I didn't know and there will be no divorce and they are crying both of them.

They should have helped their crying daughter.

Bridget

May 12, 1975

Charlotte,

I told Toran everything, finally. He cried. I've never seen him so furious in my entire life. If Father Angus Cruickshank had been here, he would have killed him with his bare hands, I know he would. He hugged me and told me he loved me and said that Father Cruickshank would never hurt me again.

Love you.

Bridget

June 5, 1975

Charlotte,
Father Angus Cruickshank has disappeared. Gone. My mother wrote me a letter and told me and said come home Bridget we want you to live with us everything will be different and even my father wrote me a letter and said come home I'm sorry I made a mistake I love you, daughter.

I wonder if that priest is dead. I hope someone killed him. I would have if I could have.

I wonder if my father did it or my mum or both of them. I cannot imagine them killing a priest. The Catholic Church is what my father lived for. He would believe he was going to hell.

But he knew the truth about Father Cruickshank when he left my flat. He knew.

My mother called me. I told her not to call me again. When my father called I said don't call me again ever I hate you both. I hung up.

Bridget

June 18, 1975

Charlotte,
My parents are dead. Toran came and told me.

They died when their car flew off the cliff outside of St. Ambrose. You know the cliff, the one on the very top. The part where it is completely straight. No curves, not a one. It was sunny. Dry. Not cold.

They are gone.

I hate them, I love them, I hate them, I love them.

I caused their accident. They were upset about me, about what Father Cruickshank did to me. I know it.

I think my father drove the car over the cliff on

purpose. His favorite priest raped his daughter and he believed the priest's lies. He took his daughter's baby away from her. He put his daughter in an insane asylum and called her a whore and a slut. Even Sister Margaret had told him but he hadn't believed her. He had dinner with the priest, the rapist of his daughter.

He had loved the church and the church had failed him.

Everything was gone for him, then. His church, his priest, his faith, his daughter. My mother was threatening to divorce him and his son hated him.

All gone.

Off the cliff.

Love,

Bridget

When I was done we sat in silence in my truck, the ocean stretching out below. This was where Carney had lost control of his car. He and Bonnie had gone over the cliff and died.

"This was not your fault, Bridget."

"I think it was."

"How so?"

"I could have forgiven my father that day. Forgiven my mother. I didn't."

"I don't think they deserved forgiveness, Bridget. Your father was a lousy, punitive, fanatical father even before you were raped. Your mother was a drunk. They didn't protect you. They shuttled you off to a pregnant girls' home, believed the lies a priest told them, condoned having the baby taken away, then allowed Cruickshank to stick you in an insane asylum when you wouldn't stop screaming."

"Even today, Charlotte, I don't think I forgive them. I could forgive them as an adult, perhaps, but I can't forgive what they did to me as a teenager. What they did to the young Bridget. . . ."

We talked until the sun went down behind us.

When it was dark, Bridget said, "I need raspberry pie."

"Me too. With ice cream and whipping cream, both."

We went and bought a whole pie and ate it straight out of the tin with two forks.

Toran asked me if Bridget and I had had a good time. I said yes.

"Do you think your parents killed Angus Cruickshank?"

"I don't. I've thought about it endlessly, all sides."

"Why?"

"Because I don't think my father would have had it in him to kill a priest. He still would have been scared of going to hell eternally."

"What about your mother?"

"No. She didn't have a violent bone in her. She was weak, too. Beaten down by my father."

I didn't know if Toran was right. When women believe their children are at risk, they turn into people they themselves don't even recognize. Bridget's mother had not protected her from a religious fanatic father, but against a man who had attacked her daughter?

She might even surprise herself.

And the timing was right. Shortly after Father Cruickshank disappears, Toran's parents' car goes over the cliff. On a straightaway. Were they trying to avoid prosecution?

"For the record, Char, I didn't kill him."

"I believe you." I did.

"There are probably many other people, people not even from St. Ambrose, who would want him dead. We may never know."

Maybe. Maybe not.

I was sure the murderer was living among us. I don't know why I was sure, but I was.

What I wanted was proof he was dead. If I ever found out who killed him, I would never turn the murderer in, but I wanted to know Father Cruickshank was not out there, preying on other Bridgets and causing cataclysmic results.

"I do think my father drove the car over the cliff on purpose. Bridget was right. He'd lost everything. He was wrong about

Father Cruickshank. He'd been devoted to the Church, and the Church had betrayed him. In turn, he had betrayed his daughter, not protected her, was friends with the man who raped her, worshiped him, then locked her up on that man's advice. My mother wanted a divorce. My father could not accept that. His entire life, filled with rigidity, misplaced devotion, and his insistence that he was right and righteous, crumbled."

"I'm sorry, Toran." Toran and Bridget, both, had been through so much. I wrapped my arms around him, then my legs. Later I brought him a slice of raspberry pie and hugged him when he went to sleep. Sometimes that's all you can do for someone. Hugs and pie.

The next afternoon I sat in the middle of my lawn in my mother's garden and read the rest of Bridget's letters that she'd written to me and had never sent. The Diary Letters. They were sporadic. Months would go by sometimes, a year, eighteen months, then another one. It was her downslide into hell. Drugs. Alcohol. Scary situations. A few bad men. Lost. Depressed. In and out of rehab. Clarity and health, coherency, which is probably when she wrote the letters she actually sent me. Gardening. She'd read my book, thanks for mailing it! Then the slide back down again. Waitressing jobs. Fired from jobs. Poverty. Toran and Pherson, trying to help, coming to get her. Slide again. And always, Legend. Where is Legend? Is she happy and safe? My Legend.

Heart shattering, that's what it was.

"I want you to give these garden designs to Lorna Lester." Bridget held two sheets of paper out to me. She was leaning against her pink pillows, her bedside light casting a soft shadow on her face. Outside it was stormy, the wind whipping around, the rain falling, the skies gray and low. Silver Cat meowed.

"Now I know you've lost your mind. You're kidding me, right?"

"No, Char. Give them to her, please. Lorna doesn't have a

pretty garden, and I know if she had one, if she had a place that was peaceful, she wouldn't be so . . ."

"You can't even say it, can you, Bridget? You can't bring yourself to say anything bad against anyone, you weird saint."

She laughed, her skinny chest shaking. "Weird saint. Ah, Charlotte. Trust me. I have not been a saint, weird or otherwise." She pushed a lock of white-blond hair back. It was lanky now, though I washed it every other day.

"Lorna tried to ban you from the village. She spoke against you in the town meeting. She told everyone that you were contagious."

"And that, Charlotte, true friend, is why she needs the drawings. Please." She held them out to me.

"No." I remembered Lorna's shrill voice. Her puffy, quivering body leaning forward and yelling, *"Bridget Ramsay should be quarantined. Quarantined! She should never, ever be allowed in St. Ambrose again! She has chosen her own death. She has indulged in sinful behavior, a common harlot, and now she's being punished, rightly so. AIDS is a curse upon this earth, sent to people who are not walking on God's road."*

Bridget laughed, a light laugh, a dancing-along-the-edge-of-death laugh. "Please again?"

"No. You can't make me, either." I knew she could.

"And I want you to bring her one of the winter pansies in the clay pots."

"Hell. No. Hell twice again. No." I crossed my arms.

She laughed.

"I don't get it, Bridget. I don't. She is a snake. And not a garter snake that eats the slugs that eat the plants. But a python-type snake."

She hissed at me, weakly. I hissed back.

"Lorna needs it."

"Why? Why on earth?"

"Because it'll help to break up her fear."

"Break up her fear?"

"Yes."

"Why do you want to do that?"

"Because as long as she's scared, it comes out as hate. She has a sad life, Charlotte. Daughter left. Husband ignores her. Her sister is Laddy. I've had fear and hate in my life, and I know how it turns out. I also didn't forgive in the past, with my parents, but I want to now. Please." She held the papers out. "Help me to show Lorna I forgive her."

I glared at her. "You are a pain in the ass."

She chuckled. "And you are wonderful."

Silver Cat meowed, as if in agreement.

I went to Lorna Lester's house. I *stomped* to Lorna Lester's house with the dumb winter pansy in the clay pot. Before I left I put on my new leather boots, new black pants, and a thick red sweater and scarf. I had learned that clothing can be armor, and when you had to do something you didn't want to do, an outfit could help you through it. I also put on gold hoop earrings and lipstick.

Lorna's home is plain. Dull. Mauve on the inside. She had a garden, but it was precise to the point of boredom. As it was now fall, almost officially winter, it was dead.

I knocked on the door, loud and hard, fully expecting her to send me away, probably with a venomous, slitty-eyed expression. I bet Malvina was a lot happier not living here anymore.

The door opened. I blinked, twice, sucked in a breath. What a change.

Lorna seemed smaller than before. She was in a dull black dress. Her slitty eyes were sagging with tiredness. Her face sagged. She sagged.

"What do you want, Charlotte?"

"Hello, Lorna. Bridget sent me."

"Bridget?"

"Yes, Bridget. The one you want to keep locked out of St. Ambrose. The one you railed against in front of the entire town and called a common harlot. Old-fashioned word, but we all understood what you meant."

Her chin trembled, her voice weak. "She might be contagious."

"Not unless you have sex with her, Lorna, and I don't think Bridget will do that with you. You're not her type."

Her face hardened, mouth twisting. She tried to shut the door. I stuck my new leather boot in. "I don't know why Bridget did this, Lorna. She's a better person than I am, I would never have done it, but she wanted you to have this." I held up the garden designs in my hands. Two pages, for the front and back of Lorna's home, filled with color and texture, a piece of art. I would have framed them, as I framed the garden plans she had made Toran and me.

"What is that?"

"It's a garden plan." Bridget had drawn intricate trees and piles of flowers; a rock pathway to the door; a picket fence; a fountain in the shape of a girl reading a book, as Malvina loved to read, surrounded by cobblestones; a circular patio; the Scottish flag on a flagpole, as Lorna was proud to be a Scot. There was a solitary red chair with a footstool in a corner. On the footstool was a pile of books, as Lorna had told her she also loved reading. There was a yellow wood table for planting flowers in pots.

"A what?" Lorna's voice had lost that ragged edge.

"A garden plan. She's drawn pictures of your garden, front and back, that you can follow to make your garden better."

I held them out. Lorna's hands shook as she took them.

She studied the drawings, the tiny details, the birds' wings, every feather outlined, butterflies flitting over a delicate rose, craggy white birch tree bark, a canopy of leaves in a multitude of colors. Her face crumbled, tears forming and spilling over. "Why? Why did she do that for me?"

"Because, Lorna," I said, aching for Bridget, "she wanted to give you something pretty. *Pretty* is actually her word. She thought if you knew what to do with your garden, you would be happier."

"I am happy."

"Right. You're happy and I'm bacteria wearing a bridal gown."

Her shoulders bent forward, her head dipped, her body shook. She cried.

I had not expected that.

I waited and watched. I had hated this woman. Hated what she'd said at the meeting, hated that she'd tried to rally people in town around her to hurt Bridget. Hated her judgmental attitude.

My hate seemed to sink out of me as Lorna became a different Lorna. She was pathetic. She was alone. She had a pathetic, alone life.

"Lorna," I said. "May I make you a cup of tea?"

"Everyone in the village hates Laddy and me. Malvina won't speak to me. My husband says I've embarrassed him and if I don't apologize to Bridget, he will move out." Lorna's hands shook so badly around her teacup, she could hardly hold it. "What I did to Bridget was unforgivable. I will never forgive myself."

"Bridget forgives you."

That undid her. She laid her head on the table, shoulders shaking, her hand over the garden designs, as if she was afraid I might snatch it back. I patted her back. I felt sorry for her. She had nothing. I would be unhappy, too.

"I do not deserve forgiveness."

"She gave it to you, anyhow."

I ended up giving her two shots of whiskey. It was the only thing I could think of to get her calmed down as she started to hyperventilate.

When she finally could take a breath, and did not need me to hold a paper bag over her face, I broached one more topic. "Lorna, there is one more person who you've hurt."

She gripped the paper bag. "I know. You. Olive. Malvina. Rowena. Kenna."

"One more."

She put the bag to her face again, tears drowning her eyes.

"Gitanjali," I said.

She nodded, then pulled the bag away. "I know," she gasped. "I know. And she has been nothing . . . nothing . . . but dear to me. I am a bad woman."

"Not bad. Sort of bad."

"Will she forgive me? Gitanjali? I will ask her to forgive me. Too late to make it up to Bridget, not too late for Gitanjali, my friend."

"You know she will."

I prefer "So long" to good-bye.

So long and good luck.

So long and good travels.

So long and good wishes.

So long, my dearest, truest friend.

I love you.

There is some pain in life that is so crushing, it is a wonder we live through it.

Bridget spent most of her time in bed, Silver Cat nestled into her side.

She cried now and then, but mostly she showed ironclad courage and strength. She drew and she read, Pherson, Toran, and I on the bed with her. Clan TorBridgePherLotte to the end.

I heard the train on the tracks. The tracks were rumbling. The whistle was piercing.

"You are my very best friend, Charlotte," Bridget said, holding my hand.

"You're my very best friend, too, Bridget." She was pale, weak, hollowing out, life leaving one breath, one word at a time. We faced each other in her bed, our heads on one pillow, the cool Scottish winter wind blowing through, a dash of salt, a hint of mint tea.

Toran, Pherson, and I had had dinner with Bridget on her bed that night. She didn't eat; we did, but not much. Clan TorBridge-PherLotte put on the crowns and capes, held the swords, wore the gold belts. We put our hands in a circle and yelled, "Fight with might, be strong, my friends."

We talked about our childhood, the games we played, the fort we built, and the battles we won against evil. We sang songs, including Scottish drinking songs. We drank Scottish Scotch.

Pherson left to go home to sleep for a few hours, Toran went to sleep in our bedroom, and I lay with Bridget, the moonlight a ray of white, like a staircase up to the heavens.

"The angel delivered the note, and I'm taking the white unicorn on out of here, Char, the one your father told us about with the gold reins. Riding it to the heavens. My room is ready up there, and the unicorn is here. Waiting for me."

I didn't know what to say. Then I decided I didn't need to say anything.

"I'll miss the ocean," Bridget said. "I'll miss the Scottish games. I'll miss Molly Cockles Scottish Dancing Pub."

I thought of the pub. The owner had announced that if there were any "idiots" who spoke out against Bridget, they could "damn well go drown themselves somewhere else, no spirits for them."

"I'll miss the garden club ladies."

I thought of Lorna. How she'd treated Bridget at first, how she treated her at the end. Last night, Lorna had brought over a smoked fish pie with haddock, cheddar cheese soup, oxtail soup, homemade hot bread, broken biscuit cake, and almond bark with sea salt. And wine. Three bottles, though she didn't let the "devil's punch" in her house. She was distraught. She thanked Bridget for the garden plans, and I have never in my life heard such a profuse, sincere apology.

"I'll miss the village."

I thought of the village. The people. How they'd treated her at first, how many of them treated her at the end, with devoted friendship and love.

"I'll miss Toran, Pherson, and you, Charlotte."

I couldn't talk, the tears soaking our pillow. The ray of white, the staircase, seemed brighter now. Ready. Waiting.

"I'll miss writing letters to you."

"I'll miss getting them." I pushed her blond hair out of her eyes.

"I'll miss Silver Cat." Her eyes drifted to the window, to the white staircase. "In some ways, I'll be glad to go. I can't live with the pain anymore. The painkillers aren't working well. I can't live feeling this ill. I'm surprised by how much I want to stay, but I have had enough of this life, too. I think of Legend every day. I know she's alive, but I can't be with her. I could have passed her on the street, at a café. I could have been sleeping on the street and her parents may have walked by with her." She smiled, a smile so sad it was as if the grief of Scotland settled on her face. "She'll come home one day. I won't be here, but she'll come. St. Ambrose is her home. It will call to her."

Her daughter might not even know she was adopted. If she did, there was no paper trail to follow home. I stroked her hair.

"She'll come," she said again, then sighed, closing her eyes. "She'll come."

"I'll be waiting for her. I'll tell her you loved her."

"I know." She squeezed my hand. "From now until I see you again, my friend, I love you."

"I love you, too, Bridget." I wiped her tears, then mine.

I watched her sleep. The white staircase grew brighter. The unicorn with the gold reins was waiting.

The train's whistle blew. It had never been louder.

Bridget died at home two days later. Clan TorBridgePher-Lotte was together, in her bed, Silver Cat beside her.

At her request, we had done nothing to slow the decline. She didn't want to eat, and we didn't push her. She didn't want to drink, so we let it go. Some might see this as giving up. I saw it as reality. Why prolong the inevitable when it is so painful for the person dying?

Before she died, after hugging Toran and Pherson, who were both emotional wrecks but trying unsuccessfully to control themselves, she held my hand. "You were always my very best friend, Charlotte," she whispered. "Always."

"And you, mine, Scottish warrior queen."

When the pain became too much, we called Kenna. Kenna had her swallow medicines from two vials.

She slipped into sleep. Silver Cat meowed so loud, a high-pitched shriek, that we jumped. She kept meowing like that, and I held her in my arms until she stopped, but her body kept shaking.

Bridget never opened her eyes again.

I wanted the train, rumbling on the tracks, to get delayed at another station. I wanted a U-turn. I wanted the engineer to change his mind. I wanted to beg, grovel, bargain.

The train came, it stopped, and Bridget climbed aboard. She smiled and waved good-bye, healthy again. The engineer was gentle but insistent. It was her time, not ours. He would take care of her now.

The whistle blew, the wheels lurched forward, the engine groaned, and the puff of steam rose in the sky, into heaven. Bridget blew kisses.

We were on our knees, hands outstretched.

Soon the train disappeared, along with the tracks and the station. There was no whistle, the steam evaporated, the earth stopped rumbling.

The train was gone.

Alone.

Alone.

So long. I will see you again.

Toran and I held each other tight. When morning came, neither one of us wanted to get up.

But we did.

You have to.

Silver Cat, after one final, loud screech after Bridget died, disappeared. We looked everywhere. We couldn't find her.

My mother called and listened to me cry. She cried, too. She wanted to come for the funeral, but I told her not to. It was too long a trip from Africa.

She called five restaurants in town. They brought us dinner each night. We received many dinners from people and had to put an extra refrigerator in the garage. People kept coming by to pay their respects, and we fed them.

My mother sent flowers the next day, too. Irises. She knows those are my favorite.

19

Bridget's memorial service would be held at the graveyard where generations of Mackintoshes and Ramsays were buried. Despite the feuds and fights, we all end up together.

It was by her request that there be no church service. Given her past, that was entirely understandable.

Toran, Pherson, and I dug Bridget's grave. I did not go to my father's gravesite. I couldn't. Not yet.

Digging her grave was one of the most depressing yet profound moments of my whole life. I stood in black farm boots, jeans, and a light jacket, which I soon took off, the clouds clearing.

We dug her grave right under a sprawling, ancient oak tree. It had seen one Ramsay or Mackintosh after another buried there.

I looked up into the branches, bare, tangled, intricate, and saw the protection, if only metaphorically, that the tree offered. The oak tree was the owner of the graveyard, not us.

Toran settled the question on the location of the grave. "She will not be buried by our parents."

Pherson nodded. He seemed to have aged overnight. He had white hairs where no white hairs had been months ago.

It is an insidious, overwhelming kind of grief that wells up when you're digging the grave of someone you love.

I shoveled the dirt out.

I remembered Bridget as a little girl, how we ran beside the meandering stream, chased butterflies, played hide-and-seek.

I remembered the imaginary games we played as Clan Tor-BridgePherLotte. We were fighters, saviors, mermaids and mermen, magical and invincible.

I remembered the Scottish sun tunneling down on our heads and the Scottish rain falling gently as we danced through it.

I shoveled the dirt out. I dug a hole to make way for my best friend.

I remembered how we wrote letters to each other as children and as teenagers before I left, back and forth, how I would write part of a story and she would draw a picture below it, how we wrote to each other for two decades as grown women.

There would be no more letters, ever. My best friend, gone, every breath gone, every thought gone, every dream, every laugh, every memory.

Gone.

I shoveled the dirt out. This was where Bridget's body would be buried.

I remembered how we felt this graveyard was so spooky, how we read the names on the headstones, how she pointed out Carney's parents and great-grandparents, and then I did the same. So many Ramsays and Mackintoshes. Some lived to be old, eighty years. One was ninety-four. Others were only babies, a day old, six months old, seven, fifteen.

Ramsays. Mackintoshes.

And now Bridget Ramsay was here, too.

I shoveled the dirt out. My tears fell, my shoulders ached.

We didn't speak, the three of us, dirt flying, inches from each other. We stopped when a truck drove up. Baen and Gowan climbed out. Toran's face tightened, and he let swear words stream out, thunder against lightning. Pherson muttered that he felt like smashing someone and those two would be the perfect victims. Pherson's grip tightened on his shovel. I knew we were looking at a fight. Baen and Gowan would be beaten to shit.

Baen held up a hand. "Please tell me to leave if you wish, man, and I will. But my son and I, we would like to help dig the grave." He ran a hand over his forehead. "For Bridget."

"Aye. We're sorry, Toran. Pherson. Charlotte. We're ashamed of ourselves," Gowan said. "You know us not to be too bright, and this time we were dumber than a rat's arse."

"Not honorable Scotsmen," Baen said. "A disgrace. Please, man, let us do this one thing."

Toran hesitated. I saw him fight with himself, not wanting them near his sister's grave, but rejecting an offer of help, kindly given, while being asked for forgiveness, that wasn't right, either. He bent his head, hand on the shovel. He was grieving too much for anger. It would come again, that anger, but not now.

He squared his shoulders. "Come on up."

Baen and Gowan walked up the hillside, hats in their hands. They nodded at me. "Charlotte. Pherson."

We nodded back.

"We're sorry," Gowan said. "Sorry for the insult to your clan and family. Sorry all the way down to the ground. This ground, right here, under our feet." Gowan stomped the ground. "Sorry to your sister, your friend. Sorry, man."

And that was it. There were no more words.

We all dug together, taking turns. I did not wipe my eyes as my tears fell into Bridget's grave.

No one bothered to wipe their eyes, no, they didn't, not even Baen and Gowan, but Gowan did give me his handkerchief. It wasn't too dirty, either.

We dug Bridget's grave, under the oak tree, away from the parents who failed her but closer to the sunsets she loved, closer to the stars spiraling and arcing across the horizon, closer to the blue skies of Scotland, so close you could scoop out the sky with your hand, like blue cotton candy.

Soon we had a grave for Bridget.

I had shoveled the dirt out, so my friend could be placed inside.

As the sun set, I climbed the hill again to the cemetery, by myself, and stood by the open grave. Bridget would be in my soul, my life, forever. Her essence, her laughter, sharp wit, humor, forgiveness, and her unending love for a baby she had hardly held, those things, they lived on.

They lived in the rocky cliffs of Scotland, the ocean waves that crashed into the shore, the fields filled with bluebells and daffodils, the sunsets that lit the sky on fire and the sunrises that covered the land in a gold and pink glow.

They never leave our hearts, the ones we love.

Where we go, they go. When we cry, they comfort. When we laugh, they laugh, too. When we grieve, when we're lonely, it's their hand we reach for, if only in our minds. We hear their voices, their advice, sometimes their reprimands. We hear their words of love and encouragement, of warning. Their love lives on, breathes on, carries on, and eventually gives us peace, the memories holding us in a hug.

"So long, Bridget," I said to her, crumbling to my knees. "I love you, I miss you. I will see you again."

"Sweetheart, Bridget asked me to give this to you."

I took the letter from Toran's hand late that night, then hugged him. We sat on the couch together, the fire roaring, as I opened it up.

> *Charlotte,*
>
> *I wanted to write you one last letter. A short one, you'll understand. But this one is all true.*
>
> *You are, and always have been, my very best friend. I love you.*
>
> *Bridget*

I clutched the letter to my chest, the sobs making my whole body ache.

I felt a hole, large and gaping, lonely and lost. True friends are so hard to find. It's so hard to trust someone completely, to find that personality that blends with yours, and now Bridget was dead.

Toran wrapped his arms around me. "There now . . . there now . . . luv . . . I love you, Charlotte. We'll get through this. Together we will."

I wondered if my whole body would ever stop aching.

That night Toran and I had wildly awesome sex. On fire. I was up against a wall. He held my legs around him as I clung to his shoulders. Afterward, we fell right to sleep, me on top of him. In the morning, I woke up cradled in his arms.

"I love you, Char," he murmured to me.

"I love you, too, Toran."

Then the tears started again.

Silver Cat did not return. It was one more ache. She was Bridget's cat, I knew that, and I missed her.

The hearse was late bringing up Bridget's coffin, so Pherson, Toran, and I were late. When we arrived, stepping over the last rise of the hill, we stopped, shocked at what we saw.

"Damn near looks like the entire town is here," Toran said.

It did. They probably were.

From the ladies in Gabble and Gobble Garden Gang, to Chief Constable Ben Harris holding Gitanjali's hand, to teachers and students we'd gone to school with, to friends and neighbors, old and young, to Baen, Gowan, Carston Chit, Stanley I and II, and Lorna Lester, and her sister, Laddy, who looked chagrined and embarrassed, outcasts now in town, Laddy's business closed for lack of customers, their eyes tired.

They were all there.

Toran bent his head, overcome. I wrapped an arm around him.

We had the vicar, Harold Mosher, who had known Bridget her whole life, a decent and compassionate man, who had seen Bridget many times during her illness, come to lead the service.

He would give the prayers, and the blessings, but Bridget's instructions were for Toran, Pherson, and I to speak.

That's what we did. I went first. I talked about our childhood, and my mother's garden, which had been the start of Bridget's love of gardening. I talked about the letters we wrote as children and as women, how funny she was, witty and smart. I talked about her artistic talents, her garden plans, her love of Pherson and Toran. I told them how beautiful Bridget's heart was and how she handled having a terminal disease with grace and courage.

Pherson talked of how Bridget was the love of his life. He could not say much more, too emotional.

Toran talked about his sister's thoughtfulness and sensitivity, her humbleness, how deep she loved, and how she saw the best in people. He talked about her enduring love for her daughter. She designed the park with her daughter in her mind and heart, for her and the people of St. Ambrose, particularly the children.

Toran played "Amazing Grace" on the bagpipes. Rowena and Kenna sang the haunting "Flowers of the Forest." Olive played her violin, a piece she composed, the notes climbing up the trunk of the oak tree, through the branches, to the blue skies, over the stream and Toran's farm, across the waves of the ocean, where they swirled up to heaven. It was sad, joyful, mournful, hopeful. I had not even known that she played the violin.

The blessing was given.

We had asked people to bring their favorite flower to drop into Bridget's grave.

The Stanleys and their wives dropped carnations. The Stanleys said, together, "Go with God, Bridget."

Rowena dropped a yellow rose and a rock necklace. Kenna dropped daffodils and a note, written on her drug prescription pad, that said, "I love you, Bridget." Olive dropped tulips wrapped with a knitted red scarf with a butterfly on it. The butterfly had two blue tears in its eyes.

Gitanjali dropped a handful of spices and said a prayer in

Hindi, her palms together. Malvina dropped white baby's breath and stood there as other people passed by. I heard her say, choked up, "I'm sorry, Bridget. I'm sorry."

Lorna and Laddy stood on either side of the grave, then tipped over a sheet filled with wildflowers. They were both crying, ashamed. I could tell by their flushed faces.

Ben Harris dropped part of a honeysuckle vine.

The reporter, Carston Chit, dropped in red gladiolas and said, "Peace, Bridget. Courageous woman."

The flowers piled up over her coffin. People hugged us, wished us well, cried.

We waited until everyone was gone, then Pherson took out Queen Bridget's crown from a bag he'd brought and placed it on her coffin.

Toran dropped in a handful of her colored pencils, his hands trembling.

I dropped in my letter to her. It was short, in a pink envelope.

I love you, Bridget. I will always miss you. You are my very best friend. Love, Charlotte.

What else was there to say?

Silver Cat trotted up and looked in the grave. I picked her up, so relieved to see her again, and held her close in my arms. Toran put an arm around me and petted her, Bridget's cat.

Silver Cat let out a wailing scream-meow. I swear that cat is a person with fur.

Before I left, I walked over to my father's grave for the first time. He had a view of the sunrise. My father had loved sunrises. A whole new day, he would tell me, then he would launch into a song or a legend or a story.

"I love you, Dad. I miss you." I kneeled on the ground, near his gravestone. "I have missed you every day. Your voice still rings in my ears, your advice, your love, your laugh, your bagpipes. I can still smell you. You smelled like Scotland. Like the wind, the North Sea, scones. I can't believe you've been gone for twenty years. Seems like yesterday. It seems like forever. You have been with me my whole life." I put my hands together. "Dad, the unicorn came for Bridget. I need you to watch over her for me. Take care of her, tell her your legends and stories. She needs you."

Just then the wind lifted my hair and I heard bagpipes, faint, light. It was "Scotland the Brave," my father's favorite. I closed my eyes as it grew louder, as if my father were stepping closer to me, his kilt swaying in the wind. I let my tears fall on his grave.

Sometimes the people who are gone come to us. I don't know how, there is no scientific explanation for it, but they do. You must only be watching for it, listening closely.

ST. AMBROSE DAILY NEWS

A LETTER FROM CHIEF CONSTABLE BEN HARRIS

To the village of St. Ambrose,

As all of you know, Bridget Ramsay passed away on Tuesday from AIDS. Bridget was one of our own, her family here in St. Ambrose for generations. She told her tragic story, with eloquence, here, in this paper. It brought tears to my eyes many times. As a man, I'm not afraid to say that.

These last months have been difficult for the village of St. Ambrose. We have wounds that may never heal. People took sides for or against Bridget, and they took them vociferously, sometimes with scant regard for others' feelings, or for Bridget's personal rights as a Scottish citizen.

It has caused much soul searching and pain for all of us, which is dwarfed by the pain that Bridget's family and friends feel. We are, I believe, different people than who we were before Bridget returned home.

Friends, Bridget is not the only villager, the only Scotsman or Scotswoman, who will have AIDS. She was the first, that we know of, in St. Ambrose, but she will not be the last. How some treated her was abominable. They reacted with fear, judgment, and disdain, disregarding medical evidence that she was not contagious. This was extremely regrettable. Others embraced Bridget with open arms, gentleness, and compassion.

We must do better when this happens to us again. We need to do better. We will do better. Not only for the next AIDS victim but for all of us. How we treat others in their moments of crisis tells us much about ourselves.

I will miss Bridget. That she reached out to people who had done her wrong, that she designed a park for all of us in St. Ambrose, that she donated her own money, in particular after what had occurred here, tells of a woman with integrity, a forgiving soul, and a love for the people of St. Ambrose.

When you enter Bridget's Park, A Place for Everyone, this spring, pause. The scent of the roses blooming will come to you. The flower beds will be a rainbow of color. The children will shout and laugh in the fountain, the orchestra will play from the gazebo, the trees will offer an oasis of shade, the grass a place for all of us to walk barefoot and relax.

Pause.

This park came to us as a gift from Bridget, with help from her brother, Toran; her best friend, Charlotte Mackintosh; her lifelong friend, Pherson Hameldon; and the villagers of St. Ambrose.

Pause.

Think of Bridget.
Thank Bridget.
Enjoy, as she meant for you to do.
Sincerely,
Chief Constable Ben Harris
St. Ambrose

I spent a lot of time thinking at our fort, on the beach, and in my mother's garden. I repainted two of my mother's birdhouses—one a log cabin, the other tall and skinny, blue, with a star on the roof—that I'd found under a pile of leaves.

Bridget had been my best friend. It had not been a normal best friend relationship where you would see each other, at least periodically. If I had been a more social person, less awkward, less of a loner, more trusting, I would have had other friends.

But I didn't. I wrote my books and I wrote letters and looked forward to Bridget's letters as I would a visit from a best friend. It's sad, in many ways, I get that.

But between Bridget, my mother, a few quirky neighbors on the island, my work, and my cats, I was content enough. Terribly lonely and alone sometimes, but content.

Yet my friendship with Bridget was entirely false in many ways. She wasn't even remotely truthful with me about her life. The letters she sent to me were fabricated, by and large. She wrote about the life she wished she had.

The only hobby I know of that she honestly loved, that I loved, was gardening, and she rarely did that.

She lied.

She lied by omission and she lied blatantly.

So was the friendship not a real friendship?

In many ways it wasn't. We didn't have truth and honesty between us; surely that is key in friendship.

But I understood why she lied. I wish she hadn't, but she did. She was raped repeatedly as a teenager. She was impregnated by a rapist, a man posing as a priest. They took her baby away and put her in an insane asylum with the help of the rapist. Her father was a punitive, religious fanatic obsessed with her virginity, her mother a weak woman who drank too much.

It's no wonder she reached for drugs. How was she to tell me that? It's no wonder there were bad men in her life. How was she to tell me that? It's no wonder her life imploded. How was she to tell me that?

Bridget wasn't who I thought she was. She lied to keep me, and our friendship, above the disaster her life had become. I was the one light in her dark life. She danced with me in her head as I danced with her, as we danced together as children. She pretended. She escaped. I would miss her letters forever, miss knowing I had a friend.

I could not imagine my life without her.

She was still, and always would be, my very best friend.

20

"You haven't written anything. All these months. In Scotland. Nothing. Zip. Zero. Be honest."

"No, I haven't."

Maybelle Courten knew about Bridget's death. I'd told her the minimum, but it had still been a long story. I gasped and choked and had the ugly cry through the whole thing. She listened. She was compassionate. She said, "Bridget's your best friend in the whole world and she died. That sucks. I'm so sorry, Charlotte, I truly am."

She sent a huge bouquet of yellow roses to me after our conversation.

But now we were back to her usual harangue.

"I know you needed time after Bridget's death, but use how you feel in a book. Give those feelings to McKenzie Rae."

"If I gave my feelings to McKenzie Rae, she would want to jump off a cliff."

"Then make her want to jump off a cliff. At the end of Book Nine, she's going to try to get back to her soul mate. Go from there. How does that happen? Where does she have to go? What does she have to do? Will it work, or does she go somewhere else in time? Back to the wagon trains, World War I, Vietnam . . . Why does McKenzie Rae Dean want to jump off a cliff?"

"Does she? I don't know."

"You have to know. It's her life. You created her. Try this one on: You've got your man, now let McKenzie Rae have hers."

"If I actually let McKenzie Rae find a way back to her soul mate, as I threatened to do at the end of Book Nine, as she's going to attempt, that could end the series. Potentially. It would be so climactic, how could I backtrack out of there?"

"I don't want you to give her up for selfish reasons. I make money off that gal. But you're my friend and I want you to be happy, and this paralysis you're feeling tells me that you're about done with McKenzie Rae."

I ran a hand through my hair and thought about that. I also thought about how nice it was to have hair that wasn't fried and tangled.

The fog suddenly cleared in my head around the block of wood called writer's block. The smoke dissipated. The haze dried up. The block broke. I felt . . . relief.

"Yes, that's it. I'm done."

"Then end her story. Give her the happy ending."

"A happy ending? Is that realistic? I have never tried to wrap up McKenzie Rae's life in sweetness. I think a happy ending would be a cliché, unrealistic, pandering."

"Everyone wants a happy ending."

"But we don't all get it."

"Sometimes we do. Shouldn't McKenzie Rae?" She paused. "Shouldn't you, with Toran?"

I thought about that while Maybelle shouted, "Eric, your teacher called today. I can't believe it. You have an A in science! Excellent work, Einstein. Sheryl wants to talk to you, Charlotte. She wants to be a writer. Hopefully she won't write about her hooker clothing. Can you talk to her?"

I could. Sheryl and I talked for a long time about writing. She was interested in historical fiction. I did not address her hooker clothing.

Afterward I sunk into the Adirondack chair on Toran's deck. The sun sank, a golden orb on a string, an invisible hand letting it drop. Color whirled through the sky as if someone had stuck their finger in pastel paint and shaped it into a curlicue. Toran was walking toward me from the large red barn. Behind him was one of his tractors, his apple orchard, his rows of blueberries, and the tunnels that would hold the potatoes come fall.

I had my happy ending.

McKenzie Rae Dean should have hers.

I waved to my happy ending.

I unhooked my bra, then pulled up my new white lace shirt and flashed him.

I saw him laugh.

The celebration to officially open Bridget's Park, A Place for Everyone, took place on Saturday at noon. It was officially winter but, miraculously, we had a sunny day, and the blue, scoopable sky had no clouds.

The red, blue, and yellow castle play structure was securely in place. The kids slid down the slides, bounced on the wood "drawbridges," climbed up the ladders, and hid in the castle towers on the second story of the play structure. They raced from the platforms to the tunnels and scooted up a winding stairway to the lookout point. They laughed, they screamed, they called to each other. Bridget would have loved it.

Separate from the castle, there were three sets of swings, two long slides, and a merry-go-round, all filled with kids. The fountain was on, and kids were playing in the water, shooting up from the ground. It was too brisk to do this, but their parents had given in to their pleas and the kids were having a splendid time.

Couples strolled through rose gardens that would be a lush swoosh of color in the spring. There were people in the community garden at the end of the park, building raised beds for summer. They would later plant corn, lettuce, tomatoes, carrots, and other vegetables.

People rode their bikes along the cement path that wound all the way around the park, the old and the young, together. Blankets were on the grass for picnics.

Bagpipers and drummers, once again with Pherson and Toran, started the festivities. A local rock band played in the large gazebo, and up next was the St. Ambrose symphony. Later there would be traditional Scottish dances, and a local harpist and violinist.

True Scots, loving our food, were also having a village potluck, with tables sprawled across the park. I have never seen that much food.

I'd had Sandra make a castle cake, then had ordered two more flat sheets to go with it, again decorated with castles. The Gabbling Gobbling Garden Ladies had decorated the park with balloons and organized games for the kids.

Later in the day Toran would speak, and we would have a moment of silence for Bridget, but for now Toran and I sat on one of the many benches in the park and watched people. We held hands.

"They're happy here, Charlotte. This is what she wanted."

"It is. She did it."

"Bridget had a vision and she took all of us along with her. She has left something that will last forever. One hundred years from now, more, this park will still be here. These young trees will grow along with these kids, those kids will grow up and have kids, and their kids will play here, too, as will the kids after that. The village will have to replace the castle, rebuild the gazebo if the winds blow it down, but it's an everlasting gift to St. Ambrose."

"It's a forever gift from Bridget."

"Yes, luv, it is. She will be here always."

We smiled. He squeezed my hand. We got one another.

I watched teenagers run across the huge grassy area, laughing, chasing each other. Bridget had not felt that she belonged after Angus Cruickshank attacked her. She said she felt shameful, guilty, depressed, scared, her mind filled with debilitating flashbacks, but she had created a place so others could feel that they belonged.

Yes, people were happy here. It was safe, friendly, welcoming. It was a place for everyone.

A place for her daughter if she ever returned. A place for Legend.

I wiped the tears off my cheeks and snuggled into Toran as the Garden Gabbing Ladies descended with wine and glasses.

"Cheers!" Rowena shouted. "The Slut broke up with The Arse and told everyone he's lousy in bed and has a small penis. Isn't that the best news yet?"

"You will marry Toran when you come back over the ocean."

"Yuck, Grandma. Then he could kiss me."

"You'll like the kisses."

"Gross." I smiled back at her.

"They won't be gross then, Charlotte." She squinted her eyes. "I see the number eight."

"Eight?"

"Yes. Eight. Eh. I don't know why."

I hugged her. We made soda bread, her mum's recipe. I gave some to Toran with strawberry jam made from my father's strawberries. He liked it. Then we played with the science beakers my mother bought us.

Toran left the next morning, the sun barely awake, to work on his farm. I would go in to the office in a couple of hours. I had found solace in numbers after Bridget's death so was well caught up with everything.

When I finally rolled out of bed, naked, as Toran had stripped off yet another negligee, I wrapped myself in a robe, slipped on Bridget's bunny slippers, and sat under the arc of the honeysuckle that Bridget had planted on one of her trips home. The blooms were gone, but the branches made a wood labyrinth above my head.

I drummed my fingers on the picnic table. Silver Cat leaped up onto my lap. I missed Teddy J, Daffodil, Dr. Jekyll, and Princess Marie. I had called Drew several times, and he told me they were all fine, and dealing with Dr. Jekyll's mood disorder.

I wanted to be with Toran all the time. Well, not *all* the time. That sounded creepy and possessive. I liked being alone, too. I liked reading books and science articles, working in my mother's garden, and cooking, but I loved being around him.

Toran was my soul mate. If we were apart again, I would be devastated. Life would feel dark, hopeless, loneliness assured. Those thoughts went against my independent, feminist leanings, but it was truth.

McKenzie Rae Dean had to live apart from her soul mate, from the man she had been married to for ten years but hadn't seen in close to two hundred years.

She had a hole inside herself. She had loved other men, on her other time travel journeys—I did give her delectable men—but it was not the same. One can love other men, but the soul mate is different because he lives in your soul.

I realized then that I had not portrayed McKenzie Rae's grief accurately. I hadn't portrayed her emotions as rawly as I should have.

Book Nine left McKenzie Rae desperate to go back in time to her love. How would she get there? I stared at the ocean in the distance. I studied the cliffs. . . . Could she?

I grabbed my Marie Curie journal and started writing. I wrote and wrote.

The sun arched across the sky. The wind blew through from the Highlands. It grew colder. The dead, brown leaves rustled, fell off, and danced away into the countryside. The labyrinth of branches of the honeysuckle swayed.

I drank more coffee and grabbed my red coat and wrapped it around my robe and me.

I wrote.

In Marie Curie's journal, I wrote. I hoped she would appreciate the creativity.

When the sun went down, amidst an artistic blast of purple, orange, and golden yellow, I went inside and wrote more in front of the fire. I was still in my robe and bunny slippers.

When Toran walked in, I said, "Hi, honey, I'll be a minute," and I kept writing. He brought me smoked haddock made with parsley and cream and kissed me good night. The kiss went longer and longer and he said, "Sweetheart, I don't want to interrupt, I know you have to work," and in response I unbuttoned his shirt. He knew what to do from there. After our naked tumble, and his, "I love you, baby," he ambled upstairs.

At the end of Book Nine I had McKenzie Rae talking to her mother, telling her she had to get back to her one true love. But in the back of my mind I thought that I would have McKenzie Rae make attempt after attempt, and fail each time, ending up in a new time period, per book . . . until I was ready to end the series.

I was ready earlier than expected.

I knew where McKenzie Rae had to be at the end of Book Ten. Between Chapter One and the epilogue, she would be tossed and turned. She would have to take a literal leap and a metaphorical leap as she jumped through parallel times, catching a wormhole here, fighting gravity there, to get back to the right time period.

McKenzie Rae Dean was done. Done saving others, because she had to save herself. Done with time travelling through the centuries, the fear, the danger. Done with attempting the near impossible while her heart wilted.

I was done, too. I was done with this series. I would write again, probably, but not for a while.

I would get McKenzie Rae back to her man so she could be happy, like me, an odd, science-studying, garden-obsessed, cat-loving, time travel romance writing author who was going to go upstairs and hug Toran, my own soul mate.

Dear Ms. Ramsay,

My name is Gracie Taggart. I live in London, where I am a student at university. I am studying art, as I love to draw and paint.

Unless there are two Bridget Ramsays in St. Ambrose, I believe that you may be my biological mother. My parents only recently told me that I was adopted as a baby. I have always sensed a secret around my birth, but they wouldn't answer my questions, so I thought I was imagining it. I do have an active imagination.

They had the legal papers and showed me your name and the village you were from.

I am sure that this letter comes as a shock. I want you to know that I do not want to upset you or your life or any of the lives of your family members and friends.

I would very much like to meet you, if you wish. I have left my contact information below.

Yours most sincerely,

Gracie Taggart

Toran and I read the letter together in front of his fireplace. He had piled on the wood to take away the winter chill, the rains abnormally torrential. I put my arm around his shoulders.

"Almost, Charlotte," he choked out. "Gracie wrote almost in time."

"Yes, she did." I put my hand to my head. It was yet another tragedy. One more wrong, the timing yet another strike of lightning against a life that seemed to insist that Bridget should suffer. The unfairness was breathtaking.

"Ah, damn. I tried several times, for Bridget, to get the information from Our Lady of Peace. They said that the paperwork was gone, lost. One of the nuns told me to accept and let it be, that she thought Cruickshank had taken it."

I held the letter as the flames crackled. "I can hardly believe this is happening now. Legend's here. Gracie's here."

"Yes, she's here, and Bridget, our sweet Bridget, is gone. It's tragic."

We watched the flames. The rain lashed the windows.

"What are you going to do about Gracie?"

A look of grief, and anger, for what Bridget had lost, crossed his face. "I am not going to let it be, that is for sure."

Dear Gracie,

My name is Toran Ramsay. I am Bridget Ramsay's older brother. I was very happy to receive your letter. Thank you for writing.

I would like to invite you to my home on Saturday at 1:00. You are welcome to bring your parents with you. I am afraid I have some unfortunate news about Bridget.
Sincerely,
Toran Ramsay

Gracie Taggart looked exactly like Bridget, with white-blond hair, her eyes pure blueberry. She was tall, like her mother, wispy, her frame thin, but strong, as Bridget's used to be. She was shy and gangly, and had a huge smile.

"My Lord," Toran breathed as she scrambled out of the car, all arms and legs. He made a strangled sound in his throat, then leaned over with his hands on his knees and took a harsh breath in. I tried to comfort him as Gracie stood, unsure of her reception, but I could hardly do a thing except pat Toran's back.

I felt faint, too. I felt unsteady. There's Bridget, I thought. There's your best friend, Bridget!

I heard Toran sucking in air beside me, still bent over.

I felt myself sway, the tears burning my eyes, then spilling over.

Here was Bridget's daughter. The baby she adored who was taken from her, literally ripped from her arms. The baby she had never forgotten, never recovered from losing. The loss was a throbbing scar on her soul as deep and cutting as if an ax had dragged itself across it.

The horrid abuse Bridget suffered under Angus Cruickshank's criminal hands would have always been a debilitating wound to live with, but losing Gracie, her Legend, this was what made Bridget lose her mind.

They should have been together, but they were not, and time had raced on mercilessly until it had shredded and eaten Bridget, cutting at her bit by bit.

Toran stood up. He sighed. He wiped his face. I put an arm around him and leaned in. He was trying to be strong, and I was trying to get control of myself.

Gracie had come with her parents. While she was tall, they were short. While she was thin, they were plump. While she was fair, her father's straight black hair was shot through with white, and her mother was a brunette.

But what they all seemed to have in common was kindness and decency. I could see it on their faces, within their worry. They smiled tentatively. Gracie beamed at us, waved, and said, "Hello there! I'm Gracie!"

Toran, his walk unsteady, went right up to Gracie and hugged her. For a second, Gracie was surprised, but then her face crumbled, and she wrapped her arms around Toran, and hugged him tight.

Poor Toran. He did not make a sound, but the tears rolled. "I cannot begin to tell you, lass, how much your mother loved you. . . ."

I wrapped my arms around the two of them, wondering if the tears in my life would ever stop. I looked up at the sky, at the heavens, at the scoopable blue and said to myself, to Bridget, "She's here, my friend. Your daughter, Legend. She's here. I will tell her you love her."

Bridget's death was too early. Gracie had known about the adoption too late.

But Bridget's love endured.

We gave Gracie the letter Bridget had written her, which explained to her why she had been forced to give Legend up, who her father was, what had happened to her with Cruickshank, and why she had been committed to an insane asylum. She enclosed the newspaper article written by Carston Chit. She gave her the three photos that the nuns had taken.

Silver Cat immediately jumped on Gracie's lap when she sat on Toran's couch, and Gracie petted her.

> *I don't want you to live with secrets. What you need to know, above all else, is that I loved you. I didn't want to give you up. I was forced to. I have*

> *thought of you my whole life, hoped you were healthy and well. Missing you has been an ache in my heart that has never gone away. I love you, Legend.*

Bridget had made one drawing a year for Gracie, 16 by 18, eighteen in all, the eighteenth finished a week before she died. Each drawing was exquisitely rendered, down to the finest detail. She had used watercolors and colored pencils, sometimes a black pen to outline here and there. They were her best work.

Bridget had mailed the drawings home as she traveled, as her life disintegrated, "for safe keeping, for my daughter. For Legend."

The first drawings, when Gracie was young, were filled with huge, smiling flowers. She later drew spring flowers, daffodils, tulips, and crocuses with tiny fairies hiding within the petals and stems. She drew a miniature village surrounded by lilies, pink cherry trees, honeysuckle and clematis, bluebells and roses. She drew a log home by a river, a girl with blond hair in front of an easel drawing the same picture we were looking at. She drew a Snow White–type house with a waterfall to the side. She drew wildflowers around a meandering river, deer, raccoon, and rabbits hidden in the grasses.

The last drawing, which I had watched her draw, was a garden design for her daughter.

A pond shimmered, with a fountain in the shape of an angel, wings outstretched, in the middle of it. Tall trees shaded an expanse of grass. A trellis, hung with both red and pink flowers, covered a yellow bench. A thriving vegetable garden in the corner seemed tasty enough to eat off the paper.

There were colorful clay pots attached to the fence and filled with flowers, a bridge across a stream, and silver watering cans attached ten feet high to a pole, as my mother had done.

Birdhouses in all shapes and sizes hung from tree branches. One was red and three stories. Another had a Japanese design, exactly like my mother's. A third was painted in Clan Ramsay colors, a fourth was painted in Clan Mackintosh colors, and a fifth was in the exact shape of Toran and Bridget's current home.

There was Silver Cat, on top of a miniature cat house. Our favorite books, *Charlotte's Web, Narnia, Beezus and Ramona, A Little Princess,* and *The Secret Garden*, were piled on a wood table on the deck. She had drawn our four gold crowns, our capes, and our swords and piled them haphazardly on a pink rocking chair. On the back of the rocking chair she wrote LEGEND.

Gracie was overcome, as were her parents. The father put his face in his hands and cried. "I'm sorry," he said, his voice wavering, gasping for breath. "I'm sorry."

"We didn't know," Gracie's mother wailed, hand to mouth. "We were told by the nuns that these babies were freely given up by their teenage mothers, who couldn't keep them. Had we known, we love Gracie so much but we never—" She dissolved into tears.

Gracie comforted her parents, gently. Her voice was exactly like Bridget's. It was like listening to Bridget. Gracie and her parents picked up each drawing again, studied every inch of them. "I love drawing and painting flowers and trees and gardens."

"She does," her father said.

"We have to buy her paints all the time," her mother said. "We've hung her work up."

Mother and daughter, both artists, both nature lovers, both gardeners.

"She did love me, didn't she?" Poor Gracie, her chin trembled, and the tears fell from her blueberry eyes onto Silver Cat.

"She loved you with everything she had and more," Toran said, holding her hand. "Don't you doubt for a minute your mother's love for you."

"Why did she name me Legend?" Gracie asked.

"She named you Legend because of all the stories and legends my father told us," I said. "Would you like me to tell you a few of them?"

She did. That poor girl. She even sounded like Bridget when she cried.

* * *

Gracie wanted to know more about her biological father.

Toran made her a cup of tea. He was kind, but honest.

Gracie's face was tormented. She hugged Silver Cat close to her chest for comfort. "What happened to my biological father? Where is he?"

"Well that story, luv, is a mystery around these parts. Don't know if it's true. The last time anyone saw him was on a Wednesday. . . ."

We all hiked up to Bridget's grave under the oak tree, the ocean in the distance, the wind cool, a dash of salt, a sip of mint tea in the air.

Gracie kneeled down on Bridget's grave and studied the marker: Bridget Marie Ramsay.

Bridget had written down what she wanted engraved on it: Sister, Friend, Mother.

"For me, then?" Gracie asked.

We nodded. "You were her only child." Dear girl, she cried and cried, which made her parents cry, so we all joined in together up there on the hill, salt and mint tea and tears mixed together.

After lunch at Toran's, we took Bridget to the park. We walked all around it, through it, three times. Even on a cold day there were kids playing, people running and biking, a kid playing a guitar, another singing as he rode a skateboard.

"My mum designed this? All this?"

"Yes," Toran said. "For you and for the people of St. Ambrose."

Gracie's lip quivered.

Her poor parents, I thought they might collapse. We sat at the table in the gazebo together, the five of us, in the middle of Bridget's Park, A Place for Everyone.

"So this is my mum," Gracie said. "This is how she thought."

Smart girl. So smart. Like her mum.

* * *

Gracie left, promising to come back and see Uncle Toran and me. She carried the drawings that Bridget made for her, the letter, the pictures the nuns took, and a stack of Bridget's gardening books. She hugged Silver Cat, then gave her back to me.

We hugged Gracie tight. She turned to leave in the car.

Silver Cat shriek-meowed, struggled to get out of my arms, and ran after her.

Gracie picked her up and hugged her.

Toran's gaze met mine.

"Gracie," Toran said. "Would you like to take Silver Cat with you?"

Oh, she definitely would.

He was nervous, anxious, his hand tight on mine.

He had brought a table down to a secluded area of the beach near sunset. It was cool, but not too cold, and we'd brought jackets and blankets.

A white table cloth fluttered, candles set out and lit. A bouquet of irises sat in a glass vase. He held my hand as we walked down to the beach and held the picnic basket with the other hand. I didn't even see the table until we were almost on it, then I said, "Look, someone's having a date at the beach."

"That would be us, my love," Toran drawled, those blue eyes laughing.

"Us?"

"Yes. It's a special day."

"Why is it special? You did this?"

"For you, Charlotte."

"Toran. Thank you. Dinner on the beach." I hugged him. "I love you, studly Scotsman."

"Love you, too, luv."

The ocean waves pounded, smooth as blue-gray silk, white lace at the edges. The sky was beginning to turn a creamy pinkish orange color, with a dash of purple, the golden sphere behind the hills. An impressive natural background that this spinning earth provides.

He reached for my hand across the table, "Charlotte, I am

not skilled with romantic words, so I will simply say what I feel."

"Okay." That was a lame response, but I was picking up on his nervousness and it made me nervous.

"Charlotte, I want us to be together for the rest of our lives."

"I want that, too." I felt my lower lip tremble.

"I want you to be in love with me for the rest of your life, as I will be with you. Every day I will work toward that goal. I can't be happy without you. You are my life, Charlotte. You're my best friend. You're funny, you're smart, you're strong, loyal, sincere. And I love making love to you." He paused, and I do think his cheeks were red, but he was smiling. "Can I say that we are compatible?"

"Yes. That would be accurate." Exceedingly accurate.

"I love how you laugh, but how you're tough, too, and fight back. I love how you work hard with me on the farm, but then we go home, and it's us. You and me, and we play chess or talk science. I love how fun you are, Queen Charlotte, always ready to do anything. Dancing, poker, walking. I love how you let me be the man in your life, that you let me be who I need to be, who I want to be, for you. I love how I feel around you, and how much I want to be with you again when we are not together."

"For a man who thinks he's not romantic . . ."

"I'm trying my best, luv."

"Your best is outstanding."

"Charlotte Mackintosh, will you please do me the greatest honor of my life and marry me?"

"Marry you?"

"Yes, love. Marry me."

Marry him. Be with him every day. Have a ceremony with my mother and Gracie and her parents and Pherson, the Garden Ladies, Ben Harris, and Stanley I and Stanley II. Live together. Work his farm, figure out another career for me, grow old together.

Have children?

"What do you say? Is it a yes or a no?"

Those blue eyes, so dear to me, blueberries and the Scottish sky mixed, now so worried and concerned. "That's a yes, Toran." I sniffled, then said, my voice all wobbly, "Thank you."

"No, my love, thank you." He stood up, hugged me, we laughed, we kissed, then he swung me around. It was like we were in a scene out of one of my own books, the waves thundering, the sun heading down amidst sky paints, the table set. How cheesy is that?

How splendid is that?

He kissed me again and again, then lifted me up, and I wrapped my legs around his waist and we tumbled to the sand.

"Thank you, Charlotte. I love you, honey, and the children are going to love it when I tell them how I proposed. We'll leave out the part about how you're on top of me, and as soon as it's dark we're going to make love right here, on the blanket I brought."

"Children?"

"Yes. What do you think of four children?"

Four?

I felt my mouth drop like someone had slipped a hook in it and pulled.

"Or five? Six? You choose."

A family. A large family. I wanted a large family, didn't I? I pictured a bunch of wild kids running around. I would never be lonely again. I wouldn't be alone. I think I could be a competent mother. I cook well. I can teach them about biology and physics, and tell them to go outside and play imaginary games. It had appeal, having children with this huge ox of a Scotsman.

Plus I would have rolling-around hot sex and a man to talk to about new research in space, new and exciting technology, even geology and time travel. Plus cells. Cells are fascinating, as Toran and I both know.

I kissed him again. "Okay, King Toran. We'll do it."

His eyes filled with tears as his smile took up most of his face. I cannot help but love that man. He is absolutely endearing. Handsome. Emotionally and mentally strong. Crazy smart and tough as can be on the outside, gentle on the inside. Plus he has an impressive, skilled spear.

"You and I, our kids, and Gracie," he said.

"Always Gracie," I said. "Always Gracie." We'd already seen her two more times. She came here again and we visited her, and Silver Cat, at college in London. She fit in immediately. It was like we'd known her forever. Maybe we had.

"Charlotte Mackintosh, this is the best day of my life. You will be my wife, I will be your husband, and we will live together in the hills of Scotland forever." He stopped. "Uh. Right? Or do you want to live on the island in Washington?"

I peeked back toward the sea, the waves background music to me. I tilted my head up toward the cliffs, to the emerald green hills, to the sun setting behind it, and up to the purple blue sky, so close you could scoop it up with your hands.

"I'll stay in Scotland," I said. "I feel like I'm home."

He laughed. "Ah, Charlotte. You are my home."

I swear, I do swear, I heard my father's bagpipes then, loud, proud, happy.

He put both hands up. I put my palms against his. We said, "Unite. As one. Clan TorBridgePherLotte Forever."

We made love on the red blanket. He slipped a ring on my finger with a bongo-sized diamond in it.

We would not tell the kids about their father's spear.

The next day the rain came pouring down. The clouds crowded in, smashed together, and opened up all at once, as if they'd been storing water for years, for centuries, all the way back to the beginning of Scotland.

On the second day, rivers flooded, streets were awash in water, trees fell in the winds, homes were threatened.

Toran worked in his office at home, and I worked beside him, writing my book. When I leaned over and kissed him, we used the time to make love in the middle of that rainy afternoon.

The rains continued their deluge on the third and fourth day, new streams winding through meadows and fields, farmland swamped. For fun frolicking, we made love again and again in the middle of the afternoon. It was an appropriate activity.

Toran said, as we lay naked in front of the fireplace, the rain pounding on the roof, that he'd never seen anything like it in all his years. I certainly never remembered it raining this hard, or for this long here, either.

On the fifth day, it looked like the ocean was filling up, the waves larger, higher, thicker.

On the sixth day, part of a hill collapsed. We could see it from Toran's house.

On the seventh day, the skies cleared and the sun popped out, as if the rains had been a joke from Mother Nature. Toran and I went out walking in the hills. It was a long walk, but we saw where part of the hill had slid straight on down, taking two trees with it. We saw black material, a scrap of white, a pair of shoes.

We walked over, cautiously, not wanting to slide down the hill.

Eyeglasses. A wallet. Keys.

He had been buried way down under, but the earth had shifted substantially, as if the Devil had opened his doors.

Hello, Father Angus Cruickshank, you horrid man.

"So there he is," Toran said, his face flushing, fists clenched. "If he wasn't already a corpse, I would kill him."

"Me after you." This man had not been a priest, he'd been the devil incarnate. I bent down and saw something. "Toran, look."

Toran leaned over me. "Can't have that being found." He pulled it out and we took it home. We would return it to its owner later.

Chief Constable Ben Harris came first after we called, followed by other constables and men and women in suits, rain slickers, and rain boots, from other agencies.

"As I suspected, and hoped," Ben muttered quietly to Toran and me. "Murdered and gone for years. I'll bet at least fifteen years, right after he disappeared, based on the remains."

"That's fortunate," Toran said. "Other girls were safe, then, from his crimes."

"I wonder who did it," Ben said. "The body's disintegrated.

We'll get nothing off of it. Dental records to identify him only. That's about what we're down to."

"Perfect," I said. "No one to prosecute."

"A shame no one will go to jail for killing a serial rapist," Toran drawled.

"It could have been anyone," Ben said. "Many possibilities."

"We'll never know," I said.

"If we find out, we should give them a reward." Toran rocked back on his heels. "I'll fund it."

"You're so handsome," I said to him.

"You mean when I'm talking about giving reward money to the man, or woman, who killed Father Cruickshank?"

"Yeah, baby, handsome as hell."

Ben laughed when I kissed Toran. He winked at me. "You're more like your mother than I think you realize, Charlotte. She used to kiss your dad all the time, too." He nodded at us when he was called over to the scene by another constable, then walked back toward us and bent his head, so that only the two of us could hear. "There is a peculiar . . . hole . . . in Father Toran's black robe, hardly noticeable. If you did know anything about that, it would be best to let . . . uh . . . the person know so she doesn't have to worry about an impending arrest. That's the type of thing that can keep you up at night, all night. Since I don't have any evidence, there is nothing I can do further here in this regard. Do you understand what I'm saying?"

Oh, yes, we sure did.

The archer froze at her kitchen table when she heard the news about Father Angus Cruickshank. Was her arrest imminent? Probably. The clue was there. It wouldn't take long.

She brought the peppermint tea to her lips. She remembered that night more clearly than any other night of her life.

"You have five seconds to start running," she had told the priest, then sighed, hating clichés, hating dramatics, in speech or in literature. Still, the instructions had to be clear. The plan was laid. It could not be changed. She brought the bow up and aimed the arrow at his chest.

Father Angus's face drained of color, as if it were being sucked out of him by a tube. She'd found that morbidly amusing. He put a hand on his kitchen table to steady himself. "No, don't do this. We can talk."

"Hell, no. I'm done talking." The archer sighed *again,* feeling impatient. Now that line sounded straight out of a movie. Was it a cliché, too? Probably. How frustrating. Never mind. She pulled the arrow back farther. "Five . . . four—"

The priest whipped around and stumbled out the back door, toward the shadowy woods. This was exactly what she knew would happen. Organization and attention to perfection are important skills in life. She picked up a few things to set the scene correctly, as planned, and set off.

The priest was in poor shape and scared witless. It was dark as black velvet, with a misty rain blowing down from the Scottish highlands and a handful of fog, but she knew the hills, every rock and tree, the towering cliffs, and the rumbling ocean below it. When the priest tootled off, panting like a rabid pig that needed to be put down, the chase began.

She had paced the priest, enjoying it, delighting in the man's insidious fear. The priest had made others feel the same way, for years. Now he deserved to feel the same desperate, hopeless terror. It was only fair. Fairness and justice were important, too.

The priest tripped over a mossy log, the moon's white light peeking through the spindly branches of the trees. He had begged her to stop. "Spare me. Have mercy on me. Forgive me, for I have sinned."

"Yes, you have, and now you will be punished." She raised the bow again, and again, as the priest kept scrambling to escape, to hide. She shot three arrows off, deliberately missing, to keep him scared. The thought of what the priest had done inflamed her. The priest was now the prey instead of the predator. That's why this chase had to happen.

"I will pray for your soul," the priest shouted, gasping, tripping. When that didn't work, he tried scripture, then he started swearing at her, that foul man, calling out the most disgusting names, threatening violence, then back to his useless pleading.

"God does not listen to the prayers of the Devil," she told him, then thought, *Excellent.* That statement was not a cliché. "I will show you the mercy you showed others."

"No, no, don't!" the priest begged, slowing down, unable to carry his corpulent self any further. "Show more, I am a man of God."

"That is incorrect, biblically speaking," she corrected him proudly. She had been taught the Bible. "You are no man of God. You attacked the innocent. I can't have that happen again."

"I won't do it again!"

"Yes, you will. You will stop only when you're in a grave."

When the priest was exactly where she wanted him, where she thought his body would never be found, the archer took aim at his sweating, panting, panicked face.

"You will go to jail for this!" the priest yelled.

"Once again, that is incorrect. No one will ever know. You, however, are going to hell."

The arrow shot through the black velvet night, the misty rain blowing down from the Scottish highlands, and a handful of fog.

She never missed.

No mistakes.

That was the most important.

Unfortunately, the archer thought, taking another sip of peppermint tea, she had made a mistake in the burial. She didn't think that monster would ever be found. He had been buried as deep as they could get him. She had taken his keys, wallet, and eyeglasses so that people would think that the bastard had run off and not look for him. You would take those items if you were running.

But now his decaying corpse and his personal items had popped up. What to do?

The archer knew she could leave the village. Hide. But where would she go?

She studied her garden. It was dull now, but Bridget, sweet Bridget, had made her such a pretty plan and she would hate not to see it to fulfillment.

Plus, would a jury convict her?

She put her shoulders back, though she had started to shake. She had done what she had to do. If Angus Cruickshank had not been shot through with her arrow, more girls would have been raped.

She was defending their innocence and taking revenge at the same time, God help her. It was an eye for an eye. She was a proud Scotswoman. She believed in her fellow Scots. They would not convict her.

She would take her chances.

The archer smiled to herself. She had won awards as a girl, and as a young woman, for archery. It had not taken much practice before she was fully up to speed again. Her aim had been true. Everyone would now know of her prowess. She could not help being a wee proud.

The newspapers had a field day. Carston Chit outdid himself.

Body of missing priest found, Part Four . . . it's almost the sixteen-year anniversary and here's the body! Murdered priest accused of molesting many girls buried in a deep grave in the hills . . . Murderer of the Catholic priest unknown . . . Who killed Father Cruickshank? Would a jury convict the murderer, even if he was found?

The village was all aflutter, especially at that last question. The consensus was that, no, a jury would not convict the murderer for getting rid of a child rapist.

Chief Constable Ben Harris kept our names out of the paper, so we were identified as the "man and woman who found the body after the storms when a hill gave way."

I thought of Bridget. She would be glad to know that Father Cruickshank had not been roaming the earth searching for other victims whose lives he could wreck. As he was in hell and she was in heaven, they would not cross paths.

I knocked on the door to Lorna's house.

"Charlotte, how lovely to see you. Please come in!"

We sat and chatted. She brought out chocolate croissants and served peppermint tea. She was nervous, though, her hands shaking, her breath coming in short gasps.

We settled into her kitchen nook facing the garden. "I'm going to make my garden exactly like Bridget's drawings."

I'd noticed that Lorna had had the drawings matted and framed, as I had. "My husband and I are saving for a proper fountain."

We chatted about gardening, but she was distracted, stressed. "Lorna, you know that Father Cruickshank's body was found."

Her lips tightened. "Yes. He was the Devil." She took a sip of tea. Her hands shook so hard she had to put the cup down.

"You know that Toran and I found the body?"

"I figured as much. It was on Toran's land."

"I thought you would want this back." I took the arrow out of my bag. "Toran and I removed it before the authorities arrived. We wanted you to know that they didn't find it. We thought you might be worried."

She paled.

"Are you going to faint?" I asked.

"I might."

"I want you to know that I'll catch you, Lorna. Would you like to lie down?"

"I hated Father Cruickshank, Charlotte."

I knew why. "Because of what he did to Malvina."

"Yes. My poor Malvina, that monster!"

"Does Malvina know that you killed him?"

"Yes. I told her. I had to. She used to be a cheerful, social, athletic girl, a wonder at archery—I taught her myself—and after the rapes, when she finally told me—he had threatened to kill me if she told—she pulled into herself.

"My Malvina changed, almost overnight. She wouldn't talk to me, and she cried all the time. I finally forced her to tell me, when she tried to kill herself two years later. I became so incensed! I knew what had to be done. I knew he couldn't live on God's earth for one more day. I had to let Malvina know that Father Cruickshank could never, ever come after her again, or threaten my life."

"So you shot him with your bow and arrow."

"I did. I delighted in it." She sat straight up. "I enjoyed seeing him frightened, begging, running. It was a fair, and just, punishment. I showed no mercy, as he had not shown any. I had it all planned out." She set down her tea, and for the first time she smiled. "I like things organized. It's important."

"Did you know that Angus Cruickshank had attacked Bridget, too?"

"I didn't. After reading Carston Chit's article, I think he started attacking Malvina about a year after he attacked Bridget. I had heard, at the time, from her mother and others, when Bridget left school, that she was training to be a nun. Given her father's fanaticism, that was not surprising to me. I later on heard vague rumors of a pregnancy but didn't believe them. Then I heard that Bridget was off at university. But during that time I was also dealing with Malvina and her abrupt change in personality, her deep depression, so Bridget wasn't uppermost in my mind, my daughter's precarious mental state was. I should have put it together, but I didn't.

"When Carston Chit's article came out about Bridget... Charlotte, I felt so guilty. Horrendous. I am a terrible woman. Terrible." She actually covered her head with her arms. "Terrible. I am terrible."

"You have been, but I'm liking you more knowing you stuck an arrow through Angus. Toran and I will never tell a soul, I promise you, but I do have one more question, if I may ask it."

"Please." She spoke through her arms, then put them down, her face pale.

"You buried the body... by yourself?"

"Laddy helped me. She is a loyal, loving sister and she was furious about what Father Cruickshank had done to our Malvina. We knew that he had to die immediately, to be judged by God. We could not allow him to rape another girl. It was our Christian duty to eliminate him and protect the innocent."

Lorna, of the imperious bottom. Laddy, grumpy lady.

"I chased him into the woods. I didn't always used to be this fat. I was quite trim then. I took aim and followed him, guiding him. I shot him rather close to our ultimate grave destination. Who knew the hill would ever give way? Curse it. Other than that, there were no mistakes. That's important, too."

I cleared my throat. "Well. I'm incredibly impressed by your aim, Lorna. A bow and arrow is difficult to shoot."

She smiled, suddenly pleased with herself. "I used to win prizes for archery."

"Something to be proud of." We drank our tea in silence. "You eliminated the devil from the planet Earth. For that, you deserve another prize."

"Thank you. I would like to be your friend, Charlotte."

"I think we could do that."

"You do?" Her voice pitched in hope.

"Yes. Let's take a peek at Bridget's garden plans again, shall we?"

It was Rowena who made up the rhymes and songs about Father Angus Cruickshank. "He attacked my friend's younger sister, Joycie, and no one did anything about it."

Olive came over one day. She handed me an article a friend had sent her. It was written by Kitty Rosemary. "Are you Georgia Chandler?"

Shoot. I didn't want anyone to know. "Yes."

"I have all your books. I love them. If only you had more animals in them, specifically pigs and chickens. . . ." She winked at me and swore not to tell a soul.

Peppermint Tea, a Soul Mate, and the Scottish Leap

A ROMANTIC TIME TRAVEL ADVENTURE

THE FINAL NOVEL

By Georgia Chandler

McKenzie Rae Dean tilted her head back and let the Scottish rain stream down her face and hair.

She was soaked. She didn't care.

The thunder pounded around her, the lightning racing to keep up, streaking crookedly through the black night. Her feet were one foot from the edge of the cliff. She would soon do what she knew she had to do.

McKenzie Rae had a chance to go back in time to the exact same time period in St. Ambrose, where Brodie was. The chance wasn't surefire, but she had to take it. She knew she could be leaping into a whole new time period in the past, a dangerous one at that, but she was tired. She couldn't live without him anymore. She had to try.

McKenzie Rae had flown from Seattle to Amsterdam to Edinburgh, then had taken the bus to St. Ambrose and a cab to her former home with the Scotsman.

Before she left, her dear, dense, clueless father chuckled and wished her an "exciting adventure in Scotland. See you in three weeks! I'll miss you. I love you."

Her mother was pale, worried sick. As a time traveler herself, she knew what obstacles her daughter faced.

The goal was to jump to the time tunnel that McKenzie Rae had whizzed through before. She had come in through the cliffs, had actually landed right here, in that spot, on a rainy, thundering night, and had walked to the Scotsman's cottage for help. This was the exact day, and month, and time, as her previous visit, endlessly long ago.

Ideally, the cosmic energy from that time tunnel would envelop her as she jumped and yank her back in. There were gravitational dynamics and pull involved, the space-time continuum,

Einstein's theory of general relativity, time dilation, special dimensions, warp speed, and faster than light backward traveling, but McKenzie Rae believed it would work.

Probably. Maybe. It could, possibly.

She peered down the cliff, the North Sea a whipped-up, frothing mess below, the gray skies churning as if they were being twisted in a mixer. The storm was a brewing disaster, lightning brightening up the sky like a galaxy lightbulb.

She and Brodie had made love on that beach at night. They had watched the sun come up. They had danced on the sand. His cottage, the cottage they had lived in together, made of beige stone, was nearby.

It was ramshackle now, the garden she had worked so hard on an overgrown wreck, except for her purple clematis, which rode the leaning picket fence like a wave. She had called it The Purple Lush. The white window shutters were filthy and askew, the red door banged up, the roof partially cratered on one side, the brick walk bumpy.

An obese man lay prone near the kitchen chomping on a chicken.

She snuck inside when he went to sleep, the chicken carcass on his shirt. His snoring was an appalling roar.

The stench was overwhelming, hitting like an invisible wall when she entered. The home smelled of layers of dust and years of decay, as if a graveyard had moved in, followed by a gang of pigs, and farts.

McKenzie Rae's stomach heaved as she silently moved through the home, a home where she had experienced so much happiness, love, and romance with Brodie.

A cat with silver-colored fur ran up and curled around her legs. She bent down and picked her up. "Hello, Silver Cat," she whispered. Silver Cat meowed.

Not only did the house smell like rotting dung, it was jammed with junk.

The couch was clearly a mice home. She heard them scurrying, having a busy day. Two cushioned lounge chairs had dark brown spots in the middle. There were three kennels for dogs, but no dogs. Inside the kennels were blankets and Styrofoam. An aquarium full of algae, half filled with water, held three dead fish, floating.

There were broken lamps and three ice chests, empty beer cans inside. Boxes of junk, including old clothes that smelled like hell, had rotted. There was another couch, gray, spotted as if it had chicken pox. Two beds had old mattresses and seemed diseased. Same with the blankets and bedspreads on them.

She glanced down at what had to be years of porn magazines.

"How does a woman walk with boobs like that, Silver Cat?" she whispered. "It's like she's got watermelons with nipples attached to her chest."

She turned a page, disgustingly fascinated. The magazines appeared to be the only things that didn't have dust on them. "Oh, for God's sake!" she thought. "That is perverted!" She shut the cover.

"Silver Cat, do not look at this, or it will rot your mind."

McKenzie Rae gasped when she saw her dining room table. It had made it through the years!

It was covered with food wrappers, a bicycle tire, a truck bumper, and a medium-sized cage. Brodie had made it. Brodie had been a master craftsman, in addition to being a successful farmer with a massive amount of land. She and Brodie had eaten there, made love right on top of it. She had made bread, jams and jellies, and cut out sugar cookies. Brodie had played the bagpipes sometimes from the garden as she baked.

McKenzie Rae walked past the obese sleeping man and found two chairs Brodie made her, upside down, near a car engine, two shovels, a tent, and a tarp. Each had a wobbly leg.

She found her armoire, which was now crooked, clothes strung across it, a kitchen sink and handlebars of a bicycle on top. Brodie had carved a honeysuckle vine into the doors, as he knew she loved honeysuckle. She had kept her china in that armoire.

In the ten years she had lived with Brodie, people said she had the Scottish Second Sight. She had been in Scotland two other times during her time travels and she knew history, so she knew what was to come. Sometimes, though, she didn't understand her predictions herself, they were often confusing, nonsensical. It had been a gift and a curse, both.

McKenzie Rae wiped impatiently at the tears that ran down her cheeks. The obese man was still snoring, like a jackhammer, the chicken bones on his chest. She headed for the cliffs through the curtain of cold rain.

The thunder was almost right above her now, a lightning strike, jagged and fierce, touching down north of her, splitting the earth.

When she was at the edge of the cliff, she peered down only briefly at the craggy rocks below.

McKenzie Rae Dean spread her arms out, as if she were hung on a cross, started chanting the day, the month, and the year in which she wanted to land, and jumped.

My grandma's name was McKenzie Rae Mackintosh. Before she married my granddad, Brodie Mackintosh, it was McKenzie Rae Dean.

She and my granddad were wildly in love. I saw them dancing together, their arms around each other, her face tipped up to his. I loved my granddad and I loved my grandma, which is why I developed an entire character around her.

I loved her Second Sight, too.

Which has, with remarkable clarity, always been right. Every time.

I mailed three chapters of my tenth novel to Maybelle.

Maybelle called me. I heard a piercing scream in the background. Then a cackle of glee. She almost blew my eardrum out, which can happen in extreme situations. She said, "Cover me with rose petals and straight shots, I love it."

21

I am selling my home on Whale Island off the coast of Washington. Toran and I will be returning to toss out all my frumpy clothes, give my furniture away, and transport Teddy J, Daffodil, Dr. Jekyll, and Princess Marie to Scotland.

I put Olive and Rowena in touch with my friend, Olga, who owns a gift shop, and she is selling Rowena's Scottish Rocks of Love and Lore jewelry. It's popular, and Rowena can barely keep up with the orders from Olga and other shops in Scotland.

I suggested to Olive that she try making knitted animal hats. Lions with dizzy eyes, elephants with trunks down the back, confused cats with drooping whiskers, inebriated raccoons with long raccoon tails. She loved the idea, Olga loved the product, and now they're in business, too.

Rowena and Pherson had a date.

Apparently it was successful. When I dropped by Rowena's a few weeks later, in the morning, to give her some cinnamon bread I'd baked, my mother's recipe, Pherson answered the door.

I looked up at him and we laughed, then hugged.

Gitanjali and the Chief are adorable. That's the word for it. He told me, "Dating befuddles me so I think it would be easier on Gitanjali and me if we were married. I do so hope she says yes. I have spent thirty days trying to find the ring. Here, Charlotte. Do tell me. What do you think of it?"

That diamond almost blinded me.

I will miss my garden and the view of the whales on Whale Island. I will miss living in Washington. I will miss living in America.

But I will miss more if I do not live in Scotland. Scotland is in my heart, with its hills that curve like green dough, the mysteriousness of the landscape, the sharpness of the ocean cliffs, the old churches that have held the prayers of people long gone, that will hold the prayers of people long after I'm gone.

The ruins of the cathedral, the ruins of the castle, are part of me, as is the village, and Bridget's Park, A Place for Everyone.

Scotland is the land of my birth, it's the land where I met my best friend and her brother, it's the land where I fell in love, truly, for the first time in my life, with a farmer.

The farmer grows potatoes, blueberries, and apples.

He has a modern cottage that looks traditionally old.

He looks sexy in a kilt. I have peeked under the kilt.

He does not mind that I need to be alone a lot, to walk amidst the fog and the raindrops, or to feel the sun on my face in silence.

We have the same interests, the same passions. We are best friends.

He loves me. All of me, and he shows me that every day.

We like to make love. We have this wild and seductive love life, then he holds me close, the wind from the ocean curling around the house, the stars spiraling through the sky, the Scottish rain a trickle from heaven, the air scented with a dash of salt and a sip of mint tea.

Our wedding is in one week. Everyone we love is coming. We have agreed on five kids. Five kids, plus us, plus Gracie is eight, as my grandma predicted.

Toran Ramsay is a man of all men.

Scottish Warrior man.

I love him, I do.

Romance Readers and Writers Magazine
By Kitty Rosemary
Books For Chicks Reviewer

BITTERSWEET AND UNBELIEVABLE!

Well, ring my panties out, my tears have run down my chin and soaked them!

Brace yourselves, readers of this column!

Writer Georgia Chandler's latest book, Peppermint Tea, a Soul Mate, and the Scottish Leap, A Romantic Time Travel Adventure, The Final Novel, featuring our favorite time-traveling heroine, McKenzie Rae Dean, is once again at the top of the New York Times *best-seller list. I started reading it on Friday night. What? Did you expect for me to have a date on Friday night? I had one date in the last month. His name was Stephan. Steph. On. Sounds like that.*

If you live in Los Angeles and a man named Stephan with a nose the shape of an owl's beak and lips like a whale's asks you out, say no. He is algae.

Anyhow.

When I came home Chandler's book was waiting for me. I was up all night reading and did not get out of bed on Saturday. Decadent!

Yes, it gripped my ever-lovin' heart like a studly Scottish man in a kilt grabbing me and slinging me up in front of him on his horse, all snug and tight.

For her millions of avid readers, I am warning you, ladies, this will be a bittersweet novel for many reasons. The ending, well, it surprised me as much as I would be surprised if honorable men over the age of thirty were suddenly in abundance.

Without any warning to her adoring public, including moi,

Ms. Chandler ended her series after ten novels. Her editors and agent are no doubt crying into their coffees and popping tranquilizers.

When I called Ms. Chandler, she told me that it was time for her to take a break from writing. She said she had writer's block for months and finally decided that McKenzie Rae Dean had finished her journey, for now. Time will tell if she comes back to us.

When I asked if the ending of this novel had anything to do with her moving to Scotland, where she lived the first fifteen years of her life, she said, "My life is changing and so is McKenzie Rae's."

When asked if she was in love, the usually insanely private Chandler said, "So in love I can hardly function."

When asked who the man was, she said, "Let's say that McKenzie Rae refound the love of her life, after many long and lonely years away, and so did I."

I asked if the people in the town she lived in knew she was Georgia Chandler.

"Not yet. Please don't tell them."

It boggles my mind, boggles it, but we're done, folks.

That's it.

It's a wrap.

I know you're probably crying in your coffee and popping tranquilizers now, like Chandler's editors and agent!

Yours in the love of books and other wild and luscious items!

Ta-ta for now!

Kiss, kiss!

Kitty Rosemary

A READING GROUP GUIDE

MY VERY BEST FRIEND

Cathy Lamb

ABOUT THIS GUIDE

The suggested questions are included to enhance your group's reading of Cathy Lamb's *My Very Best Friend.*

DISCUSSION QUESTIONS

1. Describe *My Very Best Friend* using only five words.

2. Would you have been friends with Charlotte? What would make her an interesting friend? What would make her a difficult friend?

3. Were Charlotte and Bridget true best friends, in your opinion, given the lies and distance between them?

4. Which woman—Charlotte, Bridget, Gitanjali, Olive Oliver, Rowena, Kenna, Lorna Lester, or Malvina—did you most relate to in the story? Do you see any of your own characteristics in any of them, both positive *and* negative?

5. Discuss Charlotte's character arc. How did Charlotte change from the beginning of the book to the end?

6. Do you believe in second sight, as Charlotte's grandma had? If you could see into the future, what would you want to see about yourself and your own life?

7. How did you feel about Bridget? Did you find her choices, her plight in life, believable given the circumstances? How did her drug addiction, and her lack of ability to stay clean, affect your feelings for her? Was she a sympathetic figure?

8. Charlotte said, "I had read about AIDS victims rejected by family members and friends, towns flipping out, neighbors turning their backs, schools refusing entry, and general, torch-wielding hysteria. People were afraid.

They were uneducated. Their fear often manifested itself in group think, which has never been known for rational thought. They didn't like what AIDS said about the person, either. It was against their own morality code of what they thought was acceptable. Gay? That was an easy judgment call: Sinful! It's a choice to be gay, they choose it, they die for it! It's a lifestyle! God's wrath! Amoral! Disgusting, repulsive. *Contagious!* Drug user? They got what they deserved! And in St. Ambrose? How would they respond?"

Was the way that the villagers reacted to Bridget's AIDS diagnosis realistic? Was it fair, given the time period, or was it purely hysterical and unkind?

9. Did Father Angus Cruickshank deserve to die? Was justice served?

10. If this happened today and you were on a jury, would you convict the murderer of Angus Cruickshank?

11. Did Lorna redeem herself by the end? Had you predicted that she was the killer of Angus Cruickshank?

12. What was the most romantic thing that Toran did for Charlotte? Are there men like Toran Ramsay out there? Would you marry Toran?

13. What are the themes of the story?